# Corrupted Extinction

Charly J.M

**ISBN:** 9798398205473

Cover Created by Charly J.M

Love is what makes *everything* worthwhile.

Charly J.M

# Chapter One

## Phoenix

Fifteen years… How crazy was it that fifteen years had gone by since I had announced we would be coming out to the human world, revealing ourselves.

Of course, there were those that didn't agree, but that had been expected.

A huge coven of vampires had argued this was the worst thing we could do, they would lose their source of food, they had gone years without detection and if we came out to them the humans would arm themselves to the vampires, risking their species. I had tried and tried to explain that we would work out a better way, blood banks, donations, we would sort something, but they disagreed, they wanted to keep to the old ways, sneaking in the night to take their prey, they enjoyed the fun of it. They left us, refusing to work with us any longer and then they began to attack, every time we tried to leave to speak to the human leaders they had people on watch, attacking us to the point I had to call everyone back to keep our people safe.

Some wolves disagreed too, but after long negotiations with them they decided to move their packs to areas where the humans were far from them, keeping out of it all, keeping to themselves, they did not attack, they left swiftly. I respected their decision and left them alone, making sure they knew I was here if they needed us.

After a couple of years, we decided we were going to try again with revealing ourselves, but we were stopped again, this time because a virus was sweeping over humankind, their numbers dropping dramatically. It was chaotic as we watched from a distance, I didn't want to risk the packs, we had no idea how this virus would be against us.

Masses of humans were ignoring their leaders, they didn't believe in the sickness sweeping the world, one by one they went down, dropping like flies as they convulsed on the ground.

With nearly eight billion people in the world, it was a shock when the numbers began to drop so quickly, soon enough it dropped to six billion, then to five, four, three and then two… Six BILLION people died to the virus, after countless warnings from their leaders, after trying to slow the spread they still didn't listen, they did it to themselves. Riots and looting began as jobs were lost, the economy died, and money became irrelevant.

The UK was now pretty baron of humans, only small groups were hidden around the country, either protected by us or being used in blood farms by the vampires.

I had announced war on vampires who used them as human blood bags, they shouldn't be prisoners to them, I had to protect them. But it was difficult. Really difficult.

It did turn out that we were immune to the virus though and the fae had begun testing how our blood would react with humans to save them, though most of the time they went crazy, and we couldn't work out why.

The humans knew of us now, though there were so few left it wasn't how we had hoped it to go. We had to protect them, to stop them from going extinct.

My borders had expanded, we had built more houses, for all that needed it. We had a mixture of wolves, a few vampires, guardians and very small groups of humans that we had come across. We were still searching for more.

The world had gone crazy, it was pretty much a world for the supernatural now, but I had to help them, I couldn't let them all die out like this.

# Chapter Two

## Taylor

"Bryant! Get the fuck up! Come on! Do not make me come in there and kick your arse! It's our birthday! Come on!" I bang on the door of my twin's bedroom groaning. It was our eighteenth birthday and here he was still in bed. Lazy fucker.

"Go away!" He groans.

"If you don't get up, I will go and get Uncle Kai to come to get you!" I smirk.

Kai had the knack of annoying the hell out of Bryant, he was so playful and teased him all the time. Uncle Kai was my favourite person in the world. As we grew up I loved every moment we were with him, he snuck us sweets when mum wasn't looking, helped us get into mischief, which mum always ended up glaring at him, arms folded as he looked down at the ground, a small smirk on his face as he knew he was in trouble but they were such good friends, he knew he would get away with it.

"I hate you," Bryant grumbles opening his door, his hair a complete mess as he runs a hand through it.

"Happy birthday to you too twin," I smirk as I walk in and hug him.

"Happy birthday twin," he smiles, sweetly kissing the top of my head. Boy, was my brother tall like dad, if anything he had almost surpassed him.

"So, I got you something," I go back out the door and grab the box from outside with a smile.

The box was heavy, I dropped it into Bryant's arms as he grunted at the weight, sitting on his bed, he opened up his draw and held out a present for me too.

"Thanks," I smile as he began to open his present. I was so nervous; Bryant had played a lot of pranks in his life, and it was my turn… Kind of…

"You got me a clump of clay… Seriously…" He frowns at the huge lump of clay as I giggled.

"I used my earth element to get that for you, you should appreciate it," I smirked.

"I hate you," he grumbles.

"Ok, there might be a little more to it," I grin, beginning to wave my hands over the clay as it disintegrates, revealing a beautifully hand-made blade.

"Holy shit Tay!" His eyes widen with his smile as he picks it up.

"So, not only is it hand-made for you, but take a good grip and use your fire on it," I smile. I had had a fae make it and it would use whatever elemental power we used to strengthen it. My brother favouring fire like our mother, while I favoured earth.

He lights his hand on fire, the dagger drawing it from his hand and into the blade turning the small hand blade into a fiery sword.

"HOLY SHIT!" He exclaims in wonder as he begins to move it carefully through the air.

"You like it?" I ask nervously.

“Like it… I love it Tay, thank you!” He says withdrawing his power and putting it down as he sweeps me up and hugs me.

“So, what did you get me?” I grin as he lets me go.

“Uh… It’s not going to seem as cool as this… Damn it Tay, must you always one-up me,” he says sheepishly as I open the box in my hands.

I open it to find soft wrapping tissue, moving it to the side to see a gorgeous necklace, it had a huge pendant with our family crest on it.

“Open it, it’s a locket too,” he smiles as I take it in my hand and open it carefully, I see small photos of our family.

“It’s beautiful Bryant,” I say with a tear in my eye.

“Are you making your sister cry again, Bryant?” Our eyes shoot up to the door as we both grin.

“MUM!” We call out as she opens her arms out for us, hugging us to her.

“Happy birthday my babies,” she smiles.

“Muuuummm, we aren’t babies anymore,” Bryant groans.

“You’ll always be my babies, so shut it,” mum says as I giggle.

“Alpha, you’re needed downstairs,” Alpha Cole walks up to mum as she sighs.

“What is it this time?” She sighs.

“We have news of another hideout, Alpha Hanson found it on their way here,” Cole answers.

“The alpha was coming here. Why?” I ask.

"To celebrate your birthdays of course, you're eighteen. Your wolves will be able to sense their mates, we decided to throw a party not only for your birthday but to give everyone a chance to find their mates," mum smiles.

*I didn't think about that... What if we find our mate? What if they want us to leave our home? I won't leave, we can't leave.*

**We won't be going anywhere Lily, I don't care for a mate, I'd rather stay here with mum and dad.**

*Yeah, me too, but what about the mate pull... Mum told us it's one of the strongest pulls when you meet them.*

**Then we'll reject them, simple.**

*I don't think it's that simple Taylor.*

**We'll see.**

"I bet Keeley is excited," Bryant smirks knowing how Keeley had been since she had turned eighteen.

We had all expected her and Blake to be mates and yet they weren't. Blake was devastated, he was in love with her whole-heartedly and wanted to be her choice mate, but she wouldn't have it. She wanted to wait until she found her soulmate, I wasn't entirely sure if it worked the same way with the fae, it was a grey area, Violet had said they know their soulmates, though with each of them it was different. It could be a smell, a touch, a vision or she could just sense it, Keeley had her heart set on finding the love of her life and she knew Blake wasn't it, though she loved him, she loved him as her best friend.

"Yes, though Blake is pacing his room, I don't know if he will come out tonight," mum sighs.

“Alpha, please, the others are waiting,” Cole says as mum groans.

“I’ll get Blake out, don’t worry mum,” I smile at her.

“Thank you, sweetheart, I will see you both in a bit, I love you, happy birthday,” she kisses both our cheeks before rushing off.

“Rock, paper, scissors as to who tries first,” Bryant smirks knowing Blake would be difficult. I roll my eyes putting out my hand, he never won at this.

# Chapter Three

## Blake

I can't believe she's doing this; she's actually going to abandon me. Keeley, the girl I had been in love with since we were kids was going to the party tonight in the search for her mate.

Why couldn't she love me as I loved her?! I gave her everything! Every time she was sad, I was beside her, I hugged her, told her how beautiful she was.

I never abandoned her, and she told me she loved me, but as soon as we were both of age she changed… Why did she have to change?

I will never understand girls, why must they be so obsessed with finding 'the one' when there is someone right in front of them that would be perfect for them.

*Perfect… We ain't perfect.*

**Copper, I swear to God, shut the fuck up.**

*She's not our mate, so what, you love her and can still have her as a friend, she'll always be our friend. We'll find our mate, one day.*

**I don't want anyone else! She's mine!**

*You're going insane Blake, stop letting your thirst get into your head, you're a moody git when you're hungry.*

**Fuck off Cop.**

A knock at the door pulls me from my conversation with my wolf, I groan getting up and opening the door to find Taylor standing there.

"What do you want?" I grumble, rolling my eyes as I go back inside.

"For you to be a little nicer on my birthday, come on Blake, we used to have fun, when did you get so… Old man on us, you're twenty-six, not a thousand," she crosses her arms at me. I could see she was pissed at me.

"Fuck, happy birthday. You try having your heart ripped from your chest because the girl you love doesn't want you," I flop onto my bed like a teenager as Taylor giggles at me, closing the door behind her.

"You're insufferable, you're like a teenage girl sometimes you know that?" She smirks, sitting on the bed as I kick her off and she falls to the ground with a thump.

"BLAKE!" She cries out before bursting into laughter, causing me to smile cockily.

"Call it your birthday bumps," I chuckle.

"I hate you sometimes," she smirks.

"No, you don't," I shake my head sitting up as she lifts herself back onto the bed.

"So, will you come to the party?" She smiles, batting her lashes at me.

"Nope," I shake my head.

"Oh, come on! Please! We can't celebrate without you there! Janie will finally be back from training with Alpha Hanson, and I heard they might have found a little hideout too," she begs.

"A hideout?" I perk up. I had been working with dad and the others lately in trying to find more groups of humans and we hadn't found anything.

"Yes, mum got called downstairs, come on, please come tonight," she begs again.

"Fine, but only because the whole family will be home," I roll my eyes. She squeals and hugs me tightly, I hug her back breathing her in with a sigh, she always smelt sweet, like chocolates.

"Thank you! So, what did you get me?" She grins cheekily.

"Ugghh…" I bite my lip; I had forgotten to get her anything… Again… What a shit big brother I was… Though I didn't always feel like a brother, more like a friend. Sure, I loved that mum and dad had adopted me, but I never felt the brotherly connection as strong as most would, but I loved them, but like they were my best friends. Much like Kai and mum. Mum, I would always view as a mother, she had been there for me for years and I loved her beyond all belief.

"You forgot didn't you…" She crosses her arms across her chest. Jesus, when did her boobs get so big…

*Ugh, when did you start looking at her boobs, dude! SISTER!*

**Only by adoption… Not blood.**

*STILL! What about your love for Keeley… You were raving about her a moment ago!*

**I'm a man… Cut me some slack!**

*Pfft, man… Right…*

I growl as Taylor raises a brow at me, just like mum did when she was annoyed.

"Don't give me that look, Taylor, your present is going to be awesome… When I give it to you later," I say, and she frowns at me.

"Hmm, better be. Now, get showered, you stink," she wrinkles her nose as I chuckle.

"That's my man-stench, leave it alone," I smirk as she stands up.

"Man-stench. That's one thing to call it… Get ready, if your arse isn't at the party, I will come get you and I will drag the others with me," she says with a sly smirk.

"OK! Jeez," I laugh as she walks out the room.

*She smells good…*

**Copper, I swear I will banish you to the back of my head…**

*Tell me I'm wrong, you're the one checking her out.*

**It's gross, I shouldn't have done that.**

*Not our sister…*

**She might as well be.**

*You don't believe that.*

**Cop, I swear… Enough dude. It's going to be bad enough tonight with Keeley, without us thinking about every girl around us.**

*Because you DO want a mate!*

**Of course, I do, but Keeley should be it.**

*Get over her! She's not our mate! Just stop before you drive us both crazy and focus on the family for now.*

**Fine.** I groan getting up to get ready, what the hell is going on with me?

# Chapter Four

## Phoenix

"Mum!" Janie shouts as I walk up to the council room, and she hugs me tightly. She was just as beautiful as ever, though it would seem she now sported dreadlocks instead of her wavey hair. Still, it suited her.

"Look at you, you look amazing, how was it at Hanson's pack?" I smile at her. Sure, she was thirty now, but I still loved her all the same. Even though we looked the same age now as I hadn't really changed since having the kids, thank the goddess for our ageing.

"It was amazing! He taught me SO much!" She grins.

"You should be proud Phoenix, your children seem to take after you and yet two of them aren't even yours by blood," Hanson walks up. Janie blushes with him near and I raise a brow at her with a smile.

"I am proud of them all, they will always be my children, blood or not, as the packs are my family too," I smile.

"So, Janie, do you wish to tell her or shall I?" Hanson says as my brows raise at them.

"Oh, umm, ok… Mum, Hanson is… Well, he's…" she steps back, putting her small hand in his gigantic one.

"He's your mate," I grin, and she blushes, nodding happily.

"I hope you will give us your blessing Phoenix," Hanson says with a smile.

"Of course, I couldn't think of anyone better Hanson. You are one of our best Alpha's and I'm sure Janie will be an amazing Luna to you. I will miss you; I suppose you will be returning with him?" I answer with a soft smile, taking Janie's hand in mine.

"Yes, if you don't mind, I will stay longer if you need me though," Janie answers.

"You are welcome to be wherever you wish Janie. I cannot stop you. As much as I love having you home and everyone misses you, we are all able to visit each other," I reply.

"I miss you guys too," Janie walks up to me and hugs me as I breathe in her familiar scent, squeezing her a little much, she giggles and let's go.

"As much as I know you two need to catch up, we really need to deal with this situation before the festivities tonight. I fear for any humans living in the hovel we came across," Hanson says, I nod and sit at the table with the others.

"Sorry we're late, Paul and I had to deal with a few new vampires on the south side, what did we miss?" Michael rushes in taking a seat beside me, kissing me quickly.

"Hi dad," Janie grins.

"Janie! My god, look at you, beautiful," he smiles at her softly.

"Ok, sorry guys but we should get to it, here is where the hole was found, we have several covens surrounding the area and if they get to them first, they are fucked," Cole brings out a map as I look at it.

We tried to keep track of every coven of vampires as we could while they searched for more humans, wanting to use them like cattle on a farm.

"A hole? What sort of hole?" Paul asks.

"An old war bunker by the looks of it, we couldn't get in though, we may need fae help to unlock it. That's why we didn't go in ourselves, though we didn't have enough men to protect them either, I thought the best thing would be to come here for back up," Janie answers and I can't help but feel pride as she took charge. I could see Hanson look at her with pure adoration too and I was glad she had found someone so great for her.

"None of these covens have any fae or guardian help, so the humans should be safe as long as they don't venture out," Jason says from beside Cole.

"No, but our ranks have been infiltrated before, some of our fae have been kidnapped and used for their magic, it wouldn't surprise me if they kidnap another," Jae says from beside Kai.

"Have the fae on high alert, I want extra wolves with them too, while they are here, they will be protected. I will contact Violet and let her know of this and see what she wants to do, these are her people going missing," I sigh.

"No worries about that my dear, I'm here already," Violet grins, walking through the doors, her wings sweeping powerfully behind her. She was always so beautifully regal in bright colours.

"Well, this is a full family get together," Kai sniggers.

"Keeley will be happy," Michael replies.

"Now, catch me up, I only got the last couple of sentences," Violet says as she sits with us all and we catch her up.

"So, when do we send a team out?" Cole asks.

"I would love to send a team out now, but with the festivities tonight I can't see anyone wanting to risk it. I say we leave tomorrow midday. I know most of the covens prefer skulking around at night," I answer.

"Let's hope they survive tonight," Cole sighs.

"What would you have us do Cole?" Michael growls.

"Send out help now!" Cole exclaims.

"We cannot deal with everything at once, this takes planning Cole, most humans want to kill us still! We have to be prepared, I cannot prepare everyone for a human arrival tonight on top of everything else," I say calmly.

*He's a dick sometimes, especially since Jezebel rejected him officially and disappeared.*

**I can't blame him, that hurt his wolf, Storm.**

*No need to be a dick to everyone else though.*

**I just wish I knew where she went.**

*No idea, she left the pack too, for all we know she could have betrayed us all.*

**I know.**

"You're sentencing them to death!" Cole argues.

"Alpha Cole, I suggest you reign in your tone and respect the Queen," Violet snaps at him.

"We don't know how close they are to be caught by those bloodsuckers and every time we find a new group, they get to them first. I just want to save them before they become food!" Cole says angrily, pointing towards Kai at the mention of bloodsuckers.

"Hey!" Kai shouts.

"I would refrain from calling them that if I were you, Cole," I growl. I was always protective of Kai, that hadn't changed.

"It's what they are…" Cole murmurs.

"This is not up for discussion Cole, you will refrain from tarring them all with the same brush, I have warned you before, you will apologise to Kai right now, last warning," I growl once more.

"Fine, I apologise, you're sentencing the humans to death Phoenix, and you know it. They will know we are distracted tonight, and they will attack them, I hope you know what you've done," Cole growls, storming out of the room as I sigh, leaning forward, head in my hands.

"It won't get any easier Nix, but you are right to make your decision," Kai sighs.

"As soon as the sun comes up tomorrow, we begin a search and rescue, have the word spread so people can be prepared in the morning," I murmur.

"Yes Queen Alpha," they chorus.

"So, where are the birthday twins?" Janie smiles at me.

"Probably getting ready, you know how long it takes those two, they like to look good for everyone, even if they have no interest in finding their mates," Michael answers.

"They will once they feel the pull, which should be soon right?" Trey asks.

"Yes, as soon as it gets to their hour of birth, they will be able to sense their mate, if they are here, which is going to be in… Four hours," I reply with a smile.

"It would be nice if Blake found his, he's getting worse when it comes to Keeley," Luci sighs.

"What do you mean?" Violet frowns at us.

"Keeley is so adamant on finding her soul mate that she has denied Blake's love, he's in love with her and yet she isn't his mate, he wants to be her choice mate," Luci replies.

"Ah, I understand," Violet nods slowly.

"Taylor is the complete opposite, she wants nothing to do with hers," Kai says as I frown.

"I'm going to go see them all, see you later, love you guys," Janie kisses our cheeks and then kisses Hanson passionately before running off.

"She's still as bouncy as she was years ago," Kade chuckles.

"You have no idea," Hanson smirks.

"I don't want to know," I groan, putting up my hand and he chuckles.

"Intruders north!" A warrior calls through the link as we look at each other, Michael and Paul run out the room in an instant, following close behind as we shift, running outside, heading to the north of the building.

Some of our warriors are already up against a small coven of vampires.

Leaping over one of my warriors to get to one that was about to attack him from the side, while he was distracted from the front, I tear them limb from limb, blood dripping from my mouth as we battle against them.

"Thank you, my Queen," the warrior bows in respect.

"Please! No! I beg of you don't kill me!" I turn to see Paul and Michael cornering a vampire who was on his knees.

"Why should we listen to you?" I growl into his mind, coming up behind them as they parted ways for me to get to the vampire, pressing my paw against his chest.

"I can tell you things!" He cries out.

"Tell me what you know now, and I will think about it," I order.

"They… They have one of your wolves, they threatened her, made her reject her mate because they have her daughter!" The vampire cries out.

"Who?!" I growl, pressing harder.

"A woman… J-Je… I don't remember her name it begins with J," he says.

"Jezebel?" Michael growls.

"Yes! Jezebel!" He shouts.

"Jezebel doesn't have a daughter though, does she?" Paul says through the link.

"I haven't heard about it," Michael shakes his head replying.

"Send him to the prison cells, I want more information from him," I growl the order.

"I'll deal with it," Paul nods, grabbing the vampire by the scruff of his neck, dragging him away.

"Please don't kill me!" He screams.

"Have Kai come and help you, he may squeal more with another vampire," I call out as I shift back.

"Uh, love, you... Uh... Have a little something..." Michael smirks pointing to my clothes, I was covered in blood.

"Fuck's sake," I groan.

"We'll tidy up alpha," the warrior said.

"Thank you," I smile as Michael walks with me.

"Even covered in blood, you look as beautiful as the day I met you," Michael kisses me passionately.

"That was eighteen years ago, and I pretty much look the same," I laugh.

"Still beautiful," he moans against my touch on his arms.

"Come on handsome, let's go clean up," I wink at him, and he groans.

"Shower together?" He smirks.

"No, I was going to take one of the warriors with me," I say sarcastically, hearing him growl possessively before he picks me up, wrapping my legs around his waist.

"MINE!" He growls taking us upstairs.

"Uh... Mum? Dad? Why are you covered in blood?" Bryant says at the top of the stairs.

"Later," Michael growls, bursting into our bedroom and slamming the door behind him.

"Ok! Have fun!" I hear Bryant shout as I giggle.

"You are mine; don't you forget that Phoenix," Michael growls as he rips my clothes off of me… Literally, they were ripped apart on the floor.

"That was my favourite top!" I exclaim.

"I'll get you another, it was ruined anyway," he replies, kissing my body ever so softly.

"Mmm, Michael," I moan.

"Let's have more pups," he says. I look at him in shock.

"You want more? Now?" I ask.

"Now, forever, I told you I wanted a big family. The kids are going to be flying the nest and I can't help but love seeing you with a baby on your hip, your face glowing with happiness," Michael says, kissing down my chest.

"Is now the best time?" I reply as he continues down my body, gasping as his mouth meets my pussy.

"Will it ever be the right time?" He says through the link, so he doesn't have to stop, thrusting a finger inside me as I cry out.

"Ok," reply as my stomach feels hot, his fingers and mouth working like magic before he takes off his clothes, positioning himself between my legs before thrusting inside.

"I love you Phoenix," he grunts from pleasure as I kiss him.

"I love you too," I murmur back against his lips.

# Chapter Five

## Taylor

"Uh… Is that…" I grimace at the sound of my parents having sex, I know they were loved up and I was fine with them doing it, but hearing it… Made me shiver and gag, you should never have to hear your parents going at it like that. As a human, you wouldn't hear it so much, but because we were wolves, we heard TOO much.

"Yep, can we go now?" Bryant groans, taking my hand, dragging me away downstairs.

"I see more siblings in the future," I sing.

"TWINS!" I hear a voice shout; I turn around to see Janie running towards us.

"Janie!" We grin, running to her and she hugs us tightly.

"Happy birthday! Where the hell were you, I've been looking for you everywhere," she shouts in our ears as we chuckle.

"Well, Keeley wanted to see me and give me help on what to wear tonight, so I was stuck with that. While Bryant was double checking that Blake was coming tonight and hadn't wimped out since I talked with him," I smirk.

"Ouch… Keeley on a fashion warpath again?" Janie chuckles.

"Oh yeah, she wants me wearing this dress which is all frills and bright colours, I said no and she kicked me out," I laugh.

“Ooo, no, no frills, you are not the frill type of girl, what about that red dress I got you last year? The halter neck?” Janie says.

“Actually, that’s perfect,” I grin, I hadn’t had a chance to wear it yet and it was a gorgeous dress.

“Are you two finished talking clothes or shall I grab food alone,” Bryant mumbles.

“You’re always hungry, come on, we need to catch up,” Janie hooks her arms through ours as we head to the kitchen.

“Look who it is, the birthday bandits, happy birthday you two,” Kade chuckles with Luciana by his side as we walk in.

“Happy Birthday!” She squeals coming to hug us.

“Thank you,” we say in unison.

“The way you two talk in unison will forever be creepy,” Janie points at us as we chuckle.

“Hungry?” Kade asks.

“Yes,” I smile.

“Always,” Bryant smirks.

“DUH!” Janie laughs. We all sit at the table and Kade dishes out some pancakes, luckily, it had seemed he was ready to be raided for food and made extra.

“Are you looking forward to tonight?” Luci asks.

“Not really, you know I hate too much attention on me,” I groan.

"Don't worry they won't be looking at you, they'll be looking at my sexy arse," Bryant grins cheekily, stuffing his pancake in his mouth.

"Oh, real sexy, you've got a little something there brother," I point to his chin, he wipes it as I shake my head at him.

"I take it you're still a man-whore," Janie smirks.

"Excuse me! How dare you!" Bryant fakes shock, a hand to his chest.

"He's had a different girl in his bed all week," I say as he kicks me under the table.

"Bryant…" Kade growls.

"Oh, come on! Let me have a little fun until I'm tied down for life, like you guys!" Bryant says.

"Kids," Kade shakes his head.

"How many have you slept with Kade? Before meeting Luciana?" I smirk at him.

"Never you mind young lady, I've been alive too long. I was not going five hundred years with blue balls, I didn't think I had a mate so yes, I had my fun, but you guys are barely eighteen. You have plenty of time to find yours and not give your bodies to the next girl or guy who you come across," Kade says sternly.

"Hey! Don't bring me into this! I haven't had sex with anyone!" I point at him with my fork.

"I don't believe that," Janie sniggers.

"No, it's true, Taylor here doesn't date, nor does she have any interest in anyone…" Luci says as I nod.

"You don't… Jesus woman have you become a nun?" Janie laughs.

"No, I just have no interest in it right now, as Kade said, we have plenty of time for that sort of thing, I'm not rushing," I shrug.

"Wow, I couldn't think what it's like to still have my virginity at eighteen…" Janie murmurs.

"Excuse me… Who did you have sex with before eighteen?!" Kade growls, Luci smirks, trying to calm him down with a kiss on his cheek.

"No one… Uhh…" Janie stammers.

"Janie… Do tell…" I laugh.

"Jason," she whispers.

"NO WAY! I knew it!" Luci laughs.

Kade growls, the rumble of it shaking the table.

"Kade, it's no big deal," Luci kisses him again.

"How old?" He asks Janie.

"I was just turning eighteen, it's not an issue and it was just the once Kade, seriously calm down," Janie says. Kade stands from the table and begins stomping out the door, the harsh clang of his prosthetic leg ringing through the house.

"Oh, shit…" Bryant murmurs.

"Janie, you better warn Jason what's coming," I tell her, seeing her eyes glow.

"Excuse me, I better try to calm him down," Luci runs off after him.

"JASON!" I hear him bellow out as Janie grimaces.

"Uh… I'll see you guys in a bit…" She says quickly, leaving right behind them.

"Why is Kade on a warpath?" Keeley flounces in.

"Janie had sex with Jason at seventeen…" I smirk.

"Oh…" She nods as she goes into the fridge.

"What the hell is that?" Bryant grimaces at the liquid in a bottle she was sipping out of with her name on it.

"It's just a meal replacement shake, I need to lose a few pounds," she shrugs. I look at her in shock, she was already super skinny, not an ounce of fat on her.

"Keeley, you're ridiculous, if you lose anything else you'll be a stick," Bryant shakes his head at her.

"Ugh, you just don't get it…" She says dramatically.

"Leave it, please don't set her off this early…" I say through my twins' bond.

"But she's going to kill herself doing that shit," Bryant says.

"I'll talk with mum," I say as I see him give me a small nod.

"So, will you wear the dress I chose Taylor?" Keeley whines.

"No."

"Please! You never wear things I choose!" She huffs.

"Because you choose things that are not my style!" I argue.

"You have no fashion sense," she huffs.

"And you have no sense at all," I whisper.

"Huh?" She says missing what I said, while Bryant chuckles under his breath.

"When did you become such a bitch?!" Keeley whines, stomping out of the room.

"Comes with the wolf territory!" I shout.

"BITCH!" She shouts back and I burst into laughter.

"How long until she decides to go back home with Violet?" Bryant asks.

"To be honest, that might be the best thing she could do right now, it would be better for Blake too," I sigh as I take a sip of my drink.

"Yeah, poor guy," Bryant nods.

"Fancy going for a run?" I smile cheekily, he recognised that as a challenge.

"Are you challenging me to a race twin?" He asks.

"I didn't say that, but if you want to…" I say with a grin.

"You're on!" He says, getting up quickly already leaving at a run.

"Cheat!" I shout, laughing as I run to catch up with him. Racing him outside we shift into our wolves as we bolt through the trees.

Up ahead I could hear shouting as I signalled Bryant to stop, creeping through the trees.

"Kade stop! You're going to kill him!" Luci cries as my eyes widen.

"KADE!" Janie cries. Kade has his hands around Jason's neck, Bryant and I bolt into the fray, Bryant dragging Kade from him as I growled at him in a warning.

"She was a child!" Kade shouts.

"I'm sorry, she was nearly eighteen! I-I don't know what came over me! She was old enough to make her own decisions!" Jason shouts back through coughing.

"Kade, enough," I growl through the link.

"Do not tell me what to do little wolf," Kade growls shifting.

"KADE!" Luci shifts too getting between us and I see the hurt in her eyes.

"What the fuck is going on?!" Mum bounds in as she looks between us. "Well, someone going to tell me what is going on or not?!" She shouts.

Janie begins to tell her as I see mum shaking her head in disbelief.

"Jason, get out of here, though I understand she was old enough, you should have known better, get out of my sight before I throw you in a cell for the day," mum growls and Jason nods, his head bowed.

Kade growls as mum faces him.

"Shift," she orders. He shifts, bowing to her, but I can see the anger on his face still.

"He deserved it," Kade growls.

"No, he didn't, Kade. Calm down, Janie was perfectly capable to make decisions by herself even at that age. Please calm down," mum sighs.

"Kade, let's take a run," dad walks up to us, his hand gliding through my fur as I nuzzle into his hand, he gives me a nod with a smile, and I shift back hugging him.

"Happy birthday," he says to us both before shifting, taking Kade with him.

Mum walks up to Luci and hugs her. "Go on kids," mum says, nodding for us to leave. we smile softly at them before shifting and running off once again.

"Race you," I nudge Bryant as he growls chasing after me making me laugh.

All of a sudden, I'm bowled over by a huge wolf, tongue lolling out jovially as he sits on top of me.

"Get off of me you lard-arse!" I growl, whining beneath him.

"Nope," he shakes his head.

"BLAKE! Bryant get him off of me!" I growl again, trying to move from under him as he slobbers over my face.

"Nah, I'm good," Bryant chuckles, shifting back and sitting against a tree.

"What sort of brother are you?!" I groan, giving up trying to move.

"If it means you're not bugging me at the moment," Bryant smirks at me.

"Blake! Get off!" I growl, but he still refuses.

"I'm quite comfy here," Blake shifts his weight slightly as I groan, he's crushing my ribs.

"Fine, you asked for it," I growl. I concentrate on the ground as it begins to shake, he whimpers looking down as the ground begins to move.

"Stop it! You know I hate that shit!" Blake begs.

"Get off then!" I say and he leaps off of me, leaping over the moving ground which I had made wave, changing shapes at my command, I knew it freaked him out.

"I hate that, it's so creepy like the dead are going to dig their way up," he shivers, shifting into his human form.

"Well, maybe if you listened to me, I wouldn't have to do it, you hurt my ribs, have you gained twenty stone?" I groan, rubbing my ribs as I shift.

"Of pure muscle," he grins showing me his 'guns'.

"Why is one bigger than the other?" I smirk, teasing him.

"Huh?" He frowns.

"Too much wanking probably," Bryant laughs.

"Fuck you two," Blake shakes his head, flipping us off.

"That's kinda gross isn't it, you're our brother…" I smirk teasingly.

"Not by blood so no, it's not gross," Blake rolls his eyes.

"So, you would fuck my sister?" Bryant frowns.

"No, I wouldn't, you're pretty and all, but not my type Taylor, sorry if I let you down," he smirks back.

"I'd rather stick pins in my eyes," I reply.

"That can be arranged," Bryant smirks. I throw a rock at him; he groans throwing a ball of fire at me.

"Oh, that's how we're playing are we," I smirk. We begin throwing our powers about as Blake tries to dodge out of the way flitting around us like a referee.

# Chapter Six

## Phoenix

"Nix, I'd like to apologise for my behaviour earlier. I've been feeling a little out of sorts, protective I guess you could say," Kade says, finding me and Luci in the kitchen.

"Any particular reason why?" I ask.

"Luci," he says. I frown looking to her as she smiles at me with a huge grin.

"I'm pregnant… Finally," she says. I squeal in happiness for her, they had been trying, but were having difficulties and Luci had been going to healers for years and they just couldn't figure it out.

"Congratulations!" I grin, hugging them both.

"Alpha, Paul is asking for you in the cells," a warrior walks in.

"So, he didn't ask himself because…" I frown.

"He's a little busy…" He answers as I sigh.

"We will celebrate your news soon, I swear, please stop laying into Jason, he meant no harm and does care for Janie," I say and Kade nods with a sigh.

"I know," Kade nods. I smile leaving quickly with the warrior down to the cells.

I hated this place, it reminded me of when the others were put down here and I found them, Kade literally rotting in a cell.

“Paul?” I frown as he has the vampire by the throat, Kai looking at him angrily.

“He stopped talking, won’t say another word,” Kai tells me.

“What has he told you so far?” I ask.

“Jezebel has a child, she was pregnant when she left, they’ve been using the child as a weapon against her. She’s tracking for them,” Kai says.

“Tracking what?” I ask.

“Humans,” Paul growls, throwing the vampire to the floor as he screams out in pain.

“Where? Do we know which coven?” I ask.

“No, he won’t tell us, keeps mumbling they would come to get him, kill him if he said a word, then he began to hold his head in pain screaming for it to go away,” Kai answers.

“Someone is in his head,” I say, bending to his level as he screams smashing a hand against his head.

“A fae?” Paul growls.

“I don’t know, Kai, could you fetch Rook and Jae for me? I’d like to see what they think,” I ask.

“Of course,” Kai says flitting away.

“What do we do with him for now?” Paul asks.

"Lock him up so he can't kill himself, I still want information out of him. Make sure Cole doesn't get to him though, if he finds out about Jezebel, he'll just bolt to find her, we have to be tactile," I reply.

"Yes Ma'am," he nods.

"Thanks, Paul," I smile.

"A pleasure as always my queen," he smirks as I flip him off.

I can hear the vampire screaming to be let go as I head back up the stairs.

"Shit! PHOENIX!" Paul shouts as I rush back down to find the vampire on the floor.

"What the fuck happened? I left for two seconds!" I exclaim.

"He just fell to the floor… I didn't even touch him!" He replies.

"My lady?" Rook walks down the stairs with Jae and Kai by his side.

"Who killed him?" Kai frowns.

"Not us," Paul and I say in unison.

"Did he have any symptoms?" Rook bends down at the entrance, he looks at the body, his hands hovering over him.

"He was screaming that someone was in his head, kept smacking his head with his claws," Paul answers.

"I've only ever heard of one thing being able to do that and I thought they were extinct, the closest to them is a guardian," Jae says joining Rook.

"What?" I ask.

"Witch," Rook and Jae say in unison.

"Witches… Are you serious? They're real too?" I say, running a hand through my hair.

"Again, they were said to be extinct, but I think we may have one here, they can mess with the mind and force a person to do anything if they wish it," Rook answers.

"Great, this is just great, just add it to the list of everything else I have to worry about!" I exclaim.

"Nix, calm down, it will be ok. We will deal with this one step at a time," Kai places his hands on my shoulders.

"We have the party tonight, saving humans tomorrow, we have to find Jezebel and her child and now I find out that witches are out there messing with people's minds, and they are on the opposite team! How am I supposed to calm down?!" I shout.

"My love, shh, it's ok," arms wrap around my waist, smelling Michael's scent behind me as I snuggle into his arms, breathing deeply.

"One step at a time Nix," Kai nods at me as I nod back slowly.

"It never bloody ends, does it…" I sigh.

"Jae and I will continue to discover what we can from the body. Phoenix, you should go ready yourself for the party, you are the host, after all. Do not worry about this for the moment, concentrate on your family," Rook says.

"Thank you," I nod.

I can see Michael and Paul are talking via their links, they must be talking about what happened as Michael's eyes went dark with anger, holding tightly to me.

"Fucking witches… What's next… Sirens…" he grumbles.

"Well… Some say…" Jae begins as Michael growls.

"I'm joking!" Jae laughs, holding his hands up in surrender.

"Go, enjoy your night. I have this handled. I'm not one for parties, I'll call Rodge to join me and have Jae sent back up when it's time," Rook says.

"Thank you," I smile.

"The houses are prepared for new humans too, the welcome wagon is ready for tomorrow," Jae says.

"I suppose something has to go right," I nod as we head back upstairs.

"One hour until the kids officially turn eighteen," Kai smirks, looking at his watch.

"Shit, we need to get ready!" I exclaim, dragging Michael with me as he chuckles.

"It's our party, we can afford to be fashionably late," he smirks at me.

"No, we cannot," I shake my head.

"What if…" He begins.

"No, no more tonight big guy," I chuckle, he kisses my lips, going down to my mating mark as I moan against him.

"Are you sure?" He chuckles.

"Michael! Enough, keep it in your pants," I giggle.

"Fine," he sighs playfully winking at me.

Soon we're dressed, Michael looked handsome in his suit as I bit my lip, arousal flooding my stomach as he turns to me.

"I can smell it you know," he chuckles.

"I know," I nod with a smirk.

"Tease," he laughs.

I smile as I finish my make-up, giving myself a once over. I looked pretty good, the smart jump-suit, it made me look hot and dignified at the same time.

"You're beautiful," Michael puts his arms around me, kissing me gently.

"Thank you handsome, now come on, we have a party to enjoy for tonight, tomorrow the work begins," I reply.

"Focus on tonight, the kids are our priority," he nods, kissing me sweetly before we leave our room.

"Mum! You look gorgeous!" Taylor grins. I look at her, my eyes tearing up, she looked beautiful in the dress Janie had given her last year.

"Wow, you look beautiful Taylor," I smile, giving her a huge hug.

"I wasn't sure if it would look too much at first, but I put it on and fell in love with it," she says as I notice her touch the necklace on her neck.

"Where did you get that?" I ask.

"Bryant gave it to me for our birthday," she smiles.

"It's gorgeous," I smile.

"You should see the blade she had made for me mum; it was awesome!" Bryant walks out of his room and hugs us all.

“Oh, look at you, you’re a miniature of your father,” my eyes glaze over my children, I had never been so proud than I was at this moment.

“What is that…” Keeley wanders up to us as she eyes Taylor.

“My dress…” Taylor says, rolling her eyes.

Keeley had definitely become a force to be reckoned with, she was a complete diva and reminded me of Lola from back at school. I had no idea where she got this personality from, but most of us hated it.

“You would have looked better in the one I was going to give you,” Keeley huffs.

“Keeley! Go to your mother right now!” I exclaim angrily.

“Ugh, fine,” she stomps away.

“What happened to that sweet little girl?” Michael sighs.

“She became a huge pain in the arse,” Bryant says as he and Taylor laugh.

“Yes, albeit, she is still family, so do try to be nice to her,” I sigh, though I wasn’t going to enforce it if Keeley was being a brat.

“TEN MINUTES! Happy birthday my little cherubs!” Kai flits to their sides, pinching their cheeks as Taylor giggles and Bryant swats him away.

“Thank you, Uncle Kai,” Taylor smiles.

“Thanks, but enough of the cherub shit,” Bryant growls.

“But you’re so cute!” Kai smirks and I roll my eyes.

“One day he is going to flatten you Kai, and I’m not stopping him,” I point to my best friend.

"But… you can't let your son hurt me! I'm your best friend!" Kai huffs.

"Watch me," I grin at him with a wink.

"NIX!" He exclaims. I laugh, hooking an arm around the twins as we head down the stairs. I can hear the music begin to play, right on time.

As we get to the bottom of the stairs the cheers begin, the twins are wished a happy birthday, I can already see several new mated pairs in the crowd, unable to let go of their mates.

I can see Keeley sulking beside her mother as Violet looks over at me, a disappointed look on her face.

"Excuse me a moment, enjoy the party my loves," I kiss the twins on the cheek, making my way to Violet, leaving Michael and Kai with the twins.

"Phoenix, I hear my daughter has been making a fool of herself, I do apologise," Violet says as Keeley sulks.

"No worries, I just don't know what happened to our old Keeley, she was such a happy girl. I do worry about her weight though, the twins have come to me a few times about it, all she is drinking are these weird slimming shakes," I say quietly so Keeley doesn't hear.

"Ah, I was not made aware. I will have a word with her, she is looking a little pale, I'll deal with it. Though I will say when I return, she will be coming with me, I can keep a better eye on her then and figure out what's going on with her, I know you love her too, but she needs her mother," Violet says.

"I totally understand, blood is blood," I nod with a smile.

"Go, have fun, there will be plenty of time to talk of the depressing world we have, you should be celebrating," Violet smiles.

“Thank you, I hope you enjoy the party too Violet,” I smile as I begin to walk through the crowd.

“Hey, mum…” Blake sneaks up to me as I jump out of my skin.

“I wish you would stop sneaking up on me,” I groan, holding a hand to my heart.

“Sorry, but uh, I was just wondering… When you smell your mate, but can’t work out where it’s coming from, what do you do?” He asks as my eyes go wide and I smile.

“You feel them?” I smile.

“Yes, but I have no idea who, it was like I smelt the most beautiful thing in the world just a moment ago, but there are so many people here, I can’t work it out,” he says.

“Walk with me, focus, we’ll find them,” I smile, taking his hand as we begin to walk the hall, talking to a few people as we go.

“It’s useless… I can’t work out who it is,” he sighs as we’ve been wandering around for half an hour.

“Well, how about we take a breather and go see the twins, they will want to see you turned up,” I smile. He nods slowly, his eyes darting around as we head towards the twins who are standing chatting with Kade, Luci, Kai, Jae, Janie and Hanson.

“I wondered where you went, Blake, you actually came down, I’m shocked,” Michael smirks at him.

“Blake!” Taylor grins at Blake and I felt Blake stiffen.

“Blake…” I murmur.

"Oh shit… No… No… No… I-I'm sorry, I have to go," Blake says flitting from us, going upstairs and I hear the slam of a door.

"What the hell was that about?" Bryant asks.

"Taylor… Baby… Are you ok?" I ask her through our link as she looks at me in shock.

"Mum… I think… I think he's my mate… Lily won't shut up…" Taylor says in shock through our link as I take a deep breath. Well, this just got complicated…

"Whoa…" Bryant murmurs and I follow his eye line to a girl behind us.

"Bryant?" I raise a brow.

"Mate," he says pushing past us to the girl as I hear her gasp.

"Who is that? I've never seen her before," Kai asks, but I'm too focused on Taylor, her face is that of shock.

"Taylor, baby, come on, let's take a walk," I grab her hand as Michael looks at me with concern.

"Is everything ok?" Michael asks through our bond.

"I think she's found her mate… Let me handle this," I reply as he nods. I pull Taylor with me, heading outside into the quiet night sky.

"He can't be… He's our brother…" She murmurs.

"Taylor, baby look at me," I pull her face gently to look into my eyes.

"Blake… He's…" she blubs.

"I know, I saw it in both your eyes. Now you listen to me, though I adopted him as my son he is not of blood, there is nothing wrong with you being mates.

If things had gone differently, you would have met and not have grown up together the same, but the goddess deemed it this way for a reason. You know he has never treated you as a sister as such, you were more a best friend, he never felt right calling you sister while he cared for you, plus technically we didn't adopt him as such, in the human world they use paperwork and all that kind of thing, we just… took him in. I do love him as a son, but if you two decide you want to be together, he would be my son, my son-in-law as humans call it. Do not let that taint your mind. Talk to him, make sure you both know exactly what you want before doing something silly like rejecting each other," I said cupping her cheek softly as she nuzzles into it, tears in her eyes.

"I didn't want a mate, I'm not sure I can be what a mate needs, I've never been in a relationship, never experienced love, how can I do that for a mate…" she sighs.

"You're talking to the woman who has had two mates, the first I never mated with and the second, your father, I lost my virginity to… I know Taylor, I know exactly how you feel, and you will manage, you will learn, it's a part of life, don't give up on love because you haven't felt it, open your mind to it," I hug her to my chest. I can feel Blake's anger and cry for help upstairs.

# Chapter Seven

## Blake

No, this can't be happening! Taylor can't be our mate! No way, not in hell.

*Calm down Blake, she is our mate, what are you so afraid of?*

**She's our sister!**

*No, she's not, we aren't blood, Phoenix took us in, loved us, but they are not blood-related to us. It's ok to fall for Taylor.*

**No, it doesn't feel right.**

*Really? So, when we smelt her scent and saw her that first moment, you didn't have the image of her sleeping next to us every night? Huh?*

**I... Shit... What about everyone else? What will they think?**

*You're joking, there's no way that Phoenix, mum, hasn't realised already and if she's ok with it, everyone else will fall in line.*

**What if mum isn't ok with it...**

*Then... Well... I don't know...*

**Great, thanks, Copper.**

"Blake?" A knock at the door startles me, I hear mum calling for me as I open the door slowly to her.

"Sorry… I-I… Just…" I stammer.

*Great start…*

**Shut the fuck up!**

"I know. I know you're mates, and I hope you both talk to each other about it. I'm not against it, far from it, though a little unconventional in some eyes, you are not blood, so you are free to do as you wish. You know I love you all and will be here no matter what you both decide. But you must talk to each other, I'm not saying it's going to be easy, because it won't. Taylor is just as nervous as you are, she's worried she won't be enough, she's worried she can't give the love needed to be a mate, it will be slow, but if you both decide that this calling is for you then you must talk. If you both decide you can't go through with it, there will always be another mate, though you must be sure on what you want so you don't both regret it later on," mum says as I plonk onto my bed with a sigh.

"I've always loved her, never as a sister, it always felt weird, I thought I was in love with Keeley and now this, my heart and my head are confused," I groan.

"Time, Blake, and talking, there is no rush," she cups my cheek as I sigh into it.

"Thank you," I reply with a small smile.

"Now, should I tell her to come up or would you like a moment to yourself?" She asks as I gulp.

"Uh… I… Uh… Send her up," I say nervously.

"Ok, try not to push too much, don't force it all, you'll know if it feels right, I'll be downstairs if you need me," she kisses my head, leaving the room as I groan laying on my bed, hands on my head.

"Blake…" I hear Taylor say timidly, opening the door slowly.

I've never known this girl to be so timid before, she's always so fiery…

"Hey," I gulp, sitting up in an instant as she bites her lip.

*I'd like to bite it too…*

**Copper… Not now.**

*I'm just saying, she's beautiful.*

**I know.**

"So, we're mates huh…" She sighs, sitting next to me gently.

"Yeah, crazy world right…" I reply and we sit in silence for a moment.

"We don't have to do this; I know you never wanted a mate… We won't accept each other if it's not something you want," I sigh, looking down at the floor.

"It's not that simple is it though…" Taylor sighs too.

"When has our life ever been simple?" I chuckle as she giggles.

*That giggle… My god… She's so precious.*

**COPPER! I know!**

"It's definitely not been simple, more so for you, I guess, after everything before I was even born," she replies as her eyes gaze up at me, my god, those eyes shine like the stars…

*Now, who is going all crazy over her… It's worse than you were with Keeley!*

**COPPER!**

“You’re talking to Copper, aren’t you?” She laughs.

“Yes,” I nod.

“Lily is going crazy in my head right now, she wants to see him,” she answers.

“We could… We could go for a walk, talk outside, let our wolves mix for a bit, it might help, you know, seeing how we feel?” I offer.

“Sounds good,” she nods, I stand and offer her my hand as she looks up at me nervously.

“Taylor, you’ve held my hand a thousand times before, it’s just my hand,” I chuckle.

“Yeah, but this is different isn’t it…” She says standing as her hand gently goes into mine, sending shivers through my whole body.

“Y-Yeah… It is,” I nod, looking into her eyes as I step towards her, my hand cupping her face as she looks at me nervously, my face slowly going towards her. But before our lips touch, she moves away.

“Let’s go for that walk,” she clears her throat as I sigh, nodding as we head out.

I can feel mum’s gaze on us. Is it right for me to keep calling her mum? I mean, I suppose if we mated… she would be my mum still, just a different way.

“Taylor! Hey!” Bryant shouts as we are about to leave through the front doors.

“Hey,” Taylor smiles at her twin as he is grinning from ear to ear.

“I found my mate; can you believe this?! See her, over there standing with Hanson, that’s her, it’s his bloody niece, Amanda. She’s beautiful, isn’t she?

This whole mate bond thing, it's crazy, it's like the whole world has changed in a single moment," Bryant says excitedly.

"That's really great Bryant," Taylor smiles, but he can see she's holding back.

"Ok, what's up?" Bryant folds his arms as he looks between us.

"Nothing, I just… The crowd is getting to me a little, that's all, we're going for a walk to calm my nerves a little," she answers him, he frowns and I'm sure he doesn't believe her, his eyes turn to their wolfish yellow as I see them talking through the bonds. His wolf, Ash, was just as stubborn as he was.

"Bryant, come on, leave them alone, Taylor needs to have a moment outside, let them go for their walk," mum walks up to us as Taylor smiles at her.

"Ok, but you and I are talking tonight, ok?" Bryant says to his sister.

"Yes brother," she smiles, giving him a nod as he walks off with Mum.

We go outside, both shifting as we let our wolves take over a little more.

**Be gentle, don't overdo it, Copper.**

*I know, I will.*

Our wolves began walking around the mansion while the moon sat high in the sky, our paws hitting the hard ground as Copper began moving closer to her, gently nudging her with his side, rubbing against her as we felt sparks up our side.

We stayed like that for a while as she didn't make a move to back off, our sides were touching the whole time, until she stopped, looking up at the moon as she gives off the most beautiful howl I had ever heard, it sent shivers up my spine as she looked at us, she nudged our muzzle with her nose as I stepped forward, nuzzling my head into her neck.

*They are beautiful.*

**They are…**

# Chapter Eight

## Taylor

What is this feeling? I don't understand it. Is this what mum talked about? My stomach feels queasy, my skin shivers at his touch, his head in my neck as I smell his sweet scent.

"Taylor… Are you ok?" Blake asks through our link; he backs away slowly, and I begin to miss his touch. What is with this feeling?

"I'm ok," I almost whisper back.

"Listen I'm not rushing us, we can see how this goes, we don't have to do anything you don't want," Blake says.

"Thank you… I-I don't know right now. I know we're mates, I can feel it, but this, this is weird, I've known you my whole life and never once have I wanted a mate, but this feeling, it's… Overwhelming…" I reply.

"I understand, just know I think you're beautiful Taylor, you've always been amazing to me, even though some of your power with earth creeps me out," Blake says as we both chuckled, looking into his eyes I can see him, and his wolf and I feel our bond.

*Give in… He's amazing.*

**If you could blush, I bet you would be… We didn't want a mate before… Why now?**

*I didn't know we could feel like this, I mean… we've seen it, but feeling it, the bond, it's completely different.*

"Taylor. Run with me," Blake nudges my side with a playful look, and he continuously nudges me, pushing me to stand up again. I stand and he begins to prance about playfully as I laugh and bound over him with a bark.

"Come run then," I laugh, he stands there once more, watching me before he leaps after us, paws thudding against the ground as we race through the dark woods. Barrelling through a few warriors they curse us out as we are quick to apologise but keep going.

Blake suddenly knocks me off my feet, tumbling over the grass and moss on the ground, our fur covered in dirt as he pins me on my back, his paws keeping me down as we pant hard.

We both shift, feeling the need to be in our human forms as we look into each other's eyes.

"Taylor…" He breathes.

"Blake," I say softly, his head gets ever so close to mine, our eyes looking at each other's lips and back.

"Blake! Blake! I know you're out here! Can we talk?! Blake!" I hear Keeley shout as our mouths were about to touch. Blake sighs, pressing his forehead against mine, lifting himself off of me and gives me a hand up as I see Keeley make her way through the trees.

"Oh, hi Taylor, do you mind if I talk to Blake a moment?" Keeley says, eyeing us both, we were both covered in dirt, my dress completely ruined.

"Sure, I'll give you two a moment," I smile, I didn't have a good feeling about this…

“Keeley, there is nothing you need to say to me,” Blake snaps as I’m walking away, I get to the treeline, sitting at the bottom of the trunk, just far enough to still hear them talking.

“I do, I’m sorry. I’m sorry about how I acted with you. Mum and I talked… I’ve been a bitch to you and yet you’ve shown me nothing but love. I-I-I’d like to give us a try…” she says as my eyes widen, a pang in my heart.

“Keeley… I… Jesus… This is not what I expected… Keeley you know I love you…” He says.

“Then let me try, let us try, don’t say anything, just let me do one thing before you say no,” she replies. I hear the crunch of the ground beneath her feet as she moves closer to him. My hand digs into the ground, I close my eyes feeling everything, where they stand…

They were so close… Then I hear it… They’re kissing…

*NO! How could he?!*

**He’s been in love with her for years… What do you expect? We should have seen this coming… He could never love us like he does her… It was stupid to think we could…**

*No! No way, Blake wouldn’t do this…*

**Here, let’s take a look shall we.**

I stand up quickly peering through the trees, watching Blake and Keeley embraced, kissing each other as I gulp.

How could I even think that I would get an easy mating… Of course, it had to be Blake… He was in love with her still… Might as well quit now…

*Are we going to reject him?*

**I think so…**

*But…*

**Look at him, he has a chance with the girl he loves… He's not stopping her… We were better off alone.**

I couldn't help but watch. My heart felt like it was breaking, I hated this feeling, I had never felt anything like this before, my chest felt heavy, I could barely breathe.

A small sob comes out of my mouth as I see Blake pull from the kiss, his eyes wide as he looks straight at me.

"Taylor!" He shouts. I shake my head, shifting and running towards the mansion's entrance.

"Leave her!" I hear Keeley shout to him as I race forward.

Getting to the door I shift back and push through the double doors, tears in my eyes pushing through the crowds, hearing their whispers around me as I make my way to the stairs.

"Taylor? What's the matter? What happened?" Kai flits to my side. I just shake my head and run up the stairs, rushing to my room as I slam the door shut, letting out a scream of frustration.

I should have just rejected him from the start, how could he love me when he loves her…

"Taylor! Taylor open up! Please, we need to talk!" I hear Blake shout as he thumps against my locked door.

"Blake, what happened?" I hear dad's voice call deeply.

"Taylor!" Blake shouts.

"For god's sake Blake, what happened? I won't ask again!" Dad shouts as I flinch.

*Should we reject him? I don't know… I've heard it's painful…*

**I'm sorry for this Lily…**

I take a deep breath, wrenching my door open. Blake is looking at my dad as if he's about to tell him what happened.

"I reject you as my mate Blake…" I say quickly, feeling Lily cower in my mind.

"No… Please… Don't do this!" Blake cries out.

"I have to. I am rejecting you from here on out, I no longer wish to feel our mates' bond, so it shall be," I gulp. Feeling the sting, like a snap inside my heart as we both fall to our knees.

"Oh shit! Blake, you must finish it, or the pain will never end!" Dad says getting to my level, his arms around me tightly as I scream with pain.

"NO! Please!" Blake cries out.

"Reject me, please Blake, I can't do this!" I cry.

"I-I-I am rejecting you from here on out, I no longer wish to feel our mates' bond, so it shall be," he says as we both scream out in pain.

"I've got you, sweetheart, I've got you," dad says, picking me up and going over to the bed as he sits with me in his lap, rocking me in his arms as I shake with pain.

“What happened Michael? Blake, oh my, Taylor…” Mum rushes to us, her hand over her mouth in shock as she looks between us, holding Blake’s head to her chest as she watches me.

“She rejected him…” Dad says as I cry out in pain.

“Oh, my,” mum says with a tear in her eye.

“Twin! I can feel her! Taylor! Where the fuck are you? Taylor! Why do you hurt so much?” I feel my twins’ call, but I can barely feel my body, let alone answer him.

“Phoenix, they must be separated, the closer they are the more it will hurt, they need to let their bodies relax, then once they no longer feel it they can be around each other again,” dad says.

“Ok, KADE! Help me!” She shouts as I hear the thump of his leg against the floor, seeing him looking into the room with pain etched into his features.

“What happened? Taylor… Princess…” Kade murmurs.

“They rejected each other, now help me move him, please,” mum says as he looks between us with shock before nodding sadly, helping mum take Blake away as the pain begins to disappear slightly.

“It hurts,” I cry to dad.

“I know, I know, I’ve got you,” he says holding me tightly.

“Taylor! Holy shit, are you ok? Did Blake hurt you?!” Bryant bursts into the room, kneeling in front of us, his and dad’s eyes turn yellow as I know they are talking.

“Oh, twin…” Bryant says, caressing my face gently.

"Go back to the party, to your mate," I sniff back the tears, snuggling into dad's broad chest as I used to.

"Amanda will understand, I can't party without my twin," he smiles sadly at me.

"There will always be another, you will feel it again and I'm sure it will be better, many do not get with their firsts. You know, Jae once told your mother that we all get more than one mate because some are better suited to us with a certain path we take. Perhaps Blake was not of the path you're on and you are on your way into another, life takes us in many directions, don't give up, we all love you Taylor and you will find love, as much as you reject the thought, I can feel your pain, your heart was loosening from its grip on being alone, never give up," dad says kissing my head.

"Thanks, dad, you should go to mum. Bryant you should go to Amanda, I'll be ok, it hurts, but it's bearable," I sniffle.

"I'm not going anywhere, dad you go, I've got her," Bryant says, I feel dad nod as he lifts me up, putting me on the bed softly and he kisses my head.

"Call for me if you need me," dad says before leaving the room.

"You should get changed, come on," Bryant helps me up slowly, grabbing my favourite pyjamas before I take them and get changed slowly in the bathroom. I hear Bryant sorting out the bed and I try wiping away the dirt from my dress.

I wince from pain, feeling down as I walk back into the room, climbing onto the bed where my twin holds out his arms for me to curl in.

Safe, the safest place we could be was with each other. I couldn't live without my twin, he was my other half, my best friend.

"Try to sleep Tay, I've got you," he says, kissing my head as I curl into his side.

I fall asleep in my brother's arms, pain coursing through my heart.

# Chapter Nine

## Phoenix

“What happened Blake?” I ask softly, caressing his head as he groans beside me.

“Keeley… She… Kissed… Me…”

“There’s more though, isn’t there?” I ask.

“She wants to try being with me…” He groans, wincing in pain.

“Did you agree?” I ask.

“I didn’t disagree… She kissed me and I kissed back. I didn’t want to hurt Taylor… I would never want that… I’m sorry mum,” Blake replies.

“What’s done is done, you realise Keeley is leaving to stay with her mother, right?” I say, he looks at me with shock.

“No, she never told me,” he shakes his head.

“Will you go with her?”

“I-I guess I have no choice, it may be for the best, after what I’ve done, I hurt Taylor…” He says as I see the tear in his eye. I knew he didn’t mean to hurt her; the heart was fickle and the mating bonds confusing.

“It’s up to you Blake, I will not stop you doing what you want, but we will miss you, I’m sure even Taylor will, once the pain has subsided,” I reply.

“I-I-I will think about it, can I just be alone? Please, I’m sorry I ruined tonight,” he apologises.

“It’s ok, sleep, the pain will go, good night, Blake,” I kiss his head as I head out of his room, leaning against it with a sigh, my hands running through my hair.

“How is he?” Michael walks up to me slowly, his arms wrapping around my waist gently as he kisses the top of my head softly.

“Upset, in pain, I’m sure the same as Taylor. How is she?” I ask.

“Yes, much the same, though she’s now in her brother’s arms falling asleep as they did when they were little, she’s strong, she’ll be ok,” Michael answers. I sigh into his arms as he hugs me tightly against him.

“How did it come to this? Our poor babies, I had hoped they would have an easier life than us and yet it seems only to get more difficult,” I reply.

“They are strong, like you, they will be ok, we will be right by their sides no matter what and I am right here for you my love, as are everyone else,” Michael says as I nod slowly kissing him softly.

“Phoenix… I’m sorry, this is my fault…” Keeley stands beside us as I look at her, her face filled with sorrow.

“You certainly didn’t help the situation, but I feel they weren’t meant to be. However, Keeley, if you really are going to try with Blake, don’t hurt him…” I say as she nods.

“I love him, I do. I was just caught up with the whole soul mate thing, that I didn’t realise he was beside me… I’m sorry I’ve been so awful…” She sniffles.

“Good, go to him, love him, give us old Keeley back,” I smile softly at her.

"Done," she smiles, hugging me quickly before bursting into Blake's room.

"Come now my love, I would like a dance with you tonight, before the whole party ends," Michael holds out his hand, I smile at him before quickly glancing to the kids' rooms.

"They'll be ok, won't they?" I sigh.

"They will, just as you were," Michael kisses me sweetly, pulling me down the stairs with him.

"Are the kids ok?" Luci asks as we stand beside them.

"They are facing something new, painful, but they will be fine," Michael answered for me.

"Bloody mate bonds," Trey grumbles.

"You still haven't found yours?" I give him a sad smile, taking his hand in mine and squeezing it in support.

"He hasn't even looked properly, he's been hugging the side of the room all night," Luci sniggers.

Trey growls, his wolf evident in his eyes as I feel the anger flow from him.

"Gray, calm down," I say sternly to his wolf.

"Sorry Nix," Trey groans, shaking his head.

"Will you go dance with someone?! You're making me anxious standing here; you're not going to find a mate standing here. Go Trey, just dance with someone, for god's sake even Kai is dancing with Jae, look!" Luci points to the dance floor, Kai and Jae are dancing slowly, their eyes gazing into each other's as I smile, my heart fluttering at the cuteness.

“And dance with who?” Trey rolls his eyes.

“Me, it would seem my mate is busy with his twin, so I could do with someone to dance with rather than hanging around my uncle,” Amanda says suddenly. I glance at her, she’s gorgeous, long blonde hair tied into a bun with ringlets surrounding it, she was slim, but more of a fit slim than an unhealthy stick figure.

“Oh, please Trey, she will bug me all night to dance with her otherwise, I have Janie to keep occupied,” Hanson smirks as Janie whacks his arm playfully giggling.

“Fine,” Trey huffs, taking Amanda’s hand as they walk onto the dance floor.

“My lady,” Michael bows taking my hand as I smile and we join the others in dance, I just wished the twins were here…

A few hours later and I was sat with Luci while we talked about her pregnancy, she was so nervous.

“What if something goes wrong Nix? We’ve been trying for so long now…” She sighs.

“I will have healers nearby every day, you will never be alone, nothing is going to happen Luci, it’s going to be ok,” I grip her hand in mine tightly and she nods, putting her head on my shoulder before yawning.

“You’re tired my love, we should head off to bed,” Kade walks over.

“But…” She mumbles.

“Go to bed Luci,” I smile.

“Ok, come get me if anything happens with the twins?” She says as Kade picks her up.

"Of course, go rest, good night, guys," I smile at them, they wish me goodnight and head up.

The hall was beginning to quieten down, many of the mated couples gone to mate already, others tired, while the rest were mingling.

"Mum," my head lifts quickly, seeing Taylor beside her twin, arms linked as she's in her usual jeans and vest.

"Hey baby, how are you feeling?" I say softly, tapping the seat beside me.

"Better, it hurts still, but it's getting better… We missed a hell of a party huh?" She rests her head on my shoulder as I see Bryant is watching his mate chatting animatedly to Trey, Hanson and Janie.

"You haven't missed a lot, as long as you're ok," I kiss her head softly.

"For god's sake Bryant, go to her before you burst," Taylor chuckles, shoving him forward.

"But…" He mumbles, looking between Taylor and Amanda.

"Go get her!" Taylor laughs with a grin at her twin as she hugs into my side.

"I agree, go. I have Taylor," I smile at my baby boy, he grins and kisses our cheeks before running to the others. We hear Amanda squeal excitedly as he picks her up and twirls her around, kissing her quickly.

"That's how it should be… Easy. Blake and I… We wouldn't have been easy…" Taylor sighs.

"I always believed things happened for a reason and I still do, you will find someone who ticks all the right boxes and makes you shine brighter than before, but until that day, you have all of us by your side," I kiss her head.

“Mum… Can I go on the mission tomorrow?” She asks. I bite my lip, I hated the kids going out searching for humans, it was so dangerous, but I knew they would have to grow up at some point and learn their place in the world. How could I stop them? As much as I wanted to wrap them in bubble wrap and never let them leave the house, they had to fly the nest one day.

“Yes, but you listen to Paul and Hanson, you do not put yourself into unnecessary risk and you watch your brother for me, he collared me earlier today and demanded he go too, Blake too… Will that be ok?” I answer.

“It will be ok, I don’t want to lose him as a friend, no matter what happened,” she nods.

“Good, I have to stay here with your father to protect our home while preparing ourselves for your returns, I mean it Taylor, you be careful,” I tilt her head up and kiss her forehead.

“I know mum, I promise I will do as I’m told, I’m not a kid anymore,” she smiles at me.

“I know you’re not, but you are still my little girl, and I don’t want anything to happen to you,” I hug her to me.

“I’ll be fine mum, I love you,” she says hugging me back.

“I love you too, you and your silly twit of a brother,” I chuckle, watching Bryant acting like a goofball with his mate as Taylor giggles too.

# Chapter Ten

## Taylor

I had stayed with mum most of the night, we talked about the day ahead, I knew she was nervous about Bryant and I going out on a mission without her. We were finally growing up in her eyes and I could see the love she had for us, she didn't want us to grow up, but she knew she couldn't stop it.

This morning had ended up all go as I was awoken by my twin promptly at six o'clock in the morning, both groaning it was early, but getting ready for the day ahead.

"Have you got your blade?" I ask Bryant and he lifts his top to show it sheathed by his side.

"Don't take off that necklace twin, promise me," he says as I raise a brow.

"Why? What did you do to it?" I ask, walking downstairs beside him.

"It helps keep our bond stronger than ever, with that, I will always find you, no matter how far we are," he says.

"Wow… I promise it won't leave my neck," I smile at him.

"Good," he nods.

"Good morning twins," Kai grins.

"Morning uncle Kai," I smile, hugging him.

“Are you both ready? The team are waiting in the briefing room with your parents already,” Kai says as I raise my brows in shock.

“Already… We haven’t eaten yet,” Bryant groans.

“Good thing you have me then,” Kai brings out two packages of foil from behind his back, we both moan in delight at the breakfast sandwiches.

“Thank you,” we say in unison, digging in on our way to the briefing room.

“About time you two turned up…” Cole grumbles from the front.

“It’s seven… Get a grip,” Bryant snaps at him.

“Enough, now that the twins are here, we can discuss what will happen today,” mum says, she smiles at us both before going into strategies for the day.

“Hanson will take the first team, Kai, Jae, Blake and Jason you guys will go with him and his pack, you will scout ahead for team two, with Cole, Paul, Trey, the twins and my pack members once given the all clear,” mum begins as we nod.

“What about me?” I hear Keeley huff to the side, hugging into Blake as we glance at each other, nodding briefly with small smiles.

“You’re staying here with us,” mum says.

“What?! I never get to go! Why do the others get to go?!” Keeley stomps like a child as I snigger, she glares at me.

“Keeley, you will do as you are told, you will stay back with us, end of. Janie is staying too,” Violet snaps at her daughter, Keeley huffs, sitting with her arms crossed angrily.

"Next time babe," I hear Blake whisper. Bryant bumps our arms as we look at each other.

"You ok?" He asks through our bond.

"I'm fine," I nod, watching Keeley as she sulks in her chair, her hand rubbing her head occasionally.

"When do we leave?" I hear my brother ask, pulling me away from looking at Keeley.

"As soon as possible," Cole grumbles.

"An hour, it gives everyone time to grab their gear. I want everyone to have a weapon beside their wolves just in case," mum states. I see Bryant smirk and wink at me, tapping his blade.

"What's got you looking so smug?" Dad says with a raised brow at Bryant.

"I never showed you what Taylor got me for our birthday," he smirks before pulling out his blade, swishing it around a few times.

"Very nice," dad nods.

"Oh, you think that's it?" Bryant smirks, lighting the whole thing on fire as a gasp fills the room.

"Holy shit, where can I get one like that?" Mum says as I chuckle.

"I'll have one made for you Nix," Jae smirks winking at me. I had gone to him to ask if anything like that was possible, and he had taken me to a fae that had skills beyond anything I had seen as a blacksmith.

"How come the kids get all the cool things?" Mum says as dad chuckles at her, kissing her forehead softly.

"You don't need blades, you wield enough power without the extra help," dad smiles.

"Have we all finished? We need to get ready!" Cole growls, I raise a brow at him.

"Chill dude, we'll get there," I roll my eyes.

The others begin to leave as they go to get ready to leave.

"Hey, Taylor… Are we ok?" Blake walks up to me nervously.

"Sure, we're ok," I nod.

"Thank God, I'm sorry. I ruined your birthday, broke your heart and fucked everything up all in one night," he says with a sigh.

"It's ok, we wouldn't have worked anyway, Keeley's your girl, not me, friends, yeah?" I hold out my hand, he smiles sweetly, tugging at my hand as he hugs me tightly. There's still a little sting in my heart, but it was for the best.

"Blake, come on," Keeley huffs, dragging him away.

"Good morning to you too Keeley," I snigger.

"Morning," she grumbles as they leave.

"Something is up with that girl, it's like she has two personalities," mum says coming to our side with Violet beside her.

"I have to agree, something is going on with my daughter, but what… I don't know," Violet frowns.

"Perhaps her going home will help," mum says.

"I hope so," Violet nods.

"Right, I hear I'm on twin duty," Trey grins at us.

"I don't need babysitting," Bryant growls.

"Not babysitting, just keeping an eye on you guys, helping out," Trey answers.

"Babysitting," Bryant and I say at the same time with a nod.

"Guys, stop it," mum growls in warning.

"We're just playing mum," I smile.

"You make sure you remember everything we taught you, all your training, you come back home safe, do you understand?" Dad says with a hand on one of our shoulders each.

"We will dad, we've got this, we're taking two teams, that's more than normal," I nod.

Soon enough it was time to go, I had given my parents a tight hug before my brother did the same.

"You guys be careful, take care of my man too, got it?" Janie smiles, hugging us.

"I feel like this is a goodbye hug, don't you twin?" Bryant smirks.

"Oh, shut it, just be careful," Janie smacks his shoulder.

"Let's go!" Cole shouts as he shifts, taking his spot beside Paul and Hanson ahead of the packs.

"Bye!" We shout before shifting quickly and joining them, taking our spots next to Kai, Trey, Jason, Blake and Jae.

We took off quickly, running through the trees, keeping an eye all around us for any signs of the demons hunting us.

My paws thud against the ground, feeling every branch and stone underfoot as we get further and further from home, it felt… Weird, but exhilarating too.

I sniff the air, smelling something odd as we get halfway to our destination hours later.

"Do you smell that?" I push through the links to the others as the packs begin to slow down. My nose to the air, I growl, lowering myself to the ground and walking towards the right of the group, the others right behind me.

Suddenly a loud scream pierces the air as we wince in pain, a group of vampires come flitting towards us, the screams stopping, and I shake my head to rid myself of the ringing in my ears as I bound forward with the others beside me.

I see my twin as he shifts to his human form running with his blade ablaze. I nudge his leg and he jumps onto my back quickly, swiping at the vampires around us, holding onto me tightly as we work in perfect sync, taking two down at the same time every time.

"This blade is so fucking cool!" He laughs as I tear another apart, howling with joy as the numbers get smaller by the minute.

I was so focused on my brother, that I hadn't noticed the last vampire come towards us. It swipes at my muzzle, and I whimper, Bryant is knocked off my back as he yells, getting flung from me.

I growl at the vampire as it hisses at me before Trey pounces on it, tearing it to shreds in front of me.

"I had it!" I growl at him.

"Looks like it, show me the wound, shift," Trey growls back, Gray, his wolf at the forefront of his mind as I shift.

He shifts too and grabs my face as I wince at his touch.

“I’m fine,” I growl, pushing him away.

“You’re lucky we heal quickly,” Trey grumbles as he helps Bryant up.

“You ok twin?” We say in unison, smirking at each other.

“Everyone alright?” Hanson calls out, everyone replies, stating they were ok just a few minor cuts and bruises.

“Let’s finish this,” Cole howls out before we shift again.

Bryant nudges me with his nose where the vampire had taken a swipe at me.

“It’s not healing,” he growls.

“It will, nothing’s instant,” I roll my eyes as we begin our run once again.

We were nearly to the old bunker and the wound was really beginning to sting.

“Let’s stop, rest a moment before team one heads off first,” Paul calls out as we shift, resting on the ground.

“Taylor… Shit… Jae!” Kai walks up to me, holding up my face.

“I’m fine uncle,” I say, but wince.

“Bullshit,” Kai snaps at me.

“What. Oh… Let me look at that… Can someone grab me a bottle of water?!” Jae calls out as Trey throws his own at him, his eyebrows furrowed in worry.

“This is going to sting, isn’t it?” I groan.

“Yeah, sorry…” Jae says, and he begins to pour it onto the wound as I hiss in pain.

"Is that wolfsbane?" Kai frowns.

"Yes, a basic form luckily. This is going to scar I'm afraid, but I've washed it out, luckily, it wasn't too deep," Jae sighs.

"So now they are using wolfsbane against us… Great…" I hear Cole growl.

"Are you sure you wish to continue Taylor?" Hanson walks towards us.

"Are you kidding me? A little cut and everyone's acting like I'm a kid with a boo boo," I roll my eyes.

"Just like her mother," Trey smirks at me.

"Stubborn," Jason adds.

"Michael's just as bad," Paul laughs.

"Good," Hanson smiles at me with a proud nod.

We rested for a little longer before getting into our set teams.

"We will call for you as soon as we clear the area. Stay put, ears open, there's more covens out here somewhere, we have no idea what they have with them either," Hanson says.

"Be careful," I blurt out as they are about to leave.

"YOU be careful!" Blake chuckles winking at me before taking off with the others.

Time went by so slowly once they had gone, it was quiet all around us. Some of us paced, filled with worry.

"I don't like how quiet it is," I murmur.

*I feel like something is going to happen.*

**Me too, Lily.**

"They should have cleared it by now, surely?" Bryant says to Paul, he frowns looking into the distance.

"I think we should go in Paul, it's been too long," Cole adds.

"I hate to say this, but I agree, what if they are hurt? They could have been ambushed… If they have a witch then there's no end to what could have happened," Trey replies.

"Ready yourselves, if we haven't heard from them in five minutes we go," Paul nods.

"Kai?" I push through the link.

*Why aren't they answering us?*

**I don't know, I haven't felt the bond snap, so they can't be dead…**

*Then why don't they reply?*

**I don't know Lily!**

I was pacing still, my eyes on the horizon.

"What is it twin?" Bryant asks me.

"Something doesn't feel right, they can't be dead, we'd feel the bond snap right?" I asked.

"Yes, we'd feel them…" he nods.

"So, something is blocking our communication… I've tried a few times and nothing," I answer.

"Paul! We should go!" Bryant calls out.

“Just wait!” Paul growls.

“No! We’ve waited long enough! If they were safe, they would have talked through the links already! The longer we wait the worse it could be! They could be in trouble!” I shout at him.

“I suppose you agree,” Paul says to Cole.

“I do,” Cole nods.

“Fine, twins in the middle, let’s pack up and head out!” Paul growls. We nod, getting into formation as we begin to run towards the bunker.

“I see it!” Cole calls out.

We all come to a standstill quickly, the grounds are deserted, an old bunker in the middle of an abandoned field, remnants of old brick walls crumbling dotted about. There’s nothing else here.

“I don’t understand, no one’s here…” I murmur, pushing forward a little as Paul growls at me to step back, but I don’t listen.

“Hey,” a voice whispers in my ear, my body shivers, looking everywhere for the source of the noise.

“Taylor?” Bryant calls as I step forward again.

“Get back Taylor, now!” Paul growls.

“Hey you! Come here,” the voice calls again and I keep my body low to the ground, walking cautiously forward.

“Taylor!” I hear the shouts of the others, I turn and whine in shock as I see no one there, they’re all gone! A mist begins to surround me slowly.

*What is this?*

**Keep calm, Lily.**

*Keep calm! They just disappeared in front of our eyes! Then the mist appeared from nowhere!*

"Hey! Taylor! Is that you?!" I hear Blake shout in the distance as I turn towards the voice.

"Blake?!" I shout.

"I can't see a fucking thing! Where the hell are you?!" Blake shouts back.

"Is anyone with you?!" I call back in my human form as I couldn't speak to him any other way.

"No, the others just disappeared!" He calls back as his voice gets louder.

"Blake!" I shout. but my foot hits something and I look down, screaming at the body at my feet.

"Taylor what is it?!" Blake calls out.

"But… But…" My eyes water, seeing Blake's body at my feet, blood pooling around him.

"Taylor! Answer me! What is it?" His voice calls, but right in front of me is his body… What is going on…

"I found your body… Blake…" I gulp, tears in my eyes.

"Taylor! I'm not dead, I'm here! That can't be me!" He shouts back.

"Taylor!" I hear my brother's voice in the distance behind me.

"Bryant!" I scream out.

I can see his blade swinging through the air on fire as it comes towards me.

"Taylor! Help me! Find me!" Blake shouts.

"Taylor! Run! It's not him!" Kai's voice calls next as my eyes widen.

"Taylor! RUN!" Trey shouts behind me.

"Too late," a shadowy figure slinks out from the mist.

"NO! Run Taylor!" A wolf barrels into the figure, teeth snapping at the shadowy man as my eyes widened.

"Jezebel!" I cried out, he flings her from his grasp, and she whines on the ground.

"I told you she'd come," Keeley pops out from behind him with a huge smile.

"TAYLOR!" Bryant calls out again.

"Keeley?" I frown as she just smirks at me cockily.

"Come child, come with me and the others will be safe, come with me and the world can be yours, your destiny awaits," the figure says.

"Fuck destiny," I growl shifting.

"NO! Don't do it!" Jezebel whimpers from the ground.

"Jezebel!" Cole's voice growls.

"Just kill her, she's not strong enough, you can have me, I sacrificed Blake for you!" Keeley says standing in front of the man.

"YOU! You did this! How could you?! Blake loved you! He did everything for you!" I scream at her.

"He was not my soul mate, it was too easy to split you both up, must you make everything I do so easy Taylor, you're pathetic," she laughs.

"I am tired with games," the figure snaps his fingers as she moves towards him, his fingers gripping her throat tightly.

"NO! I did this for you!" She cries as she gasps for a breath.

Blood begins to pour out of her pores as she screams in pain, I can't move, it's like my feet are stuck…

"Such a waste, now, where was I… Oh yes, Taylor…" He moves towards me, Keeley's body still in his grasp as I smell her blood, he throws her to the floor beneath my feet.

He looks menacing, a tall man with the darkest of skin, his eyes the deepest of purple, he wore a suit, which was nothing but pristine, yet he had had blood on his hands not moments ago. He was the poster child for the devil himself, his body screamed perfection and yet had the darkest of souls.

"TAYLOR!" I can hear my twin getting closer.

"Taylor! Don't look at him! His eyes are how he gets into your head!" Jae calls.

"It's a little late for that isn't it my pet, look into my eyes, I will not harm you," the man says, bringing his finger to my chin lifting it, my eyes still filled with tears.

"Don't listen Taylor! He's a witch, he's in your fucking head!" Kai shouts.

"Fuck you," I spit feeling a sudden surge of power, bringing my hand up, flinging a rock at his head as I manage to move my feet, running as fast as I can.

"Leave now! RUN!" I shout to the others.

"ENOUGH! You will join me! BOYS!" The shadowy figure shouts as the mist begins to clear, vampires surrounding us.

“Move!” I shout to the others as I spot Hanson and the others who run towards Paul and the rest of our team.

I lift my hand in the air, focusing my powers on the ground beneath me, moving it like something burrowing just under the surface as it topples vampires over, slowing them and I see the others trying to fight their way out.

My eyes catch Jezebel’s as she whimpers on the ground before someone grabs her by the hair dragging her. I shift, bolting towards her, tearing through anyone who came towards me.

“What the fuck are you doing?!” Jason barges through to me as we fight side by side.

“We have to get her!” I call as he looks ahead.

“No! Not my little girl!” Jezebel screams as she’s facing the witch.

He’s holding a small girl as she wriggles, screaming for her mother.

“LET HER GO!” I roar, darting from Jason’s side towards the witch as he raises a brow with a smirk.

“TAYLOR!” Bryant shouts. I get closer to the witch, not a single vampire touches me, they just moved around me while I notice Jason getting closer to Jezebel, tearing the vampires apart before he sets her free and they begin to run.

“Let her go now!” I growl in warning.

“Come with me,” he laughs.

I hear a blood-curdling scream in pain as I turn to Jason being ripped apart, blood spurting everywhere, Jezebel was fighting back as the others try to get to them.

"Jason! No! STOP THIS! Let them go! Please! No more!" I scream, begging. I could see some of our warrior's bodies on the ground, we'd lost half of them…

"Come with me and I will end it now, they can take the child, you'll be mine," he says.

"Fine! Just let them go!" I cry, shifting to my human form.

"Boys! Enough!" He shouts, clicking his fingers, they line up as a barrier between us and the others.

"Let the girl go," I repeat, and he drops her as she cries running towards her mother quickly.

"Selene!" Jezebel cries out as she pushes her way through the vampire barrier.

"NO! Taylor! Don't do this!" Bryant is being held back by Trey; tears fall from my eyes.

"I love you twin, go home, keep them safe," I say, feeling the witch's hand on my shoulder.

"Good girl," he chuckles, clicking his fingers and everything around us disappears.

# Chapter Eleven

## Phoenix

"Michael something doesn't feel right, we haven't heard a peep and they aren't answering back," I begin to pace around in my office.

"Phoenix, calm down I'm sure everything is fine, they are probably busy with the humans, you know what it can be like, they panic," Luci says grabbing my hand, halting my pacing.

"Phoenix! Have you seen Keeley?! She's gone!" Violet rushes into the room.

"She wouldn't have gone after the others, would she? She wanted to go," Kade runs a hand through his hair in frustration.

"Shh, calm down Phoenix, it will be ok," Michael holds me to his chest as my hands shake.

"Our babies are out there!" I murmur.

"They will be ok," he says back, but I could hear the worry in his voice too.

We continued to wait for hours, Kade and Michael were now pacing as I tried to console Violet from her worry that Keeley had indeed left towards the others. A warrior had come running into the room to warn us, but she was gone already, it was too late.

Suddenly I am pulled down to the floor, screaming in pain as I feel like someone had ripped my heart from my chest, bonds snapping one by one.

"NO!" I scream as Michael kneels before me.

"Who? Phoenix?!" Kade bellows as Michael holds me.

"Blake… Warriors… No… Keeley… Violet, I'm so sorry… Jason! NO!" I sob as Violet screams in pain, Luci and Janie trying to console her, crying themselves.

"The twins?" Luci murmurs.

"I can feel them, but Taylor… it's weak…" Michael says, I hear the pain in his voice.

"What do we do? Do we send another team?" Janie asks, sniffling from her tears.

"We can't risk that…" Kade says as I sob in Michael's arms.

"We have plenty of wolves and fae, send out several groups, pave them a safe path home," I order.

"I'll see it done," Rook stands in the corner quietly before rushing out.

Hours, it took hours before we had heard anything from the others, suddenly we were given word that they were nearly home, bodies of the fallen on their backs.

"Oh my god!" I scream out, running towards them as they break through the trees.

"Nix…" Kai flits to my side, covered in blood as I embrace him quickly, looking around for the kids.

"Mum," Bryant walks up to me slowly after a couple of bodies were taken off of his back.

“My baby,” I cuddle him to me as he breaks down, falling to his knees.

“I couldn’t get to her, I couldn’t get to my twin, I’m sorry mum,” he sobs as I take his face into my hands, tears falling from my face.

“What do you mean? Where is she? Where is Taylor?!” I cry out.

“He took her! The witch! She gave herself to him to save us all, she’s gone,” he says as tears drip from his eyes.

I can hear the roar of pain come from Michael as he shifts, howling into the air in anger.

“We’ll get her back, we will, you listen to me, we will get your twin back,” I kiss his head, hugging his head against my chest as I look around, seeing Blake’s body is carefully put on the ground next to Jason’s, his body had been torn to shreds.

I let out a sob of pain, we had lost so many today.

“Hanson!” Janie rushes out, she jumps into his arms as she sobs, her eyes looking around as she lets out a painful scream at Jason’s body.

“Hanson! Take her inside now! Don’t let her see anymore!” I shout quickly as he nods, running inside with her.

“Where is my girl?” I hear Violet call out, her voice wobbling.

“She betrayed us, she worked with the witch, she sacrificed Blake to him, she had us all trapped!” Trey growls angrily.

“Where is she?” Violet sobs.

“We left her to rot,” Trey growls once more, I hear Luci gasp.

"YOU WHAT?!" Violet screams at him. I can see Trey shake with anger, Gray at the forefront of his mind, ready to battle.

"Please, enough," I cry out.

"Actually, I brought the girl," Paul walks out with Keeley's body, not looking at Trey.

Trey shifts as I release Bryant and shift too, leaping over Paul as he hands Keeley to her mother while she sobs. Trey and I meet in the air as we tumble down to the ground, our teeth smashing angrily at each other.

"NO! Trey! Stop! That's Nix!" Luci cries to her brother, but Gray has taken over as he swipes at me angrily.

*"STOP! This will not help us! We must work together! Keeley was one of us! We loved her! She made a bad decision! Do not let that cloud your judgement! Gray! Let Trey back in now!"* Storm orders as we pin him to the ground.

*"She did this! Taylor is gone because of her! Our people are dead! Why honour her!"* Gray snarls.

"Keeley's mind was taken, the witch had hold, I can feel it, her mind was not her own," Rook says solemnly, his hand on her head.

"They took Taylor… I failed you Nix; I failed you," Trey pushes through, I see Gray has receded back, letting him up slowly.

"She's strong, we'll get my little girl back, you did what you could Trey. I know you did," I shift as he shifts and falls to the ground, deflated.

"Where is Jae?" Kai asks, frowning, looking around.

"I thought he was with you," Trey says from the ground.

“SHIT! JAE!” Kai begins flitting around.

“I haven’t seen him since the field,” Paul answers.

“Someone must have seen him!” Kai hisses.

“We’ll find him, Kai, we will,” I walk up to him as he shoves me away.

“I’m going to kill every fucking one of them if they hurt Taylor or Jae,” Kai hisses.

“You won’t find him, they move around too much, he doesn’t come out unless he has to. He needs Taylor for some crazy prophecy he’s got cooked up in his crazy head. The witch has been locked up on his own for so many years that he is beyond demented, he wants to destroy the whole human race. He started the fucking virus, he wants to rule everything, he said that he needed a powerful goddess by his side, he’s adamant that she is the one, that he had a vision of Taylor, he won’t kill her, but I am afraid of what he will do to her head,” Jezebel says, clutching both a little girl and Cole.

“We need to have a little chat,” Michael says to her sternly.

“I’ll tell you everything I know Michael, I swear, just please, keep Selene safe,” Jezebel says.

“We will,” I nod.

“Thank you,” She sobs as Cole picks her and Selene up into his arms, taking them inside quickly with a nod to me.

“Get the men inside, get the wounded healed and ready the packs for a mass funeral, tonight we say goodbye. We’re going to get these bastards and get Taylor and Jae back,” I growl.

*Let it out.*

**What?**

*Your emotion, don't hold it in Phoenix, let it out.*

Storm was right I needed to let it out, screaming out in anger and sadness I let fire burst from my hands, sending it into the skies, the sky turning red before I fall to my knees crying.

"Mum," Bryant hugs me tightly.

"We've got you, my love," Michael joins us.

# Chapter Twelve

## Taylor

I couldn't see anything, the room was pitch black, we had arrived to wherever he brought us, and I had blacked out at the click of his fingers.

I had awoken to darkness, the floor hard beneath me, it smelt damp, my hands felt around me as I squealed finding what felt like someone's leg.

"Ugghh," the person groaned.

"Hello?" I whisper.

"T-Taylor…" they groan again.

"I can't see, who are you?" I ask, not recognising the voice.

Suddenly a small flame lights the space around me as I gasp.

"JAE!" I cry out crawling over to him. His body is covered in blood, deep gashes across his body.

"Will you shut up, you're going to get us all killed," a voice growls from the other side of the dark room.

"Well! The beauty is awake! Finally!" The witch claps his hands as a light turns on in the room, my eyes widen. Several people crawl into corners, beaten and bruised, wearing barely any clothing, bodies dirty, it stank in here…

"Stay the fuck away from me," I growl, trying to move away, but I can't move far due to the shackle on my ankle.

"Sweetheart, I won't hurt you, you're mine. I will love you as if I was your true love, in fact, look at me," he says, he waves his fingers as I try to resist the pull of his magic.

"Fuck you!" I spit closing my eyes.

"You'll break eventually my dear, they all do, now as you aren't feeling so… Cooperative, I will just have to take my anger out on… Who shall it be today?!" His face lights up with glee as he looks around, my eyes follow where he looks before they come to a man across from me, he must be the one that told us to shut up…

My skin tingles.

*Uhh… What was that…*

**I don't know.**

"How about him?" The witch points to Jae with a wicked smile.

"NO! Not him, please, he's too hurt already, you'll kill him!" I beg.

"Then maybe you should have done as you were told, you will learn," he snaps before dragging Jae by the hair, pulling him with him.

"JAE! NO!" I scream out to him.

"TAYLOR!" He screams as the lights go off and the door is slammed shut.

"JAE!" I shout again and again.

"Will you shut up! Shouting for him won't help, nothing will. You're better off just being a good girl and doing as your told, that or killing yourself, though if you kill yourself, he will bring you back and you won't be yourself," the man growls out.

"What do you mean? Like… Zombies…" I ask.

"No, you won't want to eat flesh, you will just do everything he tells you; your soul won't be inside, lights are on but no one's home. Stop resisting, it's not worth it," he sighs. That's when I hear Jae's painful screams as they echo through the room, tears flooding my eyes.

"What are you?" I whisper.

"Most of us are fae, a couple of wolves and a guardian, there are humans here too, in the farm," a female voice whispers.

"You're going to get us all killed, shut up," the male growls once more.

"What are you so afraid of? You're already locked up, how long have you been here anyway? And would you please answer me, what are YOU?" I whisper.

The door suddenly bursts open, I stand up, my legs wobbly as I hold onto the wall for support.

"Here, he might not last long sweetheart, fix him up if you want him to live," the witch laughs, throwing bandages at me before throwing Jae to the ground beside me once more, slamming the door shut again.

"JAE!" I cry as I get back on my knees and crawl to him carefully. He coughs and I can smell the blood on him.

"Girls, light the room," a female says as two girls, they looked like twins, lit their fingers up with fire as the room filled with light.

"Don't help them, you'll get us all into trouble," the male says.

"Oh, for god's sake Callum, shut the fuck up," the woman snaps at him before coming over to me, taking the bandages in my hand.

"Thank you," I whisper to her as she begins to bandage Jae up.

"I'm just a guardian, there isn't much else I can do for him right now, I'm sorry," she sighs, helping lie him down in a better position before he passes out, he'd lost a lot of blood.

"Don't die on me Jae, please, we'll get you back to Kai, we will," I hold his hand.

"Who are you?" The woman asks.

"Taylor, daughter of Queen Phoenix," I whisper.

"You! You're the little princess! Jesus Christ, he's been muttering about you, what happened? Why are you here?" The man asks.

"I thought you didn't want me to speak," I raise a brow with a small smirk.

He growls moving his face, so it was into the light. The man was handsome, I was sure of it, I could see the remnants of what a chiselled jaw, muscles, gorgeous green eyes and long black hair would be.

"Don't mind him, he's grouchy, been here the longest, Callum is a wolf, he was loyal to the Queen, admired her once… Oh I forgot, my name is Evie, I'd forget my head if it wasn't screwed on," the guardian smiles sadly.

"I didn't admire her once, I still do," Callum grumbles.

"Yet you've given up," Evie raises a brow.

"What should I do? Try to get out, we've tried Evie, we've lost someone every fucking time and I won't sit here watching someone else die!" He growls.

"Well, I plan on getting out," I reply curtly.

"How do you plan on that princess?" He growls, looking me in the eye as I gasp, tingles flooding me.

*Mate... Mate! MATE!*

"Fucking hell," I whisper as his eyes widen in shock.

"No... Not happening..." He shakes his head, refusing to look at me.

"What's..." Evie asks as the twin's lights go out suddenly when the door opens once more.

"The master wants to see you little one," a vampire flits inside, taking off my chain whilst grabbing me by the neck as I wince.

I can hear Callum growl in his corner as the vampire hisses in his direction.

"Try it dog and I'll get you put in with your other friends," the vampire laughs.

"I'll be ok!" I call out as the door is slammed behind us and I'm flung onto the guy's shoulder as he flits around the building so fast, I'm disorientated.

"Put her down for god's sake, she is my Queen! You will treat her as one!" The witch snaps, slapping the vampire before gripping him around the throat as I'm dropped to the ground making me groan in pain.

"I'm sorry! I-I..." The vampire's eyes go blank.

"Oh god, what did you do?" I whisper.

"Go put a stake through your heart," the witch smirks before the vampire grabs a stake from the table behind him and stabs himself in the chest, dying right in front of me, landing on the floor with a thud.

"What the fuck!" I cry out, crawling back away from him.

"Shh, it's ok, I won't hurt you, I would never hurt you, my queen. Will you shut up! I know!" He begins shouting to thin air like a man gone crazy… He had gone crazy.

"Who… Who are you talking to?" I whisper.

"The voices, the voices in my head my dear, they whisper to me, they tell me what to do, but they don't like you, they want me to hurt you. No, no don't cower my dear, I won't hurt you, I will never hurt you, you're mine, just mine, beautiful, we are meant to be, you will love me, I swear it, you will see, we will be together once more," he nods with a grin.

"Once more?" I frown.

"Shh, no more, you don't need to worry any more, shhh, sweet one. I bet you taste sweet too, she always did, you look like her, you are her," he says.

*This guy is fucking crazy… How the hell do we get out?! I will not have him… Taste us!*

**I know! I'm working on it!**

*Work quicker.*

**You are not helping, Lily.**

"Are you talking to your wolf? Such pretty eyes, I want to see her, show me her, let me touch her," he says.

"I-I don't even know you; my wolf is a little shy…" I stand slowly, stepping back away from him, but my back hits a wall as I grimace… Shit… Cornered as he walks towards me.

"Yes, yes, my name is Maximillian, Max for short if you wish, your wolf is not shy, I've seen her in battle, she is beautiful… Show me now," he says, his eyes glaring at me as he brings up his hand dragging it over my cheek and I whimper.

I can feel his power, he tilts my head up to face him, my eyes meeting his as I can't resist the pull, staring into their dark abyss, feeling power course through my body.

"Good girl, now show me your wolf," he says backing away as I shift quickly.

*Stop! He's controlling us! STOP*

"Such beauty, you have been marked… Who did this? Who scarred you?" He snaps.

He allows me to shift back, but forces me to my knees, my eyes still following his.

"A vampire did this to me before we got to the field, he was killed," I answer.

"Good… Now, open that pretty little mouth," he says, beginning to pull down his trousers.

*NO! Don't do it! Focus Taylor! FOCUS! Mum always taught us to stay focused, use it!*

Power surged through me, I felt a sharp sting against my chest, my eyes blinking rapidly as I look down.

"Shit! What the fuck! Stay away from me!" I growl, standing and bolting for the door, but he clicks his fingers and suddenly I'm thrown against a wall, unable to move.

"How did you resist me? I had you, I know I had you, I knew you were special, oh it will be fun to break you, now look at me," he says.

"I'd rather die," I growl.

"That can be arranged, but do remember, I won't hurt you. So, the closest I have to harming you are your little buddies in your room, behave and no one gets hurt, misbehave and they are punished… Yes! I know! I will! She will be mine!" He begins talking crazy again before he focuses back on me. I gulp, feeling his erection against me on my thigh.

"I-I-I was saving myself… Please, don't do this," I whimper as he raises a brow.

"You're a virgin… Oh that is interesting, I will take you, you will be mine completely, oh how fun! I get to break in a virgin, I haven't done that in a thousand years!" He laughs.

His hand begins to caress my waist, slipping it under my top as I whimper, unable to move as he reaches my breast and squeezes hard making me whimper in pain while his eyes glow with lust.

"No, please, don't," I cry.

"Mmm, not today, but soon, I will have you soon, though I want to see your body, right now," he laughs, he rips apart my clothes leaving me bare in front of him, his eyes gazing over me as a tear falls down my face.

Please… Someone… Save me…

"Sir! We've found another group!" A voice calls from outside as Maximillian sighs.

"Give me a moment!" He snaps as he comes closer, his body pressed against mine as I close my eyes.

I feel his hands wander over me again as they get to my vagina, fingers delving into the folds, I whimper.

"Save me!" I scream in my mind using every bit of power in me as I could as my necklace began to shake a little, stinging my chest.

"Tay… Coming…" I hear parts of my brother's voice in my mind before I realise what is happening with my body.

"Please… NO!" I cry as I feel his fingers probe my entrance.

"No, you're right, not tonight, I have work to do, you will go back to your room and behave while I'm gone, but next time I see you, I will take what is mine," he grins, kissing my cheek before I fall to the ground.

I whimper as he grabs my arm and begins leading me out of the room… Still completely naked… Oh god, no, please…

"Be good and maybe you'll get some new clothes, but I like you like this, it's… freeing," he laughs, opening the door to a room, shoving me inside and slamming the door behind me as I fall to the ground, tears falling from my eyes.

"Taylor…" I hear Jae groan in the corner.

"Twins," Evie whispers as they light the room.

"OH my!" one of the other women gasps at my naked frame.

I begin shivering, it's so cold in the room and completely embarrassed from my naked body on show to everyone as I curl into the smallest form possible to hide my body.

Callum growls, slipping off what was left of his ripped shirt and putting it over me as I clung to it.

"Thank you," I cry.

"Taylor, what did he do?" Jae coughs up blood and I crawl carefully over to him.

"I don't… I don't want to talk about it," I cry, shaking my head.

"Did he… Did he rape you?" Callum growls.

"No… he… he touched me… he said… he said he would claim me next time when he gets back," I stammer.

"When he gets back… he never leaves…" Evie whispers.

"Don't even think about it…" Callum growls.

"What would you rather, that he comes back to defile the poor girl!" Evie snaps.

"Of course not! She's my mate!" He growls as the room goes silent.

# Chapter Thirteen

## Phoenix

It had been days since we had lost so many of our people, and since Jae and Taylor had been taken by the witch.

I had questioned why a male was called a witch and not a wizard, but apparently, that was irrelevant as they could change their sex when they wished…

We had scoured books about the tales of witches from ancient times as they hadn't been seen in thousands of years, everyone thought they had died out, turns out that one very bad witch had been locked up. She had been hell-bent on destroying the world, filling it with obedient slaves, wiping everything from them and creating an army that she enjoyed watching fight against themselves, she could make them do anything. She had the power to bring people back from the dead, empty shells of themselves though…

Every witch had come together to put her into her own coffin, magic shutting it permanently as they feared her, they wanted to be feared themselves, but they needed a world full of people to be feared by.

It would seem she managed to get out… As a man this time…

"So how the hell do we kill a witch?" Kai hisses as we're going through book after book, the others all continue the search for answers elsewhere.

"Burning usually works, but it's the keeping them down, that's the issue," Rook sighs, slamming a book shut.

"Mum! MUM! I heard her!" Bryant skids into the room, panic striking his face.

"What?" I stand quickly, holding him still as he breathes heavily.

"The necklace, I had it made to keep our bond stronger than ever, so we could forever feel each other, but it's been quiet the whole time since she was gone! But I felt it! I had a chain made for myself to bind us together, it shocked me! I heard her cry out! She's out there! I can feel her!" He says, showing me a silver chain around his neck.

"We can work with that, we may be able to track her through it," Rook says, taking the chain in his fingers gently.

"Are you telling me we have a way to find my daughter?" I ask him.

"Yes, hopefully. Come with me Bryant, I will need others," Rook says, letting go of the chain.

"We'll get her back, she's alive, she's going to be ok," Bryant kisses my cheek, before leaving with Rook.

"She may be alive, but she might be hurt or scared, Kai… What if…" I murmur.

"No… Don't, we have to believe they will be ok, we will help them when they are home. Nix, I love Jae and Taylor, I don't want to think of them hurt, don't do that, we can't do that," Kai hugs me tightly.

"Ok, so how do we get a witch to hold still enough, without magic to burn it? Because I'm setting this bitch on fire," I growl, sitting with Kai back at the table.

"I'll be right with you," Kai nods, looking at the books in front of him.

"Need some help?" Luci and Trey walk in the room together.

"Have you seen the number of books we have right now? Of course, we need help," Kai rolls his eyes at them.

"Ok, what are we looking for?" Trey nods grabbing the nearest to him.

"Ways to stop a witch," I answer.

Kai winces, clutching his heart as I dart to his side.

"What is it?" I ask.

"Jae… Something doesn't feel so good… I think… I think he's hurt," he says looking into my eyes, sadness and fear flooding them.

"Why would you suddenly feel that? You haven't the last few days, no one has felt a thing," Trey asks.

"Bryant felt Taylor through the necklaces… Something has helped push them through," I murmur.

"You think the necklace is pushing through the witch's barriers…" Luci asks.

"Yes, which makes it powerful…" I nod.

"Powerful enough to hold a witch down long enough?" Kai asks.

"I need to find Rook, see what he says, what we can do," I nod.

"Go. We'll keep reading, see if there's anything else on this prick," Trey growls.

I nod, rushing out of the room as I smell for Rook and Bryant, following their scents before I hear chanting in a room.

"What on earth…" I murmur as I walk in.

"They are trying to strengthen the connection to find the location," Bryant whispers to me as I join him.

One of the fae begins to scream, his body shaking violently.

"CLOSE THE LINK!" Rook shouts before they chant a final few words, letting go of each other and going to the man's side as Rodge kneels beside him, hovering his hands over the man before he stills, his breath stopping.

"Is he…" I ask.

"Yes, the witch caught on to us, he felt us probing around his magic, I feel he will be keeping an eye on it now," Rook sighs.

"Did you get a location?" I ask.

"Yes, but I fear he will have gone by the time we get there," he replies.

"Surely it's worth trying?" Bryant booms.

"It is up to you Phoenix, it is a few days away… it will not be a quick trip," Rook answers.

"Kade, can you come to me, please?" I ask through the link.

"On my way," he replies quickly.

"What if we didn't go by foot…" I answer.

"And how do you expect us to go? Do you have a magic carpet?" One of the fae sniggers.

"Kind of… Never heard of an aeroplane before?" I smirk as his eyes go wide.

"How do you intend to fly it?" Rook asks.

"You're going to make me fly a bloody plane, aren't you?" Kade groans.

"You told me once you flew one… It's the quickest way to get to them, please Kade," I beg.

"Ok," he nods.

"So, now we just need to find a plane with fuel," Bryant says.

"Yes, ready the pack, we leave tonight," I answer.

"Great, night-time flying too!" Kade groans.

"By the time we find a plane it will be morning, do this for Jae and Taylor," I sigh.

"I know, I just worry about leaving Luci behind in her state," he sighs.

"She will be well taken care of, I won't leave her alone here," I reply.

"I know," he nods and walks off.

I run about trying to organise a team to go with us and who would stay behind, so many of our people were still grieving, but their need to defeat this new evil was evident as many of them volunteered to come with us. I had to be careful about their mental state, the last thing I needed was for someone to go rogue and attack before we were ready, so some of them were placed on guard at the mansion, I made them feel special as they had to guard the house for our return while trying to keep them at distance from the battle.

"Phoenix, our son told me the plan, why am I the last to know?" Michael folds his arms looking at me sternly as I groan, feeling like a told off little girl.

"I've been busy, I'm sorry Michael. I've been trying to work out how to take down this fucking witch, how we are going to get Taylor and Jae back, plus I am sure there are others there too that need saving, there is so much to do and I feel time is running from us," I sigh.

"Then you should have come to me! She's my daughter too!" Michael snaps, a tear escapes my eye as he pulls me into his arms.

"I'm sorry," I cry.

"Shh, no I'm sorry, I shouldn't have snapped, but we are in this together, it is our family they are messing with, and we will take them down together, understand?" He tilts my head.

"Yes, I love you," I kiss his lips softly.

"I love you too, now come on, Bryant needs to talk to us all," Michael says before we walk hand in hand towards the front of the building where many are already stood waiting.

"Ah, finally, Bryant, you may begin," Rook nods at our son as I frown.

"We've been working hard on trying to figure out what will slow the witch down long enough to kill him, the necklace I gave my sister and the chain I wear seems to weaken his defences. Trey and Kai came across a few old scriptures about their kind. It talked about a precious metal, infused with the power of the fae that could weaken a witch, every one of you will be given a chain for your neck to help protect you, while we have managed to make a series of weapons," Bryant says as I hear a murmur of shock going around the pack as they watch.

"They have been busy," Michael says as Bryant and Trey hold two huge guns with wide barrels, wide enough you could probably put a child's head inside.

"This gun will shoot a net made from infused silver chains, they have been made light and can be shot from quite the distance, Trey," Bryant says as Trey turns aiming at a tree before shooting, the chains shoot out, looking like a silvery web as it shoots across and wraps around the nearest tree, glowing as it seals itself around it.

"My god," I murmur in shock.

"We've managed to make ten of these with one net each, if we had more time then we could have made more, but we are short on time. Ten shots, each will weaken the witch long enough to kill him, we have to be quick though as we do not know how long it will last. Others will be given these bad boys," Trey says, smirking and bringing out another gadget.

"You are kidding me," I laugh as he brings out a flamethrower.

"I understand that you are our resident flamethrower Phoenix, but if you're busy elsewhere we need others that can burn him alive," Trey smirks.

"I like it, you don't have to tell me twice," I nod.

"We have fifty of these, but fuel is limited, try not to waste too much on the enemy and save it for the witch. If you need to use it then use it, but be cautious," Bryant adds.

"How many are going?" A warrior asks.

"We've managed to locate an airport a few hours away that can hold around one hundred of us, we sent a few fae scouts ahead to check on fuel and the state of the plane and all seems well," Kade pipes up as I nod in thanks to him. I knew he hated to fly, he hated being a pilot all those years ago, but we needed him.

"Will that be enough? From what I heard their numbers are greater than that," another wolf asks.

"Many of you have been chosen, along with some others that are currently busy preparing for our trip, they have been chosen carefully, many have their own skills with the elements which will give us an edge. Those without, will be given one of the weapons, plus with the fae by our side from the sky, we have an extra set of eyes on us," I call out.

"My coven will be staying here while I join you, they will protect our people here, so they do not get mixed up in the battle with others of our kind," Kai calls out.

I was proud of what he had accomplished, he had managed to become a leader of a coven, a small one, but they were powerful enough with at least thirty strong vampires that just sought a normal life, they wanted no harm to come to anyone, they would take a donation of blood gratefully.

"Everyone not going with us will be called to the mansion so that all our people are in one place. It's going to be cramped, but it's for the best," Paul calls out.

"Half of my people will be here too, I will be going with Phoenix and the others with the other half, we can fly just as fast as any plane. Fae will be placed on the borders in the trees where we have set up small treehouses to keep watch while being hidden, I'm not leaving anything to chance," Violet calls out.

"When the bloody hell did she do that?" I stand in shock, I knew she had been busy, but she had avoided me for the last day or so. Had she been setting up these treehouses all this time, I assumed she was grieving for Keeley, I could see in her eyes she was ready for revenge, her baby girl had been killed, her mind controlled into killing the one man who loved her whole-heartedly.

My eyes teared up at the thought of Blake, he was gone, the little boy I had watched grow up, taken into my arms as one of my own…

Violet marches up to me, a hand over my heart as she looks at me sadly.

“We will make them pay for the losses we have gone through, we will avenge their deaths,” she says before we both hug softly, two mothers mourning.

# Chapter Fourteen

## Taylor

After everyone had come out of their shock at Callum telling them that we were mates, they began talking in hushed whispers.

“He will be a good mate,” Jae whispers, his hand in mine as I hug close to him, keeping us both warm.

“For god’s sake, she’s what… Eighteen… You’re twenty-eight, you can’t be serious,” one of the twins says.

“Yes, I’m eighteen, my mum is thirty-six and my dad is over five hundred… Age isn’t a problem in our world is it really when you're mated?” I snap as she nods slowly.

“Tilly shut up, Taylor is right, Talia don’t look at me like that young lady,” Evie says to the twins.

My eyes kept glancing over to Callum as he sat there, shivering in his corner without his shirt.

“Girls, can’t you make it a little warmer in here?” I ask the twins.

“We don’t know how,” Talia sighs.

“What… Surely you were trained?” I frown.

"We were taken as babies, we've been here years, we never learnt how to control our powers, the small flames we do, are all we can do," Talia answers.

"I will teach them," Jae groans, trying to sit up.

"You have no energy for that," I push him back down.

"If we have any chance of getting out of here, we are going to need every effort, they need to learn," Evie sighs.

"Fine, I'll teach them" I answer.

"What are you going to do? You're a wolf," one of the older male fae in the corner scoffs, speaking for once.

"My mother holds an affinity for all the elements, and I have one for earth, my twin, fire. I'm quite sure it works the same way," I snap as I hear Callum chuckle.

"Shit! Someone's coming!" A girl closer to the door whispers, her eyes turning yellow, a wolf…

The door bursts open as a group of vampires stand at the door, their eyes bright red, fangs elongated, I had seen this before, they were hungry…

"Well, well, well, while the cats away the mice will play. I fancy something a little different tonight, hmm, wolf, fae or guardian… What to choose…" One hisses out as he walks into the room.

"NO!" Tilly screams when she's picked up by the hair, screaming in pain as I stand.

"Hey! Let her go!" I growl.

"Oh! We've got a fighter, I prefer when they have a little fight in them, and she's so pretty, you're new… Mmm, nice body too," one of the others laughs, their little leader still holds Tilly tightly as tears fall from her eyes.

"Let her go, I won't say it again," I growl.

*Concentrate on the ground, I've got a plan, make holes underneath them, keep the top up though!*

I focus on the ground, feeling three wells empty beneath them silently, blissfully unaware of what was going on beneath them.

"Or what little wolf? You know what, I think we could share this one don't you think boys? She's got some pep in her step still, she needs to learn her place," the leader hisses, throwing Tilly to the wall as Talia grabs her, pulling her towards the others in the corner.

"Good luck with that boys," I smirk.

"Stand down girl!" The old man snaps in the corner.

"Shut it Greg," Evie hisses.

"Aww you've made them fight, shame we will have to beat it out of them again," the second vampire says with a sadistic smirk.

"I have a little problem with that," I walk forward almost on top of the leader as his hand grips my throat tightly.

"This will be sweet," he smirks.

"Yeah, this will," I growl, and the earth shifts beneath their feet.

The leader still has a grip on my throat as he pulls me with him, I can hear the other two being crushed by the earth already, their bodies being squished to a pulp as blood begins to spray everywhere.

“Little bitch!” The leader shouts, holding onto me tightly as I struggle to breathe. Suddenly a hand reaches down with claws as it slices through the vampire's hand, completely breaking it. I’m let go as he screams and I’m lifted back up and into a pair of naked arms.

A sudden spray of blood covers us as the last vampire dies for good.

“Holy shit…” The wolf girl near the door murmurs.

“That was amazing,” Talia exclaims.

“Tilly, are you ok?” I ask, turning from Callum, his arms still around me protectively.

“I’m fine, thank you,” she says hoarsely.

“We’re getting out of here, we really are, aren’t we? I’m Malina by the way,” the wolf girl near the door says.

“We are,” I nod wiping my face, seeing the blood on my hand.

Jae begins to cough, blood coming from his mouth as I push from Callum’s arms and rush to him.

“Malina, shut the door. Twins, concentrate on the blood on the ground, picture it is burning up,” I call out quickly, noticing the door was still open.

“Ok,” the twins answer as their hands hover over the ground.

“Taylor… Tell Kai…” Jae begins.

"No, don't you dare, you're going fucking nowhere, we are getting out of this hellhole, and you can tell him whatever you were going to say yourself, understood?!" I exclaim.

"He doesn't have long, his wounds are great," Greg the old fae says in the corner.

"How do you know?" I frown.

"I can feel it," he answers, and he turns away. I can smell the fire against the blood on the ground, I look to see it's burning up quickly.

"You can feel it… You're a fucking healer!" I exclaim, anger coursing through me, why hasn't he helped?

"I was, once," he answers.

"Help him!" I cry out as Jae begins to cough violently.

"I can't," he shakes his head, fear in his eyes.

"Why? Scared? Nut the fuck up and help him! Stop letting the fear get to your heart, just help him, stop him from dying. Just something! Just so we can get him home, please, he's family," I cry.

"Greg…" Evie snaps.

"I don't know if I can anymore, he stripped most of my powers away from me! He didn't want me healing anyone!" He shouts, his voice was hoarse.

*Didn't Rodge use power from others once, a link between fae?*

**Lily, I fucking love you!**

"We have how many fae in here? Five? If your powers have been reduced it means that they are still there, draw power from the others, work together. I've seen it be done before, please, will you help me? Jae is one of you, he's Violet's third, Rook is a friend of his and my uncle is his husband, please, do this for them if not for me or your kind!" I exclaim.

The twins make their way over, hands entwined as they look to the other two female fae behind them. They move slowly to them as they look to Greg who shakes his head.

"Greg, you can do this," Callum says facing him.

"Fine!" Greg snaps, crawling over to us as I see just how bad of a state he was in, he was skin and bones.

"Close your eyes, hold onto Greg, focus your power on him," Evie tells the others as we watch his hands shake over Jae.

Jae begins to shake, his body going into a fit as I cry out for him, Callum walks over to me, holding me back as Greg's arms shake.

Jae's body begins to calm his chest not moving.

"Tell me he's not dead… No!" I cry.

"He's not dead," Greg falls to the ground in exhaustion.

"Why is he barely moving?" I sniff, kneeling beside them.

"I've put him in a coma, he's weak. If we don't get him to a healer with more power, he will die in a week," Greg grunts as he drags himself back to his corner.

"A week… We've been in here years, and you need us to get out in a week…" Evie sighs.

"We didn't have her before…" Talia says quietly.

I wince, feeling a sting on my neck again, holding the necklace in my hand as I feel the power within it.

"That necklace seems to have a mind of its own," Tilly says, standing in front of me. She touches it as her eyes go wide.

"What?" I ask.

"It has major fae power, I can feel it," she exclaims.

"Perhaps with a little concentration, you could push beyond the boundary of the witch's spells," one of the fae women says.

"Ok, I'll try it," I nod.

"Close your eyes. Focus, use your wolf, follow the strands of the links to your pack, find the one you want, follow it," she continues, I try to do as she says, growling as the witch's spell pushes back, snapping me out.

"It's too strong," I sigh.

"Keep pushing, have your wolf work with you," she replies.

**Are you ready for this Lily?**

*Let's do this!*

Closing my eyes, I concentrate again.

"Malina, keep an ear by the door," Callum orders sitting beside me.

*I can feel Bryant!*

**Keep going!**

*It hurts!*

“Push through the pain, keep going Taylor,” the woman says, I feel her in front of me.

“You’re going to have her deplete all her energy!” Callum growls.

“Bryant!” I scream in my mind, pushing through the boundaries of the spell, my heart beating so fast as I can see what he sees, everyone is rushing about, chains of silver in front of him.

“Taylor?” He says back, but it’s broken, like a broken connection.

“TWIN!” I call as I’m thrown back into the room.

“What did you do that for?!” The fae screams at Callum beside me as I feel the pinch of his claws in my leg.

“She could have died; her nose was fucking bleeding!” He growls. I put my hand to my face, blood seeping from my nose.

“He heard me…” I whisper.

“Did he tell you anything?” Evie asks.

“He just said my name before it broke, but I saw something, they had these silver chains everywhere, guns too, like they were getting ready for battle,” I said.

“They’re coming here, Queen Phoenix wouldn’t abandon her family, she’s strong,” Callum murmurs.

“How are they going to find us? The bastard moves the compound every few weeks,” Evie murmurs.

“The necklace… Is it still true your mother has connections with Queen Violet and her people?” Greg whispers from the corner.

"Yes, they are friends, she was there the day I was taken," I nod.

"They will be able to track you through the necklace, whoever gave you that is very smart," Greg nods.

"My twin gave it to me for my birthday…" I smile.

"The power of twins," Evie smiles.

"We better rest up I feel the battle ahead won't be good, we'll need every ounce of energy we have left," Callum orders as the others nod.

"Well done with burning away the blood girls," I smile at the twins as they wave their hands. I can see the concentration in their faces as a larger flame hovers in the middle of the room, warming the air more as I see the others sigh with relief.

"We're getting out, we are," Evie sighs curling up beside Jae, keeping an eye on him.

# Chapter Fifteen

## Phoenix

"I hate flying," Michael groans beside me, his hand in mine as we sit in our seats, Kade was in the pilot's seat while we ready ourselves for take-off. Paul sat beside him as co-pilot, having had trained years ago, though not to Kade's extent.

"It will be ok, it's only an hour, focus on the kids," I squeeze his hand, fiddling with the necklace around my neck.

I could feel the plane begin to move as I took a deep breath, I'd never flown before. Most of the people here hadn't, you could feel the nerves in the air as I peered out the window, a broken and fallen city in the distance where it once would have stood tall and shining in the sun.

The plane began to shake a little during take-off, Kai began to talk loudly in the cabin, trying to make light of the situation.

"During the flight, we ask that you stay seated during take-off and landing, keep your seat upright too, but I don't remember why. Please don't annoy our other passengers as we fly through the sky, holes in the plane cannot be fixed easily and throwing your buddy off the plane is not recommended," Kai stands in the aisle. I smile at him as several cans are thrown at him, but he dodges them.

"Wow… Look at that…" A warrior mutters looking out of the window, I take a peek out the window and the clouds below us as I look into the sky. It was beautiful. It was nice to see something so beautiful still, while the world below was going to shit, it gave me hope that things could still change.

The flight felt so much longer that it had been, my legs shook with nerves as it continued.

"I'm going to go see our pilots," I kiss Michael on the cheek as he nods, talking to Kai and Violet on the other side of the aisle.

I walk along the aisle, hearing the murmurs from warriors, most in shock at the sight outside, others talking about the new weapons and the battle ahead.

I knock on the pilot cabin door as it's opened up by Paul, he smiles at me letting me inside.

"How's it going boys?" I ask.

"You're lucky I love you guys, I hate flying," Kade grumbles.

"I can't thank you enough Kade," I put a hand on his shoulder.

"Not long now, we'll be landing soon," Kade mutters.

"Ugh… Kade… What is that?" I see flashes up ahead as Paul swears, buckling up.

"This is your captain speaking, buckle up and hold on to your hats, we're in for a bumpy ride!" Paul calls through the intercom.

"Nix, sit in that seat there and buckle up now!" Kade points to the seat by the door as I sit in it quickly.

"Looks like a rough one Kade, can this plane take it?" Paul asks.

"Take what?!" I exclaim.

"A storm, a bad one at that," Kade grumbles.

"Shit!" Paul shouts as the plane begins to shake, the sky dark as rain begins to hit the windows violently.

"Kade!" I exclaim as a bolt of lightning flashes in front of us, then again and again.

"This isn't a normal storm, Kade! We have to set the plane down now! Before it wipes us all out!" Paul shouts.

Kade looks behind him to me quickly.

"Kade…" I murmur.

"We'll make it, tell everyone to hold on," Kade says. The plane shakes, fear floods me as Paul calls on the coms for everyone to hold on tight as I hear the panic from the other side of the door.

"Phoenix… What's going on? Tell me you're ok," Michael says through the bond.

"I'm fine, stay put, keep talking with Kai and don't look out the window," I reply.

"I looked out the window! Why tell me not too?! Of course, I'm going to look!" He exclaims.

"Kai! Calm Michael down!" I say through the link.

"On it," he replies quickly.

"Shit! It hit the engine; we're going down!" Kade shouts, trying to steady the plane as it descends quickly towards the ground.

My eyes fill with tears as we plummet down, everyone was going to die…

*Taylor…*

Storm whines for our family as my hands shake.

"What the hell…" Paul murmurs, the plane begins to right itself, lowering carefully to the ground. He and Kade look at each other in shock as we were so close to the ground.

The plane touches down with a huge thud, the metal creaking with pressure.

"Kade… How did you do that?" I ask in shock.

"I didn't," he shakes his head, standing slowly, looking out of the window.

"Holy shit!" Paul laughs, looking out the window as I take off my buckle and go to the window. Rook is holding onto the nose of the plane, his wings out, face red and soaked to the bone.

"The fae saved us…" I smile.

"Goddess bless Violet's people," Kade sighs in relief as he hugs me into his side.

"Let's move, we're not there yet, we'll have to do the rest on foot," I order as they nod, we make our way to the cabin to find some very sick looking wolves.

"I'll get the hatch," Paul says, pulling open the hatch door, kicking out the planes inflatable slide to get out in emergencies.

"What the hell happened?" Violet exclaims.

"A magical storm, it was bringing us down, your people saved us all," Kade explains.

"My… People… Well, I've never been so proud," she grins, heading to the hatch, flying out as I see the group of her people waiting outside for her.

"Ok guys, we aren't there yet, we've got a small trek on foot. Let's move out and watch your back, this storm isn't going to be the only thing blocking us from them, keep your eyes open and listen to everything around you, stick together, work as one and we will get through this," I call out as a series of howls echoes through the cabin before people begin to get out of the plane.

"My Queen," Rook holds a hand out to me as I'm the last of the lot, lifting me into the air before touching me gently down to the ground beside Michael.

"Oh, she gets the royal treatment, while I have to go down that bloody thing," Michael sulks as I shake my head at him.

"The weather is too bad for my people to fly, they'll be killed by the lightning," Violet says as thunder booms in the sky.

"You will ride us, spread yourself between my wolves. KAI! You're on me!" I order as I see his cheeky smile with a nod at me.

"As you wish," Violet nods, ordering her people to find someone to mount as they pair up, luckily most of them knew each other, many of them were friends so the pairing was easy.

"Let's shift!" I order as one by one wolves begin to shift, I stand at the front, looking at them all.

I let off a loud howl as they chorus along with me and we begin our journey forward, my mate and my son by my side. I had ordered Hanson to stay back, I needed an alpha I trusted to keep control back there with Janie and Luci to help him. They were safe at home.

"Let's get our family back!" Kai calls out as the rain pelts us.

The mud sloshed beneath our paws as we ran through the rain, lightning striking around us as we avoided downed trees.

“Look! There it is!” Bryant howls at a large warehouse building ahead, I howl for everyone to stop.

“It’s too quiet, I don’t like it!” Kade shouts through the loud pounding of the rain around us.

“The flamethrowers aren’t going to work in this rain!” Trey shouts. Our plans were already going to shit.

“What if they aren’t here?!” Paul calls out.

“They have to be! I can feel she’s here!” Bryant answers and that was all I needed to know, if he felt his sister here, then we were going in.

I take a step forward and the weather suddenly changes, the sky clearing…

“What?!” Michael frowns at me. I see his hair is still soaking, dripping as I take a step back, rain again…

“What the fuck…” I murmur.

“What?” Kai asks.

I move forward completely with him on my back as he gasps.

“What the fuck!” He exclaims. Others begin to walk forward cautiously.

“I don’t understand… How is this possible?” Paul frowns.

“The witch, he’s put a spell on the surrounding area to stop us… But not here, he’s got it clear. What I don’t understand is why is it so quiet?” Violet murmurs as the whole pack enters the dry pavement, fae jumping off their backs as they shake out their soaking wings.

"You spoke too soon," Kade growls, my eyes flick forward as a sea of vampires begins crawling out of the warehouse.

"I'm here with you until the very end my love," Michael says, nuzzling into my side.

"For Taylor, Jae and all those we lost!" I howl as we begin to move forward.

Howls echo as the pack begins their attack, flanking me as we tear into the first wave of vampires heading our way.

# Chapter Sixteen

## Taylor

Over the last couple of days, we've done our best to keep our energy up. We'd been thrown food occasionally, making sure the weakest got some before the others, Greg was finally beginning to perk up a little.

Half of us were barely in any clothes and as much as the others hated it, I had had an idea. I opened up the holes with the squashed vampires, their clothes covered in their blood as I stripped them. Then we made so much noise several others came in to see what the commotion was.

Callum took out the first as the other three went for him, falling into my trap as they fell into the holes waiting for them, this time having the earth hold them so we could twist their necks and get their clothes without blood all over them, and then finally sending them to the depths.

"How are we going to get Jae out?" Evie asks, my ears perk a little, hearing a loud noise outside.

"What is that?" The twins ask.

"Sounds like… A plane…" Greg frowns.

"Looks like I got home just in time for the party!" The witch, Maximillian, grins broadly, clapping his hands in the doorway.

"What the… How…" Malina looks in shock, she was always on watch.

"I teleported silly girl, now you must be punished for your behaviour, listening out for my men, are you?" He grins.

"No! I'll take it, I'll take her punishment!" I shout. Callum's hand grips onto my arm, Maximillian's eyes darting to it with a glare.

"You touch what is mine, you pay…" Maximillian says.

*Shit! No, he will not harm our new friends and mate!*

**I'm going to regret this.**

*Regret what... What are you doing?*

**Getting everyone else out.**

"No! Please! Max! Look at me! I am yours, right here, right now, come with me, take me from here. Please Max, take me from them," I beg as I pull from Callum's grip.

"Get them out," I say through the small bond between us.

"Don't do this, we'll all get out," Callum says.

"You will. Look after them," I reply, shutting off the link as my hand caresses Maximillian's softly.

"Oh, my dear, I knew you would come to me soon enough, come, you will be mine forever," he grins, taking my hand as he pulls me behind him, but he locks the door.

With the flick of my wrist, I use the earth to get to the lock, twisting it just enough to unlock before I'm dragged far from the room.

"Sire, there is an army on the boundary, what do we do?" A tall, lanky vampire flits to him.

“Kill them all, I must finish what I started,” Maximillian looks to me with a lustful grin.

“Yes, Sir,” the vampire replies, flitting away once more.

He pulls me into his room, pushing me back against the door, his hands gliding over my body as I gulp. Please let them all get out, let my family be safe.

“You don’t need to kill them all. I could stop this, tell them I want to be yours; we don’t have to do this, no one has to die!” I say as he chuckles, his mouth coming towards my neck.

I hear a loud howl from outside, Callum… They are on the move.

“What was that?” Maximillian hisses out. I close my eyes taking a deep breath before kissing his lips, imagining they were someone else's, Callum’s…

His hands begin to wander again, and he begins to unbutton my shirt as my eyes open, looking around for something to help me. His mouth kisses down my neck before he hisses in pain, his lips burnt at the touch of the necklace…

*Put it on him! Now!*

Lily growls inside me, I lift the chain from my neck quickly and shove it over his in one quick swoop as he screams in pain.

“No! You…WILL… BE… MINE!” He shouts as he goes for me, but I kick him backwards, my foot in the centre of his chest as he flies towards the wall.

“I will never be yours,” I growl. I spot a few stakes on the table, throwing them one by one at him as he tries to deflect them with magic, but his power is struggling with the necklace around his neck.

The door shatters behind me as a group of vampires hiss at me.

“Come on! Come at me!” I use a come-on gesture with my hands with a smirk as I hear Maximillian struggling still behind me.

The vampires are so stupid, they come at me one by one. Shifting into my wolf, I tear each one limb by limb, using the earth to pin down their feet.

“NO! This cannot happen to me!” Maximillian shouts as the necklace shakes around his neck.

*RUN!*

His power is pushing through the necklace, I can see it beginning to splinter. Running from the room, I dart through the corridors taking out vampires as I go. My eyes catch something, seeing the room they kept the humans in. I look forward to my way out, I whine making my decision and bursting through the door to my left. Shifting when I see the humans all connected to machines, taking their blood from them, I go the computers shutting them all down and bring them slowly off their podiums.

“Thank you,” one whispers as I get him down.

“Do any of you have the energy to move quickly?” I ask.

“Some of us have only been here an hour, we can help,” he nods.

“Get the others down, find something to defend yourself with, I’ll be back,” I say before shifting and bolting through the door, using the earth to guide me to what I needed, the armoury.

“Now this is what I’m talking about,” I laugh, grabbing several bags of stakes, knives and an array of weapons.

Shifting back once more I grab the bags with my teeth, and I surge forward towards the humans once more.

"Shit! Go back! We can't get through!" I hear Evie scream as I get to the door.

I drop the bag into the room and howl for the others, opening the link between me and Callum once more.

"Hurry up, get back here!" I order, hearing their footsteps as I shift.

"What is this?" The man asks, walking up to me slowly. I see the humans are all down, maybe fifty of them, some weaker than others.

"Weapons, arm yourself," I state as his eyes widen, nodding.

"Why would you do this?" He asks.

"Because much like my mother, I believe you should have a chance at life, no one should have to die. This is your world as it is mine, my mother is the queen of wolves, you will be welcomed to stay with us," I give him a small smile as he nods.

"Thank you," he nods, dragging the bag to the others.

"Taylor! Where is he?!" Callum growls, rushing through with the others.

"He was trapped by my necklace, but he'll break free, it won't last. I'm surprised I've lasted this long," I peek out the door.

"There are too many out there, we'll never make it," Talia cries.

"Yes, we will. Ma'am, my name is David, I owe you my life, we will follow you and would love to accept your offer of safety," the human, David says as I notice they are all armed.

"TAYLOR!" I hear Maximillian boom, my head darts towards the voice.

"We need to go now!" I shout as the humans all help each other move, lifting those that couldn't walk.

We walk quickly through the corridors, I put up several earth blockades behind us, it wouldn't stop him, but it would slow him down.

"Oh shit," I look around the corner and see the exit, filled with vampires ready to go with the next wave…

"We aren't getting through that," Evie whispers.

I look around as I see an old wall in front of us in a small room ahead.

*If we use much more of our power we're going to collapse before we're outside.*

**Once more, we have to open up another exit.**

*Ok.*

I groan as my power begins to get weaker, opening a hole in the wall carefully as I put a finger to my lips and signal everyone to go out. It led to a huge storage room, with fuel tanks everywhere.

"Are you thinking what I'm thinking twin?" Talia smirks at the tanks.

"TAYLOR!" I hear Maximillian shout, my earth barricades breaking.

"Shit!" I exclaim.

"Don't. I know what you're thinking, you aren't doing it!" Callum growls.

"Take Jae home for me, tell my family I love them, spread the fuel and burn the fucking place to the ground!" I exclaim, kissing Callum on the lips, feeling the tingle of our bond before I push away and jump back through the hole, closing it up so only a small hole big enough for them to pour the fuel in was left.

"Taylor! NO!" Callum shouts.

"Callum! Hurry!" Evie shouts.

My legs give out slightly as I weaken, my energy depleting while I shift, whining, I move forward.

"There you are," Maximillian smirks. I look to my left where his vampires are beginning to turn towards me.

I bend down slightly, letting out a whine as he comes towards me, feeling his every step as I back up to the room, feeling the fuel at my feet as he enters it.

"Move Taylor!" I hear Callum say in my mind. Maximillian goes for my throat, I leap over him, the fire chasing my arse as he grabs hold of my tail, letting out a yelp of pain as he screams at the fire beneath his feet. Clicking his fingers, he throws me into the corner, fire licking at my human body causing me to scream in pain.

"Hey! Get the fuck off my sister!" I hear Bryant as the fire disappears from my side of the room. A huge booming sound comes from his side as I see chains wrap around Maximillian, I whimper as he fights the chains, one set wasn't enough.

"We need more!" I scream out, seeing the chains are already struggling.

The wall smashes open once more beside me, another set of chains comes flying through.

"Taylor!" Trey rushes to my side as I whimper in his arms.

"Where are the others? It's not holding!" Bryant shouts as I growl, shifting back to my wolf.

"The others are trapped, there are too many vampires!" Trey answers.

With the last of my energy and pain from the pull of my burnt skin making me whine, I keep pushing on as I run past Trey and back through the hole. Darting into the throngs of battle as I look for anyone with the chain guns.

"KADE!" I howl as he's being attacked by several vampires, his skin covered by deep cuts. I bound over to him, wiping out half of them.

"Taylor!" He whines looking at me.

"They need you inside now!" I order, he whines wanting to protect me as I attack the vampires that were trying to get to him again.

He runs off quickly and I howl in pain at a vampire slicing through my skin as I tear through their arms.

"Keep it together!" I hear my mother shout as my eyes dart everywhere for her.

A deep growl sounds as a blur of black fur pounces over me, taking down a series of vampires that were coming for me.

"Callum?" I ask.

"Yes," he nods, nuzzling into my side, his eyes showing pain as he looks at me. It's not long until we have to attack once more, moving through the vampires as my body gets weaker.

"Keep moving Taylor!" Callum says, pushing me up.

"I can't," I whine as my legs give out.

"TAYLOR!" I hear my dad shout as my eyes meet his, I can see the others look towards me and they begin to push forward.

"ARGGGHHHHH!" David screams as he and the other humans come barrelling into the fight, shooting at any vampire they came across.

"You have to fight Taylor, get up!" Evie shouts as she stabs a vampire with a stake, I try to get up, but my legs give up.

"Power up princess, thank you for saving us, it's been an honour," Greg groans beside me. His hands hover over me, he shakes as I cry out, my body knitting itself together again as Greg falls to the floor, dead.

"Oh my god, no…" I cry.

I hear a scream nearby as the twins are caught between a huge group of vampires. I howl before leaping back into the action, Greg gave me another chance with his life, I wouldn't fail him…

"Use your fire!" I link to them as I leap to their aid. Fire bursts through their fingertips as vampires scream in pain.

"We need to get to those who have the chain guns now!" I growl as the others nod. We move through the battle, finding the people with guns, releasing them from battle as they are flanked by our people to the building, helping Bryant and Trey with Maximillian.

"It's working! We've got him pinned!" I hear Bryant howl happily.

"Mum!" I howl as I tear a vampire from her back.

"Taylor!" She exclaims, nuzzling into my side.

We begin to fight side by side as Callum and the others join us, mum looks at them quizzically but carries on.

"Taylor! Where is Jae?!" I hear Uncle Kai call as he flits towards us.

“Callum where is Jae?” I ask quickly.

“Evie had him…” He answers, but we see her fighting.

“Evie! Where is Jae?!” I growl.

“He’s safe… He’s… Oh no…” Her face goes into that of shock, she looks to the building that was now aflame, Trey and the others coming out with a look of pride.

“Where?!” I growl once more.

“I put him in the small storage area, beside the room that had the humans,” she answers.

“MOVE!” I growl, pushing through the others as the number of vampires was slowly dying.

“Taylor! We did it! He’s dead!” Bryant grins at me as he goes to hug me, but I push past him.

“Taylor no! It’s too late!” Mum shouts in her human form.

“No one gets left behind!” I howl, jumping through the fire, seeing Maximillian’s body burning as I’m choking on the thick, black smoke, paws blistering in the heat.

“We do this together idiot!” Bryant bursts through the flames as the fire dies down on our path.

“In there!” I rush to the door as we both slam into it, the room ablaze too.

“I can’t see a thing…” He coughs through the smoke, trying to kill the fire.

“We can’t leave him!” I howl as I feel the earth, searching for him. I yelp out as I find where he is, pushing through the flames.

“Taylor! I can’t control it! TAYLOR!” Bryant shouts in a panic as flames go back up around me.

I find Jae on the ground, covered in burns as I put out the fire on his clothes, digging my muzzle under his body and throwing him onto my back.

I whine as I can’t see a way through the fire… I’m stuck again…

“Bryant! I can’t get back through!” I call out.

That’s when I hear my mother’s scream as she expels every flame from the room, dropping to her knees in exhaustion.

“Taylor! Jae!” Kai flits into the room, he takes Jae from my back as I limp to the door, nudging my mum with my nose as she hugs my face to her.

“Why must you be so much like me?” She whispers.

“Must be in the blood,” I chuckle as I shift to my human form, collapsing into her lap and she stares at me wide-eyed.

“RODGE! I need healers now!” She screams.

“Taylor, hang in there Taylor!” Bryant says as my vision begins to blur.

“Jae needs healing… Hurt bad… Love you…” I murmur before the world goes black.

# Chapter Seventeen

## Phoenix

Seeing Taylor standing there, badly burnt, but still fighting made my heart race. I tried to get to her, we had been fighting a losing battle, people were dropping like flies, and I didn't know who was left. It didn't look good. That was until the humans gave life to us as they surged in with Taylor and a black wolf by her side, who was keeping her upright.

Humans were fighting by our side; one by one we were taking down the enemy. The witch was being taken care of by Trey and Bryant and I couldn't have felt prouder of my children than I already did.

Watching Taylor run back into the burning building, my heart had raced once more as I looked to find Michael. I couldn't see him anywhere as I ran after Taylor and her brother.

"Phoenix! Be careful!" Trey shouts as I run into the fire.

"Taylor! I can't control it! TAYLOR!" I hear Bryant shout and I burst through the warehouse.

"Bryant! I can't get back through!" I hear my daughter scream. Hearing the panic in her voice, I bound over to Bryant amid the black smoke, focusing on my power, screaming out in pain as it overwhelms me, the power draining me as the fire dies down and I fall to my knees.

Kai flits past me as he took Jae, tears in his eyes as he watched us. When Taylor passed out in my lap, panic arose once more, and I shouted for Rodge.

Bryant knelt beside me, his hand caressing his sister's face.

"You stay with me twin," he kisses her head.

"Phoenix, we should get out of here, the building may not hold," Trey says from behind me.

"Help me up," I nod. Bryant takes Taylor from me and Trey lifts me with him as we make our way out. Just as we make it out, the whole building shudders before collapsing.

"That was a little too close for my liking…" Trey grumbles.

"Oh no! Taylor!" A young woman runs up to us.

"Who are you?" I ask as she looks at Taylor.

"My name is Evie. I'm a guardian. Taylor saved us, she got us all out, I owe this girl my life," she says.

"Mate…" Trey murmurs his eyes wide as he looks at the woman.

"Oh my…" She says, her eyes gazing over him.

"I want everyone able to help the wounded, find our dead and burn the vampires!" I hear Violet shout her commands.

"Where is my mate? Where is Michael?" I ask, my eyes searching for him as Rodge begins working on Taylor and Jae with a few other healers.

"Mum… I don't see dad, where is he?" Bryant asks.

"Michael!" I shout.

"Paul is missing too!" Kade growls as he shifts and begins running around.

"Bryant, stay with them," I tell my boy and he nods. I shift and follow Kade, sniffing the air for Michael and Paul, but I can barely smell a thing with so much smoke in the air.

Kade stops suddenly as I race to his side, he whines before racing off once more shifting mid pounce as he finds Michael and Paul.

"Michael!" I cry as I run to him shifting.

"I tried, I tried to get to him, they tore him to shreds, he's like my brother Phoenix," Michael says, tears in his eyes as he sobs for his fallen brother beside him. Kade kneels beside him.

I shift and howl loudly into the air, my pack following suit as we howl for our lost. Tears fall down my face as I shift back and Michael curls into my arms.

"Taylor?" He murmurs.

"She's alive, she's not in a good state though Michael…" I sniff through the tears.

"She'll be ok, she's so much like you, our little girl will make it," he nuzzles into my neck. I hold him tightly, looking off towards the commotion that Violet is busy dealing with as she takes a glance my way, a hand over her heart before she continues to order people around.

She had this…

I can see the black wolf once more, pacing in the courtyard, his gaze on Taylor, not looking away.

"Hey! You! Who are you?!" I call as Kade and Michael glance his way.

He shifts, a man who must be in his late twenties looks at me, glancing back at Taylor, his eyes sad.

“Callum… My name is Callum, my queen,” he kneels before me as I raise a brow.

“Never gets old, she doesn’t like the whole bowing kid, stand up,” Kade gives a sad smile.

“You keep looking at my daughter… Why?” I question.

“We… Well… She… I-I…” He stammers.

“Oh, spit it out Callum, she doesn’t have all day,” Evie approaches with Trey.

“She’s my mate,” he says as my brows raise as I look him over. He could definitely do with some food, but he was handsome…

“Well, I hope you know she’s stubborn…” I smile.

“Too bloody right she is, she was adamant we would get out before these two realised they were mates, they were almost at each other's throats,” Evie smiles.

“Sounds like our Taylor,” Trey smirks before looking back at her.

Her body was covered in burns, she was still out cold.

“She’ll be ok Nix,” Trey says.

“I’m sorry, but we are gathering the bodies of the fallen, may we?” Two fae men ask. Michael sighs, nodding as they pick up Paul’s body, fixing his arm back in place quickly before carrying him away.

“Come on, your people need you, we’ve lost a lot and we need to get back home,” Kade says, clamping his hand on Michael’s shoulder, picking him up as they hug it out.

“Let me help you,” Callum extends a hand to me, lifting me to my feet.

“Thank you, for being with her, you’re all welcome to come with us back to our home, or we can help you on your own way home,” I reply.

“I have no home left, neither do the others, we would love to come,” Evie smiles brightly. I look to Trey as he smiles.

“She’s cute,” I laugh through our link.

“She’s beautiful,” he smiles. I take another look at her, she’s all bone, but you could tell she used to have a curvy frame, her face was pale where I was sure it was full of life once. These people would need a lot of care to get back to their old way, but I’d help them all.

“So, I’ve had one of my boys fly to scout for another plane, if not, we’re walking,” Violet says as we walk back over to the others.

“We can’t walk with so many injured,” I shake my head.

“We may not have a choice Phoenix, we can only do so much,” Violet sighs.

“We’ll figure something out, I’m going to call Luci and let her know what’s happened,” Kade said as he takes his phone. The further we were the more difficult it could be to contact through the links, we wore out quicker.

I walk over to those that are injured, sitting between Jae and Taylor.

“They aren’t out of the woods yet, but I’m hopeful Phoenix, they’ll make it. Though their bodies will scar, the damage is too great, Taylor’s legs will have permanent scarring, while her arms should heal, her face will forever have the scar from the vampire from the last mission too. Jae… However, I don’t know, he’s in a bad way, he was already dying and this put more pressure on his body. I don’t know if he will wake any time soon, I’m sorry Kai, he’s got a long road ahead of him, he may not make it, but stay positive, once we are home we will be able to keep an eye on him better," Rodge nods to us as he wanders off to help others.

"Jae…" Kai whispers, kissing his hand softly.

"He'll make it Kai, he will," I extend my hand over to him as he holds it tightly, his eyes looking between the two.

"We have to catch a break… Surely… I can't take this heartache anymore," Kai whispers sadly.

"Neither can I, we've lost so many, my heart feels like it's been torn apart. I felt them all, but I couldn't tell who…It was the worst thing I had ever felt," I bring my knees to my chest, resting my head against them.

"Phoenix, my men have found a plane in working order, it's a few miles out, so we need to rig something up to get them there, but we found something!" Violet calls.

"Great… Flying again…" Michael groans as he kneels beside our little girl, kissing her head softly.

# Chapter Eighteen

## Taylor

"Oh, for god's sake Trey will you stop, we're supposed to be watching over her, will you stop trying to mate me!" I can hear Evie's happy voice. Though I kept trying, I was unable to open my eyes.

What happened… The last thing I remember is being in the fire… Mum… She put it out… Then… What…

"I finally found my mate and you are being difficult woman," Trey groans as Evie giggles.

"We are not doing it here! What if she wakes up?!" Evie laughs.

"She won't," Trey growls lustfully.

Oh no. No… This is not happening… Come on! Open your eyes, Taylor, I'm not listening to him fool around with Evie… She was his mate?!

"Mmm," I hear Trey moan.

"Ughh, please don't," I groan, my eyes open finally, Evie screams in surprise as she jumps off of Trey in his seat in the corner, his erection evident in his trousers.

"Oh, shit… Taylor… I…" he grumbles.

"Save it, you're worse than my brother," I groan.

"I have to get your mum!" Evie says happily, rushing out of the room.

"How are you feeling?" Trey walks up to me slowly, shifting his trousers a little.

"I'd be better if you didn't have a stiffy," I laugh hoarsely.

"Yeah… Uh… Sorry, here," he passes me a glass of water and I sip from it slowly.

"Taylor! Oh, my baby! You're awake!" Mum comes running into the room, knocking the glass from my hand as Trey chuckles shaking his head at her before clearing away the mess.

"Hi mum," I smile softly at her as she sits on the edge of the bed, cupping my face in her hands.

"I was so scared, my little girl, I'm so proud of you," she hugs me tightly as I groan.

"I'd like to breathe you know," I groan as she gasps, and I laugh at her.

"Look who woke up," dad stands at the door with a huge smile as he walks up to me, kissing my head.

"Hey dad," I smile at him.

"How is Jae?" I ask as everyone's faces go gloomy.

"He hasn't woken up yet, he's not healing as he should, Kai hasn't left his side, we don't know if he will make it," mum says sadly.

"There's time," Trey says.

"How long was I out for?" I ask.

"A week…" Mum sighs, holding my hand tightly.

"A week!" I exclaim in shock.

"Your new friend hasn't stopped pacing outside, I'm pretty sure we have a permanent trench dug now," Trey winks at me.

"Friend… Who?" I ask.

"Callum," Evie smiles. I blush looking down, my eyes widening.

"OH MY GOD!" I cry out at the state of my legs.

"Taylor calm down honey!" Mum grabs my hands in hers.

"TWIN!" Bryant bursts into the room.

"My legs! What the hell! Why haven't they healed? They look… look… hideous!" I cry.

"Hey, twin calm down! Look at me! Taylor!" Bryant snaps his fingers in my face as I look into his eyes.

"Who's going to want a girl like me with legs like this?" I cry.

"Callum. I can tell you that right now, he's been in this room every fucking day, he's so worried about you and none of us are bothered by scars, they tell a story! You were the bravest girl I know, besides mum… You were going to sacrifice yourself to save the others, you went back for the humans, you saved them! YOU did that! You went back into a burning building to save Jae, and this is the story those scars show, they will show how brave my twin is and how she can kick arse and still go back to help save everyone," Bryant says as tears fall from my eyes.

"You saved me Bryant… They all saved me… The necklace helped me, the others helped me, I wasn't alone, we've lost so many people, Blake… Jason… Paul… Keeley and so many of the warriors, too many have had to die," I cry.

"I know twin, I know, but you're alive and we're here, we can honour the dead by moving forward, you survived, you saved so many. They are all here too, David is making a nuisance of himself in the medical wing with Rodge, but he's living because you saved him as are the others. Some are recovering still, but they made it because you went for them," he continues as he curls me into his side, hugging me tightly.

"Couldn't have said it better myself, I owe you my life little princess," David grins in the doorway with Rodge beside him.

"Yes, well you can make up for it out of my medical wing," Rodge sighs, walking to my side, his hand hovering over my body.

"So…" Mum says eagerly.

"Looks like she's all healed up," Rodge nods.

*Get up… Run… Need to shift… Let me out!*

"Can I go out?" I ask.

"I don't know Taylor…" Dad says.

"Please, he said I was healed I just need to shift… Lily needs to get out," I beg him.

"Ok," he nods as I smile at him. Bryant helps me to sit up.

"Not too fast!" Mum says as I raise a brow at her panicking.

"I'm fine mum," I smirk, standing up and groaning as my body stretches.

"Not sure the whole hospital gown look is you, hold on," Evie chuckles. I groan looking down when she darts back into the room with some loose trousers and a t-shirt, and I signal everyone to turn around for some privacy as I get changed.

"It's safe," I say as they turn back.

"Ok, come on then," Bryant hooks an arm around mine as we head out of the room.

As we walk through the halls many of the warriors bow their heads in respect as I blush, humans thanking me as I walk past their rooms.

"Taylor… You're up!" Kai calls from a room to our left as I walk in slowly, seeing Jae's body lying on a bed. He's so still, his body covered in patchy burns, luckily none were on his pretty face, I knew he'd hate that.

"Hey uncle Kai," I hug him to me tightly, feeling him sag in my arms.

"He won't wake up," Kai whispers.

"He will, I know he will, you better uncle Jae, you wake up, your family need you, Jae. I'm going to kick your arse if you don't wake up!" I say with a sad smile as Kai squeezes my hand and then goes to sit next to him.

"See Jae, it's not just me, Taylor's going to kick your arse too, wake up baby, please," Kai begs and my heart breaks watching them.

"I'll stay with him, go on your walk," mum says kissing my cheek as she sits with her best friend, consoling him.

We walk out and head downstairs before heading outside, the breeze hits me as I take a deep breath.

I'm alive… We made it… Most of us made it…

"Where are they? Blake? The others?" I ask.

"We had a funeral for them the other day. Mum did a huge speech about family, led the howl and had the fae create something a little different, come on, I'll show you," Bryant says, dragging me with him as I see a tall marble wall, names etched into the marble and painted in gold.

My hand reaches out to it, touching the smooth marble as tears fall.

"I'll never forget you all, I'm so sorry Blake," I cry.

"He wouldn't want you to cry Taylor, you know he hated to see you cry. That's why he always ran at you, knocking you over, trying to make everyone laugh, including you. He was a moron, he was family, no one will forget him or any of the others, their stories will go down in history," my twin says, and I rest my head on his shoulder.

"Taylor…" A deep voice says. I turn my head to the right to see a man, a handsome man at that, his face was that of perfection, his hair long and black, and his eyes… his eyes were the brightest of greens.

"Callum?" I murmur.

"Yeah, he's filled out a little. I'll leave you two to it, take care of her Callum!" My brother chuckles, leaving me alone with him. I look at my brother's body retreating with a small bit of panic before I gulp and face Callum.

"I felt it, you waking up, but I knew you would be surrounded by your family… I didn't want to intrude…" He says walking closer as I take him in.

"Thank you," I smile softly.

"How are you feeling?" He asks, his hand twitches as if he wants to touch mine, but he stops himself.

"Sad, happy, full of grief, in disbelief… How many emotions do you want?" I smirk as he chuckles.

"I'm not surprised, it's been a hell of a time… I'm glad you're ok," he says. He moves a strand of my hair from my face around my ear, his fingers lingering on my face, touching my scar as I wince away from him.

"Please don't, it's… It's ugly," I sigh.

"It's a scar, scars don't make us ugly, you're beautiful," he says, cupping my cheek, looking into my eyes.

"No, scars are ugly, why would you want a person like me? My legs look awful, this scar on my face will never go, nor will the ones on my legs," I shake my head, pushing him away.

"Don't do that, don't push me away. I'm here Taylor, you are beautiful," Callum repeats.

"THIS! This is beautiful?!" I cry out, pulling the leg of my trousers up as he looks at my legs.

I shift and begin to run, noticing my paws were burnt up too, my fur patchy on them as I whine, racing into the woods.

"Taylor!" I hear him call for me as I race off.

He knocks me off my feet and we tumble across the ground, landing with a thud against a tree as I shift back, groaning as he shifts helping me sit up, his eyes looking at me in a panic.

"I'm so sorry, I didn't mean to hurt you, I would never hurt you, Taylor…" He says in a panic, and I put a finger on his lips to shut him up.

"I'm fine," I sigh.

His hand comes back up to my face, caressing it with his thumb on my opposite cheek, I sigh into his touch.

"You are beautiful, don't see yourself as anything else," he whispers as he kisses my lips softly.

"EWW gag worthy! She just woke up! She hasn't brushed her teeth in a week! YUCK!" Talia laughs behind Callum; he growls turning around to face the twins.

"GIRLS!" Callum growls.

"Oops… Sorry Callum!" Tilly laughs.

"Glad to see you're awake Taylor!" They say before running off.

"Those two are a pain sometimes," Callum shakes his head with a smile, watching them carefully as they leave the forest.

"Yet you seem fond of them," I reply.

"Yes, I am. They were there from the start, you become attached, they were like sisters to me, I will forever see it that way," he nods.

"You sound like my mum, a family isn't just blood," I smile.

"Your mum is right," he smiles as he goes to kiss me again, but I put a hand to his lips.

"They were right, we shouldn't kiss. I need to wash and do my teeth, I'm gross," I giggle.

*Did you just giggle like a schoolgirl?*

**Don't start Lily…**

*He is handsome, what I wouldn't give to see him without a shirt now... Oh and in a few months as he gets back to normal... I bet he has muscles, God that's so hot, he's so hot...*

"Is that your wolf talking to you? What is her name?" He asks.

"Lily, what about yours?" I ask.

"His name is Cage, he's a little hyper sometimes, just warning you," he smiles.

*His smile is gorgeous! Those eyes I could look into alllllll day!*

"So can Lily, trust me I know," I laugh.

"What's she saying?" He asks.

"Nothing," I shake my head with a smile as I stand up.

*NOTHING! The man is a god, and you say that I said nothing! Tell him I want to lick peanut butter off of his abs!*

I laugh a little at her as my eyes go wide, Callum raising a brow at me with a gorgeous smirk.

"Nothing huh… Come on Lily, push out for me, tell me." He eggs her on as I groan, feeling her trying to take over.

"I said I wanted to lick peanut butter off of your…" she pushes through, and I put a hand over my own mouth, pushing her back.

"Lick peanut butter off of what?" Callum takes a step forward to me as my heart flutters.

"Nothing," I shake my head.

"Taylor…" He says, his voice shaking the very pit of my stomach.

"She wants to lick peanut butter off your abs!" Lily pushes through again and I growl at her.

**LILY!**

*You'll thank me later!*

"I swear to god, she's a liability…" I murmur as Callum chuckles coming forward and pulling me against him, his nose going to my neck.

"I look forward to getting to know you Taylor, Lily too. Perhaps we can make that dream a reality one day," he says, kissing my neck. I hear the lustful growl come from me, I was in shock, I had never made that noise before.

"I… Uh… I should go shower…" I murmur.

"Come on then," he smiles, taking my hand in his as we make our way back to the mansion, my heart fluttering at the electricity I was feeling.

# Chapter Nineteen

## Phoenix

I hadn't seen Kai so broken since his father died, and I hated every moment of it as I held him in my arms. Michael stayed close by watching us, but giving us the space we needed, he cared for Kai too, they'd become good friends over the years.

"I can't lose him," Kai mutters repeatedly.

"There has to be something else we can do to help him," I link to Michael.

"The fae have tried everything, something is working against them, they think magic may have a hand in it, they are researching as much as they can," Michael replies and I sigh, leaning my head on Kai's shoulder.

A giggle makes me smile as I hear Taylor coming up the stairs, hearing her giggle again was like music to my ears.

"Looks like Callum and her are getting on, they are holding hands," Michael says as I smile.

"What's got you smiling?" Kai whispers, looking at me.

"Taylor and Callum," I smile softly.

"I'll kill him if he hurts her," he says sternly.

“You and me both Kai, you and me both,” I smile as I look over him and Jae. I hoped he would wake, but as time went on it was looking less likely.

“Hey Phoenix, Hanson wants a word,” Janie smiles sadly in the doorway as I nod.

“Will you be ok Kai?” I ask.

“Yeah, go do queen stuff,” he gives a small nod and smile.

“I’ll come to see you in a bit,” I kiss his head.

“I can stay for a bit,” Janie smiles, coming into the room as I kiss her cheek.

“Thank you, sweetheart,” I say before walking out, joining Michael as he takes my hand.

“What do you think he wants?” Michael asks.

“Probably to arrange them going home,” I shrug as we make our way downstairs.

“Bryant, stop, we’re going to get caught,” I hear a giggle nearby as we go past one of the offices, both Michael and I look at each other, raising a brow before shaking our heads with a smirk.

“We won’t get caught Amanda, trust me,” I hear my son’s lustful growl.

“Take it to your room guys!” I call out as I hear Amanda squeal in shock. Bryant sticks his head out of the door, a sheepish look on his face.

“Uhh… We weren’t doing anything,” he says.

“I thought I taught you better son,” Michael laughs.

“You taught me to explore… I’m exploring my woman,” Bryant gives a cheeky grin.

“BRYANT!” I laugh.

“What have I got myself into…” I hear Amanda groan.

“Good luck with him Amanda, you’re going to need it, my children are crazy,” I smirk as Bryant gives me a look of shock.

“Crazy… How dare you!” He grins.

“I second that,” Michael nods.

“I agree,” Amanda murmurs. I see Bryant turn to her with a growl as he goes back into the room, hearing her squeal before he comes out with her in his arms, legs wrapped around his waist.

“We’ll try not to be too loud!” Bryant grins cheekily.

“He’s worse than you,” I say to Michael as they runoff.

“Oh really…” Michael raises a brow; his hand goes into my hair before pushing me up against the wall.

“Michael, not now,” I laugh as his lips catch mine.

“Is this whole building in heat?!” Kade grumbles as we separate.

“Not getting any are we?” Michael smirks at his friend.

“Oh, I’m getting plenty… With your mum,” Kade smirks as Michael and Kade both end up play fighting like children.

“I wondered what was keeping you… It seems you were preoccupied with… Whatever is happening here…” Hanson laughs at the grown men fighting on the floor.

“They may be over five hundred years old, but they are still boys,” I smirk, shaking my head at them.

"Shall we?" Hanson gestures a hand to a door, and I smile following him into the office.

"I take it this about you leaving to go back to your pack?" I ask.

"Partially, yes. We will be returning home soon, my pack also need to grieve with those of us left here, but my niece… Her and Bryant are mated, and I do not wish to keep them from each other, her parents died when she was just a baby. I'm her only family and I worry about leaving her here, she still suffers from nightmares. I worry about her as if she was my own daughter," Hanson says.

"Hanson, you know I would take care of her if she and Bryant choose to stay here, plus they are perfectly welcome to come and go as they please," I answer.

"You won't want Bryant to stay?" He asks.

"Of course I would, but ultimately it's not my decision, children fly the nest as Janie did. He is welcome to choose where he wants to be, all my children are. Every wolf here is welcome to go to another pack if they wish, I do not force people to stay," I smile at him.

"If she chooses to stay… Would you watch over her… She's acting all happy now, but she suffers so much from her own depression, her mind…" He says sadly.

"Of course I will, as if she were my own," I nod and he takes a deep breath.

"I don't know why I doubted anything else other than what you just said, you are such a caring queen and alpha, your children are amazing too. I think Amanda will fit in nicely here," he says with a smile.

"Thank you Hanson and you know you're welcome here any time. You can bring the whole pack too if you're worried about them, I can see it in your eyes, your eyes beg to go home."

"I do, my pack are my family, as you know. We feel the loss of our fallen and it doesn't get easier, does it?" He sighs.

"No, it doesn't, but we keep going, we keep our heads up and we make them proud. They fought for us and gave their lives for something much bigger than we could have believed, they died in battle for our future and the next generations," I reply.

"True, true," he nods.

"When will you leave for home?" I ask.

"We will stay a couple more days, give the kids time to think on what they want to do," he answers.

"Great," I smile.

"Thank you, Phoenix, for everything, you've done your parents and everyone proud," Hanson smiles as I hug him.

"Thank you," I smile.

"Did I interrupt? You aren't stealing my woman are you Hanson?" Michael smirks from the doorway.

"No, I don't think it would be too good if I slept with Janie and Phoenix, would it?" Hanson smirks.

"Oh, for god's sake, you're all children," I laugh pushing past Michael.

# Chapter Twenty

## Taylor

Callum had sat outside my room like a gentleman while I showered, washing away all the dirt as I sighed against the hot water cascading down me.

I was pretty sure someone had washed me down at some point as I wasn't covered in blood anymore, I just hoped it was at least mum that did it and not some random person… I shivered at the thought.

As I get out from the shower, I slowly towel dry myself, looking down at my legs with a sigh. I would never get used to it, but I knew what the others meant when they said they were just scars, but my mind couldn't deal with it. I hated them, I was so nervous about them. Why would anyone want a girl like me?

"I can feel your sadness Taylor, stop it, you are beautiful," I hear Callum in my head.

*He's so nice…*

**He is.**

I walk out into my room and get dressed, feeling a little better in my clothes before drying my hair and putting a small bit of make-up on as I would normally do, feeling a little more… Normal.

"Wow…" Callum's eyes go wide as I open my door, blushing.

"What?" I murmured, looking down at the ground.

“You are beautiful, but you don’t need the make-up,” he lifts my chin gently, his other hand goes to my waist, pulling me towards him as our eyes gaze into each other’s and he kisses me softly, sparks flying as I kissed back.

“ARGGHHHHH! GET AWAY FROM ME!” I hear a voice scream out from the medical bay. Callum and I look at each other in shock before running towards the screams.

“Kai! What’s going on?!” I ask as he’s being dragged out of the room that Jae was in.

“He doesn’t know me!” Kai cries out, panic in his eyes.

“Amnesia,” Rook said holding him back. I went to the door where Rodge was trying to calm Jae down who was looking around as if he didn’t know where he was.

“Someone get Violet!” Rodge shouts.

“Who the fuck is Violet?! Where am I?!” Jae shouts sitting up, pushing himself against the back of the bed as his eyes look around in a panic before they land on me, he frowns.

“Jae…” I murmur.

“TAYLOR! Help me, who are these people?!” He shouts and I hear Kai gasp behind me.

“Taylor come here, I need you to calm him,” Rodge says. I step into the room to his bedside and Jae’s hand shoots into mine pulling me to him.

“Shhh, I’ve got you, you’re safe Jae, you’re home,” I say holding him to me.

“Who are they… What happened to me?” He murmurs.

"Babe?" Kai says.

"That's Kai, your soulmate, your husband…" I point to Kai as Jae frowns, groaning as he holds his head.

"Why… Why don't I remember you?" Jae frowns.

"Oh my! Jae! You are awake!" Violet bursts into the room.

"Stay away from me!" Jae whimpers in my arms.

"What's going on Rodge?" Violet's eyes go wide.

"Amnesia, until we do some tests I won't know if it's permanent," he sighs.

"Permanent… He may never remember me…" Kai says falling to his knees.

"What happened to me Taylor? It hurts… Why does it hurt?" Jae says.

"I'd go slowly with information Taylor," Rook says as I nod.

"How about we let Rodge check you over first before we get into it, where do you hurt?" I ask Jae.

"Kai… What…" Mum kneels beside Kai, looking into the room as I see Callum whisper in her ear, telling her what happened. She looks to me with sadness in her eyes as she gazes over us, hugging Kai to her as she whispers in his ear.

"Too many people… Too many people… Arrgghh my head!" Jae screams, I look in panic at Rodge as his hands begin to hover over Jae's head.

"Everyone out! Except you Taylor, give us space and get me some extra healers!" Rodge orders as mum nods, picking Kai up as she begins ordering everyone around.

"Will you be ok?" Callum asks.

"Yes, would you help mum please?" I ask.

"Of course, I'll be right beside you in an instant if you need me, Taylor," he says with a small smile before he helps my mum, and she gives him a soft smile.

"At least he's awake…" I say to her through the link.

"Baby steps…" She replies before disappearing.

"It's dark, why is it so dark? There's a man… What happened to me? Why are the only faces I know are yours and a man… Who is he?" Jae whimpers.

"Who is the man? What does he look like?" I ask as Rodge frowns.

"Dark… So dark," he begins screaming again, thrashing around in pain.

"Rodge what's happening?!" I cry as he thrashes on the bed in a fit. Rodge pulls me away before trying to use his magic on Jae.

"I fear the witch may have done something to his brain," he answers.

"Dark… The witch's skin… The room we were in… They were all dark…" I mutter.

More fae healers come into the room and they begin working on Jae, his body begins to calm and his eyes slowly open again.

"T-Tay… Taylor… Have to get out… We have to get out…" He whimpers.

"Jae, hey, look at me, we are out, we're home, we got out. I swear Jae, he's dead, he's gone, you don't have to be afraid anymore, you're home," I take his hand in mine as the healers work around me.

"I can't see… Why can't I see…" he says.

"You could see earlier though… Rodge… What's happening?" I ask in a panic.

"I fear he may have a bleed that we cannot control by magic, we'll have to go in via his skull, the human way…" He answers.

"Taylor… Where am I? Taylor!" Jae calls.

"I'm right here Jae, right here," I repeat as his hand squeezes mine painfully.

"We need to do this now Rodge," a healer says as he nods in answer.

"The human, David, get him, he's a doctor. I will need that idiot to help me," Rodge sighs, he really didn't like him.

"Why don't you like David?" I ask.

"He's got too much pep in his step," Rodge grumbles as I chuckle.

"Blake… Blake…" Jae mutters as we look at him in shock.

"You remember him?" I ask.

"He died, right in front of me… I couldn't save him, I'm sorry Taylor…" He cries.

"Jae, you listen to me right now, that was not your fault, that was Maximillian's, the witch that tortured us, but we're home, he was brought home and given the send-off he deserved with the rest of them," I said.

"Others died…" He cries.

"Yes, but please don't focus on that, we need to focus on getting you better, you're going to be ok uncle Jae," I kiss his forehead softly.

"Taylor, we need to go now," Rodge says.

"Jae, stay calm, they need to operate on you. I'll be nearby, if you need me, I will be right here, stay with us Jae," I kiss his head as they take him away.

"Taylor! No! Don't leave me!" Jae screams out as I follow the healers.

"Jae, I'm right here!" I call out as he begins thrashing around again and he goes still suddenly.

"Shit! MOVE!" Rodge shouts, they run quicker into a room.

"Stay put!" A healer orders me by the door.

"We've got this Taylor," David rushes past me into the room as I sink to the floor by the door.

"Callum…" I cry, my hands shaking as I try to link with him, listening to what was going on behind the doors.

"Damn it! Come on boy, you're not going on my watch," I hear David shout as I let out a sob.

"I've got you," Callum picks me up and sets me in his lap as I sob.

Hours went by and I was still in Callum's lap. I just kept listening and it wasn't good. They'd nearly lost him a couple of times.

"DAMN IT! No, you fucking don't kid!" I hear Rodge shout once again.

"He's not going to make it like this, there has to be another way…" I hear David swear under his breath.

"There's nothing else we can do…" I hear Rodge sigh.

I stand quickly bursting into the room as they look at me in shock.

"You can't give up! He can't die!" I cry.

"Perhaps that's exactly what he needs to do…" David mutters as I growl at him.

"YOU WHAT!" I growl.

"No… I have been talking with others and they tell me of this hybrid… Blake… Is it only through birth you can make someone hybrid?" He says and my eyes go wide.

"Holy shit, we can turn him…" I murmur.

"Vampire or a wolf?" David asks.

"KAI!" I shout as loud through the halls. I can hear the rush of footsteps as he flits to me, eyes red and puffy.

"No… Don't you tell me he's dead…" He shakes his head.

"No… But he might if you don't turn him," I say urgently.

"Do what…" He replies.

"Make him a hybrid! Hurry up!" I push him in the room.

"What's happening?" Mum runs up to us in a panic too.

"Kai! NOW!" I shout as his fangs come out.

"Stay with me," Kai says before plunging his fangs into Jae's neck.

"Now what…" David says.

"Now we wait… Close him up," Rodge says as David nods and gets to work.

"What if it doesn't work?" Kai sniffs the tears back.

"Have faith," I say, taking his hand tightly.

"Why didn't you turn him, Taylor? Why ask Kai?" David asks as he finishes working on Jae.

"When a wolf bites someone to turn them, they don't always make the shift, vampires don't work the same. Plus, they are soulmates, it will be easier if they are the same," I say, and he nods in understanding. We all sit beside him, waiting for him to wake… Hopefully…

Hours we sat there as David stayed by our sides, trying to learn everything about our kind as he could.

The heart monitor begins to give off a continuous beep, Jae's heart stopping.

"NO!" Kai screams and I hold him back. His claws dig into my arms as he screams for Jae, I ignore the pain, he didn't mean it. I can hear Callum growl, his eyes on my arm as I give him a small shake of the head and he backs down.

"Wait, just wait Kai," I murmur in his ear as mum looks at us, tears in her eyes.

"Shit… I thought it would work… I'm sorry Kai," David says sadly.

"Come on Jae," I whisper.

Kai screams in my arms as Jae doesn't make a move, I was sure this would work…

Mum takes him from me as she hugs him tightly while he screams in pain.

"Jae… Come on, don't do this to me, wake the fuck up!" I shout my hand slamming against the bed.

"Taylor… He's gone…" Callum sighs, he goes to put his hand in mine I roar in anger, even the table shook at the noise.

"JAE!" I shout once more.

Suddenly he sits up as I scream in shock, falling to the ground, laughing with tears in my eyes as he looks at me with his new bright red eyes.

“Jae…” Kai says, his eyes wide in shock.

“Why is everyone staring at me like I just rose from the dead?” Jae says, frowning at us.

“You kinda did,” I grin.

“What… I… Jesus I’m thirsty… Taylor… What the fuck happened?!” He exclaims, his voice hoarse.

“Jae?” Kai murmurs walking up to him.

“Kai…” Jae smiles at Kai before Kai flits to his husband's side, kissing him passionately.

“I can’t believe that worked…” David says in shock.

“Does someone want to tell me what happened?” Jae asks.

“Yes, but first, you need to drink,” Kai nods.

“Drink… I…K ai did you bite me?!” Jae hisses, his hand moves to his neck feeling the puncture wounds.

“It was that or losing you Jae,” I sigh.

“Taylor you beautiful, beautiful girl!” Kai laughs as he lifts me and spins me happily.

“I’m going to need filling in,” Jae grumbles.

“We should let them catch up,” mum says with a relieved sigh, and I agree.

"David, you better come out. He's a newly turned vampire, we can't guarantee he won't go for you," mum says.

"And that's when I exit," he says before exiting the room quickly.

"Taylor… Don't go, not yet," Jae says.

"Ok," I nod.

"We'll be outside," Callum says, kissing my cheek before he and the others leave me and Kai in the room, but not before Rook slips in.

"I take it you may need some memory help…" Rook says.

"It's patchy," Jae sighs.

"Drink this first," Kai says, grabbing a blood bag and I watch Jae rip into it greedily, as I grimace at it.

"Gross," I grumble.

"You eat little bunnies when hunting and THIS is gross?" Kai smirks at me. I roll my eyes at him, but I can't help the smile on my face.

"He's handling it better than most," Rook says.

"You've got… Uh… A little bit… Uh… Everywhere," Kai laughs, pointing to Jae and Jae just shrugs.

"Your dinner later," he winks as I chuckle, shaking my head.

"What's the last thing you remember Jae?" I ask.

"The field…. Blake on the ground… Screaming… Pain… Fire… It's all so patchy…" He sighs.

"Taylor… Would you mind if I showed him your memories while trying to recover his own?" Rook says as I gulp.

"I…" I murmur.

"You don't have to Taylor," Jae says, noticing the fear in my face.

"Do it," I nod as Rook takes my hand and then takes Jae's.

"Guys… Don't tell mum everything… She doesn't know…" I murmur.

"What… What doesn't she know?" Kai frowns.

"Show him too," I sigh sadly as Rook nods, signalling for Kai to hold on to him as we all close our eyes.

Flashes of memory begin to whizz through our eyes, it showed a mixture of Jae's and mine before Jae's go dark when Greg had to put him out, then it was just mine. In the room with Maximillian as he touched me… I felt sick to my stomach. I tried to rip my hand from Rook as they continued.

It kept going, through the battle, every single detail was there, I could feel the tears flooding from my eyes before I dropped to the ground, and I was let go.

"Taylor…" Kai murmurs. He goes to grab me from the floor, but Callum bursts in and gets to me first, pulling me into his arms, holding me tight, growling at Rook.

"I've got you," he says as I cry in his arms.

"Taylor… You saved my life… Thank you," Jae says from the bed.

"I couldn't leave you behind," I sniff.

"We're all thankful you didn't Taylor," Kai says walking to me, kissing my head softly.

"Tell me that witch is definitely dead," Jae hisses.

"Oh yeah, he's dead alright," Callum growls.

"Trey and Bryant got him," Kai answers holding onto Jae as if he were scared to let him go for fear he may disappear.

I wince, my head hurting suddenly.

"Taylor?" Callum frowns as my hand surges to my head.

"It hurts…" I groan.

"Come here," Rook orders. Callum growls in warning at him before he helps me to Rook as his hands go either side of my head.

"STOP!" I scream as the pain gets worse.

"You've overdone it today, you're burning your mind out, we should not have done this, you need to rest, it was all too soon," Rook says.

"Bed for you then," Callum says, picking me up bridal style.

"I don't want to leave Jae," I reply.

"I'll be here when you wake up Taylor. I promise, you're not losing me again, plus I need to catch up with my husband, he's got some teaching to do," Jae winks at Kai and I giggle.

"You better not go anywhere," I point my finger at him sternly as he smiles at me.

"Never, you're stuck with me kid," he replies.

"Good," I nod.

"Good night, Taylor," they say as Callum carries me away.

# Chapter Twenty-One

## Taylor

"Taylor?" Bryant calls out as we are nearly at my door.

"She needs to sleep, Bryant," Callum says.

"I'll take her then," Bryant goes to take me, but Callum growls possessively.

"Hey, be nice to my twin," I smack his chest lightly.

"Ok, I get it, she's your mate, but she's my twin, I just want to protect her as much as you do," my twin says.

"You can open the door," Callum says. Bryant rolls his eyes, opening my bedroom door as I groan, head against Callum's chest.

"You out, I'll get her ready," Bryant says sternly, and I can almost feel the testosterone in the room.

"BOYS!" I groan, shaking my head as Callum sets me down on the bed.

"Sorry," Bryant sighs.

"I can get ready myself, BOTH of you get out," I roll my eyes, pointing to the door.

"But…" Bryant starts, and I glare at him.

"Now!" I point again as he storms out the room, Callum chuckles.

"He's so protective," Callum smirks.

"Look who's talking… Out," I tell him, he frowns, but walks out the door closing it behind him.

"Fucking boys," I grumble.

"I heard that!" Bryant shouts.

I slowly get changed, my energy depleting by the minute before I throw my pyjama vest on and flop onto my bed.

"Done," I murmur, my eyes closing already.

"Taylor I… Oh… If I pick her up, will you sort the covers?" I hear my brother whisper.

"How about I hold her, and you sort the covers?" Callum says. I smell his scent next to me before he lifts me into his arms.

"You don't need to be the only one to handle her you know…" Bryant grumbles.

"She's my mate," Callum snaps.

"I'm her twin for God sake, chill out! Taylor's never been one for relationships before, you need to chill out a bit or you just might scare her away," my brother says.

*Just let them sort their shit out themselves, I've had enough, we both need rest.*

**Yeah… I'm so tired…**

"Shit. It's Cage, my wolf, he's protective of her. After everything in that fucking place, he doesn't want anyone else to touch her, you have no idea how hard it was to stop him from jumping at her when she was holding Jae, I think the only thing stopping him was because we saw what happened to him, plus he knows he's not a threat," Callum sighs.

"I'm her fucking TWIN, I'm not a threat!" Bryant shouts. I feel Lily getting angry as they were shouting while we were trying to fall asleep.

"Guys, shut up," I groan, pulling the quilt over my head.

"Sorry Taylor, we will leave you to sleep, call for me if you need me," Callum says, I feel the quilt lift and he kisses my cheek.

"Night sis," Bryant murmurs, kissing me too as I hear Callum growl again.

"Seriously dude…" Bryant grumbles.

"I can't explain it. Cage… he… he thinks you could persuade her to stay away from us, family always win…" Callum sighs and I hear the door begin to shut.

"You treat her right and you'll have no problems from me, treat her like shit and trust me when I say, I'm not your only problem," my twin says.

"Ok, truce?" Callum says as I smile a little.

"Yeah man," I hear Bryant reply as I slowly fall to sleep.

*Finally…*

"Mmm, look at you, so sweet, so delectable, you will always be mine little wolf, you cannot escape me," Maximillian is in my room. No! This can't be happening!

I'm in my bed still as I wake up screaming, he's on top of me, burns cover his face as his hand reaches out to touch me. I can feel every bit of him as he straddles my waist, but I can't move, I can't talk, and I can't feel my wolf… Where is Lily?!

Tears fall from my eyes as his hands begin to roam, the covers suddenly fly off of me as I'm paralysed beneath him, I can smell his burnt flesh, his skin hot to touch as his hands begin to lift my top.

I can't scream now, not even a small sob can escape my mouth, I can't resist him as my flesh begins to burn with his touch.

"You are mine," he laughs as he rips off my clothing.

My whole body burns, he's now naked, his body burnt, skin singed by the chains and fire.

"You will always be mine," he says, kissing my lips as I feel him between my legs, red hot pain fills me as he burns my insides, my voice wanting to scream, my body needing to move. I want to claw him away, claw his touch from my body.

"Do you wish to talk?" He laughed, and he puts his hand over my mouth before I let out a loud scream.

"Taylor! Taylor! Wake up! It's a dream! Wake up!" A voice booms and I sit up suddenly, body soaked with sweat as I notice I'm screaming. My chest is heaving and I look around the room in a panic, looking for him, to find my dad beside me, worry flooding his face.

*I'm here! You didn't lose me, Taylor, it was a nightmare!*

"Maximillian… He… He was here… I couldn't move, speak… He was touching me and then he… He…" I sob as dad takes my hand in his.

"You are safe, he's not here, he's dead," dad says calmly, curling me in his arms as I shake.

I wince in pain as my arm touches something on my stomach, dad frowns, lifting my top slightly. He lifts my hand and I see the blood on my fingers.

"Stay put, I'll get something to clean it," he says as he goes into the bathroom.

"Dad! Dad! Don't leave!" I cry as he rushes back to my side, the emergency first aid kit in his hands. He jumps onto the bed, and I curl up into his arms, shaking.

"Hush little one, I have you, sweetheart, you're safe," he murmurs, kissing my head.

"Taylor!" I hear a few voices in the corridor as a rush of footsteps come towards my room while I sob in my dad's arms.

"Baby? Are you ok? What happened?! Why is she bleeding? Who did this?" Callum rushes in, barging past my twin as Bryant looks at me in shock.

"Callum calm down," dad growls at him.

"Oh sweet baby girl," mum comes in before pushing past Callum who goes to growl, but she gives him a stern look, he whimpers and backs off, eyes down on the ground.

"What happened?" Bryant asks as dad begins to wash my cuts out, I wince in pain in mum's arms.

"The… The… He…." I stammer unable to bring myself to say it.

"You don't have to tell us, it's ok," mum soothes me, softly.

“Taylor…” Callum moves forward, his hand reaching out as I whimper away into my parent’s arms.

“Give it time…” Bryant says, putting a hand on Callum’s shoulder.

“Show me what you saw Taylor, I will help you,” mum says through the link as she presses her forehead against mine. I can feel her trying to probe my mind as I shiver in her arms, closing my eyes before the images flash once again sending them to her as her arms close tighter around me, kissing my head, looking at dad with sad eyes.

“Mum…” Bryant murmurs.

“Your sister has been through enough lately, she had a nightmare, the witch was in it and that’s all you need to know, go back to bed,” mum says sternly.

“No, I’m not leaving her!” Bryant says defiantly and I hear mum growl at him.

“Babe?” Amanda says quietly outside the door, peering in, her hair a mess as if she had just got out of bed.

“Go, be with your mate twin,” I say through the link, wiping my face as I felt safer in the arms of my parents.

“Taylor… We always stay together when you have nightmares…” He replies.

“We aren’t kids anymore, you have Amanda and a future,” I say softly.

“You have Callum and a future too, I’m here whenever you need me, Taylor. I’m not going anywhere,” he replies, and he walks over to kiss me on the head softly.

“Good night twin,” I murmur.

"Sweet dreams sister, you're safe now," he says, then walks over to Amanda, she hugs into his arms, and I hear her murmuring about what was going on as he left slowly.

I look to Callum as he stands there sadly, looking at the floor, his eyes glancing up quickly and then back down to the floor.

"Would you like Rook to remove him from your mind?" Mum asks.

"No, I don't want my head tampered with anymore. I need to remember, I don't want to forget anything," I shake my head.

"Ok, how about I stay with you until you fall asleep?" Mum says. I look at both my parents, their eyes focused on me, but I knew they were both knackered too.

"No, go to bed, I'll be ok," I shake my head, wiping my face once again.

"Ok, come get us if you need us, ok?" Mum kisses my head.

"What about her stomach?" Dad sighs.

"I'll keep an eye on her," Callum says quietly.

"Taylor? Will you be ok with him in here?" Dad asks, I knew he was protective of me, I was his little girl.

"Yes," I nod slowly as I see Callum smile softly at me.

"You can sleep on the floor," dad growls at Callum as I have to try and stop myself giggling.

"Dad, calm down," I smile.

"I'll be wherever she needs me, I won't even touch her if she doesn't want me to," Callum puts his arms up in surrender.

"Michael, leave the man alone, they are mates, let them be. He's probably the best one to be with her right now, the bond will take over her dreams, get rid of the nightmares," mum says holding dad's hand as his shoulders slump.

"If anything happens to her..." Dad points his finger at Callum.

"It won't, I would put my life on the line for her, I owe her mine as it is Michael, trust me when I say that I will cherish her," Callum says as his eyes find mine. Butterflies fill my stomach as I smile, blushing.

"Good, I hope you will. Come on Michael, good night kids," mum says giving me a quick kiss before dragging dad behind her, closing the door on us.

"So..." I sigh, my head resting against my knees, arms hugging them to me as I look at Callum.

"Where do you want me? I will sleep on the floor if you want," he says.

"Won't that be uncomfortable?" I ask.

"You remember where we slept before right? This carpet is luxury compared to that," he smiles before frowning as I gulp.

"I... Yeah..." I sigh remembering that dark room, my eyes closing.

"Hey, look at me, we aren't there, you're safe," he tilts my head back up, I look into his eyes, a small tear escaping. His touch sends shivers up my spine as I sigh with relief at the feel of his skin against mine.

"Thank you," I whisper.

"How about you go freshen up? You'll feel better," he suggests.

"Yeah, I guess," I say, grabbing new pyjamas to replace my sweaty ones, slowly heading into the bathroom as I give myself a quick wash over. I hear rustling in the bedroom. Walking out I notice Callum is changing the sheets.

"I thought you'd want a fresh set, fresh sheets always feel better," he says nervously.

"Thank you, you didn't have to do that," I smile softly.

"I did, I would do anything for you, Taylor," he smiles back.

I notice he has made a small bed on the floor with blankets, I lift them, folding them back up he looks at me frowning.

"I need something to keep warm you know…" he says.

"You're not sleeping on the floor when there is room for us both on the bed, I trust you," I say getting into the bed as he looks so unsure.

"You're trying to get me killed aren't you…" He smirks.

"My brother and father won't touch you; they'd have to go through me first," I lay in my bed on my side facing him as he switches the light off, getting in slowly. His body is stiff as a board like he's afraid to touch me accidentally.

*For god's sake put a hand on him or something, soothe him with OUR touch for once.*

I bite my lip as my hand moves over to him, placing it on his chest and I feel him shiver under my touch, his hand entwines with mine and we both sigh with relief.

"Taylor… Can we… Can we cuddle?" he whispers.

“Yes,” I answer, shifting myself closer as he hooks an arm around me and I lay my head against his chest, listening to his steady heartbeat.

“Wow…” He murmurs.

“Yeah, wow,” I whisper, smiling as I snuggle into him. I had never felt this way before, it wasn’t like snuggling up with my family, this was so much more.

“Go to sleep baby,” he kisses my head softly.

“I don’t know if I want to,” I sigh sadly.

“No one will hurt you, Maximillian is gone, I’m right here, no one will ever hurt you again, not while I’m around. Go to sleep, I won’t sleep until you do,” he says, his fingers rubbing against my skin softly and I almost purr at his touch.

“Thank you, Callum,” I lean up and kiss his cheek before snuggling back up to his chest, closing my eyes as I feel Lily happier than ever that we were in our mate's arms.

“Good night beautiful,” he says.

“Good night,” I yawn as my eyes close, and I drift into sleep.

# Chapter Twenty-Two

## Phoenix

I hated watching everything that Taylor had seen in her dream, it made me wonder what else had happened in that building with the witch. Was she keeping things from me? Why would she picture herself under him as he claimed her… Had he forced himself on her when she was there?

Rook… Rook would know, and I would corner him to find out if no one would tell me the truth. I would ask her first of course, but I needed to know the truth.

"What are you thinking my love?" Michael says as I curl into his arms in bed.

"I don't think we know the whole story Michael, Taylor's hiding something and so are the others," I sigh.

"Why do you think that?"

"Her nightmare was of the witch holding her still by a spell as he… he touched her, to claim her as his. Why would she dream that if something hadn't happened to that extent?" I answer as he goes silent.

"I will talk to her tomorrow, you have enough to deal with my love," he kisses my head as I lean up to catch his lips in mine, kissing him passionately with a smile before curling back into his side.

"Tease," he growls.

"Maybe in the morning," I giggle as he tickles my side before straddling me.

"Maybe now," he growls lustfully.

"Michael," I moan, and he kisses his way down my neck, nipping at my skin as I groan against him, my hips grinding into him.

"BUT I WANT TO GO HOME!" I hear a shriek as Michael and I groan, his head sinking into my neck before I push him off of me, getting up and putting my dressing gown on and heading outside.

"I can't leave Amanda; my family is here!" Bryant shouts.

The two are arguing from their room and I bet most of the mansion could hear them right now. I sigh, running to their door, knocking on it as it swings open harshly.

"What?!" Amanda growls before cowering as she noticed it was me.

"What's going on? The whole pack can probably hear you… Like we need more mayhem right now," I growl.

"Sorry Alpha Phoenix," Amanda murmurs.

"Sorry mum, Hanson spoke to Amanda today about our choice of where we want to be and it seems we can't agree," Bryant says, glaring at his mate.

"MY family is Hanson's pack; you can't blame me for wanting to be there as much as you want to be here!" Amanda shouts again.

"Whoa! Enough shouting, please, you are both welcome to be wherever you want, have you both even thought of the option of going between them… One year there, one here, or however you want to do it?" I raise a brow.

"What about my twin… I can't leave her," Bryant says sadly.

"Bryant, you are both adults now, you cannot stay by her side all the time, you both need your own lives. There are many of us here to look after her, and now she has a mate too I'm sure she will be well taken care of. You need to find your own paths, you will always be connected, it's not like you cannot call each other or video call," I say, and he sighs, nodding.

"We should talk, no more shouting," he takes Amanda's hand softly.

"You realise my dad's pack isn't even that far away… It's only a few hours away, we can be here in a heartbeat if needed," Amanda smiles at Bryant.

"I know," he nods.

"Right, can I trust that you two can stop arguing tonight? I swear you and Taylor cause trouble on the same nights on purpose," I smirk.

"It's a twin thing," Bryant smirks back, I shake my head kissing him on the cheek.

"Behave you two, good night," I smile, shutting the door behind me, hearing them talk in hushed tones as I walk back down the corridor.

I get back into bed as Michael is sound asleep. I laugh quietly at his open mouth snoring, rolling my eyes as I snuggle against him. He automatically curls me into his arms, lifting me onto his chest as I lay on top of him, sighing in happiness while I listen to the steady beat of his heart before finally getting some sleep.

Stretching, I wake up slowly in Michael's arms smiling at his handsome face before kissing it softly, trying to get up, but his arms pin me in place.

"Where are you going?" He murmurs, nuzzling into my neck.

"I was going to go shower, why?" I smile, inhaling his scent.

"You're not going anywhere, Phoenix," he says, flipping us as he nips at my mating mark, sending my arousal into a frenzy, biting my lip as I moan against his touch.

"Michael... We have things to do," I moan as his kisses get lower, meeting my heat, I buck against his touch, his tongue devouring me as I cry out in pleasure.

"I need my breakfast first," he smirks, going back to licking and sucking at my clit, my hands run through his messy hair as his fingers begin thrusting inside me, making me scream out in pleasure.

"Michael... I'm going to... FUCK!" I scream, cumming over his hand and mouth as he licks up every drop, moving up to my lips and kissing me as I feel his cock at my entrance before plunging it into me with force, causing me to scream again.

Again and again, we went at it, our wolves taking over our bodies primally as we got rougher before finally collapsing on the bed, breathing deeply, sheets on the floor.

"I will never get enough of you," Michael growls into my neck lustfully.

"And I will never get enough of you Michael, I love you," I kiss him softly with a smile, nipping at his lip as he chuckles, pinching my bum and making me squeal.

"Go get ready before I make it so you can't walk for a week," he winks at me as I giggle.

"Is that a threat or a promise?" I smirk, he growls lustfully at me, ready to pounce and I get up quickly, laughing as he pins me to the bathroom door.

"It's a promise, I will tell the others you're busy and hold you here, under my body all day, writhing at my touch," he smirks, kissing my neck as I moan.

"We have things to do Michael," I groan, wanting to spend every moment in that bed with him though.

He sniffs at my neck, breathing in deep.

"Of course… You're going into heat my love," he says as my eyes widen.

"That explains it," I giggle.

"Still want more kids?" He asks.

"Yes," I nod.

"Good," he grins, lifting me into his arms and throwing me onto the bed once more.

"You're not letting me up, are you?" I laugh.

"Not until I'm done putting a pup in that belly of yours," he grins, and we start yet another round this morning.

Six times… Six more times he went at it, and I was spent. Lying beside him as we panted for breath.

"Hello! Are you two done or what?! Shit to do in this place!" I hear Kade bang on the door as Michael chuckles.

"Just got to shower then we'll be out!" Michael shouts.

"Hurry up! I'm not training the kids on my own!" Kade shouts as I chuckle. Michael and Kade had been teaching all the kids how to fight, even the humans, giving them a fighting chance as they grew up in this crazy world of ours.

"Alright! I'm up!" Michael shouts still in bed.

"LIAR!" Kade growls and I laugh, Kade knew his best friend inside and out.

"Ok! Now I am," he answers, getting up as he kisses my lips softly with a smile.

"Good! Phoenix, Violet wants a word when you're ready too," Kade calls from the door.

"Thank you, Kade," I call back.

"Michael! Out in five!" Kade growls before I hear him walking off.

"Does he think he's the boss around here?" Michael grumbles, I hear him turn the shower on.

"No, that would be me," I grin cheekily at him as he steps into the shower, gazing over his amazing, toned body.

"You coming in or just standing there?" He smirks as I walk in with him.

We end up washing each other, our hands gliding over skin as I shiver with happiness with my mate.

Once we're done and dressed, he gives me a final kiss before telling me he would talk to Taylor when he had finished with training.

Walking through the halls, it was silent upstairs, so I headed downstairs where it seemed to be getting rowdy in the kitchen.

"No! You don't put fucking pineapple on pizza! That's so gross!" Evie shouts.

"Hey! It's my body and my baby wants pineapple on pizza, so unless you want Kade to kick your arses leave it alone," Luci rolls her eyes at them.

"Pizza for breakfast, really Luci?" I laugh at the doorway.

“Wow, look who finally came out her sex dungeon, and for your information it’s lunchtime,” she points to the clock with a smirk.

“Shit…” I murmur, had we been at it for that long?

“Please don’t call it a sex dungeon, that’s the last thing I want to think of when it comes to my parents,” Bryant groans.

“Because we’ve never heard you before,” I roll my eyes, grabbing something to eat quickly, knowing Violet wanted to see me.

“How many have you slept with?” Amanda frowns as I see Taylor walk into the room with Callum.

“A few,” Bryant grumbles.

“Hey guys, oh pizza yum!” Taylor grins.

“Oh no, if you want some, you get your own,” Luci smirks.

“Aww come on Aunt Luci!” Taylor laughs.

“No, my baby and I are hungry for this, and no one is touching it,” Luci says sternly.

“You don’t want it anyway, it has pineapple on it,” Trey says, Taylor wrinkles her nose in disgust.

“You’re so weird auntie,” she laughs.

“How are you this morning, Taylor?” I asked, walking up to them as I notice they both avoid touching each other.

“Fine,” she nods with a small smile.

“Phoenix! For god’s sake where have you been, I sent Kade for you ages ago!” Violet storms in, grabbing my hand.

"Ok! What's up?!" I ask as she drags me into an office.

"I'm leaving, my people are unsettled, we need to go home now. I will be taking all those who wish to come home and ask that you still welcome those who wish to stay," she says.

"Of course, I wouldn't expect anything different, you need to grieve in your own home. Go be with your people and know you're always welcome here Violet, I truly am sorry for everything that happened with Keeley," I said as her eyes tear up.

"It never gets easier, does it? Losing a child… I know what Blake meant to you too, you helped Keeley for years as well, it can't be easy for you, I don't understand how you cope, you always seem so strong," Violet says, her lip wobbling.

"I break, sometimes. I guess I've accepted that death happens, especially when we least expect it, we need to celebrate each day we get, love those around us and fight for what we believe in. I've cried, I've screamed and I'm still grieving, although it may not show. Go home, grieve your own way Violet, you're always welcome here and you know I am always here for you," I say as I hug her.

"Thank you," she sniffs, wiping away her tears before putting on a brave front once more. She had always been so strong, so regal, she never let a tear go, but this might have been her breaking point.

"When will you leave?" I ask.

"Today, I have already sent word around to all my men and women. We will leave tonight after dinner, I was hoping we could have one final meal with everyone, maybe a buffet? Let everyone mingle before we leave," Violet asks.

"That sounds great, we'll get some people on it, it may help some of the new people feel more at home too," I smile.

"Great, I'll talk to my people, and you talk to yours," she nods.

For the next hour, I was so busy with sorting the buffet out, that I barely saw my family and friends. It wasn't until I heard someone crying that I stopped quickly, walking towards the source as I see my little girl, who wasn't so little anymore, sitting in the corner of an empty office.

"Taylor… Sweetheart, what happened?" I sit beside her; she lays her head on my shoulder.

"I can't do this; I can't have a mate. I can't be what he needs me to be, one moment I want him touching me and I feel safe, the next I can barely touch anyone, I don't want him near me. Earlier… I-I forced my hand out of his and told him to leave me the fuck alone, I couldn't get HIM out of my head," Taylor whimpers.

"Maximillian? Taylor, what REALLY happened back there? Did he… Did he touch you?" I ask softly as her hands shake. I hated to see her like this, it pained me to think of her so hurt.

"He… He… Yes," she nods as she cries.

"Right, come on," I pull her up and drag her with me as she comes with me like a toddler that follows their mother.

"Where are we going?" She sniffs.

"Rodge, where is Rook?" I pull her into medical.

"No, not Rook," Taylor sighs sadly.

"Nix? Taylor? What's going on?" Kai and Jae walk in hand in hand.

"I have no idea where he is my lady," Rodge answers.

"Taylor?" Jae frowns, putting a hand on her shoulder gently.

"TAYLOR! There you are, why did you run from me?! I had no idea where you were?!" Callum growls. Taylor hides behind Jae and I storm up to Callum throwing him against the wall.

"Carry on shouting at my little girl and you will never live to see another day," I growl.

"She ran from me! What was I supposed to do? I went to hold her hand and she pushed me away, for god's sake, we slept in each other's arms last night! Taylor, you're mine!" Callum growls.

"Growl once more pup, I dare you," Jae hisses, his eyes brighter than ever beside me.

"ENOUGH! I can't handle all of this! He's still in my head Callum, I don't want to be touched right now by you. I never wanted a mate before all this, and now I've not only been thrown into that, but I've been taken by a fucking witch, beaten, bruised, touched and burned. So, excuse me for being a little fucking broken right now!" Taylor screams before running off as her wolf.

"Jae, go to her," I say as he nods flitting away after Taylor.

"I don't appreciate your tone with my niece," Kai says behind me.

"You might be her mate, but you aren't mated yet, she can find another, she has no reason to accept you if she doesn't wish to. She's gone through a tough time, so have you and if you don't get your act together, I swear I will make sure you're never accepted around here, got it?" I growl.

"She's mine, my mate, only I can protect her," his wolf growls through him as he stands tall against me.

"Submit!" Storm growls back, but he barely moves an inch.

He roars, shaking his head, clutching it before shifting, pushing us back before bolting off.

"Find Jae and Taylor, stay with them!" I tell Kai, he flits off quickly as I shift bounding after Callum while he crashes through the building.

Callum bursts through the front door, running into Michael and the others training before running into the woods as I follow him.

"Phoenix?! What's going on?!" Michael asks through our link.

"Go find Taylor!" I reply, pouncing onto Callum's back, knocking him over as he takes a swipe at me.

Another wolf bounds over, taking him down with an almighty roar. I don't know this wolf; I've never seen him before. I howl a warning to my warriors, how did a new wolf get in our territory, unnoticed?!

Callum begins to wriggle beneath the new wolf, trying to escape but it's of no use, he's pinned. Suddenly Kade and Michael are beside me as they begin to circle the newcomer and Callum.

"Who are you?" Kade growls.

"I want the pack on alert, and I want to know how someone got through our ranks!" I growl the warning through the links.

"My name is Corey, I mean no harm to you, my Queen. Word has spread about you across the world, I have travelled a long way to meet you," the new wolf shifts as Michael grabs Callum, grabbing him by the scruff to keep him down.

He was handsome, his skin tanned, he must come from a very sunny country. His deep brown hair wasn't too short, it was swept back stylishly, his body was hidden under a pair of black jeans with a shirt, this man had style.

Callum shifts and Michael follows suit, but Callum begins to fight against Michael, kicking at him before Corey walks over and knocks him out with a single punch.

"That should keep him down a while," Corey nods at Michael.

"I don't like him," Michael growls through our link.

"Why are you here and how did you get in without my pack noticing?" I growl.

"I am here to outreach a hand; allies are important to me, and I had heard tales of you over in my country. I am from America you see, and from what I have seen over here, you are faring much better than our country. You have control, you have trust, you have people that love each other, all we have is war, I don't want that, not for my pack, not for my family. I wish to find a new place for us, away from that, have a safe place for the children to grow up and still be kids. Please, if we can just talk, if it helps, I may be able to help with your problem with this wolf," Corey says as I frown.

"What problem?" Kade snaps.

"He's corrupted, his mind has been corrupted by magic. I'm guessing for a few years, his wolf is slowly going feral, he's losing his humanity, has he been acting aggressively at all?" Corey asks.

"Yes," Michael answers.

"Possessive of something? High emotions, quickly changing?" He asks.

"Yes, how do you know this?" I nod.

"Because I am half-witch, half-wolf, my mother is a witch and my father a wolf. Now I'm guessing you've had dealings with my kind before as you've all tensed up, but with all our kinds there are good and evil. I am not evil, I will do all I can to prove this, firstly, my queen, a pledge," he holds out his hand, I place mine warily in his as Michael growls a warning.

"What do you pledge?" I ask.

"I pledge to be an ally and not an enemy of you. I pledge to respect your ruling in hope that we can work together for a new world. I pledge myself to you as my Queen, no harm will come to your people by me unless you wish it so or by accidental causes which cannot be helped sometimes," he says and I feel the familiar burn on my arm, my eyes wide as my tattoo fills with a night sky underneath the vines and ribbons that were already there. It was beautiful.

"Wow," I murmur as he smiles at me.

"So, how do we sort him out?" Michael nods to Callum, brow raised in question, I could tell he was still sceptical of Corey, I was too but with the pledge, it was certainly easier to trust him.

"I will need to consult with my mother, after checking a few things first with him, find out a few details. You may want to confine him though, he will become worse and if someone gets in the way of what's his, there will be no power on earth that may try to stop him once he has it in his head," Corey says as my thoughts go straight to Taylor.

"Lock him up, I won't have him hurt Taylor," I say to Kade, and he nods. Picking him up quickly and walking off with him, I see a couple of warriors join him and a few joins us too.

"Does he have a mate? I saw no mark…" Corey frowns.

"That's because we haven't mated yet…" Taylor's voice comes out from behind me, and I jump in shock.

"Taylor! Sorry, Phoenix she's a slippery one," Jae smirks at me before his eyes dart to Corey.

"Mum who is he?" Taylor asks.

"Perhaps we should talk inside, it's going to rain," Corey says as I raise a brow, the sky was barely cloudy.

"Oh, look the weatherman is wrong, get off our territory… Well… Shit," Kai snaps before looking to the sky as rain clouds move in, pouring from the sky.

"As I said," Corey smirks, winking at Taylor.

"Everyone inside," I say, calling for more warriors to follow us, keeping an eye on the new man. Sure, he pledged, but there are always workarounds for everything.

"This place is like a fairy-tale," Corey laugh as we walked inside.

"My, my, if it isn't the half-breed witch, I thought you died a long time ago, boy," Rook crosses his arms.

"Good to see you too old man," Corey smirks, Rook grins taking him in a hug as we watch in shock.

# Chapter Twenty-Three

## Taylor

"Mum, what's going on?" I whisper in her ear, watching as Rook and the new guy talk animatedly like they were old friends.

"He's half-witch, half-wolf, from America, he wants a safe place for his people, allies and all that apparently. He says Callum is corrupted by magic; he's going feral…" Mum says back via the link.

"Do you think I will too?" I ask, she looks at me before looking back at them.

"Corey, Rook, if you don't mind, I think we all need a chat, especially regarding Callum, Maximillian and my daughter," mum says.

"Our apologies, we got a little caught up. Corey's father was friends with my own, I thought he and his mother died years ago, seems he's been in hiding instead," Rook clapped him on the back.

An almighty roar echoes out as I hear fighting upstairs. My mum, dad and a group of warriors run towards it. I can feel him, it's Callum fighting upstairs, I can feel our pull as I walk towards the stairs.

"Don't," Corey grabs my hand, pulling me back.

"TAYLOR!" Callum's voice booms.

“He’s not your mate… Maximillian, what have you done…” Corey says. I feel warmth flood from his hand and up my arm, like a loving touch as it made its way through my body.

“Corey? Tell me, what has he done to our Taylor?” Rook asks.

“They aren’t mates, he’s made them believe they are so he can slowly tear her apart from her family, corrupt her so she takes the whole place down… He was trying to use her as a weapon, he must have foreseen his death and wanted a last moment of chaos in his name,” Corey says as I look at him and gulp.

“I’m corrupted too… Will I end up feral aswell?” I ask, looking up the stairs at the chaos as it finally begins to die down and they get Callum into the cells.

“Not if we can help it,” Rook says sternly.

“Are you telling me that she and Callum aren’t truly mates?! That Maximillian has got in their heads to destroy their minds so much that they cause chaos in our walls?” Jae exclaims.

“Yes,” Corey says, I feel the warmth in my head, and I smile, feeling relieved suddenly.

“What did you just do?” I ask with a smile.

“What?” Corey frowns.

*That guy is hot… Even when he frowns…*

“What did you just do? Your touch… I felt it…” I said.

“Taylor… I didn’t do anything,” Corey says, he looks at Rook who shrugs.

“I want men watching him twenty-four-seven!” Mum shouts the order, coming down the stairs.

"If they are corrupted, what about me and the others who were imprisoned?" Jae asks.

"More of you may need my help, I will need to see everyone who was imprisoned, but Callum could be beyond my help. Taylor, I'm sure I can help you, but his mind is too far gone, I'm sorry," Corey says, and I bite my lip nervously looking up the stairs.

"What will we have to do to him?" I murmur. Even knowing that Callum may not be my true mate because of the corruption, I couldn't help but feel for him. Was that the corruption in my brain or had I liked him myself?

"He will die, darkness will seep into his soul and drag him down until he dies from madness," Corey says sadly.

"Taylor…" Jae walks to me, a hand on my shoulder as a tear falls down my face.

"There has to be something we can do to help him," I say.

"I will consult with my mom, but I don't know how much we can do," Corey shakes his head.

"I need to see him," I say.

"That's not a good idea Taylor. the more you are around him, the worse you will get," Rook says sternly, and I glare at him, growling.

"Calm down sweetheart," mum says beside me.

My head hurts, I grab it, groaning in pain as I fall to my knees.

"TAYLOR!" Jae and mum grab me before I fall and hit my head.

“We need to get her laid down. Rook, I need to contact my mom, do you have a computer or something with a camera? She needs to see this too,” Corey says.

“Yes, we do live in this century you know, get Taylor into bed. I’ll grab the laptop,” Rook rolls his eyes.

“Come on Taylor, hang on little one,” Jae picks me up in his arms as he flits up the stairs with me, the others following behind.

“TAYLOR!!!” Callum’s roar echoes through the halls, I jump out of Jae’s arms and shift, heading to the door of the cells.

*Get to him, we have to save him, get to him…*

“NO!” Jae shouts.

Rushing down the stairs, I come to Callum’s cell, the bars shaking as he’s in his wolf form, larger than I had ever seen him.

“Callum…” I murmur, holding out my hand to him as his eyes are dark, walking to the bars as he growls deeply, teeth snarling.

*Let him mark us, Taylor, do it.*

“You are mine,” he growls, going to bite me, but my arm is torn from inside the cell as Callum lashes out, his paws missing me narrowly.

“You cannot be around him, if he mates you, you will end up just like him. Taylor, look at me,” Corey says, holding me tightly to him as I feel that warmth again.

“I don’t know what happened, I just had to come. Lily, she was pushing me to come to him… Corey, what’s happening to her?” I say as his hand cups my cheek, heat flooding my face.

"Corruption is getting to her; we have to move quickly. Taylor, I swear nothing will ever happen to you, I will save you," Corey says, looking in my eyes deeply as I find myself transfixed on his.

"Why do I feel so warm around you?" I ask.

"Later, we'll discuss that later, now come on, we need to move," Corey replies, pushing me up the stairs as Callum howls in the cell, making me want to go back, but Corey's hand on my arm seems to help calm me.

"Do you have a death wish?!" Jae shouts at me as we get further up.

"It's the corruption, she is not in her right mind, do not blame her for what her wolf is pushing her to do," Corey says in my defence.

"Are you ok?" Jae says softly to me and I just shrug.

Soon enough, we end up in my room where my parents are sat waiting nervously on my bed as Rook is hooking up a laptop and Kai is pacing outside.

"Go calm your husband, Jae," I say quietly as he looks between us, sighing before going to Kai, holding onto him tightly.

"Taylor lay down for me," Corey says as I do as he says. My parents stand to the side to get out of the way.

"Phoenix, I am afraid you are needed downstairs," Kade walks to the door, looking inside, worry-filled eyes watching me.

"I'll stay with her," dad says.

"I'm afraid I need you too buddy, but I have brought someone else with me," Kade says as Bryant walks in.

"I've got her," Bryant says sitting at my feet, his hand on my leg.

"Twin," I smile softly.

"Mum told me what happened. You, whoever you are, you better fix my fucking twin," he points at Corey.

"I have every intention to," Corey nods.

"Hello… Oh my! Rook!" A dazzling woman comes on the screen, her deep brown hair shining, eyes a bright purple and a gorgeous smile with dimples, just like Corey's.

"Hello Cynthia, so nice to see you, you could have let me know you were alive you know…" Rook raises a brow as if he's angry at her.

"Oh Rook, I wish I could have, we missed you so much, but it wasn't safe for us or you," Cynthia says.

I groan feeling pain in my head once more as I see her eyes move to us.

"Corey! Thank God you're safe and found people! What's happened, my boy? Who is the girl?" She frowns.

"Mom, this is Taylor and her twin Bryant, children of Queen Phoenix of England. Maximillian has been here, and he has corrupted minds, I fear for her, I need your help," he says.

"Oh my! It would be better if I were there in person, but if she's already getting headaches, we need to work quickly. Rook, will you channel me?" She asks.

"TAYLOR!" I hear Callum roar once again and my body sits up unexpectedly.

*We have to go! They are trying to stop us being with our mate! They will hurt us!*

"Taylor no!" Corey holds me down, warmth pulsating from where he touched me.

"You say that boy is her twin?" His mother asks.

"Yes, I am," Bryant nods.

"Then you will be of great help. Her wolf will need guidance to come back as she was, someone close to her will be the best and being as you are her twin, you share a strong bond that will help tremendously. I need you to sit beside her head, place your right hand over her head and put your palm against it softly. Corey, place yours on top of his. You two, whoever you are, you're going to need to hold her down. I'm sorry sweetheart, this won't be pleasant," she says, and fear floods my whole body.

"We're right here Taylor, you're going to be ok," Jae says by my feet.

"Rook, place your hand on Corey's shoulder and concentrate on me. Corey baby, I need you to do this, no matter how the girl reacts, if you halt in the course of this you could kill her wolf completely," Cynthia says.

"WHAT?!" Both Lily and I scream out. Lily pushes my body to try and get out of their hold, but Kai and Jae help keep me pinned.

"I will get you back to normal Taylor, I promise, beautiful," Corey says as I look him in the eyes. I can see my brother frowning as he watches over Corey.

"Ok, are you ready my boy?" Cynthia asks.

"Yes," Corey nods with a deep breath.

"Do NOT let her escape boys! Let's begin," she says. She begins muttering words I had never heard before, a new kind of language as Corey begins to copy.

"Is it even working.... ARGGGHHHHH!" I scream, the pain begins to flood my head, it feels like it will explode as my claws extend from my fingers.

"Pin her hands down!" Jae shouts as Kai pins me.

"GET OFF OF ME! PLEASE IT HURTS!" I scream in pain.

"Twin, I'm here," Bryant says soothingly, but I can see the pain in his face.

*Help! They are going to kill me! TAYLOR! Help me! He...H...*

**Lily? Lily!**

I can feel my wolf getting further away as I scream in pain, my whole body begins to shake in pain and it flickers between trying to shift, but I can't feel Lily.

"LILY!" I cry.

"Bryant! Call out to Lily, call her back! I have to deal with the corruption, you need to call Lily and keep her here!" Corey says quickly, looking at me with pain-filled eyes.

"Lily... Lily... Come on Lily, are you there?" Bryant says through our link, my body throbs with pain, I can feel magic probing my brain like bolts of lightning.

"I can't do this Bryant, it hurts!" I cry back to my brother.

"Focus Taylor, we'll get through this, you have to push for Lily too, now come on, LILY!" Bryant replies, I feel his wolf Ash probe my mind for her too.

*"Lily! Come out! We have to stay together!"* Ash calls out to her.

"I've got it!" Corey shouts, looking back to the screen.

"Is her wolf there?" Cynthia asks.

"No, I can't feel her," Bryant shakes his head.

**LILY get back here right now!**

**LILY!**

**Lily!**

*Tay... Tay... I don't feel good...*

"She's here!" I cry out.

"Lily?!" Bryant and Ash both say in my mind as tears pour down my face.

"Help me..." Lily says to them.

I can feel everything as Bryant pushes Ash forward, it's as if our wolves are right there, I can see Lily on the ground whimpering in pain as I was on the bed. Ash nudges her with his nose before nudging her up, again and again, to get her to stand.

"Come on Lily, Taylor needs you," Bryant says out loud.

*I'm not going anywhere...*

**Lily... Oh thank the goddess.**

*Mate...*

**What... Callum isn't our mate Lily; you must know that now...**

*I know... Our new mate is here...*

"Corey, finish the spell if her wolf is in her mind," Cynthia says. Corey begins muttering a few last words as warmth fills my whole body and soon I gasp at the feeling of all the pain leaving my body.

"Taylor..." Jae murmurs.

"It's gone… Maximillian hasn't got hold of me anymore…" I smile in relief, turning to face my twin as he smiles, taking me into his arms tightly.

"I have never been so fucking scared in my life," he mutters into my neck.

"You and me both twin," I reply, hugging him tighter than ever before.

"Thank you, mom, but there may be others. We have a wolf here that has been corrupted for years, he's locked in the cells, his wolf has gone feral and is only getting worse, I may need your help once more," Corey turns to the computer as I let my brother go.

"Thank you, Cynthia," I smile at her bright face in the computer.

"A pleasure my dear, you know where I am if you need me, my boy, find out who is corrupted, how bad they are and get back to me. This feral wolf though, it may be too late, the best thing you can do now is sedate him until his body succumbs to death, better than him tearing himself and others apart," she replies.

I let a sob out as Bryant keeps his arms around me, just because Callum wasn't my true mate, it didn't mean I didn't care for him at all, corruption or not, we escaped together, we survived together.

Corey turns to me as I look in his gorgeous brown eyes with a small purple ring.

*I get it now… The warmth… Taylor… He's our true mate…*

"Shit…" I murmur as he smirks at me.

"Not the reaction I thought you would have…" he laughs.

"What?" Jae frowns, he takes my hand in his gently.

"He's my mate… My true mate…" I murmur.

"OH, My baby! Finally! Oh, I have to come there now! I'll get your father, oh how beautiful! Corey! Why didn't you say something sooner?!" Cynthia exclaims, clapping her hands.

"Cynthia, calm down, they barely know each other, let them get acquainted before you even start talking of pups," Rook says as my eyes widen at the mention of pups.

"Don't worry Taylor, I don't like to rush anything, we can take it slow," Corey smiles at me as I bite my lip. A roar vibrates the floors.

"Callum got out! All warriors on high alert!" I hear mum's call before the resounding crash of the cell door upstairs.

"Oh, shit…" Bryant growls, jumping over the bed and shifting in the doorway.

"Is that the feral one?" Cynthia says looking worried.

"Yes, he's escaped," Corey answers her quickly.

"You have no choice! He must be put down!" Cynthia exclaims, I look at her with tears in my eyes.

"He's gone isn't he, his human self?" I ask.

"Yes, he's gone," she answers.

"Ok," I nod. I get up slowly, pushing past Bryant as he tries to pin me back behind him.

"Bryant, let her through," Rook says as Bryant growls ferociously.

"Bryant, I have to do this," I say, I push past him, shifting before letting out a howl.

“TAYLOR!” Callum’s wolf growls. I seem him bolt around a corner, up the end of the corridor, staring me down, teeth bared, eyes dark, no ounce of Callum could be seen in him.

“Come get me then!” I growl and he begins running at me. I bolt down the stairs as I hear him destroying anything in his path as I burst through the front doors. Warriors try to stop him but end up thrown across the ground as he leaps over my head to face me.

“Mine!” He growls.

“No! Taylor!” Mum screams as we circle each other. Dad holds her back as Kai stands with them.

“You want me! Come and get me!” I growl once more as Callum leaps for me, I could predict his every move, every slash at me as he tries and fails to wipe my legs from under me, every gnash of his teeth as he tries to bite down on my neck.

“MINE!” Callum growls again, going for me once more, but it gives me the gap to take him down as I push up against him, swiping at his belly as he growls at me, falling to the ground and I bite into his throat, tears filling my eyes.

“I’m sorry Callum, goodbye,” Lily and I flood his mind with happy thoughts and memories as I bite down hard.

“Thank you…” I hear him say back quietly… Oh Callum… He was still in there… His body drops to the ground as I let him go, backing off before lying beside him, howling into the sky. I whimper on the ground, my head under my paws as I cry.

I feel another wolf lay beside me, nose nudging me softly as I look beside me, my brother was lying beside me. I feel two more people sit beside me, Kai and Jae leaning against my side, their hands in my fur as I sigh.

*At least he can rest now.*

**Yeah, he doesn't need to feel the pain anymore.**

# Chapter Twenty-Four

## Taylor

After a while, Callum's body was taken by a couple of warriors to get a pyre ready. Corey had disappeared with my parents once they had checked on me several times, they had gone to see if anyone else had been corrupted. I had been stuck by my twin's side for the next few hours, I couldn't bear to part with him as he watched over me. Amanda joined us after a little while as I stayed quiet while they talked.

"What do you mean she's corrupted?! Phoenix! That's my mate!" I hear a voice shout, our eyes dart towards the corridor and I slowly lift myself from my seat in the small lounge we were in and went outside.

"Trey, Maximillian the witch did something to their minds and if we don't do this then she will go crazy and die like Callum did. Trey trust me," mum says, holding onto his shoulders.

"EVIE! EVIE!" Trey shouts as I hear her screams, running past them, I enter the room where the screams were coming from.

"Taylor!" Mum shouts, I see Kai and Jae are pinning her, Rook is standing in for Cynthia once more and Corey is muttering a spell.

"Taylor, you don't need to be here," Jae says.

"I do," I nod, I go round to her side as Bryant had done for me.

“Help me… It hurts!” Evie cries.

“I know, hold on Evie, it will be over soon, I promise,” I hold onto her hand tightly as she squeezes it harder than I had ever felt before.

I notice Corey grimace, frowning.

“Corey, what’s wrong?” I ask.

“She was there longer, it’s a little trickier,” he groans, his arms shaking.

*Touch him.*

**What?**

*Touch him, the mates pull will make him stronger.*

I bite my lip, leaning my hand over to his face, warmth flooding me as our skin touches. He growls as his hands shake; Evie begins screaming before going quiet all of a sudden.

“Evie!” Trey bursts in with mum on his tail, he pushes me out of the way, and I fall to the fall, groaning in pain.

“You better apologise mister” Evie groans, her hand on her head as she looks towards me, glaring at Trey.

“Taylor… Oh, shit, I’m sorry,” Trey says as Kai helps me up slowly.

“It’s ok, I get it,” I nod as I feel eyes on me. Corey was staring at me, longingly as I saw his mother smiling in the background, her eyes flickered between us and Rook at the computer.

“I think that’s enough for today, rest up my boy. Rook, take care of my son, nice to meet you all, until we meet in person!” She calls with a small wave before leaving the video call.

"How did you do that?" Corey murmurs.

"Do what?" I ask.

"You...You made me stronger... I've never... I've never felt like that before," he says, walking up to me slowly, taking my hand gently in his as if inspecting it.

"Do you feel that warmth too?" I ask.

"Yes," he nods, our fingers interlinking gently.

"Um, guys, if you two want to have a moment, better do it without an audience..." Kai smirks. I blush, taking my hand from Corey's.

"I... Oh... Yeah... Um..." I mutter looking anywhere but the people around me.

"Race?" Bryant says from the door as my eyes lock with his.

"You're on," I smile at him.

"What?" Corey murmurs.

"It's what they do," Jae laughs, I smile before racing out of the room, pushing Bryant away as he laughs.

"They will never grow up," mum laughs at us.

"Where's the fun in growing up?!" I smile cheekily at my brother as I'm ahead of him.

"Cheating as always!" He laughs as we both shift, bounding out of the mansion and racing through the trees, the feeling of the air through my fur and earth crumbling beneath my feet already making me feel better as we howl into the air.

Soon, we aren't the only ones running as mum and half of the pack join us. She takes the lead as we go on a pack run, leading into a pack howl before heading back through the trees.

"I think we all needed that," mum laughs as she nuzzles into dad's side.

"So, new mate huh…" Bryant nudges me as I shift, sitting at the bottom of a tree trunk and he does the same.

"Just one more thing to add to our crazy life, right?" I laugh, throwing a random stone.

"He seems good…" He answers.

"We'll see," I sigh.

"Taylor… I get it, with everything that's happened. Don't force yourself to be alone, you can feel the pull, I know you can, stop resisting everything, it's not all bad, he's not Callum," Bryant says.

"I know, it's just… difficult, I need to get my head straight again. It's like, it's like there's an extra piece in your head that doesn't belong, it gets in the way, it begins to try and slot itself into the wrong hole. I need to recover from that, I need to feel everything again without the corruption. I missed the funerals, I missed everything…" I say as tears mist up my vision.

"Then we will do that, together, come on," he stands quickly, holding out a hand.

"Where are we going?" I murmur.

"How do we usually let our feelings out?" he smiles.

"We fight, or race," I utter.

"Then we have already raced, so now it's time to let every bit of that aggression out before the funeral for Callum tonight, where you can say goodbye to everyone we've lost," he says, putting an arm around my shoulders.

"I don't know where I would be without you twin," I smile.

"Yeah, I know, I love you, Taylor. Just promise me that you'll always tell me stuff, don't hide it and if I'm not here you call me," he says.

"If you're not here?" I frown.

"Amanda and I, we're uh... Going to be going between Hanson's pack and here, she misses home too," he says, and I stand in shock.

"You're leaving us?" I murmur.

"Taylor... I will never abandon you, you're my twin, we will always be bonded but she's my mate..." He says as I push his arm off of me.

"Mates... Goddess, why do we have to have mates?" I groan.

"We can't be attached to each other's hip for the rest of our lives Tay. You know I love you and I will be here when you need me to be, but I also need to begin a life with my mate, I love her too Tay," he says, and I can see it in his eyes.

"I'm happy for you twin, I just wish you didn't have to go," I say, tearing up yet again as he takes me in his arms.

"Everything will be ok," he says, kissing my head.

"Bryant! Bryant!" Amanda walks happily around the corner. She bounces into his arms, kissing him as I stand there sighing, looking anywhere but them.

I look around and notice Corey sitting under the bridge with some sort of book and a pencil.

"Amanda, what's the matter?" Bryant asks.

"I needed you," she smiles seductively.

"But…" Bryant looks between us as if stuck of what to do even I could smell her heat coming.

"Go be with her. I'll see you in a bit, might as well get used to it right?" I smile sadly and begin walking down the small hill to the bottom of the dried-up river towards Corey.

I watch him for a moment as I see what he's drawing, it's beautiful… It's… Me, as a child…

"I can sense you there you know…" Corey says, looking over his shoulder at me with a smirk.

"That drawing…" I murmur walking close.

"She's pretty, right? She's been in my head for years, I always assumed it was my daughter in the future, those big, beautiful eyes, gorgeous curly hair, but then… I met you and this… This is you, isn't it? My magic was telling me my mate was out there all this time," he sighs, leaning his head back against the pillar.

"Why are you sad over that? You found me, didn't you…"

"Yes, but if I had found you sooner, if I had got to you, you wouldn't have had to go through so much pain. It kills me to feel all your pain and I felt every piece of it as I took the corruption. Taylor, I'm sorry, I saw everything," he says.

I sit next to him, taking the pad from his hands, looking at the image he had been drawing.

"There are more…" He says nodding for me to look as I open it to the first page.

"That's Janie putting out the fire when mum had us…" I murmur as I keep going.

"Who is that?" He asks, pointing to a small boy behind me and Bryant playing with our elements, the boy cowers in fear.

"That's Blake, he was always scared of what I could do with the earth. I used to tease him with it, make the earth move as if something was digging up to get him. He got me back of course," I chuckle lightly at the memories. I would miss Blake with all my heart.

"Jae was a fae right, but now he's a hybrid…" He says as I see an image of our training.

"Yes, it was the only way to save him," I nod, and I keep flicking through. I find an image of the necklace Bryant had given me, my fingers tracing the outline.

"Was that an heirloom?" He asks.

"No, Bryant had it made to protect me, and it certainly helped, I put it around Maximillian's neck," I said as he nods in understanding.

"You're lucky to have him, he's a good brother," he smiles. I find another image of me and Bryant on our eighteenth birthday.

"You have a real talent for art," I say, finding myself at the last picture, it was unfinished, it wasn't the one of me as I little girl though.

"It's not finished yet; my mind is being slow to release the image. I draw when I feel something new, but this, this is taking its time, like it's waiting for something," he says, taking the book from my hands staring at the page, a sky full of stars, a beautiful lake and clothes piled beside it messily.

"I know this lake," I say recognising it.

"Really?" He perks up.

"Want to see it?" I smile.

"Sure," he nods. I shift, his eyes glaze over my wolf, his hand going through my fur as I shiver at his touch before I yip out playfully, bolting away from him as I see him shift and chase after me, running through the trees towards the small lake a few miles out.

"Through here," I nod through a couple of bushes that hides the lake behind it.

"Trying to get me killed already?" He raises a brow as I shift shaking my head at him.

"Not yet, I still have yet to work you out," I smile softly as he shifts while I pull the bush back and we walk through it.

"Wow…" He murmurs.

"I know, it's places like these that make the world seem beautiful still in the darkness that surrounds it," I say as I sit beside a tree near the water.

"People like you do the same thing," he whispers. I blush with a small smile looking out onto the lake.

"Me, Bryant, Blake, Keeley and Janie used to all come out here when we were kids, Janie was always in charge as she was the oldest, but she was never really in charge, she was usually worse than all of us. We'd splash around in the lake until it got so cold that Bryant brought out his fire and we sat right here. Drying off under the stars, we thought we were invincible, now I'm going to be the only one left here," I sigh sadly, leaning my head against the tree.

Just then a small ball of fire drifts into my sight, sitting in front of me as I smile up at my brother in the distance with Amanda, mum, dad, Kade, Luci, Trey, Evie, Kai, Jae, Janie and Hanson behind him.

"Corey told us you were here," he says as I look to Corey in shock.

"You need your family," he says as he stands up to leave.

"Wait, don't go. Join us," I grab his hand with mine, closing my eyes at the feel of his warmth.

"Yes, do stay, we need to get to know you too!" Luci grins, winking at me as I giggle at her.

"Only if you're sure Taylor," he answers.

"Stay, please," I nod as he sits back down beside me.

"Well, with that… Let's get this party started!" Bryant hoots, stripping his top off before cannonballing into the lake as I laugh.

"That's not how you do it, watch the master," dad says. I see mum roll her eyes as she makes her way over to my side.

"Boys," she laughs.

"HA! POOR! Watch this!" Janie says as I groan.

"THIS is what she does," I say to Corey as he watches. She runs full pelt towards the lake, and I pull up a shield of earth as she splashes down, shifting at the same time to make a bigger splash, my wall stops the flow of water hitting us.

"That's my girl," Hanson laughs.

"You coming in old man?" Janie grins at her mate cheekily.

"Old man! I'll give you old man!" He answers before bounding over to her, splashing her, before picking her up in his arms and throwing her into the centre of the lake as she pops up in full on belly laughter, he swims after her kissing in the distance.

"Aww, so cute," Luci grins, sitting by us.

"What's that?" Kade sits beside his mate as the others begin joining in the fun.

"It's drawings of things I've seen, some witches get visions, they could be past, present or future, I draw everything I see," Corey answers.

"Taylor draws too," Luci says as I groan, barely anyone saw my drawings, I hated showing anyone.

"Aunt Luci…" I groan.

"What do you draw?" Corey asks, his head tilted as if he were trying to work out why I was hiding it.

"Stuff," I answer.

"She draws everything, people, places, they are beautiful," Luci grins.

"If you weren't pregnant aunt Luci I would kick your arse," I roll my eyes.

"You don't like your work?" Corey frowns.

"No, it's not that. I just, I don't like showing it, it's… personal," I shrug.

“You have a talent, and you know it, one day you will show them when you’re ready,” mum smiles at me, patting my hand.

“Hey! Twin! You coming in or what?!” Bryant laughs as he splashes Amanda.

“Fuck it,” I sigh standing up, looking down at my clothes before shrugging and running to the lake, diving into the cold depths. I grab my brothers’ foot from underneath, hearing him squeal like a girl, inhaling water from laughing, coughing my guts up when come out of the water.

“TAYLOR!” He growls, pushing me as I splash backwards, kicking my feet at him, giving him a face full of water with a grin.

I dive back into the water; I loved swimming in the depths of it. When I next came out of the water, I noticed most of the others were heading out, sitting beside a fire to warm themselves.

“Taylor come on, the others are on their way,” Bryant says from the shore, and I swim back.

“What…” I frown as he warms me up with a fresh ball of flame.

“We thought we would give Callum an old-fashioned send-off on the lake, plus Hanson and Violet are going home tomorrow morning,” he answers.

“Oh, does that mean you and Amanda are going too?” I ask.

“No, we are staying for a couple more months,” he answers, I nod with a sigh of relief.

Wolves and fae begin to walk through the trees, standing around the lake as warriors begin walking through with a small wooden raft. Callum was lying on top as they put him on the edge of the lake beside us.

“I don’t think I can do this…” I murmur.

"You can, tonight we say goodbye to them all, set your heart free Taylor," my twin says, and he backs off, giving me space.

"I'm so sorry Callum, may the goddess take you in her ever-loving arms, may you be happy. Look after all my family up there, say hi to them all, Paul, Jason, Keeley, Blake… All of them, I will see you all again one day," I kiss his head with a sigh, using my earth to push the boat into the water.

Mum leads the pack into a howl as she lights the raft on fire with my brother beside her. I drop to my knees beside the water, sobbing as I let everything out.

I feel a wolf by my side as I rest against their warmth… Corey.

"Thank you," I whisper to him, my hand in his fur as he nuzzles against my touch.

I can hear Janie singing softly behind me and I smile at our old lullaby, humming to the tune as I rest my head against Corey's neck.

Life was changing again, we were without many we loved, but had gained more too. I just hoped we didn't have to take any more heartache any time soon.

# Chapter Twenty-Five

## Taylor

A few days had gone by and saying farewell to Violet, Hanson and Janie was hard enough, but soon my brother would be leaving too.

Bryant and I had spent so much time together that I knew Amanda was getting a little annoyed from the side-lines. I knew I needed to stop hogging his time, but I wanted to make the most of it while he was here. But in doing that, I've ignored everyone else… Shit… What am I doing? I've ignored mum, dad, Corey, Jae… All of them… SHIT!

Groaning as I get up, I get ready quickly, planning to make up for what I had done.

"Morning," I smile, walking into the kitchen where everyone was sat together.

Bryant grins at me, expecting me to sit beside him, but I avoid the chair and walk over to Corey's side instead. I look to Amanda as she gives me a small smile, mouthing thank you.

"I'm sorry," I mouth back, she smiles shaking her head and taking Bryant's hand in hers as he kisses her cheek lovingly.

"What do I owe the pleasure of your company to today?" Corey smirks at me.

"I've been a little… Off with everyone. I'm sorry," I murmur.

“You needed time babe, don’t sweat it,” Aunt Luci says, and I smile at her. Her belly was really popping with her pregnancy, soon she would be having pups and you could see she was excited, Kade too, he could barely keep his eyes off of her.

“So, will I be expecting pups from my kids anytime soon?” Mum winks at me as I groan, shaking my head.

“Not yet mum,” I answer.

“Oh, I know you aren’t yet, but this one. I’m surprised he hasn’t knocked you up already Amanda,” Mum smirks.

“We will get there, mum,” Bryant rolls his eyes.

“He’d have to unwrap it first to do that,” Amanda mumbles and I look to my twin, confusion in my mind, why would he wear a condom with his mate…

“Want to explain?” I say through our link.

“I wasn’t ready… I didn’t want to bring a kid into our life when we didn’t know what was going to happen. I didn’t want to live in fear that my child would suffer as you did, I can’t deal with that,” he answers, a sad look in his eyes.

“You can’t hold back from having a child just in case something MAY happen, live your life, have pups, have a family and give me my nieces and nephews!” I smirk at him as he chuckles, shaking his head at me.

“Care to share?” Mum looks between us both as Amanda sighs, slamming her fork down before leaving the table.

“Go dummy!” I laugh at my brother as he runs off after her.

“What was that all about?” Trey frowns.

Amanda comes bouncing into the room as she darts to my side, hugging me.

"Thank you," she says, kissing my cheek before rushing back out and I burst into laughter.

"What did you do?" Dad asks.

"I told him basically to stop holding back, live his life and give me nieces and nephews," I smirk.

"Bloody kids," dad shakes his head, laughing.

"You're feeling better then," Kade ruffles my hair as I groan.

"KADE! I just straightened that!" I huff, running my fingers through my hair.

"Looks better curly," Corey murmurs under his breath.

I smile at him, slowly moving my hand to his under the table as he looks at me in shock and I steal a piece of toast from Jae's plate.

"Taylor!" He hisses at me as I stick my tongue out playfully, feeling the warmth of my mate bond through Corey's fingers.

I can feel his thumb rub over mine gently as we all talk through breakfast.

"Are you coming to training today?" Trey asks.

"Of course I am, I need to kick your arse," I smirk.

"I'd like to see you try pup," he smirks at me.

"Mind if I join you all in training? It's been a while," Corey asks.

"Of course you can," mum smiles at him, looking at me as her eyes gaze down our arms. She knows. She knows we're holding hands… I can feel it.

"Don't give me that look," I say through our link, blushing.

"What… Can a mother not look at her daughter? You're happy today, I can see it, you're… different," she replies.

"I feel it, I feel better today, day by day I'm getting better."

"Good, I think he'll be good for you. We've been talking, he wants to stay here, bring his pack over, he wants his family safe with us," she tells me.

"I'm curious, I've not heard how old you are Corey," Kade says from beside Luci, I sit up, curious too.

"Oh, I'm one hundred and twenty-eight," he says, and my eyes go wide.

"For once can't someone be my age… Other than my twin," I groan.

"Is age an issue for you?" Corey asks, I can see he doesn't want me to say yes.

"No, of course not. I get how it works, it just makes me feel like a child still," I sigh against my chair.

"You're no child, you're a beautiful, mature woman who I cannot wait to get to know," he says in my head, squeezing my hand as I smile, blushing.

"Come with me," I bite my lip nervously, I was about to let this man into my world, and by the goddess I was nervous.

"Uh oh, don't do anything I wouldn't do!" Kai laughs.

"What wouldn't you do?" Jae shoves him playfully as I giggle.

"Leave them alone guys," mum says nodding for us to go.

"Where are you taking me?" He laughs.

"You'll see," I smile as I drag him to my room nervously.

"Your bedroom... I thought we were taking this slow," he raises his brow. I chuckle, holding up a finger for him to wait as I move my bedside cabinet forward, pushing on the planks behind it as it shows a crawl hole.

"Come on, think you can fit?" I smirk, looking him up and down, biting my lip.

"I'm sure I can fit in that tight hole," he winks cheekily, I giggle crawling forward as I hear him grunt and groan as he follows me.

"Don't go checking my arse out," I laugh.

"Now you say it... It is a deliciously gorgeous one," he laughs.

I crawl out the other end of the tunnel into the small secret room that very few knew about, it was a safe room, for me, Bryant, Blake, Janie and Keeley, a safe place, but over time I was the only one who came back. Photos littered the walls as I grinned at them, then I saw them, my art books.

"If I show you this, you can't laugh," I hold my favourite one in my arms.

"Never," he says. We sit on the floor next to each other, I take a deep breath and hand the book over. His hands run over the bright purple cover as he chuckles.

"The same colour as my eyes," he smirks. I look at the purple ring around his eyes, he was right, it was exactly the same.

"Must be fate," I smile, biting my lip as he smiles, lifting the cover to the first pages.

"These are amazing," he says, looking at the pages.

"You don't have to humour me," I sigh.

“I’m not, these really are amazing. Where is this? Is this a bar?” He asks.

“Yeah, that was Kade’s old bar from mum’s old hometown,” I nod with a smile.

“This place?” He asks pointing to another.

“That’s where my mum and Kai met, their school, she burnt the whole gym down when she found her fire element, he was there with her, completely human,” I answer.

“Really… He wasn’t born a vampire?” He asks.

“No, he turned so he could stay best friends with mum forever,” I smile.

“Cute,” he smirks.

He begins flicking to pages filled with portraits of people, from a rough sketch to a full-on piece on the next page, I liked showing the stages in my work.

“You have a real talent Taylor, these are amazing,” he smiles.

“I drew this one last night,” I take another book from the corner as I flick it to the latest page. He looks at it as his eyes flicker brightly.

“How…” he murmurs.

The image was his own, I had finished it. Something in my mind last night drew me to it as I sketched the lake, clothes on the floor, every detail until I got to the people in it, Corey and I, kissing as we stood in the shallows of the water.

“I saw it in my head last night and couldn’t get rid of the image,” I smile softly.

“Taylor, look,” he pulls out his phone and goes through his gallery as he brings up a photo of his latest sketch, it was the same as mine…

“Wow…” I murmur leaning over.

“Yeah…” He whispers, I feel his breath against my skin as I look up into his eyes, his hand drifts slowly up to my face and I gasp at his touch, nuzzling into it I feel the warmth radiate over my body.

Our faces get closer as our lips almost touch before he pulls me in, kissing me softly as my body explodes with warmth as we kiss. I push the books off of his lap, straddling his legs, deepening the kiss as I moan at his touch.

“Taylor, stop,” he pulls away, placing a finger on my lips, barely able to look away from them.

“Why? Don’t you want this too?” I whisper and he rests his forehead against mine.

“Taylor, I don’t want to rush, I want to cherish every little detail. I want to cook dinner for you, tell you stories about my life, get to know you. I want to know everything, and I want you to be one hundred per cent sure this is what you want, not because of the mate pull, but because YOU want to be with ME,” he says, and I can’t help but smile wider.

“Thank you,” I kiss his finger on my lips as he smiles at me.

“Now, come on, give me the other books,” he grins, putting me on his lap facing forward, his arms wrapped around me as I reach over for them.

“No laughing, this is the one from when I was like… eight,” I said with a smile as he took hold of it, seeing all my childish drawings as he chuckled at some.

“What is that?” He laughs pointing at an image.

“That was me trying to draw my dad’s wolf. I said no laughing,” I say sternly, but can’t help but laugh with him.

“It’s cute! I swear,” he grins, nuzzling into my neck.

I giggle as his skin against mine tickles my neck, a moan escapes my lips accidentally.

“Sorry,” I murmur.

“You have nothing to apologise for Taylor, trust me, I want you just as much, but I don’t want to do this wrong,” he says, kissing my shoulder where he would most likely mark me. I could feel my arousal as I felt him shift beneath me.

“I think we should go, or this may go further,” I whisper, half hoping he would just devour my body right now.

“You’re right, come on,” he lifts me gently off of him. I smirk, glancing at the bulge in his trousers as he clears his throat, adjusts himself, before apologising and crawling out of the room.

“You have nothing to apologise for either Corey, nice arse by the way,” I giggle as I see him look back at me with a cheeky grin, wiggling his arse at me and I burst into laughter crawling back to my room.

He helps me up as I get out of the hole, holding me in his arms, kissing me softly once more before helping me push back the bedside cabinet.

“The planks didn’t go back,” he frowns.

I smile, waving my hand as the hole closes up, in truth I had a rock in there to do the work for me as I controlled it to push it closed.

“How about now,” I grin.

"Clever," he nods.

"So, your parents are coming here with your pack," I say as we begin walking out of my room.

"Yeah, my mom's excited, she hasn't stopped talking about the pretty girl I have finally found," he blushes.

"That's cute, congratulations, who is the girl?" I smirk.

"Oh, just some beautiful, brown-haired girl with doe eyes to die for, she has a major connection to her family which I think is amazing," he smiles.

"Sounds a little like someone I know," Kai flits into the middle of us, his arms around our necks.

"Uncle Kai…" I groan as he laughs.

"Sorry, I heard you two giggling and having fun. I might have got a little jealous," he grins cheekily.

"Shouldn't you be with Jae?" I laugh.

"He's busy with Nix," he sighs.

"Nix?" Corey frowns.

"It's what I call Phoenix, it's a nickname," Kai answers.

"Taylor! You coming or what?!" Kade shouts from the front door as I look to the clock.

"Shit! Sorry! I'm coming!" I call out.

"Ha! That's what she said…" Kai murmurs the lame joke; I roll my eyes as Corey chuckles with him.

"Don't spur him on," I point to Corey sternly as he puts his hands up in surrender.

"Nope, no spurring happening, I didn't do a thing," he grins at me.

"Whipped already man… Jeez…" Kai grumbles as I laugh.

"Kai! Leave them alone!" Jae shouts from down the corridor.

"Yes, babe!" Kai replies. I giggle and make a whipping noise as he picks me up suddenly, flitting away with me outside, tossing me into the air as I shift, landing on my paws.

"Oh, it's on," I growl.

"Must we start every session like this… If it's not Bryant it's Kai," Kade growls.

"I'm training, shh," I bark at him. He rolls his eyes as he waits with the other warriors, watching us.

Corey runs outside, a confused look on his face as I see Kade explain what we were doing. He was right, we usually did interrupt the start of sessions with playful fighting, but it made it more fun.

"Come on Kai, you going to attack me or what?" I bow my front down, my tail wagging behind me as he chuckles at me.

"Aww, you're like a cute little puppy!" Kai says, flitting toward me, claws out as he slices at my fur.

I can feel Corey's gaze on me and it's distracting as I go to dodge Kai, but he catches my cheek where my last scar was. I growl at him.

"Concentrate Taylor," Kade calls out.

"Fuck you," I growl back. I dart after Kai, batting him with my paw as he went flying, catching himself on his feet when he landed before flitting at me.

I dodge his punches as I snap my teeth around his arms and pull him around.

"FUCK! Taylor! Let go! I tapped out!" Kai shouts as I gasp, letting go.

"Kai, I'm sorry!" I gulp, he holds his arm which was bleeding.

"Kai go to med. Taylor, front and centre," Kade growls at me.

I walk up to him, tail between my legs.

"What the fuck was that?" he growls.

"I lost it for a minute," I shift, rubbing my face of blood.

"Taylor, you're bleeding," Corey walks up to me, rubbing his thumb over the cut as I feel it stitch together.

"Thank you," I smile.

"What distracted you?" Kade asks as I glance at Corey for a moment.

"Your scars bother you don't they…" Corey says, I notice my hand is still over my cheek.

"Yes, I try to ignore them, but some aren't so easy to ignore when Kai got this one, it made me rage," I answer.

"Taylor, you have to learn to control yourself again, think, don't feel. It could be the difference between life and death," Kade says.

"You don't think I don't know that!" I shout at him.

"I think we should get on with training the boys. Taylor, Corey, take the day off, clear her head and come back fresh tomorrow," Trey walks to us quickly.

"Fine," I say, stomping away back into the building.

"Taylor! Hey, look at me, it's ok, your emotions are all over the place what with everything going on, you're allowed to be hurt, you're allowed to be angry and lose control," Corey stops me, putting my face in his hands as I sigh at his touch.

"I hate my scars…" I huff.

"I think I can help you, well my mom can," he says as I frown, looking him in the eyes curiously.

"How?" I ask.

"She's good with healing old wounds, she may be able to reduce your scarring, when she gets here, we'll ask, ok?" he says.

"Thank you," I smile feeling hopeful. Sure, reducing wasn't getting rid of completely, but it helped.

"How about we go find something to eat?" He asks.

"Sure," I nod, he takes my hand, and we head into the kitchens.

# Chapter Twenty-Six

## Phoenix

“What are we going to do Phoenix? No one is ready to go back to this, everyone is still shaken from the last mission,” Jae says beside me as I sit with my head in my hands.

“What choice do we have? Let the humans die in some old house, rotting as they are surrounded more and more each day. They aren’t safe, vampires still want them, that hasn’t changed. We got rid of Maximillian, yes, but the danger is still there,” I reply.

“Perhaps we should discuss this with the others too,” Michael says.

“Jae, it’s only a few miles out, we could get there in minutes, it’s on our border! How can we leave them alone?” I ask him.

“Fine, see how the others feel, but I don’t think Taylor should be allowed to go yet,” Jae says.

“I agree, Kade told me what happened a moment ago at training, she’s still out of sorts, lost control a little, Kai got hurt,” Michael murmurs as Jae looks at him in shock.

“Kai got what!” Jae hisses, he flits from his seat as I groan again.

“Why did I have to be a queen?” I groan.

"Come on my love, Taylor will be just fine, Corey seems to be helping her," Michael says, and I nod.

"He's a good guy," I nod.

"I'm fine Jae! Chill!" I hear Kai shout.

"I'm going to throttle that child when I see her!" I hear Jae shout; I rush through the door finding them in the hallway.

"Touch my child and you'll face me Jae, friend or not," I growl.

"Sorry Nix, it's the whole vampire thing, amps it up a bit, you know I wouldn't hurt her, I just got angry," he sighs.

"I know, but don't you ever threaten my babies," I point sternly.

"Sorry," he sighs with a nod.

I walk downstairs with the others as we come across David and a few of the other humans.

"Queen! Have you heard? More of us have been found!" David grins.

"Yes, I've heard," I nod my head.

"Aren't you going?" He frowns.

"I need to talk to the others first David," I sigh.

"But they are there NOW, what if they get caught?!" He argues.

"David, enough, please."

"Fine," he huffs, storming off towards the kitchens.

"Taylor's in there," Kai says as I listen carefully.

"Oh, for god's sake," I murmur, walking briskly towards the kitchen as Taylor bursts through the door.

"You can't be serious about not going to save the humans mum!" She shouts at me.

"I cannot risk people who are not ready to go, we have been through enough lately, I don't have all the information yet," I answer.

"I'll go, give me a team and I will go," she says.

"No," I shake my head.

"MUM! Why not?!" She growls at me.

"Because you are not going on another mission to find humans after everything that has happened, I will not risk your life!" I shout back and she takes a step away from me.

"But you would risk their lives and those of the people you do send…" She frowns.

"No, you know that's not what I meant Taylor, you know I want to save them all, but sometimes things must be thought out a little more, especially as half our manpower has gone home," I reply.

"You're being ridiculous, we could have been half-way there by now," she stomps away, ignoring me as I call for her.

"I'll keep an eye on her Phoenix," Corey gives me a sorrowful smile, chasing after her.

"You'd think she's fifteen again," Michael grumbles.

"What a fun age that was…" I murmur.

"Please Phoenix, I beg you, send a team," David walks past me a final time before leaving the building.

"Fuck," I groan, a hand running through my hair.

"What do you want to do Phoenix?" Michael asks.

"Get me a team," I tell him as he nods walking off quickly.

I was busy talking with a warrior that had come across the humans when a shout came from outside.

"Phoenix! You better come look at this!" Trey shouts from just outside the front door as I walk out of the office.

My eyes widen as Taylor comes out of the forest and across the bridge with a couple of tired-looking adults and several kids on her back with Corey holding half of them too.

"TAYLOR!" I shout angrily as I storm across the bridge.

"Kids mum, there were KIDS," she growls at me.

"Get me the medics now!" Trey shouts as he begins helping some of the scared children off of their backs. The adults are barely responsive as I help them off too.

"Taylor, where do you think you're going?" I snap as she turns to go back.

"There are more, we couldn't carry them all, their parents are there, we have to go back," she says.

"Where's my mummy?!" One of the small girls' cries.

"Mum…" Taylor begs, whining as her eyes glance at the little girl.

"Michael, you're in charge, come on then," I call out as I shift beside her.

"I knew you would," she says happily as we charge through the trees.

"Vampires! Left!" Corey growls.

"We've got it!" Kai and Jae flit past us as they wipe out the three lone vampires that were ready to attack.

"Nice," Taylor chuckles.

"Move it, kid!" Kai smirks, racing forward together as a team.

"I guess they're back to normal," Jae smiles beside me as we continue running.

"Kai hates fighting, and Taylor couldn't be mad at him forever, she loves him too much," I reply.

"Mum, up ahead, look!" Taylor whines, seeing a house on fire.

Corey rushes forward, pushing faster as he leaps over Taylor's head, bursting into the fiery pits of the house.

"COREY!" Taylor looks at the house in a panic, I get closer, shifting as I try to calm down the flames, grunting in pain as it resists me.

Corey doesn't come back out after a few minutes.

"Nix! Look!" Kai points off to the side where a small group of humans are bundled on the ground, covered in soot.

"Go! Taylor go with them! I'll get Corey!" I order as she looks between me and the house.

"Be careful," she nuzzles into my side before helping Kai and Jae.

*Once more into the fray... I hate burning houses...*

**Let's go.**

Leaping into the fire I whine at the burn on my feet as I try to stop the brunt of it.

"COREY!" I call out, shifting into my human form, making myself smaller and harder to get burnt… hopefully.

I could hear coughing in the distance as I push through, kicking open a door as I dodge a falling beam.

"Phoenix! Get out, this whole place is going down!" Corey coughs.

"Yes, and I am not leaving you inside!" I grunt at the sting of fire, waving my hand at it as I calm it down beside me.

"I'm stuck!" He replies.

"You're a half-witch! Can't you use magic!" I call as I spot the beam on top of him.

"Yes, half, I don't know everything! I'm still learning to this day!" He coughs violently, I look everywhere for something to help lever the beam off of him.

I hear a loud howl in the air as Taylor calls for help, panic floods my chest as the fire is getting worse and I don't have the energy to wipe out the whole thing, I was still recovering from the last one…

"Just go! Taylor will always need her mother!" Corey calls.

"I am not leaving you!" I duck under another fallen beam, climbing over a burning sofa quickly as I hiss in pain from my hand.

Looking around I spot him as I clamber over a table and get to him.

"If I pull it off of you, can you get out?" I ask.

"We can try," he grunts.

"MUM! COREY! Cover your faces!" Taylor screams out as we look at each other, coughing. I move over to cover us both as I heard a noise, like a rush of dirt being thrown at a fence.

The wall beside us collapsed, I peek out as Taylor waved her hands around, throwing dirt at the fire, managing to calm it bit by bit.

"Kai! Help me!" She shouts as he flits beside her, they rush in, grabbing the beam as I stand to help.

"One, two, three, lift!" Kai says. Corey grunts under it as I pull him out quickly and they drop it back down.

Taylor grabs one of Corey's arms as I take the other and we get out of the house, coughing hard as Corey and I sit on the ground.

"Phoenix! Holy shit! Are you ok? Taylor howled for back up!" Kade kneels beside me as I groan.

"I'll be ok, check him," I cough, pointing to Corey as he is still lying on the ground.

"Get the humans back home and to medical, send for David and the welcome wagon," Taylor orders a few of the warriors as they look to me for confirmation.

"Don't look at me, she's in charge of this," I shrug, and she grins.

"I'm pretty sure you've got several broken ribs, you'll heal soon enough," Kade tells Corey as he groans.

"How did the humans get out? No one was left inside?" Corey asks.

"They started the fire, accidentally, they were cold… Thought no one was coming back for them, they managed to get out just in time, collapsing in a heap as they are seriously malnourished and couldn't call out for anyone. No one was left behind," Jae tells us.

"Good, let's get back home." I smile as I get up slowly.

"I'm starting to think we attract trouble…" Taylor murmurs as the humans have all been taken.

"I agree," I kiss her head softly before she helps Kade lift Corey to his feet, she puts a hand on his cheek and kisses him softly.

"Don't ever scare me like that again," she says.

"Ohh, I don't know about that one, need to keep you interested in me somehow, will you nurse me back to health?" Corey smirks. I shake my head with a smile as Kade raises a brow with a smirk.

"She will be the worst nurse in history, just ask Blake… Uh… I mean Bryant…" Kade says, grimacing.

"I wasn't that bad, Keeley was worse, she got out the knife, not me!" Taylor points out.

"Wait… A knife… How old were you guys?" Corey laughs before groaning.

"I was six, she was twelve… it was her idea, we'd been watching the healers work and got interested. Keeley had read some stuff about human doctors and wanted to pretend to be them instead, said they were more fun, hands-on," Taylor says.

"You weren't supposed to cut him!" Kade booms with laughter.

"THAT WASN'T ME! I was the one who stitched him up…" Taylor says.

“Is that what you call it…” I laugh.

“He healed; he was fine…” She murmurs.

“Wow… You guys were crazy,” Corey smirks.

“Oh, boy have we got many stories to tell you,” Kai smirks.

“Oh great,” Taylor groans as I smile at my daughter. I was proud of her, even though she went against my word, she took charge, she got the humans out, she saved lives today and she had her mate by her side.

# Chapter Twenty-Seven

## Taylor

A few weeks had gone by after we found the last humans in the burning house, most had survived, one died because he was so malnourished that they weren't able to help him recover in time, and he didn't want to be turned to save him. I respected that, this life wasn't for everyone, some people don't want immortality. He wasn't alone as he died, the others surrounded him as he died peacefully in his sleep, in a warm bed. That was all we could do for him. Though I had kept an eye on the little girl he left behind, she just sat quietly most days, while the other kids played, she sat quietly, looking out into the forest. I felt sorry for her.

The weeks had slowly gotten easier, I was learning to control my anger again with Corey's help. He's been amazing and I couldn't fault him at all, he's been with me every day, even though we haven't mated yet, which was also kind of frustrating… Lily was begging to get at him most days.

Bryant and Amanda left for her home yesterday and I was so sad to see them go. I had cried the moment he left as I heard him howl a goodbye. I'd see him again, sure we had video calls and all that, but it wasn't the same, I would still miss my idiot twin.

Luci was almost ready to pop, and I could tell nerves were high as mum, dad and Kade were around her almost twenty-four-seven.

"Morning," Corey yawns beside me as I smile. We'd been sleeping together the last few nights, only sleeping, but it was the best feeling in the world sleeping in his arms.

"Morning," I kiss his cheek.

"You know my mother comes today, right?" he says, rubbing a hand over his face.

"Oh shit! I can't believe forgot! I mean I totally don't have the welcome party all set up in the dining room and I haven't made sure at all that housing was prepared, how could I be so silly!" I act in mock shock.

"You're a goofball," he laughs, nuzzling into my neck.

"I'm your goofball," I say as he looks deep into my eyes.

"You are definitely mine," he grins, kissing me.

"Mark me," I whisper in his ear as I hear his wolf growl.

"I can't, not this week," he groans.

"Why? Too worried about what your parents will think if we keep sneaking off to mate?" I smirk.

"My mother wants me to have pups, and so do I one day, but we have so much to do, we can't spend all week in bed," he sighs, flopping back on his pillow.

"Ok, one week, I'm giving us one week before you mark me, I don't think I can wait much longer," I bite my lip.

*I don't want to wait!*

**Calm down Lily, we can do this.**

*But I want him!*

**No Lily!**

“Having trouble?” Corey grins cheekily at me as I notice he’s moved so he’s above me, resting on his arms as not to put his full weight on me.

“I will do if you stay there, you are not helping Corey,” I groan.

“So, this doesn’t help… Or this…” he says, kissing down my neck.

I flip us over, pinning him to the bed as I straddle him.

“You tell me,” I growl lustfully as he moans beneath me while I copy what he was doing.

“Taylor,” he moans beneath me.

“You started this,” I kiss his neck as I move my way down his body.

“Fuck it,” he growls. He flips us over once again and I giggle, biting my lip with arousal as his fingers begin to drift over my body, tweaking my nipple as I gasp at the pleasurable pain.

“What are you doing?” I gasp as his hands go down further.

“You still want to mate?” He asks as my eyes go wide.

“Are you serious?”

“Yeah, I can’t wait a week longer, I want this, do you?” He asks, looking into my eyes.

“Yes, mark me, Corey,” I say. Kissing him passionately on the lips, our hips grinding together as he rips open my top, kissing down my neck until he gets to where he would mark me.

“Mine,” he says before he bites into my neck. I wince at first before the pleasure floods my body, my own canines extending as I grip him against me, marking him too as I moan under him, feeling the bond explode in our body, heat flooding our bodies with every touch.

When I woke up, my body was hot with need, and I growl. My hand hits the bed as I looked at the other side of the bed, it was empty. The dream had been so real, everything was true, except for Corey sleeping with me. We had gotten closer and closer day by day but still, he was denying us mating, saying he wanted it to be special.

Today his family would be here, and I had organised an amazing welcome with mum and Luci. We'd been so busy to make it perfect.

*That dream was way too real... We need him!*

**I know, I can feel it too Lily.**

I groan as I get up, feeling the heat of my arousal between my legs as I walk into the shower, my fingers glide down my body. I imagine Corey doing it to me, moaning against them as I release my arousal in the shower.

"Tay! You up?!" Evie shouts through the door as I get out of the shower, wrapping my body in a warm towel.

"Just got out the shower!" I call out.

"Are you decent?" She asks.

"I have a towel on…" I reply with a chuckle as she walks in quickly before shutting the door.

"Corey is pacing…" She replies.

"What?" I frown.

"He's outside, pacing," she says.

"Why?" I smirk.

"How should I know?! Why haven't you two mated yet?" She exclaims, looking at my neck. I could see her mark clearly; she loved showing it off.

"He's waiting to make sure it's special," I replied, rolling my eyes.

"That's cute, but you two are going to go mad if you keep this up, you'll go into heat and he'll… Wait… Are you in heat now? That might be why he's pacing…" She replies.

"I-I don't know… I've never had it before…" I murmur.

"Ah, you're in for a tough ride, and being unmated with it too, you'll have all the males at attention for you," she says.

"No, no, no, no, that is the last thing I want!" I groan.

"Then he needs to mate you soon," she says.

"Great, how do I do that?" I sighed sitting on the bed.

"Give me a minute," she says, leaving the room quickly as I hear hushed whispers outside.

The door bursts open as I was grabbing some clothes, almost losing my towel in the progress when I saw Corey standing a foot away from me as Evie winks and closes the door.

"So… Morning Corey," I smile, blushing.

He walks forward, his nose hitting my neck as he takes a deep breath in.

"You're coming into your heat Taylor, I can smell it coming," he groans, pushing himself away from me and walking to the other side of the room.

"It wouldn't be so bad if we were mated, I'm going to have to watch my back," I sigh, going into the bathroom, hiding away from his sight as I pull my clothes on.

"If anyone touches you…" He growls.

"Again… Not my fault," I roll my eyes.

"Are we seriously going to have this argument?" He sighs.

"Not much of an argument, I'm going into heat, it's going to suck, unmated wolves are going to try it on, some more forcefully because I'm not mated because what…You want it to be special… The mate bond in itself is special, we are given our perfect half of our soul to mate with for eternity, yes sometimes we have multiples, but it depends on what paths we take. YOU are my path Corey, can't you see that, because, in the short amount of time we've known each other, I have," I say as I come out of the bathroom to face him.

"Hey! Lovebirds! Time to ready up, we leave in twenty!" A bang on the door makes me growl in frustration.

"We'll be there Uncle Kai!" I reply.

"Don't do anything I wouldn't do!" He chuckles.

"There's nothing you wouldn't do!" I call back.

"Fair point! Have fun!" He laughs before I hear him flit away.

Corey still hasn't said anything as I shake my head and begin drying my hair quickly before tying it into a ponytail. I quickly put on my make-up before turning to Corey.

“Nothing to say?” I ask, looking at him as he says nothing. I shake my head and take the door handle in my hand before his hand slams against the door, keeping it shut, I can feel him right behind me, his breath tickling my neck.

“Taylor… I am trying to stop my wolf from devouring you right now. Coal wants you just as much as I do, but I want to do this right, I want to prove myself to you, to your family, you have no idea what it’s like to not be accepted in a hard and cruel world. You were brought up in this place, right in the open, people will come for me and my mother for what we are, and I don’t want you in the crossfire… Taylor…I-I-I love you,” he says as I turn around to face him, looking in his sad eyes.

“Tell me that again,” I whisper.

“What… That I love you?” He smiles lightly as I grin before kissing him deeply, my arms going around his neck as his go around my waist.

“You are one of us, Corey. Sure, I was brought up here, but you’ve heard the stories of everything my parents have been through, I have been through shit too and you know it, it’s not the same but I get it. My family do accept you; you wouldn’t be here if they didn’t, my family, the wolves, fae and vampires, all of them here are my family and we will welcome every single one of you in. You’re family too now, if you’re under fire, we are too and for the record… I love you too,” I smile.

He lifts me into his arms as I squeal happily, he kisses me with a passion I had never felt before.

“How long have we got?” He asks as I giggle.

“Ten minutes,” I answer looking to my clock quickly.

“Not enough time,” he growls in disappointment.

"Hold on," I hold up a finger.

"Hey mum, do you know what that stuff was to calm your heat down? With everything going on today that's the last thing I need right now," I ask through our link.

"I will have it made and brought down for you when you're downstairs," she replies after a couple of minutes.

"What are you doing?" Corey tilts his head in confusion.

"My mum knows of a potion that helps reduce a wolf's heat… She's having it made for me," I smile.

"Good, because I need to show the rest of the world that you are mine," he grins, throwing me against the bed as I fall with an "oof" before giggling into a kiss with him.

"You're mine too," I smile, I see his canines elongate as mine copy.

*Yes! Finally!*

"I love you," he says, biting down as I cry out, first in pain, but then in pleasure as I join him, he lets out a roar in passion.

"I love you too," I say through our stronger bond as I felt his wolf closer than ever.

*Hi Coal!*

I can feel our wolves reach out for each other as we kiss on the bed, hands gliding over each other's bodies.

"Two minutes!" Kai pushes to me as I groan.

"I'm going to kill my uncle," I growl as Corey chuckles.

“Come on princess, let’s go get my family, I want to introduce my mate to them,” Corey grins, pulling me up, kissing me softly once more before grabbing my brush and fixing the end of my messy ponytail.

“I could get used to this,” I smile.

“I’m at your every beck and call my lady,” he bows, and I giggle.

“You might regret that,” I point at him with a smirk.

“I will never regret this,” he puts his arms around my waist as I look into the mirror at us, we fit each other perfectly.

I wince in pain as I feel a sting on my stomach, lifting my top as I look in shock, sat on my belly was a moon filled with the night sky.

“What the hell…” I murmur.

“Ah… I forgot about that… Witches have a mark of their own that appears when they finally accept their soul mates,” he says nervously.

“Wow… I love it,” I grin.

“Seriously?” He smiles.

“I really do,” I nod as he kisses me.

“Good, now come on, before Kai comes in here to get us himself,” he chuckles as he grabs my hand and leads me out of the room.

“FINALLY! You’re two minutes were up two minutes ago! Holy shit… You two… You… Welcome to the family dude!” Kai shakes hands with Corey as I giggle when he hugs me.

“Taylor, you’re heating up babe,” Corey says, his hand touches my skin as I groan.

“I need to get to mum,” I say. He nods as we all head downstairs quickly.

“Nix!” Kai calls as we see her, David is stood next to her with a small vial.

“Oh dear, Taylor drink this,” she runs over with it as I groan, holding my stomach as the pain began. I guzzle the liquid down as Corey holds me in his arms.

“It may take a minute to work,” she says with concern.

“This sucks,” I growl.

“I heard it was like having six human periods all at once, and they suck normally…” Mum says.

“I hate women hormones,” Kai grumbles.

“You used to like them once, I remember you being quite the player Kai,” mum winks at her best friend.

“Less said about that the better,” Kai mumbles.

“Well, he’s mine now,” Jae says, walking towards us. I begin to feel better, my body doesn’t feel so hot and the pain is beginning to subside.

“It’s going,” I say as Corey takes my head in his hands, kissing me lightly.

“Come on guys! We’re going to be late!” Dad calls from the door with his booming voice.

“Sorry, dad!” I call back as I smile at Corey, taking his hand in mine as we all begin making our way to the door.

“Right, Kade, you’re in charge, Luci is resting in bed and David will be going to her now to stay with her. Jae will be here with you, Michael, Kai, Trey,

Taylor and Corey will be going with me with a few warriors, if you need us back, we'll come back," mum says.

"I can take care of the pack while you're gone. Go, you're already late. Congratulations by the way," Kade smiles at me and Corey.

"Thanks," we say in unison.

We all shift as Kai jumps onto mum's back with a cheeky grin as she nips at his feet.

"Whoa! Come on! You used to let me!" He laughs.

"Let's go!" Mum orders as we begin our journey. I look back as I see the human little girl, just watching us as she waves at me, I let out a howl back at her as she smiles.

"That's the first time I've seen that child smile," dad nudges my side.

"Baby steps dad," I nod as our paws thud against the earth.

"Taylor… You have a new marking on your fur!" Trey says, budging Corey out of the way.

"Wait what?!" I exclaim, trying to look, but nearly fall over a tree stump as they laugh at me.

"It's the witches mark, it comes up as a streak against your fur, you have a bright line of dark purple along your side," Corey explains.

"Whoa… Cool," I yip happily as we carry on our journey.

"Where are we meeting them all?" Trey asks as we go on a trail I had never been before.

*I don't like new places… We haven't checked it…*

"Mum, are you sure this is the right way?" I ask uneasily.

"Yes, we are meeting them on the coast, they have come by boat, don't worry Taylor, we scoped the place first, what sort of idiot do you think I am?" Mum says as I sigh with relief.

"Can I answer that?!" Kai smirks. Mum bumps him off her back, he falls to the ground, avoiding our paws trampling him as we leap over him.

"Bad move uncle," I chuckle.

"Aww come on!" He hisses, standing and catching up with us in a sulk.

He continues to moan at mum as we all run through the forest, my ears perk at the slightest noise, I look to my right and see a glowing pair of red eyes.

"MUM! Watch out!" I howl, leaping into action and a spear is thrown towards us as I bite at it, catching it in my teeth as it snaps at the force. I growl in warning, standing in front of mum as dad stands beside me.

"I've got this," Kai says, flitting into the depths as suddenly a yell is heard, and a vampire is thrown to the ground in front of us.

"Was it just the one?" I tilt my head, ears perked for more.

"Yes," Kai nods.

"Listen, it's nothing against you, I'm hungry," the vampire hisses.

"So that calls for you hunting us…" I snarl, teeth bared in anger.

"You took all the food! What am I supposed to drink?" He shouts as Kai squeezes the back of his neck making him yelp out.

"Plenty of deer around here, start there," Kai says.

“But you know that doesn’t help! It doesn’t curb the craving!” The vampire cries out.

“What do we do?” Dad asks mum.

“We can give you a home, a chance to live OUR way, you will get blood donations from our humans. If we even get a small hint that you are against us or working against us, we will kill you,” she steps forward.

“You’re seriously giving this guy a chance! He tried to kill you!” I growl.

“I swear, I just need blood, please, I have nowhere else, the covens don’t even take me in!” The vampire begs.

“Why?” Kai frowns.

“I don’t kill… Usually. I wasn’t aiming to kill, by the way, just spill blood,” he answers.

“What’s your name?” Dad asks. I look at Trey as he seems to have the same stance I had, unsure of this new vampire.

“They can’t seriously be thinking of bringing him in right…” I say through the link to Trey.

“Looks like it, we’ll keep an eye on him, I don’t like this either,” he nods at me.

“Kai, give him your snack,” mum smirks as she shifts.

“But that’s mine!” He huffs bringing out a blood bag as he passes it over.

“Lewis, my name is Lewis, thank you!” He says as he drinks the whole bag quickly, a shiver goes down his spine and I see the relief in his face.

Corey nudges my side before he nuzzles into me, and I relax a little.

"You will come with us, we have to collect some people and then head home," mum says as I sigh, shaking my head.

"Give him a chance to prove himself, he may surprise you," Corey nudges me as I roll my eyes, pushing through them with a yip at Trey as we begin our run again.

# Chapter Twenty-Eight

## Taylor

I could hear Lewis chatting between Kai and my mum, my senses were on alert, Lily didn't trust him, no matter how much they seemed to so quickly.

*Give him a chance… A chance to kill us… Sure, great idea!*

Corey howls, he rushes past me, bouncing slightly on his feet as he runs excitedly towards the shore as we get to the edge of the sand.

A large vessel is docked at what was left of a long pier. I could see a huge group heading towards us on lifeboats as that was the easiest way to get to us because half of the pier was gone, its wooden boards succumbing to the sea.

Corey stops suddenly as he barks out at me, tilting his head for me to follow him.

"Go," Trey nudges me forward as I feel the sand beneath my feet…

I had never been to a beach, I stared into the horizon, the sea was as far as I could see, the feeling of sand under my paws was the weirdest sensation I had ever felt.

"Taylor! Come on!" Corey laughs as he shifts, holding out a hand.

"I've never… I've never been to a beach before…" I murmur as his eyes widen.

“I forget you have so much of the world still to see, come on, we’ll explore it soon, I promise, but my family are coming into the shore, I want to introduce you to them,” he says as I walk towards him, I feel my paws sink into the sand as I take it step by step.

I hear my mum yip happily as she and dad bound across the sand happily past us, already getting to the water's edge as they swim through the water to drag the boats to shore quicker than them rowing.

I shift as I get beside Corey as he takes my hand in his and we walk towards the group of new people as my mother seems to be introducing herself to Cynthia already as they hug happily.

“Oh! My baby boy!” Cynthia shouts as she makes her way to us quickly, hugging Corey to her tightly as she puts his head in her hands with a loving mother’s eye.

“My, my, Cynthia dear, don’t forget the girl hanging off of his hand, my name is Reginald, afraid we haven’t met before,” a bigger, older version of Corey stands holding out his hand to me and I shake it nervously.

“Don’t be nervous dear, he’s a big teddy bear,” Cynthia smiles as she hugs me too.

“Mom, dad this is Taylor, my mate,” Corey smiles brightly, taking me into his arms, his nose into my neck as I see his mother’s eyes widen at the sign of my mark.

“OH, MY BABY BOY! You didn’t tell me you marked her! How could you not tell me?!” She huffs. smacking his arm as I giggle.

“It was only this morning mom,” he groans.

"You… This… This morning… But you're not in heat… How is that possible?" His dad frowns in confusion.

"I can explain that one Reginald. I knew of a guardian that could make a potion to help stop the heat for a while, we thought it best that she takes it, she didn't want to be in heat as we came to get you," mum smiles at me.

"COREY!" A little boy squeals happily as he bounds over the sand to us.

"Little man! Look at you! You've grown so much! Have you missed me?" Corey grins, picking up the boy with the biggest of grins.

"I really missed you! Momma said you might not come back, I told her you would!" He says with a smile before it turns into sadness.

"Where is Eva?" Corey asks, looking around the group of people.

"She didn't make it…" Corey's mother says sadly.

"How?" Corey asks. I feel his sadness seeping through his body, placing my hand on his shoulder as the little boy looks at me curiously. I stick my tongue out at him and he giggles, hiding his head into Corey's chest.

"She got sick, she was shot by some new bullet, we tried to keep her alive, but not even my powers could stop the poison," Cynthia answers sadly.

"What's your name, little man?" I ask.

"Hunter," he murmurs.

"Hunter, since when are you shy?" Corey laughs.

"She's a girl…" Hunter whispers.

"Hunter has taken a liking to pretty girls," Reginald smiles at us as he ruffles Hunter's luscious long blonde locks.

"She's beautiful, isn't she?" Corey smiles at Hunter nodding to me.

"Yes," Hunter whispers before hiding his face again.

"Aww thank you handsome," I kiss Hunter's cheek and he blushes hiding up into Corey's chest again with a giggle.

"What about me?" Corey says in mock shock.

"Hmm, you're alright I guess," I smirk, shrugging my shoulders.

"Excuse me a minute little man," Corey puts Hunter down who goes to hide behind Cynthia. She turns from talking to my mum to see what he's hiding from as she smiles.

Corey grabs me by the legs as he flips me over his shoulder and begins walking over to the sea.

"Don't you dare!" I squeal.

"I'm alright, am I? Well let's see how alright you are after I dunk you," he laughs as he proceeds to throw me into the water with a scream. I land with a hard splash against the water as it splashes everywhere.

My eyes sting under the water, what the hell?! I come up for air as I groan rubbing my eyes, choking on the most disgusting tasting water I had ever known.

"Why does it taste so bad?!" I groan.

"It's seawater, what did you expect?" Corey laughs, swimming over to me.

"Less salt," I grimace.

"Kids get out! There are jellyfish in there!" Trey points beside us and I see a huge group of jellyfish coming our way with the waves.

“Shit,” I say as Corey and I begin to swim back to shore, narrowly missing getting stung.

“Well… That was different…” Corey laughs.

“Yeah,” I nod, wringing out my hair.

“You still look beautiful, even drenched,” he smiles, kissing my lips.

“You’re still alright,” I smirk as he tickles my sides and I burst into laughter.

“OK! OK! You’re the sexiest man in the world!” I call out between laughs as he stops, scooping me into his arms.

“Better,” he grins.

“Shall we take these lovely people to their new homes?” Mum raises her brow at me as I grin cheekily.

“Yes mum,” I nod as Corey lets me down.

“Need drying or will you do so naturally?” She asks.

“If you don’t mind,” I smile as she brings out a ball of flames which hovers around us, drying us out quickly with the heat without burning us.

“Impressive,” Cynthia says to my mum.

Trey whimpers as my eyes dart to him.

“Luci… She’s in pain,” Trey says in a panic.

“The baby is coming! We need to go now! Something doesn’t feel right!” Mum says as she howls shifting.

“Mum you and dad lead, Corey and I will take the rear!” I call as she nods.

Corey's pack all shift except for Cynthia as she climbs onto Reginald's back, who is a massive black wolf, bigger than I had ever seen.

"Whoa…" I murmur as I shift.

Mum howls as we begin our trek back, I hear Trey whimper again as he pushes faster than ever before.

"Something's wrong Corey," I tell him.

"Go, you're faster than most of them, run," he says. I nuzzle into his side before sprinting past.

"Trey shift! Jump on! I'm faster!" I order, he shifts mid-air jumping onto my back as Lily takes over completely, leaving the others in our dust.

"Be careful!" Mum howls out as my feet almost glide across the ground.

I can feel Trey wince at his sister being in so much pain.

"Taylor! Hurry up!" He groans.

I knew his pain, I knew the pain of feeling everything your twin felt as a wolf, he must be in agony.

"LUCI!" He roars out as we see the mansion, he leaps off of my back, bursting through the doors, skidding across the floor towards the medical wing.

I run up the stairs after him quickly, shifting back to my human form as we bolt through the corridors to find Kade on his knees on the floor outside a room.

"Kade! What happened?!" I ask as Trey stands in the doorway.

"They… She started labour and then she was bleeding… We can't find David; we only have a couple of fae healers who stayed. Rodge went home," Kade says with tears in his eyes.

"Who is in there with her?" I ask.

"Jae and Evie with a couple of our healers," Kade answers.

I hear Luci scream as I see Kade and Trey both want to tear the door down. The door opens as Jae comes out covered in blood.

"She's losing too much blood, I couldn't handle it," he shakes.

"Shit!" My hands curl into my hair.

"The baby?" Trey murmurs.

Jae shakes his head and I hear Kade sob.

"Cynthia…" I murmur as Trey looks at me.

"Do you think she could help?" Trey asks.

"Stay put and make sure they keep her alive!" I order. I shift, I could feel myself getting tired, but I had to do this for Luci. I bolted back out the house towards the oncoming group of wolves who were still at least a couple miles out.

*Tired…*

**Keep going Lily, we have to do this for Luci.**

Newfound energy seems to push me as I go quicker, seeing my mum at the head of the pack as they rush towards me. I bark at Cynthia; she frowns at me as I run side-by-side Reginald.

"Corey tell your mum I need her help! Luci will die otherwise!" I push through the link as I see him look on in shock. Cynthia gasps and jumps onto my back, holding tightly as I bolt away once more.

I can hear Cynthia muttering on my back as I feel something snap into place inside me.

"Now you can bond with me directly, tell me now, tell me quick, what has happened?" She says and I begin to tell her what had happened.

"Do you think you can help?" I whine.

"Yes, it may be too late for the baby, but I will help your aunt," she says. I see the mansion once more, not even shifting as I dart up the stairs with Cynthia on my back as warriors rush to the sides of the corridor to let us past.

"TAYLOR!" Trey shouts for me. Cynthia jumps off of my back and with a flick of her wrist the door opens and she heads in as I shift and collapse on the floor, breathing heavily, exhausted.

"Thank you," Kade sits beside me, his hand holding mine tightly as I rest my head on his shoulder.

"She'll make it uncle Kade, we're not losing her too," I say between breaths.

"Holy shit, I can feel her magic… Taylor, she's doing it!" Trey says excitedly as he helps Kade up to his feet.

The main door opens as I hear a rush of feet downstairs, mum and the others must be here.

"She's out of danger, you must be Kade, she's asking for you," Cynthia gives him a small, sad smile as I hear Luci's sobs in the room when he goes in.

"The baby?" I bite my lip.

"Is small, but healthy…" Cynthia smiles. Trey hollers through the halls as I tilt my head back, laughing in relief.

"Thank you so much, Cynthia," I smile.

"We owe you, Cynthia, for saving my sister's and my niece or nephew's life," Trey smiles at her.

"You owe me nothing, I would not let harm come to people so precious. Go, be with your twin," Cynthia says.

"Thank you! Taylor, you too!" Trey grins as he goes in the room.

"I've not seen a wolf move so quick, you have a real talent," Cynthia says.

"Being surrounded by so many competitive people I had to keep up, my twin and I used to race all the time, he's just as quick as me," I smile.

"Quite a few twins around… Something must be in the air," she laughs.

"Taylor! Oh my god! Is Luci ok?!" Mum runs to our sides.

"She is fine, she will take time to heal, but she and the baby are out of danger," Cynthia answers.

"Oh, thank the goddess," mum sighs with relief.

"You are so fast! Damn princess, where were you hiding that?!" Corey smiles coming up to us with dad.

"Is everyone alright? Was David struggling?" Dad asks as my eyes go wide.

"David… Shit, Kade said they couldn't find him…" I answer as dad frowns.

"Well, today is going well…" Mum rolls her eyes.

"Not quite the welcome party we had hoped," I reply.

"Don't worry about it, family come first. Now, who is this David?" Cynthia asks.

"Our human doctor, he's trained with a fae healer and our own, he was learning everything, he should have been here," I answer.

"Michael, have the warriors search for him," mum tells dad as he nods.

"Look after Luci, I'll find him," he answers, kissing her on the head before running off.

"Taylor, you and Corey should take them to their new housing, let them get settled in and rest, show the grounds," mum orders.

"I'm going to need a minute," I hold up a finger, my body still exhausted.

"I've got it," Corey smirks as he lifts me into his arms bridal style.

"TAYLOR! Wait!" Kade peeks out of the room.

"Yeah?" I reply.

"Luci wants you to meet our little one," he smiles. Corey lets me down carefully in front of him and I groan at my muscles resisting.

I walk in slowly as I see Evie is busy cleaning up most of the sheets of blood.

"Taylor… Hi," Luci whispers, she looked pale, but her eyes still held their sparkle.

"Hey, how are you feeling?... Stupid question," I groan, putting a hand to my head as she and Kade laugh.

"Better than earlier, come meet our little girl, she's alive because of you Taylor. I'm alive because of you, thank you," she says. I walk to her, and I peer into the blankets to see the cutest little bundle I had ever seen.

"Oh Luci, she's gorgeous," I smile.

"Just like her mother," Kade kisses her head.

“You guys need to rest; I will come by later. I have to help Corey with his family, she really is beautiful Luci, I’m glad you’re ok,” I kiss her head.

“You look exhausted Taylor,” Trey smirks at me.

“Well, I carried your fat arse here, didn’t I?” I smirk.

“You… What…” Luci frowns.

“Trey will explain,” I smile.

“I think Luci needs to sleep and be retold everything when she’s a little more with it,” Kade chuckles.

“Get some rest, I’ll see you later, congratulations!” I grin as I walk out the door as my mum is pacing.

“How are they?” She asks.

“Fine, tired, go in,” I smile pushing her to the door.

“I don’t want to intrude…” She replies.

“Mum, go, she’s one of your best friends. I can guarantee she wants you beside her,” I smile.

Mum goes inside as I hear her cooing over Luci and the baby.

“Where the hell did the others go…” I murmur, noticing the hallways were quiet.

“Corey?” I call through the bond.

“Kitchens!” He answers and I head slowly down the stairs.

I can see Kai holding Jae in his arms, Lewis standing right behind him.

“Jae… You ok now?” I ask.

"He'll be fine, I'm going to take him and Lewis for a quick drink," Kai nods. My eyes dart to Lewis with a glare.

"I know you don't trust me, but I mean no harm," Lewis says with a sigh.

"One fuck up and I will tear you limb from limb, understood?" I growl.

"Understood," Lewis says in a high pitch with a gulp.

"Stop frightening the poor kid… Taylor, calm down," Kai laughs.

"I better go see what the newbies are doing to our kitchen," I smile at Kai and Jae, hugging them both before walking off towards the kitchens.

"There she is!" Corey grins, picking me up and spinning me, kissing me like he hadn't seen me in a lifetime.

"Sorry Taylor, I can see your people have been preparing something special, we just needed a quick bite, some of us haven't had a good meal in some time," Cynthia says.

"Our home is your home, it's fine," I grin as I look around the room, there were at least thirty of them.

"Princess!" Hunter giggles as he hands me a small daisy.

"Thank you, Hunter," I grin as he runs off to hide back behind Cynthia.

"He's a good kid, I can't believe it about his mom though, Eva was great, she was like my aunt, of sorts," he says.

"Like Luci?" I ask.

"Yeah, exactly, mom and Eva were best friends," he nods.

"So, would you show us our new homes?" Reginald smiles at me as I nod.

“Of course Sir, right this way,” I bow with a smirk as he chuckles.

“I like her,” he nudges Corey.

“I love her,” Corey says, and I hear Cynthia gasp happily.

“Does this mean my dream will come true soon?!” She says excitedly.

“What dream?” I ask as I lead them all out of the house.

“Grandbabies,” she grins.

“Cynthia, stop it, they only mated today and haven’t even completed it yet… Calm yourself,” Reginald says as I have to laugh.

“Having one of these would be good though, wouldn’t they?” Corey smiles, picking up Hunter with a smile.

“Hmm, yeah, but I couldn’t eat a whole one,” I smirk as he laughs at me.

“NO! You can’t eat me!” Hunter cries out.

“I’m joking Hunter,” I giggle, kissing his cheek as he blushes.

We walk across the bridge towards the new field where we had built new housing ages ago but had no one to fill it. We thought it would be perfect for them as it gave them so much space to do their own thing but be close enough they could be in the mansion within minutes.

“Oh, my,” Cynthia gasps as the people behind her all begin chatting loudly, also impressed at the sight.

“I hope you like it,” I bite my lip nervously.

“Are you serious Taylor? This is better than anything we’ve had in years… It’s beautiful,” Reginald says as he and his people begin rushing towards it happily.

"You and your family are amazing, I'm glad my son found you," Cynthia says, kissing my forehead before joining her mate.

"Mom, dad, we'll let you settle in, don't be afraid to ask for anything," Corey calls out.

"The houses are fully stocked with various clothing in different sizes, food and anything you'll need. If you need anything specifically, let one of the warriors know and they will get it for you or direct you to the right place," I call out.

"THANK YOU!" They grin as they go towards the houses.

"So, how long do you think we have until someone wants us?" Corey says, turning me to face him.

"Depends… What were you thinking of doing?" I smirk.

"Making you mine completely," he growls lustfully.

"We'll be disturbed if we go to our rooms," I bite my lip.

"I have an idea," he grins, picking me up and begins he walking as I giggle in his arms.

# Chapter Twenty-Nine

## Taylor

"You brought us to the lake," I smile as he sets me down.

He looks into my eyes before his head dips down to me, catching my lips in his as his hands travel from my neck down. He lifts my top, lifting my arms for it to come off, our lips separating for just a moment before they move again, tasting him on my tongue as I moan.

I can feel him as he unzips my trousers, slowly kissing down my neck, over my mates' mark and down to my breasts as he takes off my bra and begins to suck and lick them as I step out of my trousers.

"We're going to get caught," I say breathlessly.

"No, we won't," he says, kissing down my stomach, I can feel his hands go down my legs which makes me jolt.

"Don't, not my legs," I murmur.

"Taylor, you are beautiful, you know I love every single bit of you, scars and all," he says as he lightly kisses over my arousal before kissing down my legs.

"Corey, please don't," I sigh.

"Ok, you will love yourself one day, for now, I will love all of you," he says. He pulls down my knickers as I'm left completely bare, I gasp when his mouth hits my slit, his mouth suckling on my clit as I moan, my legs barely able to stand as his fingers graze my skin up to my wet pussy.

“Fuck,” I moan as my hand clutches at his head.

I groan as he stops, standing up as he strips his clothes too before picking me up into his arms and my legs go around his waist.

He wades into the water with me, kissing me deeply as one of his hands begins to finger me slowly, opening me up for his huge cock.

“Corey, fuck, please, I want you,” I moan as he bites at my neck.

“Are you sure?” He asks.

“Yes!” I moan as he kisses me.

“If you need me to stop I will, ok?” he says as I hear the care in his voice.

“I love you,” I nod. I feel the tip of him at my entrance, gasping as he pushes in, wincing a little at the sheer size of him. My head goes into the crook of his neck as I hear him moan against me.

Slowly he pushes deeper, the pain subsides and pleasure kicks in as he begins to thrust in and out at a steady pace, causing us both to quiver in pleasure.

“Faster,” I moan. He growls lustfully, moving us closer to the grass bank as he settles me down on my back, continuing to thrust, harder and faster as I cry out for him, our mouths fight for dominance his claws digging into the ground.

“FUCK… Taylor, I’m not going to last much longer,” he moans.

“Cum with me,” I cry out as he pounds into me harder, biting my mark and causing me to scream out as we both cum hard.

He kisses me gently but deeply before moving to my side and curling me into his arms.

"Wow," I murmur as he chuckles.

"I love you," he whispers into my neck.

"I love you too Corey," I smile, feeling better than ever before.

We lay there for a few minutes in silence, looking up to the clouds, enjoying each other's warmth. I loved this, the feel of his body against mine.

My phone rings from my pocket and I groan, sitting up as I crawl over to my phone, grabbing it from my pocket before going back to Corey's side.

"Hello?" I answer without seeing who it was.

"What the hell did you just do twin?" Bryant exclaims as my eyes go wide. Oh shit… I didn't block the twin link…

"Ughh… I… Well… I'm mated…" I bite my lip.

"TAYLOR! For fuck's sake! Why didn't you close the twin link? Seriously, I don't need to know that you're fucking your man! Gross! But… How does it feel? Different?" He laughs through the phone.

"I'm not having this conversation right now Bryant," I laugh.

"Oh, come on! Wait, are you two still… Oops sorry Tay! Talk soon!" He says before hanging up as I shake my head.

"That's not awkward at all, how much will he know?" Corey grimaces.

"General emotion, major arousal… He will probably have to go find Amanda right now…" I chuckle.

"Shut the link next time," he smirks.

"Will do, trust me," I laugh.

Corey's phone is next to go as I laugh.

"This solitude didn't last long…" I smirk as he grabs his phone before placing one side of his head against my chest, listening to my heart as he placed his phone on the other.

"Hey, mom, what's up?" he rolls his eyes at me as I giggle. "No mom, she's with me why? None of your business… Ughh, yes, please don't start that again… No… Mom! Seriously calm down on the pups thing! Yes, I know, I know, yes, we will see you in a few minutes, love you too," he says before hanging up, burying his head between my breasts as he groans.

"Quite comfortable there?" I giggle.

"These are the comfiest breasts ever," he moans as I giggle.

"Glad I can help," I smirk.

"My mom and yours are talking, they want us back at the mansion for the party," he groans.

"We knew it wouldn't last, come on, we can continue this later and we'll talk about the whole pup thing," I push him off me playfully as I stand up to grab my clothes.

"Wait… Tell me now, where do we stand with that? I know what I want, do you?" He asks.

"What do you want?" I ask.

"I want a family, a big one, with you," he says, grabbing me around the waist pulling me to him.

“Good thing I’m so used to a big family. I didn’t know I wanted it, but now… Now I do. You’ve changed so much for me Corey, so if it happens, it happens, though I wouldn’t be against adoption either,” I smile as he grins, spinning me around making me giggle.

“You just made me the happiest man alive,” he kisses me deeply.

I can’t help but smile around him, he has this effect on me which I love so much. The warmth of his touches makes me go into a frenzy, his gorgeous smile, handsome face, sexy body… It drives me insane.

“We better get dressed,” I say as he nods, kissing me again before spanking my bum as my eyes widen at the arousal I felt with it.

“You liked that didn’t you… Jesus woman, you’re going to be the death of me,” he growls, biting at my neck again as I moan, leaning into his hold.

“ARGGGHHH! SHIT! GET SOME FUCKING CLOTHES ON! MY EYES!” Kai shouts as he flits into the clearing, turning quickly, covering his eyes with his hands as we both gasp in shock before rushing to put our clothes on.

“What the fuck Kai…” I growl.

“What the fuck me? What about you two? Bloody exhibitionists! You’re lucky it was me and not some other weirdo! Uggh I’m never getting that image out of my head,” he groans.

“We’re dressed,” I sigh as he turns around, slowly peeping out of his fingers.

“So… Your dad found David, drunk on the floor of his bathroom… He doesn’t remember ever picking up the bottle, when Rook turns up tonight, we’ll have him check his head…” Kai says.

“That’s what you wanted to tell us…” I raise a brow.

"That and I was sent to find you to come back," he says.

"Bullshit… You just crave chaos," I smirk.

"Hey! I did not expect to find you two completely naked by the lake, I mean seriously, take her to bed and make love… Not in the lake we swim in!" Kai groans.

"It was meant to be, trust me, we have pictures to prove it," Corey smiles as I remember our drawings.

"Ooookkk, I will leave you two with your… Pictures, I don't need to see any more of your bodies… Though Corey…" Kai winks.

"UNCLE! You have JAE!" I growl.

"I'm playing, jeez, get a mate and you get all tense," Kai laughs, flitting away.

We both end up shaking our heads at him as he leaves, Corey takes my hand in his as he kisses me and pulls me towards home.

As we get closer to home, I hear whimpering in amongst the trees and I frown.

"Did you hear that?" I ask.

"Yes," he answers as we walk towards the noise as we find Amelia, the human girl that lost her father.

"Amelia?" I kneel beside her.

"Go away," she murmurs.

"Not a chance," I shake my head, moving her hair from her face, gasping at the bruise on her cheek.

"Don't tell, please," she whimpers.

"Who did this to you? Amelia, please tell me what happened," I ask. I look at Corey, who looks angry, just as I was.

"I-I-I live in the big house with lots of people and… and one of the men… he… he got angry with me for getting in his way. David tried to help me by telling the man off, but he got pushed, he wouldn't wake up, the man picked him up and took him upstairs and I just ran. I was scared, I'm sorry," she cries as I gasp, taking her into my arms as she sobs.

"The man, do you know who he is?" Corey asks.

"Umm… Long black hair, but it's going grey at the top… he… he had this scar on his arm, like this," she swept her finger over her arm.

"Corey, do me a favour and take Amelia into the mansion, you're not sleeping in that house any longer, not on my watch," I pick her up and put her into Corey's arms.

"Wait! What… What will you do? I don't want him to hurt you too!" She cries as I cup her cheek.

"He won't hurt me. I'm a wolf remember, and you know who my parents are right? Well, you know there are rules we live by, and he went against them. Don't worry, I won't be alone, I promise. Go inside with Corey for me and go find a little boy called Hunter, he's five and he lost his mummy not long ago, so I need a big girl to take care of him, can you do that for me?" I ask.

"Yes, but the other kids don't like me… He might not either," she sniffles.

"He will love you," Corey smiles at her, giving me a look which I knew was that he was worried about what I was about to do.

"Don't worry, I've got this," I kiss his cheek and cup Amelia's cheek lightly, a growl emanating from my chest at the bruise on her cheek.

"Dad, meet me at the human camp, we've got a problem," I link to dad.

I shift as I make my way through the woods until I got to the human camp.

"Taylor, what happened?" He asks bounding up to me as Trey stands beside him.

I press my head against him as I show him exactly as I hear his growl and then Trey's as he shows him too.

"No one does this and gets away with it," I growl.

"After you Taylor, this is your show," dad says, nodding for me to go ahead as we walk into the busy street, kids were playing, adults were chatting, and they were all happy.

"Taylor, this house," Trey nods to the biggest house.

Shifting back to my human form I bash my hand against the door as I feel eyes watch me, dad and Trey staying as their wolves.

"Taylor, how are you dear? I heard about David, I hope he's ok," one of the teen girls says opening the door as I notice a bruise on her cheek too as I growl.

"Where is he?" I growl.

"Taylor, he has a gun, don't," she holds my hand.

"Guns don't scare me," I growl, I push past her as I see others looking nervous when I walk through the rooms one at a time. I saw several bruises and broken bones.

"How long has this been going on? Is it just him?" I ask the girl.

"Just him, the last month. He thinks we deserve more, that we should be up at the mansion, with you all here, we don't agree, you saved us all, we love it here, he's stuck in the old ways, he's been threatening everyone with the gun, no one dared tell Phoenix." She whispers.

"Which room is he in?" I growl.

"Room twelve, be careful Taylor, please," she begs as I nod, heading up the stairs as the people downstairs walk quickly out of the house.

"Do you need us?" Dad asks.

"I've got this," I answer as I get to room twelve, bashing my hand against it, claws extended already in anger.

"Well, well, well, look who it is, if it isn't the wolf princess, what do you want?" He only opens the door a sliver.

"Let me in," I order.

"Why would I do that?" He laughs.

I can hear the click of his gun, I know exactly where he has it pointed, too easy.

"I just want to talk, come on, please," I bat my lashes at him.

"I don't fuck mutts," he rolls his eyes at me.

"Good, I don't fuck men like you either," I growl, punching my hand through his door, grabbing his gun before it goes off as it crumples in my hand. I throw it to the ground, kicking the door open as a girl screams in the corner, naked, battered and bruised.

"Now… Now… Listen… they want this… Kinky little things… They begged for it…" He backs up as my growl gets louder.

"How old are you?" I ask the girl as I pass her the blanket to cover herself.

"Four… Fourteen," she cries, and I growl again, grabbing the man by the throat.

"Get out of here sweetheart, you don't need to see this," I say as I hear her rush out the room.

"You won't kill me! You're too much of a pussy," he laughs.

"Oh really…" I tilt my head.

"You mutts shouldn't be in charge, we should, this is OUR land, OUR home," he shouts, spitting in my face.

"How about we see what everyone else thinks?" I say, grabbing him by the back of the neck, my claws slightly puncturing his skin as I drag him outside.

"What's going on?!" Mum runs up to us with the others not too far behind her.

"Just in time mum," I smile as I kick the man to the ground, kicking him straight in the crotch as he screams out in pain. Most of the humans around me look at him like he was a piece of shit, and he was.

"How many of you has this man hurt?" I shout.

At least twenty hands go up as I see mum's eyes turn to rage.

"How many has he raped?" I growl. At least five…

*How did we not see this?*

**I don't know, but I'm going to fix it…**

"We do not tolerate this! We do not tolerate this disgusting behaviour; we are here as a community! We are here as a family! I will not stand idly by as this man tries to take everything, your community is still separated, but no longer!

This WILL become a mixed community, we are ONE FAMILY, if something hurts one of us, it hurts us ALL. Do you agree?" I call out as they begin to cheer.

The man tries to get up, but dad puts a paw on his chest, pushing him hard to the ground.

"This man will answer to his crimes, but the only thing we must do together is decide WHAT will be done…" I shout.

I hear a lot of people calling for death. But that seems too simple.

Cynthia and her people walk towards us too now as the street is getting crowded. The kids didn't need to see this…

"He will be placed into the deepest cell until his fate has been decided, I hope all of you can now rest in peace knowing he will be dealt with. If anyone should ever need help you need only ask, any of us. You are all invited to our welcoming party at the mansion, we have plenty of room and food, I will make sure living arrangements are looked over again and make sure everyone is where they want to be," I call out, grabbing the man again as they cheer.

"SCUM! The lot of you! You'll regret this!" he says. Reginald walks up to me, he holds up a finger for me to wait as he lifts the mans' head and punches him straight in the jaw, outcold.

"For god's sake Reggie," Cynthia shakes her head at him as I smirk.

"Nicely done," I laugh.

"I don't like men like him," he growls.

"Me neither," I nod, dragging him with me by the scruff of his shirt across the ground.

"Well, this has certainly been quite the day," mum catches up to me.

"Never simple, is it?" I laugh.

"We'll take him to the cells," two warriors smile, and I thank them as they drag him, hitting his head against a wall or two… Accidentally… Of course… I couldn't help but smirk, he'd feel that when he woke up.

My stomach grumbles loudly.

"I think that means you need some food, go get cleaned up and the party can start. I'm proud of you," mum kisses my cheek. I smile, walking inside and head upstairs.

"Hunter! Ready or not here I come!" I hear Amelia giggle before she runs past me, hearing Hunter giggle next as I spot him under the little table nearby. I put a finger to my lips at him, but he giggles louder as Amelia turns quickly to find him.

"BOO!" She shouts as he laughs loudly.

I couldn't help but smile as I remembered my childhood when we all did similar things. Bryant and I would always have the best spots to hide, Keeley would get annoyed and stomp off because she couldn't find us. Blake would search everywhere for us while Janie pretended not to know where we were for him to find us.

"Taylor… Corey is in your bedroom," Amelia giggles at me.

"Thank you, sweetheart, you be careful ok," I kiss both their heads and head to my room.

"I wondered how long until you came in," he grins, shutting the door behind me and pins me against it.

“Miss me?” I smirk as he locks my door, picking me up and taking me into the bathroom as he puts the shower on.

“Always. Now, you have to get ready and I’m going to help you,” he smirks as he strips me slowly, kissing my skin as he goes. Stripping himself of clothes he picks me up again as we get in the shower. The warm water cascading down us as we kiss before he sets me down, turning me around as he gently wets my hair, kissing my neck and I moan softly.

He begins washing my hair as I shiver at his touch with a smile, his hands over my body felt perfect as I could feel his arousal against my arse.

My body tingles as he touches me and it feels amazing, I notice a small bottle on the rack where my soaps are. I frown, I had never seen that there before…

“Taylor, what is it?” He asks noticing my gaze.

“What’s that? That’s not mine,” I point to it. I notice his hands are covered by it, it smells sweet, like sickly sweet medicine, like the one's parents try and coerce their kids to take.

“Close your eyes for a few more minutes and I will tell you,” he says. I frown but do it as I feel his hands glide down my body, flinching as he touches my scarred legs.

“Corey, no, you know I don’t like them…” I groan.

“Taylor, look down,” he says, nuzzling into my neck as I open my eyes and look down.

My eyes widen in shock as I see my legs, the scars… They are gone! Mostly… A couple of scars still remain, but it’s like they are just from cuts, not burns.

“COREY!” I cry, tears filling my eyes.

“It wasn’t me, mom made it,” he smiles.

“But you must have told her, oh my god, thank you,” I kiss him hard, wrapping my legs around his waist and my arms around his neck as he pushes me against the shower wall, fucking me hard against it as we both moan.

“I love you no matter how you look, but I knew you needed this, for you, I’d do anything for you,” he says, kissing me once again, our tongues battling for dominance.

“I love you too,” I say breathlessly with every pounding of his cock before we both cum together in a tangle of limbs.

“I guess we need to really wash now,” he chuckles, kissing my nose as I giggle.

“Yeah, they might wonder where we are,” I bite my lip as I hear him growl lustfully.

“I’m sure they know,” he laughs as we actually begin to wash properly, washing each other as I looked down, I still couldn’t believe it, my legs looked normal again.

# Chapter Thirty

## Phoenix

"Your daughter is a very impressive young lady," Cynthia sits beside me with her mate by her side.

"She is, she's grown a lot lately," I smile.

"She's more like you now, it's kind of scary Phoenix," Michael chuckles.

"She'll be a strong leader, just like I've heard about you Phoenix, your family is blessed by true leaders, you've raised them right," Reginald says, and I feel a beam of pride inside me.

"I've done what I can, I wasn't alone in raising them, the family is a big part of our life," I smile.

"So, I can see, but I can't help but think we are putting you in danger being here. As soon as people begin to hear rumours of witches being alive still, we could end up being hunted once again for our power, I don't want to put you into any danger," Cynthia sighs.

"Cynthia, we've had our fair share in trials and grief, we protect our own, you are part of us now and we will fight for you, tonight you will meet more of my pack. It's a surprise for Taylor too, I know she's missing her twin already, several of our alphas are coming to show their allegiance to us and outreach a hand of protection to you and your people. You will be safe with us," I hold her hand in mine as a tear falls from her eye.

“Thank you, we can’t thank you enough, whatever we can do, we’ll do it, we’ll do our fair share. My men are great warriors, though a little out of touch with it as we’ve been more on the run than the attack,” Reginald says.

“You’re all welcome to train with us. Kade, Trey and Michael all deal with training, though Kade may be away from that for a while due to the baby, thank you for that once again Cynthia,” I reply.

“That would be great, it’s been a while since I’ve had a good training session. I will be honoured to join your ranks, though I hope you don’t mind that I stay alpha of my own pack rather than palm them to you,” Reginald says.

“That’s fine by me, I have many alphas who I work with, it will be great to add another Reginald,” I smile.

“Call me Reggie,” he smiles.

“Ok, Reggie it is. Now as an alpha you will need to come to certain meetings, we usually have major ones at least once every two months with all the alphas, whether it be via face to face or computer, otherwise we talk most days casually if there are issues, we work together to solve them,” I explain.

“Sounds just to me,” Reggie nods.

“Look what the cat dragged in!” The door to the office bursts open and I see Rook stood there with the biggest grin on his face.

“Rook! Brother!” Reggie laughs as he gets up and they hug.

“Oh, look at you Rook, you haven’t changed a bit, it’s so good to see you!” Cynthia hugs him next.

“I don’t think I’ve ever seen such a big smile on Rook’s face before,” I chuckle in Michael’s ear.

"I agree," he smirks.

"Phoenix, as always, a pleasure. I'm afraid it's just me though as the others have stayed behind, we're having a few issues back home," Rook says.

"Will you stay or go back home? What's happened?" I ask.

"More of our people have gone missing. Violet is leading a team to find them, she asks for you to keep your eyes peeled and your ears opened at this time for anything of her people, I will be staying for the time being, if you have no quarrels," he answers.

"You're always welcome here, I will have my warriors on high alert and let our alphas know tonight of the fae plight, we'll find them Rook," I give him a sad smile.

"Thank you, now, would you mind if I steal these two from you, I have much to catch up with them," Rook smiles, clapping Reggie on the back.

"Of course, don't say anything too mean about me Rook," I smirk.

"Wouldn't dream of it Queen Alpha," he bows with a smirk.

Rook takes Cynthia and Reggie with him, leaving Michael and me alone as I hug into his warm embrace.

"I can't believe how fast Taylor ran today… I've never seen her go THAT fast," Michael says into the crook of my neck.

"I know, I don't know how she does it, she's a speed machine," I laugh.

"Must get it off me," Michael winks at me as I giggle.

"Oh, you're a speed machine in a whole other way," I laugh as I move to straddle him.

"I can't wait until you have another baby in this belly," Michael growls lustfully.

"Me too, though I have this feeling two others may announce pregnancy tonight," I say as Michael frowns at me.

"Who?" He says.

"Janie and Bryant, call it mother's intuition," I laugh.

"Taylor will be excited, have you seen how she acts with Hunter and Amelia? She reminds me of you with the kids when they were smaller," he smiles, kissing my lips softly.

"I have. She'll be a great mother one day too, but I don't know how she will feel about it, she needs to explore. I just wish our world was a little better, so we don't have to worry about who is coming at us next. I'm glad she has Corey, but there is a whole world out there," I sigh.

"She loves being here at home, she does things in her own time. I'm sure she will explore as all the kids have, she'll be safe with Corey too, he's a good lad," Michael says.

Someone knocks on the door as I sigh, getting off of Michael's lap with a quick kiss.

"Come in," I call as Michael tucks himself under the table to hide his hard-on as I try not to giggle.

"Phoenix…" Jezebel and Cole are at the door as I look at them in surprise, jumping from my seat, I hug them both, they had gone with Hanson and his pack, Cole standing down from his position as alpha to look after her and their child.

"You came! How are you? How is the little one?" I ask excitedly.

"We're ok Phoenix. Selene is doing great, much happier now she has us both, though she gets a little nervous around big groups," Cole smiles as they take a seat together.

"I'm so glad you're both ok, I was worried I wouldn't see you guys again after everything," I said.

"We weren't sure whether we wanted to come back honestly, to begin with, but we needed to, this is still our home," Jezebel answers.

"I'm glad you did, we all miss you guys, and I can't wait to see Selene again," I smile.

"We were wondering…" Cole murmurs.

"Yeah?" Michael answers.

"Can we come home?" Cole asks.

"Of course you can, this will always be your home, plus I could do with my best technicians back," I smirk.

"At your service my lady," Cole chuckles.

"That's the problem, service issues, our connectivity is abysmal," I groan.

"I'll have it sorted in a few days Phoenix," he smiles.

"Great, now we have to get ready for the party, will Selene be there?" I ask standing.

"Yes, though she will no doubt be attached to our sides," Jezebel answers.

"I'm sure she'll get used to it. In fact, I think I know a couple of kids that might be able to help bring her out of her shell tonight. I'll speak to Taylor to set it up," I smile.

"Taylor… Why Taylor?" Cole raises a brow in question.

"She's quite… Attached to the two kids," I smile.

"Great, well we'll see you both later then," Jezebel smiles hugging me.

"It's good to have you guys back," I reply.

"It's good to be back," she replies as they leave.

"Let's go get ready," Michael takes my hand and leads me out of the room to our bedroom as we get ready for the party tonight.

# Chapter Thirty-One

## Taylor

"Taylor! Taylor! Look! A nice lady found this dress for me to wear!" Amelia giggles as she spins showing off a pretty polka dot dress.

*Isn't that Keeley's?*

**Yeah, it is...**

"COREY!" Hunter leaps up the stairs towards us as he jumps into Corey's arms with a giggle.

"You look gorgeous Amelia, and don't you look handsome Hunter," I grin.

"Who gave you the dress Amelia?" Corey asks. I knew he could see I was looking at it.

"I did," Malina stands there, her arms crossed as she glares at Corey.

"You should have asked first," I say sternly.

"Should I get dressed into something else? I don't want to upset Taylor," Amelia whispers to Corey.

"I'm not upset with you Amelia, I promise. That dress was one of my friend's from when we were younger, how did you even get it, Malina?" I frown, I had barely seen her since we had got back here, I knew most of them kept to themselves. The twins, Tilly and Talia I saw occasionally, they seemed happy enough and waved every time we saw each other.

“I heard some kids being mean about her clothes, so I went rooting about, sorry if that wasn’t ok,” she sighs, but I can still see she’s glaring at Corey.

“That’s fine, but maybe ask next time… Hey kids, how about you go find my uncle Kai, you know who he is right?” I say, turning to the kids.

“Yeah, why?” Amelia frowns.

“Because he always has sweets, tell him I said you could have a treat, our little secret,” I put my finger to my lips as they squeal happily. Corey laughs putting Hunter down as Amelia takes his hand and leads him away quickly as I see them speed off, making sure they were out of earshot.

“What the fuck is your problem?” I growl at Malina.

“Taylor…” Corey murmurs.

“You keep giving my mate a look like you want to burn him at the stake. Tell me now Malina, do I need to worry about you?” I snap.

“He’s a witch, one of those arseholes like Maximillian. They will never be good, it’s in their nature to destroy, you’re putting this whole pack at risk by bringing not only HIM here, but his mother too!” She argues. I growl, storming up to her as she gasps when I get in her face.

“They are not here to hurt this pack, they are not evil, all species have a good and evil, Corey and his Mother Cynthia are not evil! You will not treat them this way or I will make sure you are cast out, understood?” I growl.

“Maybe you should do your research. Cynthia isn’t as innocent as you might think, sure she’s healed your legs, I’m not blind, but there will always be the witch's darkness in there somewhere and when they let that out, I will be right here telling you I told you so, watch your back Taylor," she growls back, pushing me away from her as she storms down the stairs, shifting and barreling through a group of people as they come inside.

"Arggh she is unbelievable," I growl, throwing a punch to the wall as it puts a small dent in it.

"Hey, Taylor, calm down princess, come here," Corey pulls me into his arms before checking my hand quickly. I can feel his unease though.

"What she said about witches being dark… Have you… Has your mother…" I stammer.

"There are some things we've had to do to survive that would be counted as dark magic, yes, but we don't take to it lightly. Taylor, you have to believe me, we won't hurt you or your pack," Corey cups my face as I sigh, nodding.

"I trust you," I murmur as he kisses me softly.

"Now let me fix this before your mother throttles the pair of us," he chuckles, waving a hand over the dent in the wall as it pulls back out and is fixed right in front of my eyes.

"That's cool," I smile.

"You look beautiful in that dress Taylor. I'm having to withhold my wolf from wanting to rip it off you right now," he growls lustfully, his nose nuzzling into my neck.

"Behave, Corey, later," I giggle.

"Yeah, you should put my sister down for a minute man," I hear behind me as I turn, eyes wide. I squeal happily, running at my twin as he laughs hugging me tightly.

"You're here, why are you here?!" I grin happily.

"It's a party… Of course I'm here, plus I had to see my newly mated twin, thanks for that," he groans, rolling his eyes as I blush.

"Sorry Bryant," I giggle.

"Nothing I haven't done to you; now do I need to threaten you as her brother or are we good?" He smirks at Corey.

"No problems with me Bryant, we're good," Corey chuckles as they slap each other's back in a bro-like hug.

"Who else is here? It sounds busy down there," I say as the voices begin to get louder.

"Mum kind of went overboard…" Bryant smirks.

"She invited every pack, didn't she?" I laugh.

"Yep," he nods.

"Hold on, does that mean Janie is back too?" I grin.

"Yeah, she's around somewhere, looking rather… Plump…" He says.

"SHE'S PREGNANT!" I say excitedly.

"Oh, for god's sake Bryant, I thought we were telling your family together!" Amanda smacks his arm as my mouth opens in shock.

"Wait… You're pregnant too?!" I exclaim.

"You weren't talking about me, were you…" Amanda groans.

"No, but now we are! Congratulations! Oh my god, my twin is going to be a daddy! Are you sure this is what you want? I mean he's a kid himself most of the time, he's hardly a grown-up," I wink cheekily, Bryant laughs before getting me in a headlock.

"We'll see about that Taylor," he laughs.

"Do NOT mess up my hair!" I cry out, elbowing him in the stomach as he loosens his grip enough for me to flip him over and he thuds against the stairs.

"Jeez Taylor cut down on the steroids," he groans, rubbing his ass.

"Obviously you need to work out more," I smirk.

"No seriously Taylor, you weren't that strong before," he says as Corey gives him a hand up.

"It's probably their mating bond, you take strength from your mate, depending on how strong Corey is, Taylor could be channelling some of his power," Amanda says.

"Makes sense," Bryant says.

"We'll test that out later, but for now, we have a party to get to," Corey kisses my neck as I struggle not to moan from it.

"Uhh… Taylor… Your legs…" Bryant looks at me in shock as I smile.

"Corey and his mum did it," I grin.

"Wow… You look good twin," he smiles.

"Thanks, not too bad yourself. How did you get him to wear a decent shirt, Amanda?" I smirk as I curl my arm through hers and lead us all down the stairs.

"It took a LOT of persuasion," she winks at me as I laugh.

"I hope you got a good deal out of him," I laugh as we get to the bottom of the stairs, my eyes glaze over the huge number of people who are near the main hall.

"I did, now go on, we're here for a couple of days so go enjoy your party, you two can catch up later," she smiles, pushing me to Corey.

"I'll catch you later twin, I need to find mum and dad, tell them the news," he grins.

"I'm so happy for you," I hug him tightly as he smiles walking away.

I introduce Corey to a few of the other alphas as they greet me happily, some of them I hadn't seen in person since I was a child as we talked about how their packs were doing.

"Taylor! There you are! I've been looking for you everywhere," mum says pushing through the crowd, apologising to some as she walks to our side.

"Queen," the wolves that had been talking to us bow and leave us.

"Have you seen Bryant?" I ask.

"Yes, are you excited to be an aunt?" She grins.

"Unbelievably," I nod happily.

"Listen, I needed to ask for your help, the kids, Hunter and Amelia, I need you all to help me with something," she says, and I raise a brow in question.

"Help with what? What do you need the kids for?" Corey asks.

"Jezebel and Cole are here, their little girl Selene too, but she's shy, she still suffers from when they were imprisoned. I said I would talk to you and see if you could get Amelia and Hunter to help cheer her up and feel more comfortable here," mum says as my eyes go wide.

"They're back?! Of course, we'll find the kids, are they staying permanently?" I ask.

"Yes, they are coming home," she nods.

"Wait… They weren't checked for corruption… We did everyone, but Jezebel and Selene were taken by Maximillian too…" I say as mum's eyes widen.

"Shit," she growls.

"Don't worry, I will talk to my mom, and we will work on checking them immediately. Taylor go find the kids, I'll grab my mother," Corey kisses my cheek.

"Thank you, Corey," I smile as he nods and heads into the crowd.

"So, where could the kids be?" Mum asks as she peers into the crowd.

"Depends… Where is your best friend?" I raise a brow with a smirk.

"Kitchen," we say in unison as we laugh and head towards the kitchens.

"Taylor!" Hunter giggles stuffing his face with cake as mum looks at Kai with a stern glare.

"This was HER idea!" Kai points to me.

"Hey! I said sweets, not fill them with cake!" I laugh.

"Cake is sweet… But you little lady said she told you that I should get you guys cake," Kai smirks, pointing at Amelia as I see her grin cheekily. I love the smile on her face, it was nice to see it after her father had died.

"Oops," she giggles.

"Ok, right, enough cake. Kai help me clean them up please, we need their help," mum says grabbing a cloth and wetting it from the tap as she begins wiping Hunter's cake covered mouth before bopping his nose as he giggles.

"You need our help?" Hunter frowns.

"Yes, there is a cute little girl that is REALLY shy, she needs a friend, I was thinking you guys could help us, could you do that?" I smile, picking up Hunter and putting him on my lap.

"I be a good friend!" He giggles.

"Me too!" Amelia smiles.

"Great," I grin as I put Hunter on my hip.

"Looks good on you," mum smirks at me as I smile, bouncing Hunter on my hip.

"He's super cute, it helps," I laugh as Hunter blushes, hiding his head in my neck.

"Taylor, where are you?" Corey says through our link.

"Kitchen," I answer as I can already smell him nearby as he walks in with his mum and dad by his side.

"Oh, look at you guys! So cute!" Cynthia smiles, pinching Hunter's cheek as he giggles.

"So, anyone want to tell me what's going on?" Kai asks.

"Mum, you explain, do you know where Jezebel and Cole are?" I say.

"Will do, they are with your father, Hanson and Janie by the buffet table," she answers.

“We’ll deal with this and see you in there when you’ve explained what’s going on to uncle clueless,” I smirk as Kai flips me off with a smirk.

“He did a bad thing,” Hunter whispers in my ear.

“He’s a very naughty boy isn’t he, bad uncle Kai,” I poke my tongue out playfully.

“Bite me,” Kai laughs.

“Rather not,” I scrunch my nose up at him.

“Come on, the quicker we do this, the quicker we can enjoy the party,” Cynthia smiles as I nod.

“Surely if they were corrupted, they would have gone feral by now right…” I ask Corey through the link.

“Sometimes it’s slow, better to be safe than sorry, but I would say yes, I feel they will be fine,” he kisses my head as we walk through the crowd to where dad and the others are standing. I pass Hunter over to Corey as we make our way over.

“Oh my god! Look at you, Janie!” I grin as I see her baby bump, hugging her tightly.

“I know! They are growing so quickly. I’ve seen it happen, but it really doesn’t compute until it happens to you,” she giggles. Hanson smiles at me as he continues to talk to dad who gives me a quick cuddle before I face Cole, Jezebel and little Selene.

“It’s great to have you guys back,” I smile as Jezebel hugs me tight.

“How are you?” She asks.

“Getting by day by day, a few teething problems, but I’m working on it,” I say as I see the sadness in her eyes.

“Anger?” She asks.

“Yep,” I answer.

“We can work on it together, I’m the same. Cole has been helping so much,” she says. I look down to the little girl behind her leg, hiding behind them with fear in her eyes.

Cynthia and Reggie are busy talking to them as I bend down carefully, trying not to flash anyone from under my skirt.

“Hi Selene, I’m Taylor,” I wave with a smile.

“Taylor… Is that her?” Hunter taps my shoulder as he peers under my arm.

“Yeah. Hunter, Amelia, this is Selene,” I introduce them as Selene who hides behind her mother's leg further.

“Mummy, too loud,” Selene whispers.

“She’s not too keen on loud noises, perhaps we should leave this room, too many people,” Jezebel says.

“That would be better for us anyway. While we check you guys over, Taylor and the kids can watch over her,” Cynthia nods as Jezebel picks Selene up in her arms. We all make our way out and into a quieter room as Cynthia and Corey have Cole and Jezebel sit down.

Selene is standing behind Jezebel’s legs as Hunter walks forward towards her.

“Hi,” he says waving with an adorable smile and Selene can’t help but wave back with a small smile.

"Selene it's ok, you're safe in here," I smile at her sitting on the floor.

Amelia bites her lip nervously as she looks to me as if she didn't know what to do.

"Selene, come sit with us?" Hunter holds his hand out to her as Amelia sits beside me. I look around for something that might catch her attention as Cynthia is trying to work around them with difficulty.

"Want to see a trick?" I call out as she peeks out further, nodding.

"Come sit with me," Hunter smiles as she walks out from her mother's legs and walks over, she's unsure as he takes her hand softly and leads her over.

"Look," I hear Cole whisper to Jezebel. Selene walks over to us as I place a hand on the ground, feeling for the dirt deep beneath the building.

Amelia shifts over quietly to Selene's side as I smile at the kids, their backs to what was going on behind them. I see Cole grimace at Corey's touch as Cynthia was working with Jezebel who wore a painful expression, holding a hand against her mouth to muffle her cries.

"What's this trick?" Reggie asks as he smiles softly at me, kneeling just behind the kids so if they looked back, they wouldn't see around his huge body.

"Watch," I smile. My hand begins to vibrate as the floor beneath it shakes, a hole opens up as Selene gasps, her eyes wide as she watches.

"What's in the hole?!" Amelia asks as she goes to peer inside.

"How about… A wolf…" I say, pulling the earth up with my powers, making it into the shape of a wolf as it bounds around on the floor, running over the kid's laps as they giggle happily.

"Cole is fine, but Jezebel is corrupted. We have to take her somewhere else away from the kids," Corey says through the link, and I see Jezebel crying behind them.

"Cole, come play with us, we'll distract Selene, so she doesn't notice Jezebel is gone," I say. He nods, kneeling beside Reggie as he tickles Selene, causing her to giggle loudly as they take Jezebel out the room.

"What else! What else!?" Amelia laughs. I notice her eyes peer around as she frowns, looking between them leaving and Selene. She was a smart kid, she moved closer to Selene as they giggle at the earth wolf run around.

"What else should I do?" I ask.

"Tiger!" Amelia grins.

"A tiger… Let's see if I can make a tiger… Can you make a noise like a tiger?" I smile.

"ROAR!" They all shout. I bend the earth to take shape of a tiger as I make its mouth roar with them.

"Whoa!" Hunter says, eyes wide.

Selene's hands were getting a little shaky and I noticed she started to look behind her, Cole intercepted her as he put her into his lap, gulping as he looked at the door.

"She can feel Jezebel…" Cole says in my mind.

"Mummy?" Selene turns in Cole's lap, he tries to stop her, but she slips under his arms.

"Selene…" Cole murmurs.

"Where is my MUMMY?!" She screams as the whole room begins to shake, I can feel her shake the earth, she can use the earth element!

"Selene! Calm down sweetheart," I kneel in front of her, grimacing as I try to calm the earth from taking this whole place down.

"Where is my mummy?!" She screams.

"Selene, she'll be back! Listen to me, you have to breathe, in and out, control your power, you're shaking the whole room sweetheart," I said taking hold of her hands.

"I want my mummy!" She cries.

"She'll be back, she's helping Corey, she'll be back," Hunter says as his hand goes on hers and I feel the earth calm.

"Reggie, could go check everyone else is ok?" I ask.

"Will do," he nods, heading out of the room quickly.

"Selene…" Cole murmurs. He looks at me in shock as I grimace, I can feel her power, she was going to have a strong earth element.

"Are you an earth bender like Taylor?" Amelia asks.

Selene just nods and I feel her slowly beginning to calm down.

"Can you make the tiger move?" I ask her. She shakes her head, face filled with tears.

"I bet you can!" Hunter grins, wiping away her tears with his sleeve as my heart melts.

"Selene, try this with me a second, give me your hand," I say as she whimpers walking over to me and she places her hand in mine.

"Nearly finished Taylor," Corey pushes through my mind as I sigh with relief.

Reggie comes into the room, his brows furrowed as I raise a brow.

"They didn't feel a thing… No one knew the ground shook," he says in my head.

"Selene, close your eyes and think of the tiger, imagine it leaping around, concentrate on the ground, make it move for you," I say as she frowns, her hands shaking. My eyes widen at more earth coming from the hole as the tiger gets bigger and bigger.

"That's big enough Selene!" Cole exclaims.

"Selene! LOOK!" Hunter laughs at the tiger that was almost as big as him.

"I did it!" Selene grins, jumping up and down.

"Oh my," Cynthia walks in with Jezebel behind her who looks pale and tired.

"Mummy! Look! Look what I did!" Selene jumps up and down as she pulls on Jezebel's arm.

"Wow baby," Jezebel whispers, I could see she was exhausted.

"Will she be ok?" I ask Corey through the link.

"Yeah, she just needs rest, it was deep, but we got it," he replies as I sigh with relief.

"Mummy, I made a HUGE tiger!" Selene giggles.

"Ok, Selene do you want to help me put it all back in the ground where it belongs?" I ask.

"YES!" She grins, coming back over to me as Jezebel snuggles into Cole's arms.

"Close your eyes, concentrate," I say. She sits in my lap, her hand in mine as the earth begins to fall into the hole before I seal the whole thing up.

"THAT'S SO COOL!" Amelia grins.

"Ok, I think that's enough earth for today, Selene. Mummy needs to rest. Are you coming with us, or do you want to stay with your new friends?" Cole asks, kneeling beside his daughter as she frowns, looking between the kids and her mum.

"They're my friends?" She says.

"YES!" Amelia and Hunter grin.

"You guys can stay with me if you like, we can take you to see mummy and daddy whenever you want," I tell her.

"I want to stay with mummy, can we play tomorrow?" Selene whispers.

"Yes! We can show you all the best hiding places, me and you can hide, Amelia finds us!" Hunter claps.

"I'd like that," Selene smiles at him.

"Well then, come on sweetie, let's get mummy into bed as she's tired, I will read you a story," Cole says picking her up.

"Wait!" Hunter shouts as he stands in front of me, his arms up as I frown, picking him up.

"What do you want to do?" I smile.

"Go to Selene," he whispers in my ear. I nod, walking to Cole, putting Hunter next to Selene as he leans over and kisses her on the cheek.

"Night night Selene," he smiles, blushing as my heart melts once more. These two were so cute! She might be a little older than him at six, but they were made for each other.

*Like Keeley and Blake?*

**Kind of, I just hope they have a better end.**

"Good night, guys" I smile at them.

# Chapter Thirty-Two

## Taylor

“Thank you guys, you did a great job,” I smile at Hunter and Amelia.

“I wanted her to stay and play,” Hunter pouts.

“I know, but she’s shy, she’ll play tomorrow, but you need to take care of her, ok?” I say, cupping his cheek.

“I will,” he nods, hugging me around my neck as I cuddle him to my chest.

“I need a drink, let’s get back to the party, shall we?” Cynthia says as she walks with Reggie out of the room. Hunter drags Amelia with him, leaving Corey and me alone.

“Well… That went well,” I breathe deeply as I drop into a chair.

“Dad said you had an earthquake in here… Is she that powerful?”

“Perhaps more powerful than me with training, the whole room shook as she screamed, I thought she would bring down the whole house. I don’t understand how no one else felt it,” I reply.

“Are you sure she’s Cole’s?” He asks.

“What are you trying to say?” I frown.

“What if Maximillian did something to Jezebel? Altered the DNA, he could have done it, she may have started as Coles’ but if he altered it… She could be half-witch,” he replies.

“Can we find out?” I ask, my hand running through my hair nervously.

“I will talk with mom later. Selene seems ok, we’ll keep an eye on her for now, if she is half-witch then I’ll train her myself, make sure the darkness doesn’t creep into her mind,” he says.

“What if that… That was the darkness inside her?” I murmur.

“We’ll help her, I swear,” he says cupping my face, his thumb stroking my cheek.

“Things get better and better,” I sigh.

“Everything will be ok,” he kisses me softly.

“I-I need a minute alone, go find your parents and mingle, I’ll be back,” I kiss his cheek and head out of the room quickly, surging past everyone as I make my way outside, taking a deep breath as the door shuts behind me.

*Nothing is ever easy…She’ll be ok though, Selene will be fine, we’ve got this.*

**I hope so.**

It had been a few days since the party and everyone was still here, but most were planning to head home in a few more days. The halls were always busy and I was trying my best to keep a cool head, but I kept seeing Malina skulking around and it unnerved me.

Corey was helping with Violet's issue; mum had heard that she was having more and more fae go missing and she was begging for help. The packs began to go on hunts further away so they could scope out new areas. Cynthia had managed to help give them directions at least, when her magic was able, it wasn't an exact science sometimes… Several of Violet's fae were in the medical wing healing before they would be escorted home with a team of wolves to help with the perimeter.

I had been busy all day helping the kids play as Selene was still shy, but she was getting better. I had left them with Jezebel, needing a break as she had smiled at me with a knowing look. She was happier to be home now, and you could tell Cole was too.

"I'm telling you; we have to get him out of there, we need to leave. I'm a wolf and I hate this place, they want to play happy families, but where is the revenge? Witches are here, they will succumb to the darkness and kill us all, they will bring forward a horde of vampires with them and we will be pushed into the dirt!" I hear as I frown, creeping around the corner as I spot Malina with two other wolves and two humans, one wolf was imprisoned with us, the other I recognised as one of dad's old recruits, the two humans I remember from in the house with the guy who had been beating the kids.

"It's busy most of the day, we could probably get in and out without them realising," the wolf says.

"Dad, we have a problem," I link to him, focusing on our bond, letting him see through my eyes.

"I recognise them, stay put, keep listening," he replies.

The second wolf tilts his head, I hear footsteps behind me as I turn quickly noticing it's Jae and I slam a hand on his mouth.

"Did you hear that?" Malina calls.

"Move now!" I mouth as Jae nods, and we rush towards the doors.

"What the hell was that?" He says.

"A problem, a huge problem," I say. Hearing the door being pushed open, I lean against the wall casually as I begin talking about the kids with a huge smile on my face to make it look like we had been there the whole time.

"Dad, they are on their way in," I link to him.

"I have extra guards on the cells. Cynthia and Corey are beside me; they know what's going on, I don't know where your mother is though…" He replies.

"Bryant, do you know where mum is?" I ask through our link.

"Haven't seen her for the last half an hour, why what's going on?" He asks quickly.

"Get Amanda and go to dad now," I reply.

"Oh, hi guys," Malina smiles. She hooks an arm around the second wolf, giving him a passionate kiss before giggling and walking off.

"Jae, I need you to get Kai and find mum, now," I whisper as he nods.

"What about you?" He asks.

"Malina's mine," I growl.

"Be careful," he says flitting off.

The hallways were busy as normal. Wolves, fae, vampires and humans mixing as they chat happily.

I follow Malina and her little friend as they head upstairs, her friend keeps twitching weirdly and I frown.

*That's weird... What if he's corrupted?*

"Corey, did you check EVERY prisoner from Maximillian's?" I ask.

"Yes, I believe so... Why..." He asks.

"Look," I push the image through our link.

"I've never met that wolf before Taylor, are you sure he was there?" He asks.

I think back and I remember him clearly, he was always near Malina.

"He was there, I remember, but I haven't seen him since..." I answer.

"Kai and Jae have your mother. She's safe, the two humans are being watched, they are outside trying to cause mischief, throwing bottles like drunks," dad says to me.

"They are trying to distract us... Malina's up to something," I say as I speed up the stairs, having realised I had lost sight of them.

"Shit," I say out loud as I sniff the air.

"How cute... It's such a shame we couldn't get to the Queen... This will have to do. Take her. Run," I hear Malina whisper. I walk briskly towards them, noticing they were in Luci and Kade's room.

"Where are Luci and Kade?" I ask dad as I can't smell them up here.

"Kade brought her down for a moment, they left David with the baby," dad replies as the door opens and the second wolf comes out, blood covering him as he holds a bundle.

"Just give me the baby, Malina, wait…" the wolf growls as he comes out of the door.

"I'd think very carefully before you make your next move," I growl.

"I could say the same for you, Taylor. I hold Annabelle, all it would take is one big squeeze and her guts would be all over the floor, now you wouldn't want that to happen, would you?" She laughs as she steps forward.

"Give me the baby and you can go," I growl.

"No, I don't think I will. Jered, do me a favour, kill the little princess," Malina kisses his cheek with a smirk and Jered shifts, snarling at me.

"Here pup," I pat my leg as I growl, claws out ready for his attack.

"There's no need to fight guys. Taylor, let them go, now," I whirl around to see Lewis with a huge smile and the kids in his hands as the human from the cells was beside him holding Amelia, blood all over him.

"I hope you're watching this still dad," I mutter through the link. "I knew you were trouble," I growl at Lewis as Jered grabs me by the neck hard.

"Your mother is too soft; I WAS trying to kill her. I would have succeeded too if it weren't for you, but look at us now, you WILL die, and I'll take the kids. We'll destroy your world and create a new one of people who aren't afraid to get their hands dirty, like Corvin here," he smirks, pointing to the human man who had beat the girls. He was stroking Amelia's hair, his hand touching her a little too much for my liking as my chest vibrates with a protective growl.

"You want someone who gets their hands dirty? How's this? Close your eyes kids!" I growl. I throw my head back against Jered's, he lets go of my neck as I punch my fist through his throat, grabbing at his spine, my feet pinning his down as I feel every single bone pop out of place, pulling it from his back as he tries to scream before he dies. Blood covering me completely as I throw it to the floor, teeth bared angrily.

"Well done, Taylor, I have to say I'm impressed, what do you think Malina? Can we keep her?" Lewis laughs as I hear a growl behind me.

"You killed my mate!" She snarls, rage filling her eyes.

"Put the kid down and fight me like a real wolf," I growl as she screams out, she drops Annabelle to the ground, I gasp, she screams, still alive as Malina runs towards me.

"Hold them," Lewis says behind me.

"Two of you at once, fine, come on then!" I growl. I don't even shift, I stay human but keep my claws out, teeth bared as they both come for me.

I hear shots come from a gun nearby and I feel the pain of someone I love being shot, whining as I duck from Malina's attack, I slice at her belly as she shifts, bowling into the kids and Corvin.

"Kids! RUN! HIDE!" I shout. I notice Lewis going for them, I bite his arm and he slashes at my face causing me to howl.

"Hunter come on!" Amelia screams.

"Annabelle!" Hunter shouts. He runs past me again as Lewis slams me against the wall, smacking my head against it hard, dazing me for a second as I see him go for the kids again.

I leap onto Lewis's back as he claws at my arms.

"GO!" I shout to the kids as they run off down the corridor and I see Malina is finally getting up.

"Little help would be nice!" I howl to my dad.

"Having trouble contacting daddy, are we?" Malina laughs.

Lewis throws me off of his shoulder as he slams me into a wall, I gasp in pain from my side.

"Get up idiot," Malina kicks Corvin as he groans.

"Shame we have to kill you, baby girl, you would have been fun," Lewis smirks at me as his eyes flash red, licking the base of my throat of blood. I growl at him.

I see Cole and my brother up ahead; they signal for me to stay quiet and not look.

"We're still having fun arsehole, I'm not dead yet."

"Corvin! Get the kids!" Malina slaps the guy as he goes to smack her back but backs off and goes running in the direction of the kids, the complete opposite direction of Bryant and Cole.

I try to get to him, but Lewis has other ideas as he grabs my arm, snapping the bone and I scream out in agony.

"TAYLOR!" I hear a series of roars come from downstairs.

"Can we hurry this up? Lewis just kill her, I'll get the kids myself," Malina storms past as Lewis holds me by the throat, nails digging into my throat.

"Kill me then, I dare you," I spit in his face as he gets angrier, he pulls back his other hand and I smirk.

My brother whistles behind him as Lewis looks behind him.

"Night night arsehole," Bryant growls, snapping his neck.

I rub my throat, nodding at my twin before I just run, ignoring the pain of my broken arm and I sniff out the kids.

“Here little ones, come to aunt Malina. We won’t hurt you; we will keep you safe, I promise,” I hear her call up ahead.

“She’s way off. Bryant go that way, Blake’s favourite spot,” I point as he nods rushing off for the kids.

“They’ve messed with the wrong people, you ready?” Cole asks as he puts a hand over my mouth, pulling at my arm as I feel it pop, trying not to scream in pain.

“Arsehole…” I growl in my mind, but nod in thanks as we stalk forward.

I signal for him to stay put as I walk out into the room they were in.

“Looking for someone to play with, try someone your own age,” I growl.

“How the fuck did you survive? If you need a job done, do it yourself,” Malina growls.

“Malina, look at what I have,” Corvin grins, pulling Amelia from a cubby hole.

“Amelia…” I gasp.

“Where are the others?” Corvin snaps.

“Bryant, tell me you have Hunter and Annabelle…” I ask through the link.

“I have them, but no Amelia…” He answers.

“She’s here…” I answer as I growl at Malina.

“Put the girl down,” I demand.

"I don't think so, I've taken a liking to her, she's pretty," Corvin says, his hands hold her against him as she cries, screaming to be let go.

"First, you're going to die for even touching her and you are going to die slowly," I point to Corvin first and then Malina.

"Try your best sweetheart, we have more people on our side, they'll keep coming," Malina smirks.

Suddenly I hear a gun go off, I hear Cole yelp before falling to the floor, looking at him in shock as several of the humans we had saved step forward with guns.

"Ready to go miss," they smirk.

"Bring the girl Corvin," Malina smirks.

"I'll take care of her, I promise," he winks at me as I snarl at him.

"We've got to go now!" A male shouts as gunshots begin to ring in my ears.

Malina runs for it, dragging Corvin behind her as her army of humans follows her quickly.

"AMELIA!" I roar as I shift, nudging Cole as he whimpers on the ground.

"GO! Get her back!" He urges. I nod leaping towards the humans that were shooting at any wolf that dared go near them.

A warrior went down beside me as I darted between the bullets, using the earth to knock as many as I could from hitting anyone.

My fur was still soaked in blood as my feet pounded against the ground, I was joined by a series of wolves as I saw Malina shift, throwing Corvin and Amelia on her back.

"Kill them all!" I howl as we lept into the group of humans, tearing them apart while they tried to shoot at us.

I saw Bryant come into the fray, swinging his flaming sword as it melted a gun in two as he searched for me.

"GO! Save Amelia! I've got this!" He shouts as I nod, leaping out from the battle. I begin running through the forest as fast as I could, dodging every tree and branch before I hear them.

They've stopped, pausing for breath as I keep myself low, stalking them like a predator. I am a predator.

"You're going to get us killed Malina, my men are dying out there! We didn't stand a chance!" Corvin shouts at her.

"Oh, shut up and get on with whatever you're doing with the kid, we said we'd wait for the others here," she snaps as I see them. Amelia is on the ground, body shaking with fear, and I have to stop Lily from growling.

"Fine, they better hurry up or we're dead," he snaps as he walks towards Amelia.

"The pack are too busy with the humans, they won't notice the coven hitting them from behind," she laughs, and my eyes widen.

"Coven incoming from the rear!" I roar in my mind to every pack member I could push it too.

"I've got the rear, Bryant stay up front, Hanson flank left, Kade flank right!" I hear mum order through the bond as she controls the situation from home.

"Taylor! Where are you?!" Corey says in a panic in my mind.

"Look after my family, I have something to deal with, I love you," I say praying I wasn't over my head with this.

"You might as well have led us all to the slaughter Malina," Corvin snaps as Amelia screams, he picks her up and throws her over his shoulder.

"What are you doing?" Malina snaps.

"I am not playing with her in front of you," he says as he begins to walk away from her, and I bare my teeth in anger.

*He's not playing with her at all.*

I stalk around to where he's heading, seeing a large rock that he's placed her on as I stalk around behind it.

"Now, this will only hurt a little sweetheart, you'll enjoy it soon," he laughs as I hear his belt buckle.

"HELP! NO!" Amelia screams her hits on him barely affecting him. I leap over the rock and pounce on Corvin, ripping into his stomach as I tear him apart while he screams in agony.

"What the fuck… Corvin?!" Malina shouts as I hear her coming this way.

I turn to face her, Amelia behind me as I guard her with my body, dripping with fresh blood.

"T-Ta-Taylor?" Amelia cries as I turn, nodding at her as she cries, shaking like a leaf.

I hear a snap to my left as my ears perk to the noise.

"Amelia, do you hear me?" I say, trying to push a link with her as I knew we could do, but I had never tried with a human before…

“What… Was that you?” She says, eyes wide.

“Yes, get on my back, close your eyes and hold on tight, can you do that for me?” I say, I feel her climb onto me as she slips slightly on the blood with a scream before finding a patch of fur to cling to.

“Taylor… This is blood right…” She says shakily.

“Yes, I need you to be brave and hold on, can you do that?” I gulp, hearing footsteps coming to my left, they were fast… Vampires. I could hear Malina wandering about too.

“Yes,” Amelia nods.

“Good, hold on sweetheart,” I say, lowering myself to the ground. I spot Malina as she glares at me, shifting as she comes for us.

# Chapter Thirty-Three

## Phoenix

I couldn't believe what was happening, we were being attacked, Taylor was somewhere out there fighting, I could feel her, she was in pain.

Gunshots began to boom in the mansion, humans came in fully stocked with weapons that looked to be stolen from our armoury as warriors began to fight back.

"Michael! Duck!" I scream as one aims at him in the hall, I see him go down, eyes wide as I shift, howling for everyone to get to the mansion to defend it.

It was then that I saw Taylor rushing after the humans as the wolves rallied to her.

"Come on Phoenix, we'll get him in there," Cynthia rushes to my side as we drag Michael into the nearest office, and she begins to hover her hands over him.

"Coven incoming from the rear!" Taylor roars in my mind as my eyes widen.

"Oh shit… I have to go, we're under attack, can you save him?" I ask with tears in my eyes.

"I'll do what I can Phoenix, I'll keep him safe, go," Cynthia says as I kiss Michael's lips before darting out of the office.

"Prepare for battle! I've got the rear, Bryant stay up front, Hanson flank left, Kade flank right!" I order.

"On it!" Bryant answers. I shift heading towards the back of the mansion, seeing the oncoming vampires heading our way.

"Thought you could do with some backup!" Reggie runs beside me.

"Thank you," I nod as his wolves help in defending our home, vampire after vampire coming at us.

"MUM!" I hear Janie scream as a vampire has her trapped, I see Reggie bound over to her, knocking them flying as he frees her.

He stays by her side; I continue taking down vampires as the numbers begin to decrease and they begin to retreat.

"TAYLOR!" I hear Corey roar into the air.

"We've got this, go!" Reggie says, batting away another as I nod, my feet pounding against the ground as I run through the house without a care for the furniture, feeling that my daughter was in trouble.

"Corey, move it," I growl beside him as he and Bryant both join me, we dart through the trees, and I hear more rushed footsteps.

"Don't forget us," Jae says, flitting to our side with Kai, Trey and another team of warriors. Rook is flying in the sky, bow poised as he begins to shoot towards the ground in front of us as we see Taylor in the centre of a whole coven of vampires, Malina facing off with her.

"Not my fucking daughter!" I howl, the vampires turn in shock as Malina goes for Taylor and the battle begins.

I can hear Taylor's snarl as she and Malina are fighting, Amelia is hanging on for dear life on her back as she cries. Taylor trying not to crush her.

"Rook! Get Amelia!" I howl as he nods swooping down, he snatches her up off of Taylor's back with a scream and then Malina bats Taylor while she's distracted, sending her flying into a rock.

Taylor howls, I feel the ground shakes as half the vampires sink into the ground making it easier as Taylor falters in her steps.

"NO!" I howl as I fight to get to her.

"YOU WILL DIE!" Malina howls, slicing at Taylor bit by bit. I feel it bite into my very soul as I can't get to her, fighting and fighting.

Taylor howls suddenly once more as she shifts.

"Come on! Fight fair! Fight as though you were human!" Taylor laughs and I see her get up unsteadily, arms open wide.

"Taylor! NO!" Corey howls as their eyes meet.

Malina shakes her head, I can almost see her laugh even as a wolf. I growl, snapping at the vampire that tries to snap my neck as Bryant pounces onto it, we all try to get closer.

Malina pounces and it's like time slows down. I hear Taylor scream as Malina bites into her neck, blood spurting everywhere.

"NO!" I howl as I feel her pain. More of the pack end up running to our aid as we take down every vampire before Corey can get to Taylor and Malina.

"Taylor!" Corey shouts. He grabs Malina by the scruff as he throws her, what I didn't expect was for her chest to be open wide, her heart gone as I look at Taylor, she's soaked in blood, heart in her hands as she breathes heavily.

"She really was a heartless bitch," Taylor says with a small laugh and Corey lifts her into his arms as I shift.

“Taylor, are you ok? Jesus, I can’t tell what’s your blood and what’s hers,” I say in a panic, sliding my hand over her face to rid some of the blood from it.

“Honestly, I think some is Lewis’s too, not to mention Jered’s…” She grimaces. I feel a pang in my chest as I turn back.

“Mum…What happened to dad?” She asks, her eyes wide.

“MUM! We need to get back!” Bryant shouts.

“Have you got her?” I ask Corey.

“Always,” he answers as he begins running with her.

“Amelia?” She asks.

“With Rook,” he answers while I shift and run towards home.

Bodies were everywhere, a mixture of human, wolves and vampires. I felt the pain of loss in my chest as Bryant ran ahead of me. He shifted, running towards the office where Michael was with Cynthia.

“DAD!” He shouts as my heart burns, I see Cynthia frowning as her hands shake.

“I don’t know what was in these bullets, but they are resisting me,” she says.

“The chains… We made bullets against witches… They must have used them so we couldn’t use Cynthia to save them!” Bryant says.

Corey walks up to us, Taylor groans, jumping out of his arms and Cynthia looks at her in shock.

“Sorry about this dad,” Taylor says, extending her claws and pushing her hand into his wound and he wakes up screaming.

"Hold him down!" Cynthia tells Bryant as I watch them pin him, Taylor digging into his flesh as she screams out.

"Taylor! What are you doing?!" I cry as Corey holds me back.

"She's on the right track, wait," Cynthia holds up a finger and Taylor pulls out a bullet.

"Now Cynthia," Taylor exclaims. Cynthia hovers her hand over him as he begins to calm and passes out again.

Michael lets out a long breath before I feel agony go through my heart as Bryant and Taylor cry, looking at each other.

# Chapter Thirty-Four

## Taylor

Dad's heart gave out as I looked at my brother and Cynthia in a panic.

"I don't have any energy left to bring him back," Cynthia says with sadness in her eyes as if trying to work out what to do.

"Twins are powerful energy sources, right?" I ask as she nods.

"Use us," Bryant grabs my hand and I hold mine out to Cynthia.

"Taylor, this could kill you, you've already got so little energy," she says.

"I don't care, bring my dad back," I gulp as I look at my twin.

"I've got you," he nods. I close my eyes, lip quivering as Cynthia takes my hand.

"I love you all," I whisper. I feel Cynthia draw power from us as Bryant begins to cry out in pain before it hits me, an unimaginable intense pain as I scream.

"MOM NO!" Corey shouts, she flicks her hand up, holding both him and our mum back as I open my eyes and look at them.

"Siblings do things together!" Janie bursts into the room, seemingly getting past the barrier as she places her hand onto mine before screaming out too. Dad takes a sudden breath and I feel Cynthia's power leave us as I collapse to the floor.

"Taylor! Baby, come on, open your eyes. Taylor, please, come on, open them! Taylor, don't you dare leave me!" I hear Corey shout as I feel his hand tap my face.

"P-Pho-Phoenix," I hear dad stammer and I feel the relief that he was alive.

"Get the wolves that have been shot brought in, have the bullets removed by hand!" Bryant shouts out.

"Taylor, can you hear me, sweetheart? Corey lay her down, someone get me some water!" Cynthia shouts the order.

"Cynthia, tell me my daughter isn't going to die," I hear mum cry.

"You'd be lucky…" I whisper, forcing my eyes open finally, groaning at the pain flooding my body.

"Taylor!" They all shout as I groan, head resting on Corey's chest.

"Janie, you're a fucking idiot…" I grumble as I see her looking panicked at the door, looking worse for wear.

"Siblings," she says with a sad smile, holding her stomach.

*You don't think she lost it, do you…*

**I don't know, she'll say when she's ready…**

"Janie, go get checked out by medical," mum orders sternly as she nods and runs off.

"Go, help them," I push Corey away. He looks at me, shaking his head.

"No, I'm not leaving you," he says.

"GO! Help our people, please, find the kids, check them," I push him again, groaning.

"Oh my god! She wasn't kidding!" Evie walks in, a slash across her cheek as she runs in with cloth and water as she stands beside me.

"GO!" I growl at Corey.

"You stay put, understood?" he says.

"Just go idiot," I laugh. I hiss with pain as Evie begins to help clean me up.

"Phoenix, you too, our people need you," dad says as I see him looking at her with adoration.
"You stay alive, understand? No more trying to die on me," mum cries, kissing him softly.

"I don't think the twins would let me," he chuckles groaning in pain.

"Not on my life dad," I smile holding my hand out as he holds it tightly in his.

After a while, I hear cries of pain outside as Evie has me sit up.

"You shouldn't have done it," dad says.

"Done what?" I hiss as Evie looks at me sheepishly.

"Saved me, you could have died," he growls.

"And leave us without a father and mum without a mate, we can't live without you dad. Ok Evie, that's enough, I need a shower, not a wash down by that bowl," I growl as she sighs, nodding.

I get off of the table with a groan, testing my weight on my legs as they still feel a little wobbly.

"For god's sake," dad growls as he sits up too.

"Guys! What are you doing?!" Evie exclaims.

"Going to our family, they need us," I answer, and dad shakes his head at me.

"Why must you be so much like me and your mother?" He laughs as he wraps an arm around my waist.

"They are going to kill me," Evie groans.

"Don't worry, it's two against one," I roll my eyes.

"Fine, I need to find Trey… Wait… Taylor… I can't feel him…" She says, her eyes widen as I look at my dad.

"Trey?!" I call out through the links, searching for his.

"NO!" Evie screams as she runs out of the room.

Dad and I make our way out as we see warriors being patched up.

"NO! TREY!" I hear Evie scream; I wince but run towards her ignoring my pain as dad tries to keep up.

Luci is sobbing beside her brother as Evie screams next to his face, pale and cold.

"No… Trey…" I cry as I kneel beside Evie, putting a hand on her shoulder.

I can see mum up ahead, she moves through warrior after warrior before her eyes land on Trey too, eyes glistening with tears at her lost friend.

"Luci!" Kade booms as he scoops her up, his body covered in deep lacerations, and she sobs in his arms.

Evie shoves my hand off as she lays on Trey's chest sobbing, and I get back on my feet looking all-around at the devastation around us.

My hands shake as I feel like I'm going to be sick, I go to the corner of the building, puking my guts up as I cry.

"That's it, bring it up, oh baby girl, it's ok, I've got you," dad rubs my back as I sob, falling to my knees as I scream out in pain, the very ground beneath my feet shaking like when Selene had done it.

I look at my arms, the blood drying on my skin as I scratch at it.

"Stop! Stop Taylor, come on, let's get you in the shower," dad pulls me up with a grunt of pain, leading me into the building and up the stairs. I see the blood-soaked corridor, Jered still on the ground, his spine on the floor.

"That's just crazy, do you see this? She ripped his spine out! That's fucking cool!" A warrior exclaims.

"Boys," dad growls, they look up in shock before rushing to get back to work as dad leads me to my room, turning the shower on for me.

"Michael, I've got this, be with your mate," I hear outside before I feel Corey's hands on my body, stripping my clothes as he pulls me into the shower, grabbing the shower head and he washes away the blood from my body, not saying a word.

I stand there, crying as he finishes before he pulls me into his arms, letting me sob into his chest.

"I've got you," he says, holding me tight.

I can feel Janie's pain, my thoughts confirmed she'd lost her baby.

Corey lifts me out of the shower as he dries me off, grabbing me some new clothes as I put them on, numb to the bone.

"Taylor, princess… Look at me, please," Corey says quietly, turning my head towards him as I look into his eyes.

"I-I-I tried, I tried to warn everyone in time, but it didn't help, they still died…" I cry as he hugs me into his chest.

"You were so brave, you got the kids back, they are safe now because of you. You did everything you could, there were so many of them, it wouldn't have mattered if we were double in numbers, people would have died or gotten hurt, you can't save everyone, death is part of life and we live in a scary world right now, but you, you did everything you could. You even risked your life to save your father, you are beautiful, brave and the strongest woman I have ever known, I love you, Taylor, so much," he says, kissing my lips softly as I cry in his arms.

"The kids…" I murmur.

"They are with Jezebel," he says.

"COLE!" I exclaim.

"He's alive in medical, he's fine," he caresses my cheek.

My hands shake as my heart hurts within my chest, I take his hand in mine and walk out of my room slowly, lip quivering again before I take a breath and stop it quickly.

I walk down the stairs, people are clearing up the mess of the battle, bodies are being sorted, our people moved separately so we can give them a proper goodbye as the ones that attacked are thrown harshly around.

"Taylor, perhaps we shouldn't be down here," Corey says.

"No, I need to be, I'm helping," I say, letting go of his hand. I see a huge pile of dead vampires and I notice them keep adding to the pile. I wave my hand over the earth, groaning as they suddenly dropped down through the deep hole.

"Nice," a warrior nods at me.

"Add a little fire," Bryant clicks his fingers, setting them alight from deep in the ground.

"Twin," I sigh as he hugs me tightly.

"We lost a few good people today, but you helped save a lot more. Without your warning it would have been a slaughter, I know you blame yourself, but don't, we couldn't have done anything else. We will remember them all as they join the others with the goddess as they watch over us. Don't let the grief take over your heart, you still have family here, friends, we're here beside you," Bryant says, cupping my face.

"It's so fucked up," I cry.

"I know," he sighs hugging me.

"Amanda… Where is she?" I ask.

"She's with Hanson, consoling him and Janie," he says sadly.

"Who else did we lose?" I ask.

"David, about twelve warriors, we haven't found Kai yet… Jae is frantic…" He says.

"YOU WHAT? What the fuck are we doing then?!" I growl as I shift, shaking out my fur before sniffing the air as I dart towards where mum had sent him.

"KAI!" I howl out as I search through the bodies.

Sniffing the air I catch a whiff of his scent, my senses zero in on it, darting into the trees as I howl for Corey and Bryant, they follow close behind.

"Taylor, there!" Bryant nods towards our left as we turn sharply towards the body on the ground.

"No, not you too Uncle Kai, come on!" I shift. Noticing a branch in his chest pulling it out in one swift movement, I hear him gasp in a breath, blood once again over my arm.

"Took your time," Kai coughs out blood.

"He's not healing," Corey states.

"Kai, you need blood," Bryant says.

"Go get some then!" I shout.

"We don't have time, he needs it now," Corey replies.

"God damn it, Kai, you owe me," I bite into my wrist, watching it bleed, putting it against his mouth as his eyes go bright and he latches on to it as I hiss in pain.

"Not too much! You've done enough risking your life today! Kai! You're done! KAI!" Corey says as Kai keeps on sucking the blood from my wrist.

"KAI!" Bryant yanks my wrist from him, I cry out in pain as it rips the skin away too, Corey rips a bit of his shirt, and he wraps it around my wrist.

"Taylor… Oh no… I'm so sorry!" Kai says in a panic.

"It's ok," I reply, groaning.

"Let's get you both back," Bryant growls at Uncle Kai as he looks at me sadly.

"Shit…" Kai murmurs, looking around as we get closer.

“Not the half of it,” Bryant murmurs.

“Who died…” Kai asks, looking between us.

“Trey…” I whisper as his eyes go wide and he flits away.

“Let’s get you stitched up,” Corey says.

“I don’t need stitches, it will heal,” I roll my eyes.

“Stubborn,” both of them say in unison before shaking their heads.

“I don’t like this whole ganging up on me thing,” I point between them.

“Let’s just get inside, mum will need us,” Bryant says, pulling me along with him.

“I’m surprised you haven’t asked to see the kids yet,” Corey says as I help an injured warrior to his feet, putting his arm around me.

“Thank you,” he mutters quietly as he groans.

“I doubt they want to see me, not after what they saw me do,” I sigh, shaking my head.

“Actually, Amelia is begging to see you, they all are. Hunter is frantic, he wants to make sure his favourite girl is ok,” Corey says with a soft smile.

“Those kids have taken a liking to you Taylor, no idea why, you’re fucking weird,” Bryant smirks at me and I growl playfully at him, setting the warrior on a chair inside as a healer rushes forward to help.

“They saw me rip a wolf’s spine out. I told them to close their eyes, but I know they didn’t. How will they get over that? How will Amelia get over Corvin touching her and Malina trying to take them with Lewis?” I sigh.

"I should have got to you sooner, then I could have got to them, you wouldn't have had to do that," Bryant grumbles.

"It's not your fault Bryant, our family seems to attract trouble, I just wish we didn't have to lose so many of our loved ones in this god damned corrupted extinction," I growl.

"Young lady come here," I hear a deep voice say. I turn to Reggie as he stands beside his mate.

I walk to them; he tilts my head up before kneeling in front of me as I frown.

"What are you doing dad?" Corey frowns.

"I Reginald, Alpha of the Rebel Pack would like to announce you, Taylor, as my beta. I've never seen a wolf fight so hard, be powerful, just and downright badarse as the young ones say. I would be proud to have you by my side and pledge to help you in every endeavour, including if you wish to finish this… Corrupted extinction… Is that what you said?" He smiles and I stare at him in shock.

"Beta… You want me… To be beta… Surely that should be Corey… I… Shit… Yes, corrupted extinction, they tried to corrupt our people to fuel their plans and yet we're corrupting their plan, we're taking the covens down and anyone else who wants to wipe out the races…" I say.

"Taylor, you're babbling," Bryant chuckles as I gulp.

"Corey will be Alpha one day, but yes, he is also my beta, there are two of you, should you accept," Reggie says.

"Can I do that… What about mum?" I look back at my brother.

“My understanding would be that you will still be linked to both packs, of equal standings as you are the child of a Queen,” Cynthia says.

“Just accept it!” Bryant says.

“I accept the role as a beta for the Rebel Pack,” I smile, feeling a huge ping in my heart as I join their pack, power surging inside me.

“Whoa…” Bryant says as I turn to him.

“What?” I ask.

“Taylor… Lift your top…” Corey says, I frown looking down as I see a sliver of my stomach covered in an image as I lift my top and gasp. The witches mating mark had expanded across my stomach and up my side, a mixture of my mother’s vines and bolts of electricity.

“Holy shit!” I exclaim.

“You get more beautiful by the second,” Corey walks up to me, kissing me as he lifts his sleeve to show me a tattoo of a bolt with his packs name.

“Well, we will need to talk soon, but go be with your family,” Reggie smiles, hugging me.

“Welcome to the family,” Cynthia grins, hugging me before walking off with Reggie as they help the warriors.

“Hunter! I said no!” I hear a shout; my head turns quickly to the stairs where Hunter is running as fast as his feet can carry him.

“No, he doesn’t need to see all this,” I say before rushing to the stairs as his eyes widen at the sight of me, I pick him up quickly.

“Taylor!” He exclaims, hugging me tightly.

"Hunter keep your head against me," I say, running up the stairs quickly to my room as I close the door behind me and sit him on the bed. I kneel in front of him as he leaps forward into my arms and doesn't show any signs of letting up.

"I got Annabelle," he mumbles into my shoulder.

"I know, you were so brave, do you know that? I'm proud of you, your mummy and daddy are proud too, I know they are," I cup his face gently in my hands, his eyes begin to water before I pull him back into my chest hugging him tightly, kissing his head as I pull him into my lap properly, rocking him back and forth as he cries.

"Shhh, it's ok, I'm here," I coo.

"I miss my mommy," he cries.

"I know, but she will always be watching over you, do you know what I do when I miss someone?" I say as he shakes his head.

"What?" He sniffles.

"Come on, I'll show you," I say, lifting him as I pull my bedside cabinet out, pressing on the door as it opens, and his eyes go wide.

"You got a secret cave…" He whispers.

"Yeah, come with me," I say, crawling in as he comes in slowly behind me as his eyes stay wide at the small room.

"Whoa!" He says open-mouthed.

"Here, this is what I do when I miss someone, I draw them, I could teach you," I say, sitting him on my lap as I slowly turn the pages.

"Who's that?" He points to me and Blake as kids.

“Me and one of my best friends, Blake, he was also like a brother,” I say.

“What do you mean?” He frowns.

“Well, when he was younger, he was adopted by my mummy and daddy as he didn’t have any, they made him their son. So, he became a brother to us, same as Janie, she’s not my sister by blood but she is still my sister,” I say as he frowns.

“People can get a new mommy and daddy?” he says.

“Yes, they don’t replace the ones you’ve lost though, they just… Make a bigger family. They take care of you like you were theirs from birth, do you understand?” I ask as his brows are furrowed.

“Can I choose a new mommy and daddy?” He asks, standing up as I put the book on the small table.

“Do you want new parents? You live with Cynthia and Reggie, don’t you… Don’t you like them?”

“I like them… But…” He murmurs as he begins rocking on his heels.

“But what Hunter?” I ask, cupping his chin softly.

“I want you to be my mommy,” he says, and I sit back in shock.

“Me…” I murmur.

“Please…” He begs with tears in his eyes.

“Corey…” I say through the link.

“Yes, princess? Is everything alright?” He replies.

“You want a big family right…”

“Yes… Why…” He replies as I hear footsteps outside the hole.

"Hunter wants me to be his mummy… And… I-I can't help but want it too," I reply. I hear someone shuffle down the crawl space as Corey smiles when his head pops out.

"So, I hear you want Taylor as your mommy, what about me?" He says as Hunter giggles.

"You'd be my daddy!" Hunter grins.

"What do you say, princess?" Corey says, sitting beside me.

"I say, I'd love to be your mum," I smile as Hunter squeals in delight, jumping on us, tears flooding from both our faces.

"I love you, mommy," he says as my heart explodes, kissing his head softly.

"I love you too buddy," I reply.

*We're turning into mum…*

**Yeah, so? She's epic!**

*True…*

# Chapter Thirty-Five

## Phoenix

I couldn't believe I was doing this again; setting alight the funeral pyres as everyone surrounded us. Tears flow as the torch sets alight to Trey's body, my eyes looking to our dead as I drop it, falling into Michael's arms before I hear Taylor come to my side as she shifts.

She howls loudly into the air, the packs follow suit, they were just as proud of her, after what she did with Malina and the others. She was their warrior princess and now she was beta to Reggie's pack too, she was more powerful than ever.

"Tonight, we say goodbye, tonight we grieve for our dead as they go on to their next journey, following in the footsteps of our predecessors! Our pack, our people, our FAMILY are strong!" Bryant bellows as he joins his sister up the front, she shifts, linking hands with him.

"What are they doing?" I whisper.

"Tomorrow, we begin training! We will train every single person here, it will be hard and gruelling work, we will not go easy because the enemy will NOT go easy!" Janie joins them.

"I implore every one of you to look around you, look at the people beside you, what would you feel if they were on these pyres? Would you want to avenge them? I certainly do, Trey was like an uncle to me, to us. He was kind, he was fun, and he was a heck of a fighter and he lays there now! Dead, because of those monsters out there! The fight is far from over and it's time we truly fight back! Honour them with me and fight in their names!" Taylor roars out as I stare at them in shock, the whole crowd roars in applause.

"Did you have any idea about this?" Michael asks.

"No, I didn't," I shake my head.

"Do you agree with them?" He asks.

"I do, it's time we fought back, properly," I nod as I walk up to them, standing between the twins and they look up at me.

"Tomorrow is a new day! Tomorrow, we begin training, we will get this world back in order!" I bellow as the twin's smile and kiss my cheeks before they hug Janie tightly.

"I'm sorry mum, we would have said something, but there wasn't time," Janie says.

"It's been a rough couple of days, I understand, I'm proud of you all," I smile at them as they hug me all at once. I look behind them at Trey's pyre, a tear falling as I remember one of my best friends while I hear the cries of his mate behind me.

"Evie doesn't look so good, she won't eat, sleep or let anyone touch her," Janie says.

"Time… All we can do is keep trying and show her we are still here," I sigh as I see Evie walk to the pyre, dropping to her knees as she sobs.

"I'm going to miss him," I hear behind me as Luci stands there, tears flowing freely as I walk to her, wrapping my arms around her tightly.

"Me too," I whisper as she sobs.

"I'm sorry about the baby Janie," Luci hugs her.

"Thank you, it hurts, but we will try again. One day when he talks to me again…" Janie sighs.

"He still hasn't said a word to you?" Bryant asks with a frown as he spots his mate standing with Hanson.

"No, he blames me I think, he told me to stay behind… I didn't listen… When Reggie came to help me, I had already been hit by a few of the vampires, I felt their heartbeat disappear… If I had stayed behind like Hanson said, then our baby would be alive right now," Janie cries and I pull her into my arms.

"I'm going to go talk to him," Bryant growls.

"NO, give him time, he needs to grieve his way too, he will come around," I grab my boys arm tightly.

"MOMMY!" I hear a cry as Hunter darts past us all and jumps into Taylor's arms, her eyes widen, looking at me in shock.

"Mummy?" I raise a brow.

"Surprise… We adopted him…" She says, biting her lip nervously.

"You're joking…" Luci murmurs.

"Oh, she's definitely Phoenix's kid… Adopting the strays," Kade walks up to us passing Annabelle to Luci as she's fussing for a feeding.

"Kade, don't call him a stray," Taylor growls glaring at him, he grimaces before holding his hands up and apologising. I raise a brow and smirk at him.

"What happened, little man?" Corey asks as Hunter cries in Taylor's arms.

"Let's go inside with them," I say as I lead them all in.

"You don't approve, do you mum?" Taylor says through our bond as I turn to her in an instant when she puts Hunter in Corey's arms.

"Of course, I approve, I think this is a beautiful thing you've done, you're going to be an amazing mother. It just surprised me, that's all, I'm so proud of you, I love you, silly girl," I kiss her head as she hugs me tight.

"NO! I want to go back to MOMMY!" Hunter screams, kicking at Corey.

"Whoa! What's with the tantrum baby?" Taylor cups his bright red face.

"My head, it hurts," he cries.

"Corey?" Taylor murmurs as she presses her hand against his head.

"I think he may shift for the first time," Corey answers.

"Is everything ok?" Cynthia walks quickly over to us as she frowns at Hunter's painful expression.

"Corey give him to me," Taylor says as he passes Hunter back over and she places him on the ground in front of her.

"It hurts!" He cries.

"I know baby, I know, it will only hurt the first time I promise, can you hear a little voice in your head?" She asks as I see warriors peering over in interest.

"Perhaps we should get him somewhere with more space, without watchful eyes," I say.

"We'll deal with the crowds, mum take them with you," Bryant says as he, Luci and Kade begin to work the crowd.

"Where shall we go, outside is usually the best option… But…" Taylor bites her lips.

"The perimeter is being watched, we will be fine, come on," I say as she picks up Hunter as her, Corey, Cynthia and Reggie follow as we all go back outside, moving past the pyres before we get to the side garden.

"Hunter, can you hear a voice?" Taylor asks again.

"Yes," he cries.

"Good, that's your wolf baby boy, you talk to him," she says as he falls to his knees screaming.

I hated watching this, I hated it when my kids shifted for the first time, to sit there and watch as there was nothing we could do but talk them through it and be with them.

"Taylor, shift so he can feel the bond between you as wolves," I tell her. She kisses his head and shifts, laying on the ground as he shakes beside her.

"I always hated this part," Cynthia sighs.

"Me too, to see them in pain, it hurts me," I reply.

"Hunter, try not to resist, let your wolf in, just let your body do what it needs to do little man," Corey kneels beside him as Taylor nudges Hunter with her nose, whimpering.

Hunter screams, hearing the cracks of his bones as they shift for the first time.

Suddenly, he turned into a beautiful white and grey pup as he collapsed to the ground, Taylor curled herself around him as he whimpered.

# Chapter Thirty-Six

## Taylor

"Hunter baby, you ok?" I wrap my body around him protectively as he snuggles in close, whining.

"Am I a wolf…" He says before looking down, yipping as he sees his new wolf feet, getting up on wobbly legs and used to his new way of walking with four instead of two.

"Yes baby," I nudge him as he begins bouncing around me.

"Well, looks like someone found his legs," Cynthia chuckles as he bounces around.

"His name is Dash," Hunter yips as he nuzzles into my front, curling up under my head and I nuzzle him back.

"Dash! Hi Dash, I'm Lily!" Lily pushes through to him, I could feel our heart melt as he snuggles closer.

"I think it's been a long day; we should all get some rest. Hunter, concentrate on your human form and shift, it won't hurt this time, I promise," mum says. I nod nudging him out from under me as he yawns.

"Shift baby boy," I nudge him, his eyes close and he begins to shift as I follow suit.

"I did it!" He grins before jumping into my arms.

"You did Hunter, I'm proud of you," I smile, kissing his cheek as he lays his head on my shoulder.

"Bedtime," Corey smiles, kissing my head too.

"Night mum, sleep well guys," I say to the others as they hug us goodnight, while I carry Hunter upstairs with us.

"I don't want to sleep in my room," Hunter murmurs.

"Why not buddy?" Corey asks.

"I want to stay with you," he hugs me tighter.

"One night won't hurt," I say to Corey through the link.

"But I wanted to show just how much I love you tonight…" he says with a lust-filled look. I smile at him wanting nothing more, but I knew that Hunter needed us too. It had been a rough day.

"One night Corey, look at his little face, how can you say no to him?" I bat my eyelashes as he smirks.

"OK, but just tonight, ok?" He says to Hunter.

"Yay!" He grins as we head to our bedroom.

After getting changed in the bathroom, I find Hunter giggling in one of Corey's shirts and it looked like a dress on him.

"Did you shrink in the wash, Corey?" I gasp in mock surprise.

"I'm not daddy!" He giggles as Corey pounces on him, with a huge grin on his face tickling him on the bed. I giggle, joining them as they settle down, Hunter snuggles between us as Corey wraps an arm over both of us, I kiss Hunter's head before pecking Corey on the lips.

"Good night baby boy," I whisper into Hunter's ear as he nuzzles into me.

"Night mommy, night daddy," he whispers.

"Good night little man," Corey looks at me as he kisses Hunter's head.

"You want to add to the family, don't you?" I smirk, talking through our link as Hunter slowly falls asleep.

"Of course I do," he smiles.

"We will," I nod as I imagine our family growing.

"Go to sleep princess," he kisses me once more before turning off the light and snuggling up to us as we fall asleep quickly.

It had been months, and it was almost Bryant and I's birthdays once more, training took up most of our time and if it wasn't that it was family. Janie and Hanson had finally reconciled after some very angry rough sex, which the whole house heard. The next day they came back down in a whole new mood, they were sad about their loss, but they were happy together again.

Amanda and Bryant had had their baby, Bailey, and she was the cutest little thing in the world! They had decided to stick around here for now as most of the packs stayed too. The packs were on a path to redeeming humanity, and it didn't seem like we were stopping any time soon.

Amelia, Hunter and Selene were never far from each other as Selene was finally coming out of her shell, between me and mum we were teaching her how to control her powers and boy was she powerful.

Amelia had been adopted and she was so happy. Kai and Jae were feeling like they needed to expand their own family and wanted a little one to call their own and Kai had gone from crazy uncle to protective dad unbelievably quickly. They were great together though, Amelia was so much happier, and I knew they were worried about her being human when they were vampires, so they discussed it with her and decided when she turned eighteen, she could decide whether she wanted to be turned or not. I think I already knew what her decision was as she watched them every minute, it was like she was learning how they moved, and I could see the excitement in her eyes when they would flit around.

"Taylor! Would you mind looking after Annabelle for a little while? I need to go find your mum about something," Luci says with a cheeky grin.

"Uhh… Sure…" I nod, taking six-month-old Annabelle as I coo at her while Luci runs off.

"You gained another child…" Cynthia laughs as she spots me with Annabelle.

"Luci needs to see mum and asked if I would watch her," I shrug with a smile.

"Taylor, Corey was talking to his father earlier and I don't wish to put any stress on you but are you feeling well? He noticed you haven't come back into heat recently and he's concerned about you. I know you both want a family but does something seem amiss to you?" she asks.

"I… Well… I just thought it was taking time… Things aren't always straight forward. It took a lot for Luci and Kade to have kids," I answer.

"Luci had a defect since birth, she didn't know about it until recently. Taylor, most wolves conceive pretty quickly," Cynthia says.

"Are you trying to say I can't…" I gulp.

"Perhaps I should take a look at you later sweetheart, just in case," she answers, cupping my chin.

“I can’t, we’re going out on a search later. I won’t be back for a couple of days,” I sigh.

“Then we do it now…” She says as she puts a hand on my back softly.

“What about Annabelle?” I murmur.

“She will be fine in my arm, I only need one hand,” she answers as we walk to my room.

“Cynthia… What if I can’t have kids? Corey will be devastated…” I say, my eyes fogging up with tears.

“Then you will build your family by other means, there are a few ways to have a family and no matter what I am sure my son will stay by your side. He loves you, Taylor, now lay down for me, give me Annabelle,” she orders, and I pass Annabelle over gently before laying down.

“Is this going to hurt?” I ask.

“It may sting a little, but it shouldn’t hurt, stay still,” she says. Her hand hovers over my stomach before it falls on it, a searing heat burns at my skin as I cry out in pain, her eyes scrunch up.

“STOP! It hurts!” I cry.

“One more minute Taylor, hold on,” she says as she presses harder.

“MOM! What the fuck are you doing to Taylor?!” Corey bursts in with Kade beside him.

Kade takes Annabelle quickly, Corey shoves Cynthia away from me as I cry, bent over in pain on the bed.

“A life for a life… My god…” She mutters.

“MOM!” Corey shouts as he picks me up into his arms.

“Balance, there has to be a balance, a life for a life, we brought Michael back… He wasn’t supposed to live… A life for a life brought back… There is a reason you haven’t had any children Taylor…” She says as I look at her in shock.

“Tell me I wasn’t pregnant that day…” I murmur.

“What the hell is going on?!” Kade booms.

“Your body hasn’t registered the loss yet… It’s still inside you, I’m sorry Taylor… Corey baby…” She says, looking at us sadly.

“She was pregnant…” He whispers looking at me, his eyes sad.

“I can help her body heal and get the baby out, then we will pray you have the same chance to conceive,” Cynthia says.

“Are you telling me that when you did your magic shit on bringing Michael, my best friend, back from the dead, you killed her child?!” Kade booms.

“Kade, calm down,” I gulp, tears in my eyes.

“Your child Taylor! Your father won’t like this!” Kade says. He goes to leave; I get up quickly grabbing his arm as I drag him back inside.

“You can’t tell dad, please Kade, it will kill him! He’s already finding it hard enough with Janie losing her baby, after everything he went through in the past, losing his kid with his first mate, we can’t put this on him!” I beg.

“You let this happen,” Corey snaps at his mother.

“Corey how was I supposed to know what would happen?! I was just trying to help baby boy!” She cries as he glares at her.

"You killed my fucking kid!" Corey growls, claws out as his eyes change colour to a deep purple.

"Corey! Stop! You're letting the darkness win, look at me baby, look at me," I stand in front of him, cupping his cheeks as I try to force him to look at me.

"I'm so sorry, baby boy," Cynthia cries.

"You'll pay for this," Corey growls as he pushes me to the side.

"NO!" I shout. I shift, pouncing on him as he goes to slash at his mother's throat, slicing into my leg instead as I pin him to the ground, snarling. I watch as his eyes change again, fear showing in his face.

"What have I done…" He whispers.

"Taylor, let him up," Cynthia says as I slowly climb off of him.

I stand between them, still as my wolf, I growl in warning.

"I'm sorry, I'm so sorry," Corey murmurs as he rushes past and bursts out of the room.

"Corey! Wait! Taylor, if he loses control and lets the darkness in, he could do some serious damage! You have to calm him down!" Cynthia says. I nod bursting out of the room, bounding down the stairs as I see him shift at the front door.

"COREY!" I howl, racing after him.

"Taylor! What's going on?!" Bryant shouts as I see him training with the others.

"No time, ask Cynthia, go check on her!" I reply as he nods rushing off, shouting to the trainees to take a break.

My leg stung from Corey's slash, but I pushed on chasing after him as the sky began to darken, rain falling to the ground, the mud sloshing against my feet.

I was gaining on him as I used my earth power to make him slip, he tumbled to the ground as I saw his eyes a deep purple again.

"Stop, you have to stop! Corey, baby, please, don't let it in!" I hold him down as he snaps his teeth at me.

"Get off of me!" He howls as he bites at my leg, I howl in pain before he kicks me off making me slam into a huge tree as he goes running off.

"COREY!" I howl into the air, whining, trying to get up, my front leg was broken as I whimpered.

"Taylor! My god! Where is he?" Reggie runs up to me, his fur soaked to the bone.

"That way," I nod in the direction he went.

"Get back, I'll find him," he replies.

"Reggie, be careful," I whine standing up, unable to put any weight on my front leg.

"He'll be ok, this happened once before and we got him back, we'll do it again, I promise, go," he nudges me gently before running off.

I whine while I try limp back home, the searing pain in my leg was unbearable when I noticed it glow like electric was pulsing through it, but it was purple.

*What did he do to us...*

**Cynthia will fix it.**

*Perhaps we should shift, it will be your arm injured, make it easier to walk.*

**You're right Lily.**

I try to shift, but pain surges through my leg.

**Lily, why can't we shift?**

*I don't know, I feel stuck, Taylor it's the magic, it's stopping us from shifting!*

**SHIT!**

The next thing I know is I hear a howl before flashes of lightning in the distance, the sound of two wolves fighting.

**Shit! They're going to end up killing each other!**

I turn back around, trying to get to them as quick as I could, but the closer I got the more pain I was in. I kept moving, whining in pain as I saw Corey and Reggie up ahead fighting as they clawed at each other, tearing flesh.

"COREY!" I howl as I collapse on the ground.

It distracts him for just a moment as Reggie swipes at his face with a thundering crack, Corey falling to the ground.

"COREY!" I howl again looking at them in shock. Please don't let him be dead!

"He's not dead, knocked out. I'm sorry, it was the only way," Reggie says, grabbing him by the scruff of his neck, dragging him over.

"I don't feel so good Reggie," I whine on the ground.

He drops Corey to the ground, and he lets out the loudest howl I had ever heard.

"Stay with me Taylor," he nudges at my face as I whimper.

"Taylor! Holy shit what happened?" Hanson runs up to us before shifting as Reggie shifts back to his human form too.

"Help me get them back, I need to get Corey pinned, we're going to need those chains of yours," Reggie tells him.

"Oh! Taylor…" Janie bounds up next as she nudges me.

"Can you shift?" Reggie asks me.

"I can't, I'm stuck," I whimper.

"How the hell did this happen?" Hanson snaps as he glares at Corey's unconscious body.

"Darkness, he let it in in a moment of sadness, magic is a powerful thing and if unchecked it can turn into darkness, we should have seen it coming, but we missed it, we can deal with it though, he'll be back to normal in no time," Reggie says.

"What about Taylor?! He hurt her!" Hanson growls.

"Hanson, stop, can we get home? Please," I whimper.

"Fine," he growls as he shifts. He takes one side and Janie takes my other as they prop me up between them.

As we made our way back, our fur was covered in the thick mud as the rain continued to plummet down to the ground. Even through the thunderous sound of rain hitting the ground, I was able to hear something to our right.

"Hanson," I growl in warning.

"Janie set her down," Hanson says as they help sit me on the ground, my eyes open for what was coming our way.

"There's more," Reggie growls as he puts Corey beside me.

"Behind you!" I howl to Reggie as a vampire comes flitting at him, he roars out in pain. Hanson jumps over, ripping the vampire from his back tearing it limb from limb.

"Help..." I hear in the distance, my ears perked up, the voice was young...

"Janie..." I whimper as I get up weakly.

"Sit your arse back down now Taylor!" She growls at me as she howls for back up.

"Janie! MOVE!" Hanson barks out, she manages to jump out of the way of a spear being thrown at us as it lands just in front of me.

"We have to get out of here now!" Janie says as she helps me back up.

"Reggie go! I've got this arsehole," Hanson growls, grabbing Corey as he flips him over and manages to get him on his back as we begin to move through the trees.

"Janie, watch it!" Hanson howls. I notice another spear fly towards us and I use what little energy I had to snap it out of the sky, snapping it in my teeth.

"Hanson, we have a problem... We're surrounded," Janie says, looking all around.

"Wake Corey up," I order.

"How do you want me to do that? Why would I do that?" Hanson growls.

"REGGIE! Wake him up!" I growl as my lips curl in a snarl at the vampires moving towards us.

“Sorry son,” Reggie says, biting him hard on the ear as we cower at the loud high-pitched howl that shook through the ground.

“Corey!” I whine as the ground shakes.

His eyes meet mine, a mix of yellow, purple and his normal brown, fighting a battle of dark and light.

“TAYLOR! Watch out!” Reggie howls, bowling me over as a vampire flits towards me, taking a swipe at me but catches Reggie instead. But then I hear a snarl behind us as Corey stands snarling at the vampire, his yellow eyes bright as his wolf takes over.

“Coal,” I breathe out as he tears the vampire limb from limb.

“Taylor, I don’t know how long I can keep the darkness at bay, I’m doing what I can, I need mom’s help, we need to get out of here now!” Coal, his wolf replies.

I let out the loudest howl I had ever done in my life, and I heard a reply nearby, back up was coming.

“We’re coming!” Bryant answers.

Corey… Well, Coal begins attacking the vampires around us as they came at us one by one.

“Why are they attacking one by one?” I murmur, looking around.

“They’re watching us…” Janie replies.

“Why… Why are they watching us?” I reply.

"Corey… They can sense the darkness in him, these could be some of Maximillian's vampires, if he controlled them with his darkness they would sense it in others, they will crave it, it's like a drug," Reggie answers.

"We have to get him back to normal," I say as I hear the pounding of wolves coming our way.

Bryant and his team charge into the vampires as they begin trying to flit away like cowards. The odd one kept trying to attack us as we made our way over to Bryant.

"Knock me the fuck back out!" Corey growls as I turn to see his eyes turning purple.

"HANSON!" I bark out as he takes a swipe at Corey, but he dodges it, eyes deep purple.

"Corey no!" I snarl as he attacks Hanson.

Using every bit of my energy I had left I pounce onto Corey's back, biting at his neck as he tries to buck me off.

"TAYLOR!" Reggie howls as he joins me, trying to take Corey down. He throws me off of him once again, flying towards another tree, but not before Bryant gets in front of me and cushions the blow as we both howl in pain.

"GET HIM DOWN!" Reggie barks as Hanson and the other warriors help pin him down.

"GET OFF OF ME!" Corey shouts as I see his fingers glow purple.

"NO!" I bark out as he goes to use his powers, but Hanson shifts, slamming a rock into his head. I whine as I can feel his pain.

"He's still alive," Bryant nudges me gently.

"We need to get back now," I whimper.

"Bryant, Janie, help Taylor get back. You two help Reggie, the rest of you surround us, keep your eyes open and ears listening out, I've got Corey," Hanson orders as Bryant and Janie help me up.

"Hanson did you really need to use a fucking rock? You could have killed him," I growl through my mind as we make our way through the trees, I limp side by side with my siblings.

"Oh, I am sorry, what did you want me to knock him out with?" he snaps back.

"Guys, stop it, what's done is done, Corey will be fine," Janie says as I shake my head, I can see the mansion up ahead.

# Chapter Thirty-Seven

## Taylor

I could see my mum rushing out with a team of healers and Cynthia right on her tail.

"Oh my!" Cynthia gasps, she looks at her son who is knocked unconscious on Hansons back before walking over to me, her hand running over the fur of my leg.

Everyone else shifts, mum looks at me with a confused gaze.

"Why aren't you shifting?" She asks.

"I can't," I whine.

"It's the darkness, you see the purple glow, that's part of the darkness that was inside Corey, No doubt, you helped his wolf get through while out there, but we need to destroy it before it destroys you. Someone take Corey and chain him up, I must work on Taylor first, he would want it that way," Cynthia says as Reggie nods, kissing her on her cheek before helping Hanson drag Corey away.

"This is going to be a really shit day, isn't it?" I sigh.

"It's not going to be pretty," she replies.

"Bryant, you need to lead a team to surround the territory. Take the Rebel pack with you, get everyone inside the inner boundaries. Michael, go get the weapons for the humans," mum orders as they nod.

"You take care of my daughter," Michael growls at Cynthia before shifting quickly.

"Call on me if you need me, twin. Together we are strong, don't be afraid to use our energy," my brother nudges me with his muzzle before running off too.

"Let's get her inside… We do have a problem, where are we going to lay her? She's much larger as a wolf," Cynthia says.

"The main hall," mum says as Cynthia nods.

"Mum, she doesn't have enough energy to move," Janie says while I'm slumped on the ground.

"I've got this," Kade's gruff voice says, I yelp when he picks me up with a grunt.

"Luci, keep the kids away from the main hall, keep them busy with something a little noisy," mum says.

"Why… Oh… Taylor!" She gasps, seeing me in Kade's arms still in wolf form.

"FUCK!" I yelp as a surge of pain runs through my leg.

"Hurry!" Cynthia says as everyone moves quickly.

I can feel him… Corey… He's awake and in so much pain…

"Stop struggling Taylor," Kade growls as I try to get out of his arms.

"No," I snap, biting his arm as he drops me, limping away.

"Taylor, no!" Cynthia snaps her fingers. I still, my whole body frozen.

"You couldn't have done that earlier," Kade growls, grabbing me once more.

“The more I use my powers now, the less I will have to help her and my son,” Cynthia snaps back, he grunts before walking to the main hall as I’m placed on the ground.

“I’m going to need her pinned down, she will thrash about, and I need her as still as possible without using my magic for it,” Cynthia says.

“What the hell is going on? Why are there vampires waiting in the trees?! It’s like they are waiting for something!” Kai and Jae flit inside, their eyes wide as they see me laying on the floor, Kade, Janie and mum trying to keep me still.

Mum’s eyes flash yellow as I hear Kai hiss out.

“Jae, help them. I will go out and help Bryant,” Kai kisses his cheek before flitting outside.

“I need to get to Corey!” I howl as Kade forces my head down and I snap at them. Lily was furiously trying to get to our mate, making me snap when I didn’t want to.

“Be still Taylor! Right, I must start, be warned this will get worse before it gets better,” Cynthia warns.

“It’s going to be ok baby girl,” mum says, her hands gripping my fur tightly.

“Here we go,” Cynthia takes a deep breath before muttering nonsense words, pain surges through my body as I howl out, body shaking as they all struggle to keep me down.

“Shit! We need someone else! Watch out for her paw!” Jae says, warning Kade before he grabs at my paw. I’m howling in pain, the ground shaking beneath me.

"TAYLOR!" Corey's voice vibrates through the whole mansion as Cynthia looks up in a panic before muttering her words quicker.

A rumble comes from outside, I can feel the power making its way to us as Corey is coming.

*He's coming for us! We need to help him! I'm scared for him!*

**He's our mate don't be scared!**

*Taylor, for god's sake, think about this, concentrate! He's letting the darkness in! I'm scared FOR him not OF him!*

"Taylor," Corey growls in the doorway, covered in blood.

"No… What have you done?!" Cynthia shouts in shock.

"He wiped the vampires out! It's not our blood!" I hear Reggie shout.

"He's right, the pledge he made would have killed him otherwise," mum agrees.

Cynthia nods as Corey's eyes are in a deep battle before he comes to my side, shouting out his mother's words as I feel the darkness leave me, my body healing.

"NO! He's taking the darkness; he's not destroying it!" I shout as I can shift once more.

"Corey no!" Cynthia says, watching as Corey stands, his eyes darkening.

"Don't worry Taylor, I will always love you," Corey says before shifting and bolting.

"NO!" I scream out, I try to get up, but my legs wobble weakly beneath me.

"Stay here," Reggie says running after him.

“Cynthia!” Jae says, flitting to her as she falls to the ground.

“Cynthia, what can we do?” Mum rushes to her side as Kade and Janie stay with me.

“Rest, I need rest… Taylor, I fixed it all, everything, you’re healed…” Cynthia says weakly.

“Doesn’t matter now, he’s gone, I can feel him getting further and further away,” I say sadly.

“What else was healed?” Mum frowns.

“Nothing, just my wound,” I shake my head giving Cynthia a stern look.

“Do NOT lie to me!” Mum shouts sternly as I gulp, she rarely got angry and when she did, she was a force to be reckoned with.

“Taylor, you have to tell her at least, fine you don’t wish to tell your father, but you can’t handle this alone,” Kade grips my shoulder.

“So Kade knows, and I don’t…” Mum says in shock.

“Mum… I…” I murmur as I hear footsteps rush inside.

“They’re gone, every single one of them, Corey killed them all!” Bryant bursts inside with Kai by his side, both covered in blood.

“He’s fighting it…” Cynthia says with a small smile before falling to the ground.

“Take her to the medical wing!” Mum orders as Kade stands up, scooping her into his arms and giving me a stern look before leaving the room.

I sit down with my arms around my knees hugging them to me as Janie pulls me into her arms, a look of confusion on her face.

"Will you tell us what's going on?" She asks through the bond.

"I-I-I can't," I stammer in reply.

"What on earth is going on?!" Violet's voice calls from the distance.

"Janie, take Taylor upstairs, I'll speak with you later young lady. Kai, Jae if you could help with clean up, Bryant check on the troupes," mum orders.

"Are you ok?" Bryant tilts his head at me.

"No… Not really," I sigh in our link.

"Bryant, I've got her," Janie says with a nod to him as she pulls me up. I stagger a little, weakened from everything that had happened.

Mum had disappeared to find Violet as Janie helped me up the stairs.

"So, tell me now, what's going on?" Janie cups my cheek as a tear falls from my face.

"The battle, when dad died… We helped revive him, but… Cynthia… She said today, she said… a life for a life… I was pregnant too Janie…" I cry as her eyes go wide, pulling me tightly into her arms.

"Oh Taylor," she murmurs, tears falling from her eyes too.

"Girls…" Reggie stands in the doorway, a sad look on his face, covered in mud.

"He's gone, isn't he…" I say quietly.

"Yes, he's gone, but he'll be back, I can feel it. Chin up, he will return one day," Reggie says.

"Cynthia is in the medical wing, she passed out. You should wash up and go see her," Janie says softly.

"I will, but I need to speak to Taylor for a moment. Would you mind?" He says as she nods kissing my head, walking out the room as Reggie shuts the door.

"What is it?" I ask.

"There is a chance that my son may not return the same as he was. Trying to fight the darkness may change him and the last time he did so, he was a wreck. It took a long time for us to return him to how he is… was… But if you love my son, I hope that you will help us because I believe you may just be the answer to helping him. We will find him, even if we have to search for him ourselves to bring him home," he says.

"I love him, Reggie, always will, I want him back. We have a son together now too, Hunter is as much a son to me as a blood one would be, we have to get him back," I answer, wiping my face of tears.

"We will, I promise we will, but we must also have patience. You are the daughter I never had, and I promise to protect you with my life, you are so strong, and I can see where you get it from, but you must tell your family the truth. They must know what you're going through, only then can we all pull together," he says, cupping my chin softly.

"I know, I'm just scared… If I tell my dad… It will hurt him so much," my lip wobbles as I hold back a sob.

"It will hurt, yes, but if he was then to find out later that you never told him, it will hurt more. The family must heal together, you will be stronger together, our bonds help us heal," he replies.

"I'll tell them," I nod slowly.

“Good girl, but for now, you must rest, tomorrow we can all sit together and talk through it all. I must go see Cynthia, rest now my beta daughter,” he kisses my head as I smile sadly at him.

“Thank you, thank Cynthia too,” I reply as he nods leaving the room.

“How are you feeling now Tay?” Janie walks in as she climbs onto the bed, pulling me to her as I curl into her arms.

“Not great, tired, sad, my body yearns for him,” I sigh.

“It will. Go to sleep Taylor, rest,” her fingers graze across my arm, my eyes close when she begins to sing the lullaby from when we were kids.

# Chapter Thirty-Eight

## Phoenix

"Violet what are you doing here? Are those ALL your people?" I ask, looking outside to see a huge group of fae surrounding the mansion.

"It is time to stick together, we are losing too many, we must fight back. I had heard what your children were doing, teaching the others to fight so we come here to join you, though it seems we came at a rather difficult time…" Violet raises a brow.

"No kidding," I sigh.

"Phoenix, Janie is with Taylor, she's sleeping, Cynthia is also resting. Reggie has suggested we talk tomorrow about everything," Michael says, taking me into his arms.

"I just don't understand what's going on right now…" I reply.

"We will figure this out, as we always do my love," he replies, kissing my head softly.

"Plus, you have us now too," Violet says.

"Jae, would you mind catching Violet up for me. I need to go for a walk," I say, my head spinning.

"Of course," he nods.

"Want company?" Michael asks.

"No, I just need peace for a moment," I hold up a hand before kissing his lips and walking out of the building.

*Something is going on, something is wrong with Taylor, what is she hiding?*

**I don't know Storm, hopefully, she will tell us. She hides things to protect others. She's stubborn.**

*And what about Corey, he was a danger to all of us, if this darkness fills him, we could end up with another Maximillian on our hands.*

**I know Storm, but it's not that simple! He's our baby girl's mate, we can't just kill him.**

*He's going to get us killed.*

**Storm enough! He killed all those vampires not any of our people, his wolf still has some control and so does he, give him the benefit of the doubt for now. We protect the pack and everyone here and we continue our work. Make sure the kids are ok first.**

*Ok, ok, sorry for me being worried...*

**You're not the only one scared of losing it all Storm.**

Taking a walk around the perimeter, I notice the slaughter of all the vampires around as their bodies are being dealt with. I couldn't believe the sight in front of my eyes, had Corey done this on his own?

Without realising I had walked inside and found myself outside of Taylor's room. I opened the door slightly to see her curled into Janie's arms and then little Hunter in hers, I could see his face was red and puffy from crying. They must have told him Corey had gone.

"She is a brave girl your Taylor, I am honoured to have her as my beta and my daughter-in-law as the humans would say," Reggie surprises me by sneaking up beside me.

"She is, but I can't help but worry about her, she's only just going to turn nineteen and she's been through so much, more than myself in some ways, I didn't want this kind of life for her, I wanted to give her a happy life," I sigh closing the door.

"You think she isn't happy? She has the brightest smile around, she works hard for her family and people, she sees the world in a bright light where people can be saved from corruption. Taylor is going through something traumatic, but she will push through it as you have with troubles in your own life. Phoenix, your family is one of the strongest I have seen in my lifetime, and I am honoured to be a part of it now. Do not look to the future with sadness, things will right themselves, it is mere moments of time," Reggie says with a soft smile.

"What happened to my little girl?" I ask quietly, gulping.

"That is not for me to tell, with great power comes great sacrifice, tomorrow may be a difficult day but with each other, but we can get through this," Reggie says.

*What the hell is that supposed to mean?*

**No... I-It can't be... Taylor... She's had trouble conceiving... What if... No, I won't believe it.**

*WHAT?!*

**What if she lost a baby... Bringing Michael back...**

*No... Surely not... she would tell us.*

**Not if she didn't want to hurt him, we already lost Janie's baby, Taylor wouldn't want anyone else to hurt anymore. Especially her daddy, she's a daddy's girl, she hated seeing him so hurt by the loss of Janie's.**

*Oh my god... Our baby... I think... I think you may be right, reach out, can you feel that, her pain? The loss as she holds onto Janie. Feel Janie too, they feel the same.*

"She lost a child, didn't she?" I whisper, looking to Reggie as he sighs looking down sadly.

"A life for a life, the balance is a fickle thing, I'm sorry for your losses Phoenix, I know you have lost a lot recently. I will be forever by your side when you need me. We are family," Reggie nods, while I wipe away a tear.

"Thank you," I nod.

"Go spend time with your family, Bryant is coming," he says as my baby boy walks towards us.

"Mum?" He frowns.

"Hey, are Amanda and Bailey, ok?" I ask as Reggie walks away.

"Yeah, Bailey is sound asleep, and Amanda is trying to calm her uncle down. Hanson isn't happy about Corey escaping," Bryant replies.

"He left, he didn't escape, there's more to this, I know there is," I say, cupping his cheek.

"Taylor..." He says as I nod.

"Yes, tomorrow we will all have a discussion and find out what's truly going on. For now, Taylor is in there with Janie and Hunter. I'm going to go in and check on them properly, coming?" I ask as he nods following me, we walk quietly into the room but Janie's eyes pop open, hugging Taylor to her tightly, protectively until she realised who it was.

"Mum…" Taylor grumbles as her eyes open slowly. I sit on the bed beside her, I caress her face gently with my fingers as Bryant sits on the other side with Janie.

"Shh, go back to sleep," I hush her as she shakes her head.

"I don't know how I am going to do this alone mum, we adopted Hunter together, he misses him already and I just don't know what to do," she says as the little boy curls into her further, snuggling into her chest.

"One day at a time, we are all here twin, we will help," Bryant smiles at his sister.

"He's right, we will take everything one day at a time. No matter what, family will always be first, though I have to say it's going to get a little cramped around here again," I say.

"How many people did Violet bring?" Janie whispers.

"All of them, they packed up and jumped ship for now. We share our home with around five hundred new fae, though I have been assured they will spread about and help with anything. Plus, most will probably join teams to scout and find their people," I answer.

"Five hundred, that's a lot of mouths to feed," Bryant mumbles.

"We'll manage, some of their people are born with the gift of growing, so our farmland should do well…" I begin but am interrupted by little Hunter's eyes opening slowly as he wipes them.

"Why everyone in here?" He mumbles, looking around.

"We were just checking on you and Taylor, I like to check on my babies," I smile softly at him.

"Daddy left…" He whimpers.

"I know buddy, but hopefully he'll be back soon, so how about until he comes back you can come train with me every day with your wolf. Then you'll be super strong when he comes back?" Bryant says.

"YEAH! I'll get bigger than him!" Hunter giggles.

"Well, that sounds like a plan then, you'll train with Uncle Bryant and get bigger than daddy," Taylor says kissing his head, I can't help but notice the sadness in her eyes and the hand that goes to her stomach.

"I'm right here, I know," I say through the link while I squeeze her hand that's on her stomach.

"How…" She replies in shock.

"I'm your mother and there were signs…" I rub my thumb across hers gently.

"Dad… He's going to be devastated," she says as I see her lip wobble.

"He will be upset, as we all will be, but he loves you and he wants to see you grow. You'll have a child when the time is right, though you have Hunter now too," I smile at the boy who is now jumping all over Bryant as we giggle at them.

"Mum! Are you watching?!" Hunter grins at Taylor before jumping onto Bryant's back as he fake falls to the floor, tapping out.

"No, how could you?! I'm done for! Let me up, big man!" Bryant says, laughing.

"I took Uncle Bryant down! Did you see it?! I'm super strong!" Hunter grins happily before bouncing on the bed next to Taylor.

"I saw Hunter," she smiles, cuddling him.

"Are we all having a family meeting without me?" Michael smiles from the doorway.

"Never without you daddy," Taylor smiles at him as he comes in to kiss her head.

I could see her eyes gaze at her father sadly as she tried to put on a smile, I knew the next day was going to be difficult and the future was unsure, but we would make it through this like every other time.

# Chapter Thirty-Nine

## Taylor

Last night had been nice having the family all chatting and playing with Hunter, it gave me a sense of relief that they would always be there, no matter what.

Today though, I was beginning to worry about telling dad how his life and my child's had been traded. Mum had assured me she would keep him calm, and we would get through this, but I knew he was going to be in so much pain with it.

Jezebel was looking after all the kids with Tilly and Talia who had taken a liking to playing with them all, showing them tricks with their fire.

"Taylor," Cynthia says as she rests against Reggie, a tired smile on her face.

"Cynthia, how are you feeling?" I ask.

"Better, a little tired, but better. I should think you feel the same?" She replies.

"Tired, definitely," I nod as I notice the council room was getting fuller by the minute.

"Come, let's get this over with," Reggie says, gesturing for me to go first as my hands shake.

I sit beside my parents at the front as the last of those who were to come sat down.

“Good morning, today we come together to… Evaluate… What has happened and what our next steps are. There will be personal matters which are going to be emotional for some of us and I ask that you all respect those involved as these matters are all linked, Violet,” mum calls out.

“Thank you, Phoenix. Firstly, I would like to thank Phoenix and all of those who have taken my people in already, while our homes are under fire, we thought it best to move to a safer location where we can defend each other. I hope you all take in my people as you have done before, we are all looking for peace and to get the world back in order, so I do hope we can work together once more,” Violet pipes up.

“How will we have room for everyone?” A wolf asks.

“Preparations are already being made on housing, including local towns, such as the one our Queen once lived in. They are abandoned and can be remade while we mix our forces to keep everyone safe,” Cole answers, mum nods in gratitude.

“What of the boy… The one of witchery! Are we just letting him loose, surely, we should be out there trying to find him!” One of the fae shouts angrily.

“That is not an easy subject, and I will ask that you keep your anger to yourself until things have been explained. Corey is family. However, I understand that you are all worried after yesterday’s events, but my daughter will be clearing up a few things with the help of his mother and father, Cynthia and Reggie,” mum says as I gulp, standing up shakily as I feel dad’s hand grip mine gently.

“Witches, as we know, can suffer from darkness, though it is possible to keep at bay, sometimes there are days where it is a little harder to handle. I guess it’s much like depression, some days are easier than others to control your own mind. In our last battle, a lot of things happened. We lost a lot of our people and one of them was my father…" I breathe deeply as I can feel the tears well up.

"While Michael was on the table I was able to use my magic to revive him, but only with the help of Bryant, Taylor and Janie who stood together as siblings to help revive their father," Cynthia continues for me as I nod at her, knowing I would have to tell the next part.

"The issue with this was… was that there must always be a balance, a life for a life…" my lip wobbles and I feel my dad's hand tighten.

"Stay calm Michael," I hear mum whisper.

"For those of you who know me, you know I lost a child, I can hear you all muttering. My child died during the battle, where I should not have been," Janie pipes up as people are whispering about her.

"No, the life for a life was closer to me, that day Corey and I lost our child, it wasn't until recently that we found this out… This… This caused Corey a lot of stress which caused him to lash out and lose control…" I say as dad's hand drops from mine, turning to him as a tear falls from his eye, he shakes his head, his head drops into his hands as mum rubs his back softly motioning for me to keep going. I can feel his pain, making my chest well up inside.

"Corey is still inside his mind, his wolf is fighting with him to control the darkness and he left to keep us safe, he killed all those vampires yesterday to keep us safe. I know some of you may believe he is a danger and yes, if he lets it control him then he will be dangerous. But I swear if that happens… if that happens…" I struggle to finish the sentence.

"If it comes to Corey being a danger to everyone and turning into a monster like Maximillian, we will deal with him. We will not let him destroy everything we hold most dear, even if it means killing him," Reggie stands, nodding at me as a tear falls.

"What's to stop HER from becoming a danger?" Someone snaps, pointing at Cynthia.

"Because my powers are failing me, as I awoke this morning, I felt that my power was ebbing. I am old and though most would believe we get more powerful as time goes on, when you get to a certain age, your body begins to lose it, especially if you don't use it for a long time and then suddenly use it nearly every day," Cynthia calls out.

"Wait, so if you have no magic will you…" I murmur.

"Die… Yes," she nods.

"We'll deal with that when it comes to it, I've always fancied having you become a wolf like me," Reggie kisses her head.

"ARE WE JUST SKIPPING OVER THE FACT THAT TAYLOR LOST A BABY FOR ME?!" Dad bellows, people grimace at his shouting as I shook.

"Daddy, I couldn't lose you, I didn't even know I was pregnant at the time, please don't be mad," my hands shake.

"Let's take this outside, go for a run," Kade puts a hand on dad's shoulder.

"Come on dad," Bryant pulls him up.

"Daddy," I cry.

"You shouldn't have chosen to save me, I should be dead, I cheated death and you paid for it…" He says storming from the room.

“Dad!” I shout as I push past my brother, shifting as I chase after our father, he runs into the trees, snarling at anyone who got in his way.

“Leave me alone Taylor!” He growls as I push myself harder.

“NO! Stop! Daddy please, I love you, please stop,” I whimper as I ignore the tiredness in my body.

“You traded your unborn child for my life! Cynthia should have known!” He turns suddenly to me.

“She didn’t know, not then, none of us did. I didn’t even know I was pregnant. We couldn’t lose you, I’m not the only one who needed you, we all need you dad,” I say as he paces in front of me.

“So innocent… No child should have to die before they’ve ever lived, this is my fault,” he whimpers, falling to the ground as I wander over, curling into his side.

“It’s not your fault daddy, you didn’t ask for this, we did this, it was our decision. Don’t blame yourself for something none of us knew would happen,” I nudge his muzzle with mine.

“My baby girl, oh my sweet little girl, what a horrible world we brought you into,” he says, rubbing his forehead against mine softly.

“We can make it better; we can do it together. I will always miss my unborn child, but we can make this world a better place for the next, for all of us,” I reply.

“When did my little girl grow up?” he says as he shifts, sitting on a log as I shift too, huddling into his side.

“Growing up sucks,” I sigh, which makes him chuckle, nodding sadly.

“It does,” he kisses my head, wiping away the stray tears in his eyes.

“I still have a son that needs his grandpa, Hunter loves you,” I hold his hand in mine.

“He is quite the boy, reminds me of Blake a lot…” He replies.

“I bet Blake is looking after the babies up there, Trey and the others too. Paul is probably stood there all menacingly like he loves to do, making the kids behave, Keeley will be dressing them up,” I chuckle at the thought.

“May our goddess look after them all,” he nods.

“Mommy?!” I hear the calls of Hunter as my head darts towards the sound.

“Hunter…” I frown as we both stand.

“Mommy, I felt you were sad, don’t like you sad,” he sniffles, rushing through the trees and jumping into my arms.

“I’m ok baby boy, I promise,” I hug him tightly as dad runs a hand through Hunter’s long, blonde hair gently.

“I think we should all go back inside and have something nice and warm; it’s getting a little colder out here,” dad says.

“Hot chocolate?” Hunter smiles at dad cheekily.

“Oh, I think we can do that. How about you go get the other kids and bring them down to us while we go finish our meeting, how does that sound?” Dad says to him.

“YEAH!” Hunter grins, wriggling in my arms as I giggle and let him down as he shifts so easily, bouncing around while he runs to the door, almost falling over his own feet as we follow behind.

“He’s a good kid,” dad nods.

“Yeah, one of the best, Corey should be here,” I sigh.

“He’ll come back, we have to believe it,” dad frowns.

We go back into the mansion as dad wraps an arm around my waist, keeping me by his side as we make our way through the crowds of people about.

“They can’t be trusted!” A voice shouts angrily as we step into the council room once more.

“None of the pledges made to me have been broken, which means they are not a threat to us!” Mum shouts back as I see who she was shouting at.

A young fae boy stood angrily, his fists clenched as he glared at Cynthia before I saw flames from his fingers. I push through the people as I grab him by the throat firmly.

“Try it, I dare you,” I growl a warning as he stares me down.

“Witches are a threat,” he snaps.

“The only threat I see right now is you, turn the flames off now before I tear you a new one,” I snap. The flames on his hands get bigger as people begin to back off.

“You’re all weak! Witches will destroy us!”

“Stand down now Ere!” Violet says angrily.

“No, I will not stand here and wait for them to kill us all… Surely there have to be others like me who feel the same!!” He calls out, but no one answers, their heads cast down, refusing to look at him.

"Ouch, looks like you don't have anyone to back you up, I wonder why…" I smirk as his eyes darken before he takes a slash at me with a burning knife in his hands. The crowd disperses in shock.

"Ere! Stand down!" Violet orders again.

"You are no longer my queen, I abandon the fae realm and challenge Taylor for her position," he snaps at her, before smirking at me.

"You are joking Ere, she's a beta for the Rebel pack and the child of a Queen, you have no chance," one of the other fae hisses.

"Taylor, do you accept his challenge?" Violet asks walking to my side.

"Yeah, I accept," I growl at him.

"No wolfing out though," Ere smirks as his hand shakes slightly… Odd.

"Fine by me," I roll my eyes.

"No time like the present, shall we take this outside?" Ere gestures the door.

"Taylor, something doesn't feel right with him," Bryant says, and I glance back with a small nod.

"Let's go," I gesture him forward, walking beside him as our footsteps echo through the mansion as everyone follows silently.

"Reggie, watch his hands," I link to my alpha.

"Corruption," he answers as I glance at him, nodding.

"If he's corrupted… How many others could be?" I reply.

"I will get Cynthia and Rook to help me. We'll grab Violet now and try to work this out. Taylor, if he's corrupted, he could be more powerful than normal…" He answers.

"Dad, take mum and go spend some quality time with the kids, maybe take Cole and a few others with you," I link to him as Ere walks past me, out the front doors as a blade of fire erupts from his hands and he begins to draw a large ring in the dirt.

"Challenge is to the death, if you leave the ring it's forfeit, a free shot, which could be fatal," Ere smirks.

"Weapons?" Rook steps forward, looking at us both as he gives me a small nod.

"Name one," Ere signals for me to choose.

"Hand blades," I answer. It was one of the things Bryant and I had trained with for years, though he was the better one with them.

"Nice choice, I think I'll stick with this lovely sword I had made a while back," he smirks as he swings it around, the blade red with heat.

"There are several other possible corrupted fae Taylor, we're working on them. Warriors are trying to sneak them out, if Ere hears us he may go deeper into his feral side, he seems to be the leader so far. Maximillian still has corrupted people out there; these are some of them. You need to distract him from us," Reggie says as I take a deep breath. Bryant throws me a couple of blades before pressing his head against mine.

"Keep moving, keep low, only take a big shot if there is no risk to you, remember how we trained Taylor," he whispers, kissing my forehead.

"Mommy… What's going on?" A small voice calls.

"No, Hunter baby, I need you to go play with grandpa for a little while. I have to deal with something first, ok baby?" I kneel beside him as he glares at Ere.

"He wants to hurt you…" He whispers.

"He challenged me, but listen to me, I am going to finish this challenge and come right back inside, you hear me? Now, be a good boy and go inside with Uncle Kai and find grandpa, tell him to give you extra marshmallows, ok?" I cup his cheek, rubbing it with my thumb. I look behind him as Kai nods at me, grabbing his hand.

"NO! MOMMY! NO!" He cries as I try to hold back the tears of Kai taking him inside kicking and screaming.

"Mummy loves you!" I shout after him.

"Oh, how sweet, it sickens me. Shame you will have just lied to him, you're not getting out of this circle alive," Ere smirks and I hear the rumble of anger around us.

"If I die, kill him, find Corey and look after Hunter," I tell my twin as he nods kissing my forehead and I twist the knives around in my hands.

"Taylor!" The crowd cheers.

"Power of the twins, power of family, don't forget," Bryant says in my mind.

# Chapter Forty

## Taylor

“Rook, state the rules, let's make this official,” Ere calls out.

“The fight shall be to the death, if you exit the circle, it will cause a forfeit where the opposition is allowed one free hit. This hit may NOT be fatal. There will be no shifting into your wolf, and YOU cannot fly… Am I missing anything?” Rook calls out.

“I said hits COULD be fatal on forfeits!” Ere snaps.

“Don’t make it too easy Ere,” I smirk at him, and he scowls at me before nodding.

*Use my senses.*

**No, he wants this without a wolf, he’s got it. I’ve got this Lily.**

*Be careful.*

“Sounds good to me,” I clutch my knives in my hands as I feel them drawing power from me. Bryant you sneaky boy… He had given me matching knives to that of his sword, but these ran from my element.

I can see him smirking from beside Rook as he nods at me.

“Don’t reveal it too soon,” he says.

“Thank you,” I reply.

"Let's get on with this," Ere nods.

"Challenge between Ere of the fae lands and Taylor, Beta of the Rebel pack and daughter of Queen Phoenix will now begin!" Rook shouts as the crowd begins to get rowdy. We circle each other, I watch my footing carefully, the last thing I wanted to do was give him a free hit.

"You wanted the fight, why not start it, big boy," I smirk, egging him on.

He laughs before his sword bursts into flames, swinging it around wildly as I can feel the heat from it already as he lunges towards me. I duck under his blade when he takes a swing at me, slicing at his leg as he hisses in pain, I roll and get back up once more, knees bent and ready to move.

"Looks like it stings a bit, do you need a band-aid?" I pout at him, batting my eyelashes as I hear some of the others booms with laughter.

"Distract him!" Reggie calls out, I can hear a scuffle as Ere goes to look around, but I use my earth to trap his leg, his eyes going wide pulling his leg from the earth with what sounded like a war cry as he swings at me once more. I dodge his blade and elbow him in the face as blood spurts from his mouth.

"Ouch buddy, not looking too good for you, is it?" I smirk as he glares at me.

*Seems a little easy…*

What I didn't notice was his leg sweeping out knocking me off of my feet, his blade slicing through the air as I pull my element into my blades, they solidify with stone becoming huge swords when they clash against his. His eyes widen in surprise.

"Nice try arsehole," I grunt as I push him from me, kicking at his chest before jumping back onto my feet. Getting used to the new weight of my blades in my hands, he watches me carefully.

"You think you're so smart, little Taylor, daughter to the Queen, Beta to a deserter. My master told me you were smarter, you were destined for greatness. I don't see it, I see a weak little girl pining to be saved," Ere says and I see something in his eyes change.

"His eyes… Taylor, his sword is changing…" Hanson says, walking to the front as I see him eye a fae standing beside him. The sword was turning black, the flames turning black too, I had never seen anything like this before.

"You need to get that guy too, don't you," I link back while keeping an eye on Ere.

"Yes," he nods.

"No one's saving me Ere, so come on, fight me like a man!" I shout, getting rid of the knives on the ground as he laughs at me, kicking them out the circle.

"Bad move, I never said I was dropping mine; you make this too easy," he laughs, swinging the sword at me as I dodge his moves, I hiss as I feel it burn my shoulder as it whizzes past a little too close.

"Hey! You've got dust in your eyes!" I shout, using my element to throw the dirt in his eyes as his sword flies into the air and narrowly misses me. I take a step back and I hear a gasp.

"Ooh, you went out of the circle!" Ere laughs.

"Forfeit, one shot. NOT FATAL!" Rook shouts.

"On your knees, Taylor," he smirks at me as he picks up his sword.

"NOT FATAL Ere!" Rook bellows at him.

"You ruin all my fun," Ere chuckles as he hits me with the hilt of the sword dazing me.

“That all you got?” I groan, standing up, ignoring the blood trickling down my face from the cut on my head.

“Oh, look at you, blood dripping down your face, no weapons, weak,” he laughs as he swings his sword at me once more. I barely dodge it but manage to grab his wrist and push against his elbow until I hear the snap of it bending the wrong way as he screams out, falling to his knees.

“I’m… Not… WEAK!” I growl, kicking his knees from under him making him flat on the ground.

“NEITHER AM I!” He shouts, pushing off of the ground as I hold onto his neck. He pulls at his arm as I hear it crunch several times before he flexes it.

“He’s healing! How is that possible? He’s not a healer!” I hear someone call out in shock.

“Dark magic, always fun to play with. Maximillian might have passed on a thing or two,” he chuckles as my hold on him doesn’t seem to faze him.

“Let’s see how you manage using it underground,” I growl as I open up the earth beneath him, letting go of his neck, but he grabs my hair dragging me with him. His sword lodges itself in my shoulder causing me to scream in agonising pain.

“TAYLOR!” Rook steps forward but is thrown back as I try to keep myself from falling in the hole completely, struggling against his hold.

“FUCK YOU!” I snap, my hands shake against the ground while it pushes up against him, the walls closing in.

He shouts out as he presses against the sword, pushing it in further.

"DIE DOG!" He shouts as he hits the walls while they begin to break around him, giving him room to move as he flies out, fist upper cutting my jaw as I fly backwards, almost hitting the circle barrier. I cough out blood as he lands in front of me.

"Taylor, get up!" Bryant howls out.

"Weak little pup, you're going to die, then I'm going to kill your family and then I am going to take over the packs, all because you are weak," he smirks, coming closer.

"There's one problem with that Ere," I growl as I ready myself to move.

"Oh really?" He laughs maniacally.

"Yeah, I've got your fucking sword," I say, pulling it from my shoulder with a painful shout and swing with everything I have left, straight through his stomach, slicing him in half. His face is that of shock, before his body falls to the ground.

"Heal from that dickhead," I spit blood at him as the crowd cheers.

"Taylor!" Rook tests the boundary as he is allowed through, showing that the battle was truly over.

"Fuck, it hurts!" I groan, holding my shoulder.

"Show me!" He says as he tears at my t-shirt, looking at it, I can see it's seeping a thick, black liquid.

"I don't feel so good, Rook," I cough blood, falling back on my knees, he grabs me before I fall any further.

"What the hell is that, Rook?" Hanson asks as he picks me up in his arms.

“I don’t know. Janie, go get Cynthia, quickly, we’ll take her to the medical wing,” Rook orders as Hanson carries me inside as the crowd disperses quickly.

I continue to cough, coughing out the same thick black liquid that was coming from my shoulder.

“Rodge!” Rook shouts as I am placed on a gurney quickly.

“What the… What happened?” Rodge bursts inside as they tear open my top.

“Here, I brought the blade, thought it might help,” my twin says, rushing to my side.

“Make it stop!” I grip the edges of the gurney.

“It’s spreading down her arm, I’ve never seen anything like this before,” Rodge lifts my arm making me scream out in pain.

“Taylor! Oh no! We have to stop the spread, it’s a poison!” Cynthia exclaims, rushing in.

“How?” Hanson asks.

“The arm is lost, we have no choice but to amputate it, the chest I can control, bleed it out, I’m sorry Taylor, but we need to do this now,” Cynthia says.

“You’re going to chop her arm off now! She’s still awake!” Bryant growls.

“By the time we knock her out, she will die,” Rodge says as he grabs an axe… An AXE!

“Pin her down,” Cynthia says.

“Can’t you magic her to sleep?!” Bryant says as Hanson grabs my legs, Rook my other arm and Bryant stays by my head.

"If I use any more power, then I won't have enough to heal her from the poison," Cynthia says sadly.

"HURRY UP AND DO IT! IT HURTS!" I bellow out, gritting my teeth as I breathe through the pain.

"I am sorry for this princess," Rodge says as he swings the axe, slamming it just below the shoulder and my scream floods the halls, body writhing in pain as they try to hold me down.

"We have to let it bleed, Rodge get some blood to infuse her with once I'm done," Cynthia says as she begins muttering words, my eyes begin to shut with the amount of pain.

"No, stay awake twin, you have to stay awake," Bryant grits his teeth, obviously feeling some of my pain.

"Taylor! No! My baby!" Mum cries as she rushes into the room eyes wide with shock.

"Phoenix, stay out of the way," Rodge huffs as she hovers around me.

"I think I'm h-armless now," I cough out as I hiss in pain.

"She's healing, Rodge get the blood," Cynthia says.

"That was the worst joke you've ever made twin," Bryant leans his head against mine, tears falling from both our faces.

"I WANT MY MOMMY! SHE'S IN PAIN!" I hear Hunter scream in the distance.

"Bryant, go, calm him, please," I grunt as Rodge sticks a needle into my left arm.

“I will, don’t you go anywhere,” he kisses my forehead and rushes out.

“Was an axe necessary?” I groan.

“Quickest and the sharpest thing I had at the time princess,” Rodge grimaces as I glare at him.

“Mum… I don’t feel so good…” I mumble as my eyes flutter.

“No, Taylor, no, wake up, don’t sleep, Rodge hurry up with the blood!” Cynthia says, tapping my face.

“Come on baby, stay awake, mummy is here, stay awake for me,” mum rubs my cheek with her hand as she shakes with worry.

“I’m still here mum,” I say before passing out.

# Chapter Forty-One

## Taylor

I woke up alone, lying on one of the medical wing beds as I look to my shoulder seeing the stump of what was left. It was crazy, it was like I could still feel it was there, but I knew it wasn't. I could feel pain in my fingers that weren't there either.

My fingers… Oh no, my right hand was the one I would draw with… I would never draw again.

*Of all the things to focus on, you focus on, oh no I can't draw…*

I can almost feel Lily rolling her eyes at me as I pushed myself to sit up uncomfortably with my left. The wound had closed up, it was red and sore, but closed. Cynthia must have really used her magic on me.

My chest was bandaged up underneath the gown I was wearing, my trousers were still on though… Weird…

I groan standing up, feeling weak as I go to walk forward, I notice the empty blood bag attached to me as I pull out the needle with a wince.

"Fuck," I hiss.

I walk unsteadily out of the room, a cry of a child makes my head dart up as I walk towards it, it's Annabelle in Kade and Luci's room. I knock but hear no answer as I peep inside to see her sat in her cot, crying.

"Hey sweetie, it's ok," I coo as I walk in.

How the hell do I pick her up with one arm? I groan as she puts her arms up to be held.

I try to pick her up, sliding my hand under her, but I struggle to keep her still as she wriggles out of my grip.

"Come on," I sigh trying again as I manage to lift her, her head in the crook of my elbow, while my arm supported the rest of her as my hand laid against her bum to lift her.

Pulling her up, I wince at the muscles in my chest protesting the movement but do a little happy dance as I pull her into my chest with a smile, kissing her cheeks as she begins to settle.

"Losing a limb takes getting used to, yet you seem to be doing well already…" Kade's voice booms in the doorway as he walks in slowly.

"I heard her cry," I whisper.

"Thank you, but you shouldn't have. You should be back in your room resting Taylor, you lost a lot of blood," he says as he takes Annabelle from my arm.

"How long was I out for?" I ask.

"Two days," he answers with a sigh.

"Two days… Jeez… Hunter…" I say as I go to walk out.

"Taylor, slow down, stop thinking about everyone else and think about yourself for a moment. Hunter is fine, he hasn't left your brother's side for the last two days and he can manage a few more moments. You need to rest," he says sternly.

"I need to be with my family… I nearly died… Again…" I snap back.

"I'm not arguing Taylor, medical wing NOW!" he booms, frightening Annabelle as she screams.

"What on earth is going on?" Luci walks in going straight for Annabelle before she looks up at Kade's face, turning around. "TAYLOR! Oh my god! You're awake! What's going on? Why are you in here? Are you feeling ok? You look pale you should sit down, I should get your mum, never mind she's on her way already," she says quickly.

"I'm ok…" I sigh as I feel a little light-headed.

"No, you're not," Kade rushes to my side, grabbing me before I fall.

"Just tired, that's all," I grumble as he pulls a chair over.

"Why can't you just sit still for once in your life?" He sighs.

"Taylor… Taylor!" I hear mum shout.

"Nix! In here!" Luci calls out as mum rushes towards us, seeing me sat in the chair as she kneels in front of me.

"What are you doing in here? What were you thinking?" She says, cupping my cheek.

"No one was in the room, I got up and heard Annabelle cry, I came in to soothe her," I yawn.

"Come on, we're getting you back to bed. Luci, could you find Rodge, I have a feeling she needs more blood," mum says. Kade scoops me into his arms as I hiss in pain when my shoulder hits his chest.

"Sorry, shit I'm sorry Taylor," he says in a panic.

"It's just tender… It's ok," I grunt from the pain.

"I'll have Rodge check it, it should have healed better than this," mum says, walking towards the medical bay, opening the door back for Kade as he lays me down in the bed that I had woken in.

"I heard a certain girl is awake," Rook walks in with Rodge right behind him.

"Rodge, she's complaining of pain in her shoulder and she's so weak, she might need more blood," mum utters by my side, holding onto my hand.

"She needs nutrition, food, drink, she doesn't need any more blood. Your wound, however, I will take a look at," he says coming around with a frown, hands hovering over it as I hiss once more, jaw clenched.

"Infection, I will sort out some anti-biotics for you and we will keep a close eye on it, I will be back shortly," Rodge nods, heading out quickly.

"You've caused quite the chatter amongst every one Taylor. Everyone wants to have you as their friend, everyone wants to be part of your team, your pack. You've become a strong, powerful, beautiful warrior to them all, you should be proud," Rook says.

"Maybe if I was stronger, I wouldn't have lost my arm," I sigh.

"Don't you dare talk like that young lady, or I will beat you with my FAKE LEG!" Kade says sternly.

"Noted," I nod with a chuckle. "How is Cynthia? What about all those who were corrupted? Did you get them all?"

"Whoa, slow down there Taylor. Cynthia is weak but resting. We got… Most of them, some ran so our warriors are keeping a close watch on all the grounds. The ones we managed to get have either been detained or healed," Rook says.

“The ones detained…” I murmur.

“It is too late; Cynthia doesn’t have the power after healing you to get to them all so it was decided who would be healed. Violet made some difficult decisions with your mother, but I have to agree with the both of them, they chose the right ones,” Rook nodded solemnly.

“If Corey was here, he could have helped…” I growl.

“Do not dwell on that right now Taylor,” mum says, caressing my head trying to calm me.

“NO! HE LEFT! HE LEFT ME! HE LEFT HUNTER! His parents… his family… We could have helped him, he should be here, with me…” I cry as she holds me tightly in her arms, hushing me softly.

“I know baby girl, I know,” she coos at me as the others look at me sadly.

“MOMMY!” I hear down the hall.

“Hunter! Wait! Shit,” I hear my brother curse as a little bundle of fur leaps into the room.

“Hunter! Be careful!” Kade manages to grab him as he shifts back to his human form, struggling in Kade’s arms.

“Let me go!” Hunter hits Kade’s chest.

“Give him to me Kade,” I nod, wiping my eyes as he puts the wriggling boy on the bed.

“Mommy,” Hunter cries as he crawls up my body and plants himself on my chest, his arms around my sides and I try not to hiss out with pain as he catches the edge of the wound coming from my shoulder.

“I’m here baby boy, I’m here, I’ve got you,” I caress his head softly.

“I’m sorry I… TAYLOR! You’re awake!” Bryant grins at me as he bolts to my side, kissing my forehead.

“Hey twin,” I smile softly at him.

“Here we go… Oh… More guests…” Rodge walks in with a thick, creamy looking liquid in a glass.

“I have a feeling that will taste disgusting… Am I right?” I grimace.

“I’m afraid so,” he nods.

“Drink up,” Rook smirks as I take it in my hand before downing it, trying not to puke it up all over Hunter.

“Worst… Thing… I’ve ever tasted,” I gag.

“It should work quickly though,” Rodge nods, taking the glass back.

“Mommy where’s your arm?” Hunter lifts his head as he looks at my shoulder.

“No one told him?” I ask.

“We didn’t want to worry him,” Bryant shakes his head.

“That man hurt you, didn’t he?” Hunter says, looking me in the eyes.

“He did, but he’s gone now, mommy dealt with the bad man so she could keep you and the others safe,” my thumb wipes a tear from his cheek.

“I want to be big and strong and protect you!” He huffs, hugging me tightly once more.

“One-day baby boy, one day,” I mutter, yawning as I suddenly felt exhausted once more.

“Hunter, we should leave mummy to sleep,” Bryant says going to grab him.

“NO!” Hunter snaps, hugging me tighter.

“Hunter, let up a little, be careful,” I grit my teeth before breathing a sigh of relief as he lets go.

“Sorry,” he whispers.

“Can I stay in my bed, then he can stay with me?” I ask.

“Yes, but you must call if you need something,” mum nods.

“I will check you through the day too, to make sure the antibiotics are working,” Rodge says.

“Hunter, come on, get off of Taylor so we can take her to her bed,” Bryant says. Hunter grumbles as he jumps down from the bed.

“It’s ok sweetie, you can come spend some time with me in my bed,” I ruffle his hair as he smiles up at me.

“I will get you something to eat and drink, we need you to build your strength back up,” mum kisses my head and walks out.

“Come on kiddo, I’ll help you to your room,” Kade says, carefully helping me up as we walk to my bedroom.

# Chapter Forty-Two

## Phoenix

It was good to see Taylor back on her feet, but I could see the sadness in her eyes still when looking at her shoulder. She kept her smile though for little Hunter and I had to say I was so glad they had each other. He could make her smile with the slightest touch; she truly loved that boy like he was her own.

As the days went by Taylor was getting stronger, but she didn't venture far from her room, she hated the stares of people as they looked where her arm once was. I knew she was so nervous about it. She didn't know how to BE without it. It was her main arm, she wrote, drew and swung a sword with it. I was sure she could retrain her other, but she was nervous to get started.

I needed to do something for her, perhaps the fae could make something as they had for Kade, though an arm may be more complicated with all the finger functions…

"Violet, can I ask you something?" I asked, walking into the common room where she and a group of fae were sat, chatting happily.

"Of course," she nods with a smile.

"The leg that was made for Kade… Could something be made for an arm?" I ask.

“I don’t see why not, though I’m not sure how… functional it will be. We could definitely do the basic movement, but fingers moving as they should, might be a little more advanced, though I would be happy to try,” she smiles.

“I would appreciate it, it’s the twins’ birthday in a couple of days and if I could give Taylor something to get her confidence up, that would be great,” I reply.

“She’s still having trouble?” Violet sighs.

“Yes, she’s barely left her room,” I nod.

“She’ll be ok Phoenix; she just has to have a little time to adjust. Plus, it doesn’t help with all this Corey craziness. Have you seen the groups that flew in this morning, my people have been missing for weeks and suddenly they arrived this morning, claiming they were saved by a large black wolf of magical power that wiped out every enemy he came across. Corey is getting our people home,” Violet says.

“Why wasn’t I notified?” I frown.

“I had it covered, and you were busy, I was going to tell you when I saw you,” she says and I roll my eyes.

“Next time have someone tell me as soon as you know Violet,” I sigh.

“As you wish, I apologise. I will talk with my men about the arm, have a good day Phoenix,” Violet smiles before leaving the room.

*That woman can be a real pain in the arse.*

**She can, but she’s still a friend.**

I couldn't help but think about what she said about Corey, he was out there saving lives while my little girl was suffering without him. He needed to come home.

"You look deep in thought my love," Michael surprises me with a soft touch on my hip and a kiss on my neck as I sag into his arms with a happy sigh.

"Corey has been saving people…" I say.

"How do you know?" He asks, turning me in his arms.

"Violet's people, some of those who were taken arrived today telling of a wolf that saved their lives… It was Corey. He's out there doing what we should be doing and not spending time with his family."

"Where were the last ones saved from?" He asks as I raise a brow.

"What are you thinking Michael?" I ask.

"I'm thinking of finding the bloody boy myself," he answers.

"He could have moved on to somewhere else by the time you get there," I state.

"That's true, perhaps we need someone who knows the boy a little more…" He answers.

"No one knows that boy better than his father, right?" Reggie sneaks up to us.

"Taylor will never agree with it, she won't want you guys risking your lives to find him," I run a hand through my hair nervously. She needed Corey and I wasn't sure if he would come back of his own accord…

"Then we don't tell her," Michael says.

"You would lie to our daughter?" I scoff.

"No, not lie, twist the truth. That a team is being sent out on a rescue mission, Reggie and I will make a strong team, she won't be any the wiser," Michael says.

"It's time my son came home, even a few days has been too much. Their bond will grow weak if they continue this way, he needs his family and his family need him," Reggie adds.

"What of Cynthia? What will she think?" I ask.

"She misses her son and wants him home, she would do anything to have him back," Reggie answers.

"Get a team together, send someone to find out exactly where he was last seen, but you must promise you will be careful and all of you get home safely. I can't bear to lose anyone else, not now," I say, cupping Michael's face before pressing his hand against my stomach.

This morning I had found out I was pregnant once more; I was excited and scared at the same time.

"You… You're…" Michael stammers.

"Yes, another pup," I nod with a smile.

"Congratulations Phoenix," Reggie smiles at me.

"Thank you," I reply. Michael picks me up, twirling me around in the air.

"I promise I will come home; nothing will stop me from getting home to you and our children," Michael kisses me softly.

"I'll get him home Phoenix, him and my bothersome son," Reggie nods to me.

"Make sure you come home unscathed too," I smile.

"I'll do my best, now I better let Cynthia know what's going on, I'll have a few of my boys find out where Corey was last seen," Reggie says, leaving us alone.

"I can't believe we're having another pup, is it bad I don't want to leave anymore? But I have to do this," he presses his forehead against mine.

"For Taylor, you will be back soon enough, and you can enjoy this with me once more," I kiss him as his hands graze my stomach, I can feel the love coming from him.

"You be a good little pup for your mother while I'm gone little one," he kisses my belly as I smile with adoration.

"Go on, you need to tell our children where you're going…" I shoo him away.

"Thanks… Give me the difficult job," he rolls his eyes playfully.

"I love you," I smile.

"I love you more beautiful," he grins, kissing me passionately before walking away as I sigh happily. That man was my life.

"Well little pup, now what…" I sigh.

"Talking to yourself is a sign of madness you know?" Kai smirks at me as he sticks a lollipop in his mouth.

"Who said I was talking to myself?" I smirk back as my hands go to my belly.

"YOU'RE PREGNANT! I'm gonna be an uncle again! YEAH!" He cheers with a grin.

"And now the whole place knows," I shake my head at him with a smile.

"Oops… Michael knows right?" He grimaces.

“Yes, luckily for you, idiot,” I swat him around the head.

“Congratulations bestie,” he puts an arm around my shoulder as we walk through the mansion.

“Is it true?!” Janie runs over to me with a huge grin.

“Is what true?” I raise a brow.

“I’m getting another sibling! Why, what else would there be?” She asks.

“Yes, I’m pregnant and I’m taking your father hasn’t told you about his little trip yet…” I reply.

“What trip?” Kai and Janie say at the same time. I sigh and I tell them both the truth, I knew I could trust them both not to blab… Well Kai might to Jae…

“Taylor will go nuts if she finds out what dad and Reggie are doing. She’s pulling her hair out now, her wolf wants out, but she won’t let down her guard,” Janie says once I finished.

“She needs Corey, what else do I do?” I sigh.

“We need to work on getting her out, a walk in the woods at least, once she’s out there she may let go,” Kai says.

“You’re her favourite uncle, you try,” Janie smirks.

“OK,” he nods, flitting away.

“Didn’t think he’d actually do it,” she says as I laugh.

“He likes a challenge,” I shrug.

“KAI!” Taylor bellows out a growl as Janie and I run to the bottom of the stairs.

Hunter is laughing his head off as Kai has Taylor over his shoulder. She's thumping him on the back with her hand.

"What did I just walk into?" Luci smirks at the sight.

"Trying to get princess Taylor from her dungeon," Kai chuckles, walking past.

"Kai! I swear to the Goddess, if you don't put me down, I will tear you limb from limb!" Taylor growls.

"Go on then," Kai smirks, taking her outside.

"Kai…" I murmur, unsure of how far he was going to push it.

"PUT ME DOWN!" She shouts as Hunter hugs my leg with a grin.

"Hey buddy," I ruffle his hair as he giggles.

"Mommy needed to go outside, Kai is so funny," he giggles.

"KAI!" Taylor shouts again as they get outside. We follow them as he drops her to the ground, her hair a mess as she blows it out of her face.

"Fresh air, see, feel better?" Kai smirks.

"Fuck you," she groans, getting up as she tries to move past him, but he grabs her and pulls her back.

"No, you stay outside," Kai says.

"Kai… What are you doing?" Kade comes around the corner from doing a patrol.

"Getting the princess from her tower and making her stand in fresh air once again, her wolf is begging to come out," Kai replies.

"I am NOT shifting!" Taylor huffs angrily.

“Why not?” Kai asks.

“Because… Because… Because I’m scared… Ok, is that what you want to hear? I am scared of what people will think of me, I’m scared I will never be the same again,” Taylor answers and I see a tear fall down her cheek.

“Taylor, come on, come on a walk with me, we need to talk,” Kade says to her as he places a hand on her shoulder.

“I don’t want to, just let me go back in,” Taylor shakes her head.

“Taylor, come,” Kade says sternly.

She lets out a scream in frustration before stomping like a child and following him anyway.

“I haven’t seen her do that in a while,” Janie laughs.

“Why must all my children be so stubborn?” I laugh.

“Grandma! Can we have hot chocolates? Go and get the girls too!” Hunter grins.

“Go on then, go find the girls,” I nod with a smile as he shifts and bounds off playfully.

“He’s a lot like Blake isn’t he,” Janie says, laying her head on my shoulder.

“He is,” I nod sadly. I missed Blake, I missed all of them, I would never forget any of them.

# Chapter Forty-Three

## Taylor

I couldn't believe Kai did that, he just burst into my room after dad had left from telling me that he was leaving on some mission. As if I didn't feel bad enough that I couldn't go with them, he drags me outside like a child and now I'm stuck with Kade!

"Come on, hit me with it," I sigh, rolling my eyes.

"You're being a brat," he says sternly.

"Is that all?" I shake my head.

"TAYLOR," he growls at me as I sigh.

"I'm sorry," I bite my lip nervously as I see more warriors around, feeling unsure of myself as my hand covers my shoulder.

"Stop it, embrace it. It's difficult, I know, but people see you nothing less than a hero Taylor, they aren't looking at your shoulder, they look at you because of what you did. They look at your shoulder because they cannot believe how you have lived through such events. They ADMIRE you. Stop. Look around, look at how they truly look at you, how we all look at you," Kade says, tilting my chin so I look ahead.

Looking forward I can see many of the warriors, wolves, fae and human as they gaze over with smiles on their faces, some even wave as I give a small wave back.

"You will learn once again how to live without your arm, I will spend every minute helping you learn with your left arm, train it to be just as strong as your right was. I will work with you, and you will continue to be the strongest girl we've known. You are fierce, you have such a passion inside you that it even surpasses your mother sometimes, your mother is amazing, but you are everything she is and then some because of how you have grown up, you have heart, you're fierce, you're strong and you can get through this. Corey or no Corey, you are an amazing parent to Hunter, you love with passion, please Taylor, come back to us, be YOU," Kade cups my cheek as a tear falls.

"I'm scared," I whimper.

"I know, trust me, it won't be easy, but we are all here, every step of the way, you with your arm and me with my leg, we'll keep on going," Kade says.

"Ok," I whisper with a nod.

"Good girl, now time to push the boat a little, shift," he says, and my eyes widen.

"NOW?!" I exclaim, looking around me.

"Yes, now, a wolf can run on three legs, it's difficult, but possible. Come on, I'll even take off my leg for you," he says as he begins to unlatch his leg from the stump, laying it carefully on the ground, hopping about.

"You aren't joking…" I murmur.

"Shift Taylor, Lily needs it," he says as he shifts, shaking out his fur as he nudges me softly. My hand shakes nervously as I notice people are watching. Kade growls at them as they make themselves busy.

With a deep breath, I slowly begin to shift, falling straight onto the ground.

"Up," Kade nudges me as I try to push up with one leg, it wobbles, and I fall again.

"I can't," I shake my head.

"No such word, get up, listen to your wolf," he says.

*Get up, we can do this Taylor, come on, feel your weight and counteract it.*

I sigh, trying again, groaning as my front paw wasn't used to taking the full weight of my front, but this time I hadn't fallen to the floor at least.

"Balance yourself with your back legs and take a step," Kade says.

Moving my back legs, I take a small hop with my front leg.

"That's it, keep going, watch me, it's just how you have to do it, but in reverse, yours is up the front, mine the back," Kade says as he begins walking off, I watch him carefully and I begin to move slowly, my feet were wobbly as he came over to help steady me.

"I'm doing it…" I say in shock.

"You are, keep going," he yips happily as I try to go a bit faster, but wobble, toppling into him as he keeps us both up.

A playful yip sounds ahead of me as I see my twin with Amanda and baby Bailey.

"You're walking!" Bryant howls happily.

"Slowly," I chuckle.

"How does it feel now?" Kade asks.

"Exhausting, but good," I nod.

"Good, you CAN do this, shift back," he says as I nod shifting back while Bryant grabs his prosthetic for him.

"You did it, twin," Bryant hugs me.

"You'll be back to missions in no time," Kade smiles at me.

"Thank you, Kade," I hug him.

"Any time sweetheart," he kisses my head softly.

"Are you guys coming in for some hot chocolate with the kids?" Kai flits towards us.

I walk towards him and smack him on the arm hard before hugging him.

"Thank you, you're an arsehole, but I love you, Uncle Kai," I say as he chuckles.

"I wondered if you would hate me," he says.

"Never," I shake my head with a smile.

"Let's go enjoy something to drink then," Kade claps a hand on Kai's shoulder.

"Can I… Can I just have a moment alone? I'll be in soon," I say.

"Of course," Kade nods, dragging Kai with him as Bryant and Amanda take Bailey inside with them.

I walk into the woods, enjoying the fresh scent of the ground, it had rained recently, I could smell it on the earth.

"Corey, where are you?" I whisper to the wind, closing my eyes, trying to feel even the slightest part of him through our bond.

I could feel his power, it was surging, but not of darkness, something bright and beautiful, he was out there somewhere…

"You feel it too?" A voice makes me jump in surprise.

"Cynthia, you scared me," I say with a hand over my heart.

"Sorry sweetheart, but you feel his power too, don't you? It's not dark, it's something new, something I think because of you, your light, your passion is driving him away from darkness into something we've never seen before that's even more powerful, this could change the world as we know it," she says grabbing my hand softly in hers.

"I just want him to come home," I say softly.

"He will. Can't you feel it, he's working towards it, he's out there trying to make a better world," she says.

"I can feel it, but I miss him," I say as she cups my cheek.

"As do I," she nods, hugging me softly to her chest.

"I better go inside before the other descend on me again," I smile.

"Go then dear," she nods, looking up to the sky.

"Do you want to come?" I hold out my hand to her.

"That would be lovely dear," she says as she puts her hand in mine. Her hands are frail and skinnier than they were before.

"Cynthia… Are you sick?" I ask.

"I am not destined to last much longer Taylor…" She sighs.

"Then we must try turning you, please Cynthia," I beg.

"I have lived a long life, Taylor, I don't mind greeting death," she smiles softly.

"What about Reggie and Corey? Hunter too," I say.

"They will keep going, they will be fine," she shakes her head.

"Yes, they will keep going, but none of us wants to lose you. Please Cynthia, fuck the magic, join the pack by trying to be one of us, become a vampire, anything to keep you by our side," I beg.

"I will think about it Taylor," she nods, but I wasn't convinced.

"Live to see your grandchildren, because they deserve to have a grandmother and with Corey not here you can't leave yet, because I haven't had pups yet," I say sternly.

"Oh, Taylor, you drive a hard bargain. I said I will think on it and I will, no more of this," she taps my hand before walking off ahead of me.

"Corey come home, we need you," I say in my mind, trying to push it through to him, but I doubt he would get it, he was too far.

"Mommy! Look! I got EXTRA marshmallows!" Hunter's eyes are huge, just like the mug of hot chocolate in front of him.

"I am not dealing with him when he's hyper later, just saying," I laugh, pointing at Kai who looks at me with a cheeky grin.

"You were the same, so don't go there," mum chuckles.

"So, it's our birthday in a couple of days, what's the plan?" Bryant grins.

"How should I know?" I shrug.

"Party?" Amanda asks as she feeds Bailey.

"Can we keep it low-key?" I ask.

"No big parties got it, I could do with a quiet birthday for a change too," Bryant nods.

"How about a good old barbeque by the lake?" Luci asks.

"Sounds good to me," I nod.

"Has dad already left?" Bryant asks.

"Not yet, but any minute," mum nods.

Hunter grins at me as he climbs onto my lap at the table, dragging his drink towards him before diving back into it, whipped cream all over his mouth.

"Is any of that going inside your mouth or just around it?" I giggle as Cynthia throws a cloth over for me to wipe it.

"NO! I was going to lick it off!" Hunter whines.

"HUNTER! Come play!" Selene grins with Amelia beside her as they had already finished their drinks.

"I'm still drinking," Hunter huffs.

"Hurry up!" Selene whines.

"Girls are so bossy," Hunter murmurs under his breath as I burst out laughing, kissing his head.

"You'll get used to that little man," I chuckle.

"Hey, Selene, how about while we wait for Hunter, you show us some of your new earth tricks," Kai smiles at her softly.

"I'm not allowed to do it indoors," she sighs sadly.

"That's because your powers are too strong, you'll bring the house down," Cole chuckles, walking in as he places a kiss on his daughter's head.

"Let's go outside then," Kai takes the girls hands in his, leading them out as they skip happily by his side.

"He's a good daddy," Luci smiles.

"Yeah, I just feel sorry for anyone who falls for Amelia, he's so protective," Luci giggles.

"My girls," Hunter mumbles.

"What?" I frown.

"They are mine, my girls," he repeats.

"Aww, Hunter do you love Selene and Amelia?" Amanda smiles.

He nods, blushing as I hug him with a smile.

"That's so cute," I giggle.

"Phoenix, can I have a word in private?" Cole asks as we're teasing Hunter.

"Of course," mum nods, she kisses both Bryant and I's cheeks, leaving the room.

Annabelle begins to whine in Luci's arms before full-on screaming.

"Oh no, not again," Luci sighs, bouncing her on her hip.

“Let’s go take her outside for a bit, she always calms in the fresh air, she doesn’t like being cooped up,” Kade kisses his mate.

“I’m going to play! Love you, mommy,” Hunter kisses my cheek, jumping off of my lap and running off towards the girls and Kai outside.

“Then there was five…” Janie laughs.

“I’m going to put Bailey down for a nap, so I will leave you guys to it, you siblings could do with some time together anyway,” Amanda kisses Bryant and walks off with a smile.

“Down to three…” Janie laughs.

“Wait… When did Cynthia leave?” I frown, looking around.

“Not long after Cole took mum,” Bryant answers.

“She’s dying…” I sigh.

“What?! Explain now,” Janie says, sitting closer to me as I explain what had happened in the woods.

“Perhaps, mum could talk her around. Though it is her choice, she’s been around for a long time, I’m not surprised she wants to rest in peace,” Bryant says.

Our heads all dart towards the entrance of the mansion as several howls echo in the air.

“Dad’s leaving,” Janie says.

“Such a lovely goodbye we got,” I say sarcastically, rolling my eyes. Both their eyes turn yellow as I frown. “Want to keep me in the loop?” I raise a brow.

“Nothing Taylor,” Bryant says, but I could tell he was lying.

"Bryant…" I growl.

"Shit… Damn this twin link, dad's going to find Corey," he answers as I look between them in shock.

# Chapter Forty-Four

## Taylor

"HE'S WHAT?!" I slam my hand down on the counter as I push off from my seat.

"Taylor! They are doing it for you!" Janie calls as run from the kitchen, looking all around as I burst through the front, seeing mum, Cynthia and Cole at the bridge.

"DAD!" I shout as they all turn to me, I try to run past them, but Cole grabs me, stopping me.

"You don't have enough strength to go with them," Cole says.

"Fuck you, get off of me," I shove him off.

"Taylor, sweetheart…" Mum murmurs.

"Dad lied; you knew what he was doing… How could you? You're putting them at risk!" I snap.

"He's trying to bring Corey back; Corey has managed to save a huge amount of fae lately. Violet only told me this morning, your father didn't lie, it is a rescue mission, he's going out there with Reggie to get Corey and a possible group of humans again. They will be ok," mum says walking towards me.

"You're pregnant and dad left, it's stupid," I huff.

"He'll be back, you have to trust in that," she replies softly, cupping my cheek as I growl in frustration.

"I should be out there!" I growl.

"You will be, one day," Cynthia says.

"That doesn't help right now though, does it…" I sigh.

"They are perfectly capable of going on a mission. They will be fine without you, they've been doing this longer than you have," Cole says.

"Ugh, fine," I sigh as mum hugs me tightly to her.

"I know you're angry with me Taylor, just know I love you and I'm doing this for you, take care of your mother," dad says in my head.

"Make sure you come back home dad," I reply.

"I will do everything in my power to," he replies.

"You better or I will find you and kick your arse."

"I don't doubt that," I can almost hear him chuckle before they get too far for the mind link.

Now I was finally out of my room it would seem everyone wanted to keep me busy to stop my thoughts travelling to my father, Reggie and the others who had gone to find Corey. We hadn't heard a thing yet and it was making me anxious.

"I'm glad I caught you before dinner, would you mind if I checked your shoulder?" Rodge snags me before heading to dinner.

"Sure," I nod as he leads me to the small office nearby.

His hands rub over the stump softly as I grimace, not from pain, but from it being touched by another.

"Did that hurt?" He asks.

"No… I just… Don't like it being touched…" I sigh.

"Ah, I understand. Do you still feel it? Like a ghost limb?" He asks.

"Yes, I'm wiggling my fingers right now," I nod.

"It will take some time to get used to it, your brain will figure it out," he nods.

"Have you heard from Evie? How is she doing? I haven't seen her since the funeral," I ask.

"She's… Struggling still. She doesn't like to see anyone, she's not herself right now. I have her under close observation in the medical wing as she was a danger to herself for a little while," he frowns.

"I wish she would let us see her," I sigh.

"Grief can cause a lot of mental instability. Give her time," he says.

It was crazy to think that most of us from Maximillian's had died, the only ones left were the twins, Talia and Tilly, Jae, Evie and me. Albeit a select number of humans were still left, but they kept to themselves.

Once Rodge was done checking me, he wandered off and left me to join the others at dinner.

"Mom, look, we drew these for you!" Hunter grins, passing me a stack of paper with drawings.

"Oh, wow guys," I smile going through them.

Hunter's were messy, but I could see what he was trying to draw at least, his family. Selene's were basic, she didn't have an artistic flair when it came to drawing, she was artistic with the earth instead and then there was Amelia, hers were amazing, she had a talent.

“They aren’t good like yours Taylor,” Amelia says sadly.

“You’re joking right… At your age, I couldn’t draw like this, these are so good,” I smile.

“She’s talented right?” Jae grins, hugging her.

“Super talented,” I nod.

“I’m not good at anything,” Hunter frowns.

“Don’t start that shit mister, I’ve seen how fast you run,” I bop him on the nose.

“You’re going to be a strong warrior Hunter and you’re an amazing friend, that’s what you’re good at,” Amelia smiles at him as he blushes.

“So cute,” I hear Luci whisper happily.

“Can you show me how to draw better?” Amelia asks.

“I mean I can’t actually show you, but I can tell you, I have to relearn…” I sigh.

“You can do it, I think we should do some training soon with your left arm soon,” Kade says from the other side of the table.

“Training it is,” I nod.

The rest of the day went so quickly as I gave Amelia a few tips for her drawing before everyone went to bed. Hunter had taken a permanent position in my bed as he didn’t want to leave me alone, though I think he just wanted to cuddle.

The next day I spent with Kade and Kai, trying to work with my left arm, which was proving difficult.

"Swing harder Taylor," Kade growls at me in the gym.

"Don't you think I'm trying?!" I growl back.

"Use your anger," Kai says.

I growl, punching the bag Kade was holding for me, what I didn't count on happening was my claws extending and splitting the bag, the insides spilling out.

"That works I guess," Kai laughs.

"Sorry Kade," I smile sheepishly.

"It's a start, though maybe control your wolf next time," Kade chuckles.

For hours he kept drilling me with my arm, using weights and training to use it better. It would certainly take a while though.

By the end of the day, I was hot and sweating like a pig, heading upstairs for a shower. I stood still, sniffing the air, confused by the metallic tang in the air… Blood.

"Taylor… You smell that?" Jae flits to my side.

"I do," I nod as we walk along the corridor, we reach the room where the stench of blood was coming from, a note taped to the door.

*To everyone,*
*I am so sorry, but I cannot handle life without my love, my brain holds too many dark and terrible memories. I can't do it.*
*Do not mourn me, I want this, this is my choice.*
*Thank you, Taylor, for everything. You gave me a chance at happiness, and I am sorry I haven't spoken to you since the funeral. None of this was your fault.*

*Phoenix, thank you for taking me in when I had nowhere else to go.*
*I do hope you all a long and happy life, but I need to be with Trey.*
*I love you all.*

*Evie x*

"NO! EVIE!" I shout passing the note to Jae as I try to get into the room, the door was stuck. I slam against it with my left growling in frustration.

"Let me help, ready, one, two, three, now!" Jae says as he slams into it with me, but it still didn't budge.

"She's a guardian, could she have put a ward on it?" I ask.

"It's possible. But if it's still up then she's still alive," Jae he answers.

"Go get help, I'll keep trying," I say as he flits away.

Lifting my hand I focus on the wall, cracking the old brick around the door frame.

"COME ON!" I growl as my powers struggle against something that was counteracting me.

"Taylor move!" Rook rushes along the hall with Violet by his side, their hands press against the door, my chest heaving as I had used so much of my energy.

Mum was next to bound to us as her wolf as Jae follows quickly.

"EVIE! Take down the wards!" Jae shouts.

"She's not going to last much longer!" I exclaim, smelling the amount of blood as I join Violet and Rook at the door. My hand pressed against the door as it vibrates, the wall cracking once more.

"That's it, Taylor, it's working, keep going," Rook calls out.

“EVIE!” I howl out as I push my element more than ever as the door frame comes loose from the wall. Mum and Jae move it as we stand at Evie’s barrier, still unable to get in, but we could see her, lying on the ground, wrists cut, barely breathing.

“Evie please! Don’t do this!” Jae shouts.

“Trey…” She mutters quietly.

“Evie! It’s Taylor, please, don’t do this! Let us help, we’re your family too!” I beg.

“Tired, so tired…” She mutters.

“EVIE!” Tilly and Talia rush down, their eyes filled with tears as Jae grabs them before they look inside.

“Evie, please, take down the ward, we can help you, we love you girl,” I call.

“It’s been good… But I can’t…. Goodbye Taylor,” she coughs before I hear her heart slow.

“NO!” Jae and I shout. The ward comes down as we rush to her side.

“She’s gone…” Rook shakes his head.

“I should have helped her more, we should have been there for her more,” I cry.

“There was nothing you could have done, she refused to see anyone, shut herself off, only let in Rodge, nothing could have been done,” Violet lays a hand on my shoulder softly.

“She just wanted to be with her mate…” Tilly says, crying from the crumbling space in the wall.

“She’ll be happy now,” Talia adds.

My wolf whines as I sit next to her body, hand caressing her head as I cry.

“I’ll have a pyre made,” mum says softly.

“Make sure she’s added to the monument,” I say.

“Of course, she will be added,” Violet nods, getting up and heading out with mum.

“I’ll have someone come to get her body, get her wrapped up and ready,” Rook sighs sadly.

“Taylor… You’re covered in blood,” Jae says softly.

“Go clean up, we’ve got this princess,” Rook lays a hand on mine.

I kiss her head gently before getting off the floor slowly.

“Twins, you don’t need to be here,” I say softly.

“We want to light the pyre,” they say in unison.

“I’ll make sure you can,” I nod as they hug me, tears in all our eyes.

I walk to my room slowly, my heart hurting from yet another loss, why did we have to suffer so much? I suppose they were right though, at least she was with Trey now.

I shut the door of my room as I lean against it, tears pouring from my cheeks.

“Corey, come home, please, I need you,” I cry.

Suddenly I feel a warmth spread through my body as if being touched by my mate, hands gliding over me.

“What the…” I murmur.

"Coming…" I hear him in my mind, a single word, but that single word meant the world to me. Corey was coming home!

I showered quickly and left my room to find my twin outside waiting for me.

"How are you? Mum told me what happened," he asks.

"I can't believe it… I'm sad, but I know she will feel better being with him and the goddess," I sigh.

"Come on, the others have all gathered already," he says.

"That was quick…" I murmur.

"You were in the shower over an hour Taylor…" He says.

"What… An hour… No," I frown, how had I lost so much time?

"Something has you distracted, not Evie though," he frowns, looking at me.

"Corey… I felt him, I heard him," I reply.

"You heard him! Dad called mum, they only just got to the building he was last seen, they haven't found him yet," he replies.

"Just one word, he said coming. What if he's on his way here already and they missed him?" I ask as he links our arms.

"We'll let mum know and she can call them back," he says as we walk quickly down the stairs.

"Mommy!" Hunter runs up to me crying as he jumps up, clinging to my neck as I hook my arm under him.

"Hey baby boy, it's ok, I've got you," I coo at him. "Bryant, speak to mum, I need to deal with Hunter."

“Will do,” he nods, ruffling Hunter’s hair before running off.

“Evie died…” He cries as I bend down, placing him on the stairs as he cries into my shoulder.

“I know baby boy, but she’s happy now, she’s with her mate, the goddess and she’s going to be really good friends with your mummy and daddy up there, I am sure,” I cup his cheek gently.

Hunter was so sensitive when it came to death, he hated to lose anyone, even though he had barely ever seen Evie, he felt every loss around him because he was just so caring of everyone.

“You sad?” He murmurs, wiping his eyes before wiping a tear that had escaped my own with his sleeve.

“I am and that’s ok, we are allowed to be sad,” I give him a sad smile.

“I love you, mommy,” he says, hugging me tightly again as I pick him up, his legs wrapping around my side.

“I love you too, come on, we need to go say goodbye,” I kiss his head as I walk outside with him where everyone was stood around the pyre. Tilly and Talia were stood next to mum waiting for the last people to arrive.

“Hunter, why don’t you come with me? Taylor needs to lead the howl,” Amanda holds out her arms to take him, but he snuggles harder into my neck.

“He can shift with me and stand under me,” I smile thankfully at her.

“I howl too?” He asks quietly.

“Yeah, I need your help to howl,” I answer as he nods, taking my place next to my mum.

“Today we grieve for yet another loss, but we also celebrate the life she had and the eternity she will have with our loving goddess above, joining her mate Trey in the heavens above. Our futures are forever uncertain, and we should all cherish every memory and moment we have. Taylor,” mum nods to me as I take a deep breath, putting Hunter on the ground before shifting, sitting on the ground as I was still a little unsteady on three legs, Hunter shifted and sat between them. The other wolves followed suit before I let out a loud howl into the sky while Tilly and Talia lit the pyre.

Hunter’s howl vibrated through my chest as he tried to keep up with me, but his little lungs couldn’t hold enough oxygen to match me.

“Good job Hunter,” I nudge him gently as he nuzzles into my chest.

People begin to talk, most shifting back, but I felt the need to stay as my wolf, Hunter stayed as his too as I laid there with him, nuzzled into my chest.

“I have called your father; Reggie is trying to call out to Corey. They will stay put for the rest of the day, they need to rest, if they haven’t heard from him soon, they will move on. There are no signs of him anywhere, the rain has washed them all away,” mum walks up to us, her hand drifting through my fur.

“Ok,” I nod.

Luci walks over with Annabelle in her arms as she places the baby against me, small hands gripping my fur. Hunter yips happily at Annabelle, his nose poking her sides as she giggles at the pup.

“Thought you could do with a smile, she always helps me,” Luci smiles softly at me.

“I’d give you Bailey too, but I don’t want her on the ground just yet,” Amanda looks at me sheepishly before sitting with us.

“I don’t blame you,” I link to her as Bryant shifts into his wolf, curling around his little family.

We all sat there quietly for a little while as the pyre continued to burn, Evie’s ashes flowing off into the wind and over the forest as one of the wind users kept it from flowing over other people.

# Chapter Forty-Five

## Taylor

The next day was really quiet as I spent most of it with the kids, trying to cheer myself up. Bryant had had to remind me that it was our birthday the next day and I wasn't looking forward to it. It didn't feel right celebrating without dad, Corey and the others, but I had to for those that were still here and wanted to celebrate.

"TWIN! You up? Come on lazy! Happy birthday!" My brother shouts through the door early this morning as I groan, getting up quickly as I wrench open the door.

"You realise Hunter is asleep too right…" I hiss.

"Oops… Sorry," he peers around me at Hunter, who I could see was waking slowly, hands rubbing his tired eyes.

"Happy birthday twin," I hug him.

"Mommy…" Hunter murmurs as I walk over to him.

"Morning baby boy," I smiled, kissing his cheek.

"Happy birthday mommy and uncle Bry," he smiles up at us.

"Thanks, little man," Bryant grins.

"I told you not to wake her yet! For god's sake Bryant, why are you such a child on your birthday?" Mum walks in, clipping him around the ear making Hunter giggle as he snuggles into my side.

"Morning mum," I smile as she hugs me tightly, kissing both Hunter's and I's heads.

"Morning baby girl, happy birthday," she wears a huge grin on her face.

"Uh oh, I don't like that grin she has twin," I laugh.

"Oh, you will," he smiles too.

"Ok, well I need to get us ready, so if you don't mind," I gesture the door.

"I'll sort Hunter out, you get yourself ready, wear something nice," mum winks at me as she holds her arms out for Hunter, he climbs into them happily, he adored his new grandma.

"Kiss mom first," Hunter said as she went to leave. She leans over so he can kiss me before they wave and head out.

"Shouldn't you be with your mate and child?" I laugh.

"She's busy sorting something out," he shrugs.

"Ok, well as much as I love you brother, get out," I smirk, shoving him out of the room. I shower before getting dressed as I go to put make-up on, I stand there stumped… Literally, I had a stump for an arm…

"Shit…" I growl. I look at my make-up, not knowing how I was going to do it myself with one hand, I knew it would be possible somehow, but I had yet to even try…

"Mum, can you help me?" I push through the link before a few minutes later I heard a knock on the door.

"Your mum was busy, she sent me, what's up?" Luci walks in.

"One hand and make-up…" I murmur dejectedly.

"Ah, yeah, makes that kind of difficult. Sit down, I've got you today, but I'm sure you will figure it out soon," she smiles, grabbing my make-up as I sit on my bed.

"Doesn't feel right with dad not being here," I sigh.

"I'm sure he will call you at least," she says as she concentrates.

We continue chatting as she finishes up my make-up with a smile as I look in the mirror in shock.

"Whoa… That's… Wow… I look…" I murmur.

"Beautiful, happy birthday," she smiles, hugging me.

"Thank you," I smile.

I had put on a gorgeous deep blue dress that went to my knees, putting on a pair of black boots with it. So, what they didn't go with it… it wasn't a fashion parade, and they were comfortable…

"I don't know how you do it, but you make mismatched look good," Luci giggles as we walk out.

"I am not wearing uncomfortable shoes all day," I laugh as we head downstairs.

"I don't blame you," she laughs. A howl outside makes our heads turn sharply to the door.

“Dad…” I murmur, running out of the building.

“Vampires on the boundary, get to positions, my mate is out there with casualties!” Mum’s voice echoes in the distance.

“Mum! What’s going on?!” I shout as Luci and I run to her.

“Your father and the others were on their way home and they were cut off by a coven, I’m sending warriors out now,” she replies.

“Casualties?” Luci says.

“I don’t know who yet,” she shakes her head.

“You coming, twin?” Bryant asks swinging his blade around.

“You have to be joking, she’s not ready for that,” mum says.

“I… Fuck… Give me a blade,” I say to my twin. He throws me a blade and I catch it by the hilt with my hand, swinging it carefully in awe of it.

“Oh, by the way, that’s your birthday present,” he winks as I notice it was a specially made sword.

“Thanks, you’ll get yours later,” I grin excitedly.

“You aren’t strong enough for this!” Mum says.

“Watch me, I am not leaving them out there, that’s our dad, my alpha and our packs!” I exclaim. I see Kade about to head out as I run over, jumping onto him, surprising him.

“Little warning next time, walk yourself,” he groans.

“I’m not ready for that yet, but I will kick some arse,” I tell him as he looks back to mum who looked angry at me.

"Your mother is going to kill me," he shakes his head as Bryant shifts and joins us before darting into the trees with the other warriors.

"Count it as training," I smirk.

"Stay close, don't do anything stupid," Kade growls as they dart through the trees.

"Up ahead!" I call out seeing a group of wolves fighting off vampires. I growl, swinging my sword without catching Kade before standing on his back as he leaps into the fray. Jumping onto a vampire I stab my blade into its chest.

I can hear the screams of panic behind me as I whirl around to see several humans cornered into a huge clump of trees and no one else to get to them.

"Bryant! Look!" I call out, but he's too busy taking down his own vampires.

I can see dad try to get to them, but he's mowed down, claws tearing at the vampires attacking.

"Shit… Sorry Kade," I say as I slice at every vampire around me, getting used to my new sword, it wasn't easy and I was depleting my energy quicker, panting with exhaustion, but I had to do something.

"HEY!" I shout at the vampires cornering the humans.

"Mmm, tasty wolf treat. You get her, I've got these, she'll be easy, she's one-handed," the vampire in the middle laughs.

"Come on then," I smirk cockily as they flit towards me, my sword swings through the air, hardening with the help of the earth, claws reach out for me as I slice his hand off as he screams in anger and pain.

"BITCH!" One hisses, he slices at my side, drawing blood as I take another swing, lodging my blade into his throat, but it gets stuck.

"Shit," I growl, trying to pull it out with one hand.

"Aww look at her," one of them laughs.

"Taylor!" I hear dad growl out.

The rain suddenly begins to pour, clouds darkening to a deep black all of a sudden, lightning crashing all around us as the humans scream.

A huge black blur of fur pounced, tearing every vampire around me to shreds, looking at me for mere moments before darting to the others as I watched in shock, his fur coursing with golden electric power.

I hear the humans behind me, scared. I run over to them quickly, keeping an eye on the wolf darting around as my heart beats like crazy.

"It's ok, you're safe now, I promise," I put my sword down, checking them over as one of them comes out with a baby in their arms.

"Thank you," the lady nods with a small smile.

"He's cute," I smile.

A deep howl sounds behind me as I turn quickly, the battle is done, the big black wolf standing in the centre, fur brimming with energy.

"Go to him, I have them," Bryant shifts, taking the sword from the ground pushing me to the centre. Dad nuzzles into me gently as I go past.

"Slowly Taylor, his wolf is very powerful right now and I don't know how much control he has," Reggie links to me as I nod at him.

I get closer, feeling his power flood towards me. He looks to me, his eyes dart to my missing arm, a growl vibrating angrily from his chest.

"Corey… It was losing my arm or my life," I whisper out as he growls.

“Taylor…” He says through the link as I almost cry at the sound of his voice, hand reaching out, ignoring the sting of the golden bolts.

“You came home,” I cry as he suddenly begins to shift. My eyes widen, he was broader, his muscles pulsing under my hand, golden bolts of lightning wrapped around his arms as a tattoo.

“I’m so sorry,” he looks at me sadly, his eyes not leaving my shoulder.

“Stop, this was not your fault, it’s ok, you’re home Corey, you’re home and I love you,” I say as his eyes meet mine.

“I love you too, I’m never leaving again, I swear, I will protect you with my life,” he says as I let my hand glide around his neck, kissing him passionately. I had missed this, I missed him.

“TAYLOR!” Bryant gasps out as my eyes open, Corey was almost glowing with the golden electric, but it wasn’t stinging me anymore as bands of it twisted around my arm too as a matching tattoo.

“Holy shit,” I murmur in shock.

“You made me good Taylor, your love turned my darkness into something better, you make me better,” Corey smiles, caressing my face gently.

“We need to get the humans back, sorry to interrupt…” Reggie chuckles, clapping his son on the back as I let go and they hug it out.

“I really am sorry, to all of you, but someone tell me that Taylor losing an arm wasn’t my magic… The last I saw… The purple fire…” He gulps.

“It wasn’t you; it was a corrupted fae… We’ll discuss it when we get back,” Reggie shakes his head.

"You didn't do this Corey," I kiss his cheek softly, happiness flooding me that he was home.

"Happy birthday twin," Bryant gives me back my sword as I grin.

"Happy birthday brother," I laugh as they shift once more, putting the humans on their backs as I get onto Corey's.

"Feels good to have you against me again," Corey says in my mind lustfully.

"You're never leaving me again," I reply.

"Never," he answers as everyone begins the run back to the mansion.

"MICHAEL!" I hear mum shout as we come through the trees.

He shifts before she jumps into his arms, kissing him roughly. Bryant shifts, fake gagging, making me laugh before I drop off of Corey's back for him to shift, his arms wrapping around my waist.

"I miss you, I missed your smell, your touch, your taste," he growls lustfully before nipping at my mark, causing me to gasp at the touch.

"Corey! My baby boy!" Cynthia calls out as she walks tiredly from the mansion.

"What happened to my mother…" He asks, unwinding his arms and heading to her as Reggie holds her in his arms, Corey, putting his hands in hers, glowing with power as she cries out, her eyes turning a brilliant gold.

"Corey what have you done…" I hear her gasp.

"Breathed life into you, you can't leave, please mom, I won't see you die, not now," Corey says.

"She's not going to be happy with him choosing for her," Bryant says by my side with a whisper.

"I think there's more to it, he's seen something," I reply.

"Oh! You… Taylor! OH!" Cynthia grins as she looks between us.

"Told you," I murmur.

"What did you see Corey?" I ask through the link as he turns, walking to me as he presses his head against mine.

"Our future," he smiles as the images begin to flood my mind.

It was sunset and we were sat at the lake, the kids, Hunter, Selene and Amelia playing in the water as it shifts to us a baby in my arms… Wait… Arms, as in plural?!

"How is that possible…" I murmur as I come out of it.

"Well, you come into heat and we…" Corey smirks.

"NOT THAT! My arms," I laugh.

"That would be your birthday present I'm guessing," mum grins as I turn to her confused.

"What?" I ask.

"Come on," she takes my hand, dragging me away as the others follow us with a chuckle. I can hear Corey ask his parents what happened, and they tell him how I ended up with one arm. I can feel the rage in him as he runs to my side, winding an arm around my waist as we walk briskly with mum inside.

"Ah, there you are, ready?" Rook grins at mum.

“Yep,” she nods. We’re led to a room where several of the medical team and the weapon forging team were waiting.

“What’s going on?” I ask.

“You are getting an arm, just like Kade got a leg,” mum grins as Rodge brings out a gorgeous looking prosthetic.

“Holy shit…” I murmur.

“Fitting it might be a little uncomfortable, but we have to make adjustments,” Rodge nods to me as he places a couple of leather straps over my head to hook it around my chest as I feel the prosthetic clamp over my stump of a shoulder. I wince at first as Corey growls protectively.

“It’s ok,” I grip his hand on my waist gently.

“It won’t be able to move as your fingers once did, we don’t quite have that power, but you will be able to use it to grip,” Rodge says.

“I can fix that,” Corey smirks as he closes his eyes, hands wandering over the prosthetic as it moves a little against my shoulder as if moulding to it.

“Try moving your fingers baby,” Corey smiles at me.

“You’re not serious,” I laugh nervously.

“Just trust me,” he nods.

I look to the arm, thinking about moving it as it raises with me, flexing my fingers as I look at it in shock, crying in happiness.

“Think you can make my leg better like that?” Kade chuckles at the door.

“Of course, I will see what I can do,” Corey nods as his hand waved in the air as his eyes narrow in on Kade’s leg.

“My God,” Kade says in shock as he moves his leg around as if it was normal, ankle circling at his command.

“I think we need to talk about your magic young man,” Cynthia laughs happily as she admires the arm I had.

“The arm should be able to be strengthened by earth too, Taylor, much like your sword,” Rook says.

“This is THE BEST day ever,” I grin.

“Happy birthday beautiful,” Corey kisses me sweetly.

“Thank you!” I hug everyone tightly as they chuckle happily at me.

“OH! Come with me, sorry guys, but Corey has to come with me a second,” I grin taking his hand and dragging him away as I lead him upstairs.

“If you wanted to take me to bed you could have just said so,” he chuckles.

“Not why I’m bringing you up here, though tempting,” I wink.

I knock on Selene’s bedroom door, knowing I would find the kids inside.

“Mommy… DADDY!” Hunter screams in shock as he barges past me and into Corey’s arms laughing as Corey hugs him tightly.

“Oh, little man, I missed you,” Corey says as I look at them with a smile.

“Whoa… Your arm is so cool,” Amelia gasps.

“Huh… Whoa…” Hunter gasps, getting down as he takes my new hand in his as I grip it softly.

“You have your arm back!” Selene gasps.

“Daddy! Where were you? Mommy was upset, I was too…” Hunter pouts.

"I'm sorry little man, I had to deal with a few things. I had people to save, I'm not going anywhere now, I promise," Corey kisses my cheek and ruffles Hunter's hair as I smile at them.

Best birthday ever…

# Chapter Forty-Six

## Taylor

## 5 years later

It's crazy to think just how quickly time flies when your life is a whirlwind of events. The last five years had flown by, and things were really looking up once more.

It hadn't taken long to get used to my new arm what with Corey's newfound power, he and Cynthia had been working hard to test it.

I had been on several missions in the last month, but now I had to slow down, now my life had to change for a while. Corey's vision had finally come true, and I bore him a child. He was the most gorgeous little thing on earth, and everyone was besotted with him.

"Mommy! Look!" Hunter shouts happily from in the lake with the other kids, splashing around just like we all used to do.

"I'm watching," I call out with a giggle as I kiss little Luke on the head, his beautiful eyes gazing up at me and I smile brightly. I couldn't be happier right now.

"SIS!" A little voice giggles from the bushes up ahead as my little brother, Logan, jumps from them, Corey and mum behind him.

"Hey!" I grin as he cuddles up to my side.

"Hi beautiful, I hope the kids have been behaving," Corey smirk, knowing full-well the kids were a handful.

"Oh sure, they've been angels…" I roll my eyes playfully.

"Bryant is on kid duty tomorrow, so you get a break," mum smiles, kissing my cheek before taking Logan into the water with her, joining the kids.

"How are my beautiful mate and our bouncing boy?" Corey grins before kissing my neck.

"We are great," I smile, sighing contently.

"Are you still up for a mission tomorrow?" He asks.

"Yes, I need out, as much as I love all the kids, they are driving me around the bend," I giggle.

We sat there for a while as we watched as one by one more people turn up to the lake, playing in its waters before it became a full-on cookout. I was so happy at this moment.

Missions had been going well ever since Corey had returned, his new power helping to destroy anything that apposed us easily, we hadn't had more than ten casualties in the past three years, all of those recovered too.

Life was finally getting to normal, Violet and her fae had finally decided they could return home, taking a mixture of humans and wolves with her too that wished to join them.

People were beginning to spread across the country again, towns slowly being built once more, farmlands had been regrown with the help of fae powers and I had seen so many new babies being born already with our numbers building every day. We'd even managed to get some of the people from overseas to us, to safety.

"Hey Taylor, I hear you've been training with Cole and Hanson, think you can take me now?" Uncle Kai chuckles at me as I raise a brow.

"With one hand tied behind my back," I smirk.

"Take your arm off, might be easier," he winks playfully.

"Fine. Corey, mind helping me?" I smile as he takes Luke from my arms while I unclip my arm and take it off. I had been training with and without my arm recently, just in case and my left arm had grown so much stronger.

"Kai, you're an idiot," Jae shakes his head.

"What's going on?" Kade asks, coming forward with Luci.

"Kai pretty much challenged her to a fight with one arm," Corey smirks.

"She won't take me down babe," Kai kisses Jae.

"I bet he lasts a minute tops," Kade smirks.

"HEY!" Kai shouts.

"I could take you and someone else down in… Three minutes," I smirk cockily.

"Fine, let's see… Who wants to help me?" Kai calls out.

"I'll do it," Cole smirks.

"You know my moves… But fine, let's do this," I shrug before everyone circles around us. This wasn't a battle to the death, but I knew everyone was still intrigued by how I battled with just one arm.

"You tap out, you leave the ring," Kade calls out as we all nod.

"Let's see how well your training has gone," Cole smirks.

"Oh, for god's sake, this will end up in tears again," mum sighs, rolling her eyes at us as I giggle.

"Come on then," I gesture for them to come to me with a smirk as we circle around.

Kai flits at me first as I dodge him, sticking out my leg so he was knocked to the ground, he grabs my ankle pulling me down but I roll out of it, using the earth to smack against his wrist as he hisses out in pain, letting me go before Cole comes at me, kicking at my side. I pull the earth to me, pinning his foot by my side before pulling it back as he hops on one leg, grabbing him by the shoulder before flinging him from me as he lands with a thud on the ground.

"I didn't teach you that," Cole grumbles as they both stand together opposite me, in position to attack at any moment.

"No, I did," Hanson smirks, arms folded with pride as he nods at me.

The battle went on as they kept coming at me again and again, they got in a few good hits, but we were all getting tired.

"Tapping out… You win…" Kai taps on the ground, breathing heavily as I pin him to the ground. Cole was blocked by the earth as it was trying to pull him down like quicksand, though of course, I wouldn't let it hurt him.

Cole taps the ground too with a smirk as I lift him back out of the ground, the crowd cheering happily for me.

"Now who needs training…" Kade smirks at Kai, helping him up.

"Apparently me…" Kai grumbles. I chuckle as I hug my uncle.

"I've still got it," I grin as Corey walks over with Luke in his arms, whining for food.

As I feed him, I look around at my family surrounding us, I was happy to be here and have them all by my side, even those we had lost, they were here, in our hearts and memories.

The battle was far from over, there would always be a balance of good and evil, we just had to continue and fight with every last breath.

The future was unsure, but when can we ever really know what will happen, we had to live for the now, work for our future and make our dreams a reality.

We watched as the sun went down slowly, my head resting on Corey's shoulder as I sighed happily, the kids surrounding us giggling and playing together. I would fight forever for them, for their happiness, their futures, the corruption would no longer be ours, or anyone's extinction, not while I still breathed on this earth.

# Also by Charly J.M:

**Zombie Apocalypse Duet (Can be read as stand-alones)**

- *Screechers*
- *Bleeders*

**Contemporary Romance / New adult**

- *Piece By Piece (Stand-alone)*

**Contemporary Romance / New adult Duet**

- *Little Ruby Red*
- *Red Rider*

Printed in Great Britain
by Amazon

27175289R00245